NOT THE DEATHS

IMAGINED

Anne Pettigrew

RINGWOOD PUBLISHING
GLASGOW

First published in Great Britain in 2020

by

Ringwood Publishing, Glasgow.

www.ringwoodpublishing.com

mail@ringwoodpublishing.com

ISBN 978-1-901514-80-3

British Library Cataloguing-in-Publication Data

A catalogue record for this book is available from the British Library

Printed and bound in the UK

by

Lonsdale Direct Solutions

To Norman, a husband without equal

*This book aims to help Plan UK in its endeavours
to improve the education and independence of girls
worldwide.*

Find out more by visiting www.plan-uk.org

Also by Anne Pettigrew

Not the Life Imagined

'When a doctor does go wrong, he is the first of criminals.
He has nerve and he has knowledge.'

– Sir Arthur Conan Doyle

Chapters and Timeline

One

Something About Mary

Oakfield Surgery, 26th October 1992

It was an ordinary Monday morning in leafy Bearsden. Well, almost. From the waiting room I could see the office was cluttered by strange objects. A life-size plastic skeleton swayed on a pole behind the reception desk, a scary pile of rubber spiders graced the filing table and several ghostly and ghoulish dressing-up outfits swayed on coat hangers dangling from record shelves. A witch's hat lay atop Alison's computer. My irritation was complete when I opened the office door and tripped over two broomsticks on the floor.

'What the hell?'

'Sorry, Dr S. It's stuff that the girls have brought for my Guides' Hallowe'en party tonight.'

At least my practice manager, Ellen, had the grace to look shamefaced. Sick people coming in wouldn't appreciate these macabre reminders of mortality.

'I've never liked Hallowe'en,' I grumped. 'As a kid, I was terrified bodies would rise up and chase me from the cemetery beside my house.'

Young Alison, the typist, huffed. 'I love it!'

Since Monday mornings aren't a good time to antagonise staff you're dependent on, I back-tracked. 'But dooking for apples is OK ...'

Raising a scornful plucked and pencilled eyebrow, Alison resumed typing. Ellen handed me a mail mountain topped by the usual pile of curling, hot-off-the-fax lab reports. Juggling coat, bag and mail, I manoeuvred back out into the corridor over the broomsticks, wondering if this might bring good luck. It didn't, on many fronts that day. The day I met Mary.

My first mistake was taking a handful of jelly monster sweets from the front desk. On bending to open my room door, those which rolled off my precarious mail mountain were later to be found stuck to my hall carpet via my shoes. My next error was to expect anything to work in my freezing room: the heater switch turned ineffectually, the blinds jammed rakishly at half-mast and the computer blinked into life to offer only the blank blue screen of death. As a final straw, my filing cabinet key wasn't in my desk drawer, denying me access to vital stationery and lab request forms. Considering my irritability might be due to hypoglycaemia from missing breakfast, I scoffed my remaining two sets of Dracula teeth and three red jelly devils. Morning surgeries need all the energy you can muster.

First surgeries of the week always last longer – or seem to. Emergencies demand fitting in as extras after pre-booked surgery appointments. Many patients appear to have spent all weekend brooding and catastrophising symptoms, yet still prevaricate when getting to the point with me. Or maybe I'm inordinately slow after switching off at the weekend, though I might have done some brooding myself, worrying I'd dismissed someone too hastily on Friday to get away. Could that 'backache' have been a potentially fatal aortic aneurysm? Either way, come Mondays I'm either guiltily super-thorough or ditheringly indecisive as I face patients needing convinced that what they *want* isn't necessarily what they *need*. My partner Charles MacTavish has no such qualms. He whizzes through all his surgeries, curtailing the wordy and ushering out the loquacious he calls COUs: Centre of the Universe patients. But I find Closed Monosyllabic Patients trickier.

By swearing and fiddling, I achieved a readable screen and called in my first patient, a definite CMP (I, too, can use acronyms). I like to walk out to greet patients in the waiting room, having been taught it helps early diagnosis of breathlessness or limping, and forewarns of their mood. But Mary didn't smile or look grumpy, just walked beside me silently.

I directed her to the seat at the side of my desk. Here I also differ from Charles, who prefers patients at a distance across the desk, as befits specimens of scientific interest. And he runs to time. My ten-minute slots expand elastically as I explore how an illness affects a patient's life. Different approaches suit different patients: some complain Charles proffers a prescription before they've finished talking, others love his decisiveness. Mary had never seen him. There was nothing in her case sheet. She wasn't listed on the computer.

Her lined face was expressionless. She remained standing. Was she deaf? Or spaced out? I doubted she had taken anything. She had normal-sized pupils and didn't look drowsy. I patted the seat. She sat on its edge, ankles crossed, legs tucked under, shoulders down, hands between her thighs.

'So, how can I help?'

'I'm not sleeping, Doctor, I'd like some Mogadon, please. I've had them before.' Quiet, apologetic, wan smile.

'You know, Mary, sleeping pills aren't always useful. They wear off quickly and can be addictive. Why aren't you sleeping? Is anything troubling you?

'No, nothing unusual,' she nodded. Why nod for no?

'Well, anything usual?' I leaned towards this thin woman with a pretty face, though her fine, scraped-back blonde hair needed a wash. She wore a crumpled black jersey midi-dress, a faded sheepskin coat, red-patterned tights and open-toed snakeskin shoes. Her date of birth shocked me. Did I look this old? Life can't have been easy for this woman. I ploughed on. 'So, what goes through your mind at night?'

She looked down, raised her eyes, briefly caught mine and shook her head sideways. 'Nothing.'

Desperate to get her to talk, and following teaching advice, I 'gave a little of myself.'

'You know, if I'm worried about my family, I have trouble getting over. Or I wake early. Is that how you are?' She nodded. Did that mean yes or no? I waited, left a vacuum. Another trick. Most folk hate silence and fill it. She didn't. 'I get the feeling you're a bit down about something. Would you like to tell me about it?' She gave more rapid head shakes. I sighed. Head shakes outnumbered words. As I looked to the ceiling for guidance, she blew her nose loudly making me jump.

'Well,' she swallowed, 'there's nothing anyone can do about it.'

'About what?'

'My husband. There's no pleasing him.' She breathed in deeply. 'I, well, I'm afraid he ...'

'Does he hit you?'

'No, though I have worried ... I think he finds marriage ... constraining.' There was a long pause. 'His father and his mother had a troubled relationship. I believe he, well, he likes control. I worry that he has, what do they say nowadays? Anger issues. Yes, he has anger issues.'

Such a tumble of infuriatingly vague, unfinished segments. Conscious of the full waiting room outside, I didn't follow up any particulars here, only asking softly, 'Would he consider counselling?'

'Oh dear, no, never! It might affect his work.'

'What does he do?'

'It doesn't matter, I'm sorry, Doctor. I know he has a very responsible, difficult job. I should be more understanding. No wonder he gets frustrated with me at times. I shouldn't question things. He says I have too much imagination, he's probably right. Sorry ...'

'I see.' I didn't, but deciding I'd had as much as I was going to get on the husband information, I rattled through

4

my depression catechism asking about mood, energy and appetite.

She shrugged. 'Not so good.'

And then the million-dollar suicide question. 'Do you ever feel you can't go on?'

She stared into middle distance. 'Never, Doctor, I wouldn't because of ...' To my delight she looked at me intently. I awaited a meaningful revelation.

'Sorry, Doctor, your gum is bleeding.'

I rose to look in the mirror. Ghastly red gooey sediment streaked my teeth and gums. Sitting down, I muttered about silly sweets and threw in the last tricky question in the 'depression' litany. 'And sex – any problems there?'

A swift response. 'Oh, we haven't done it for years. Not since ... It's fine.'

'Since ...?'

She looked down, shaking her head. 'It's not important. Please may I just have some pills.' The curtain had closed again.

'I think you have depression, Mary.' She frowned sceptically. 'And you look very tired. Are you working? If so, some time off might help.'

'Oh, no. I've just started a new job. I like it much better than the hospital. That's how I met ... Sorry, no thank you.'

Sadly, pressurised by the thought of twenty-two patients to come, I didn't follow that up, but vowed to get her to return. Prescription printed, I handed it over. 'These dothiepin will help you sleep, then in ten days or so, make you feel brighter. Can you come back in a fortnight and we'll see how you are?'

In retrospect, I think at this moment she looked at the script and mouthed 'Prothiaden', dothiepin's trade name. A clue lost. Silently, she rose and left.

I noted that her records lists her occupation as housewife. Tucked in the back there was a month-old Well

Woman Clinic cervical smear report marked 'Normal' and a microbiology one showing a urinary infection. But it wasn't stamped with the 'P' indicating a prescription had been left. I could find no listed phone number. Ellen could check, and chase her previous medical records. Though registered for a year, we had received no old notes. Her last address was in Edinburgh, yet she'd sounded English.

I ploughed on till lunchtime. In the staff room I asked if either of the boys had seen her. Young Gerry McColl thought not, but my senior partner, Charles, chipped in.

'Truscott? An unusual surname, isn't it? Think I've only heard of it once before. That guy Nancy had a run-in with at Asda's whilst you were on holiday – a husband maybe?'

'What run-in?'

'Nancy came back one afternoon spitting blood. This fellow had given her laldy for parking over the lines in Asda's car park. I must say he probably had a point. Have you seen how she abandons her car out there?' He nodded towards our car park. 'What really got her goat was his claim that women were rubbish drivers since they lacked "spatial awareness!"' Charles laughed, stirring his coffee with an up-ended biro while snatching the last digestive. Mean: he'd already had a cheese sandwich and a Tunnock's Teacake.

'Hey Charles – I needed that biscuit!' I protested. Gummy sweets have no staying power.

Young Gerry grinned his cheeky-monkey sort of grin. He rose and chucked that week's copy of Pulse at me. 'Article in there about coping with aggressive patients, Beth.'

'This woman wasn't aggressive, quite the opposite. Blood-from-a-stone taking her history. I'm worried she's abused. Anyway, I haven't got time to read newspapers! How come you do? And finish your stuff so quickly?'

It was a mystery to me. Gerry usually had half the mail Charles and I suffered. He wasn't exactly a skiver, but his smaller workload was annoying. My husband Ralph reckons it's a key skill acquired at Fettes. Ralph should know, being ex–public school himself and wont to swan through life as a GP professor while doing only three token surgeries a week to 'keep his hand in.'

Gerry laughed. 'Pure efficiency and genius, of course!'

Charles lifted his biro to point at Gerry, splashing tea droplets on to a Scottish Office directive in my hand, albeit a boringly unimportant one. 'Wasn't there something else odd about that guy, Gerry? Yes!' He slapped his knee then pointed at me, always theatrical. 'A Bible basher! Quoted scripture about "a woman's place" and that kind of thing. You can imagine how that got Nancy going! She said she'd muttered "Christ on a bike" if I recall, whereupon he ranted about not taking the Lord's name in vain. Told her she should "repent and atone for her sins before it was too late!" or some such. Would've liked to be a fly on the wall at that. Didn't help the situation that he was English.'

'What difference did that make?' I laughed.

'No idea, but he wouldn't let it go, thrust on her a card for some church he ran in town – that's how she got his name. The card said he was a Doctor Truscott from some evangelical set-up in Garnethill I'd never heard of. Probably bought a mail order PhD in Bible-bashing. Heard you can buy one for anything in Florida. Nancy checked our list, but he wasn't ours. Wherever he's registered, bet he's lodged one of those scripture-misquoting Jehovah's Witness leaflets about refusing blood transfusions and what not. Does she have one?'

I checked inside Mary's folder again. 'No. And by the way, why isn't she on the computer? She registered well before Jess started.' Jess was the nurse we'd hired to summarise and computerise our records. We'd had to abandon doing it ourselves, largely due to the boys' priorities of golf and rugby at weekends.

Leaning against the door, Gerry shrugged. 'Oh, who

cares! You're an impatient bunny, Bethany, aren't you? We'll get there eventually!'

I scowled. I loathed my 'Sunday' name, but after spotting it on official mail, Gerry used it whenever he could. 'Anyway, we're at "T" now, though we'd have been long finished if you'd bothered your ginger! Though I do worry what we'll do in power cuts with no paper notes.'

Gerry shrugged again and left whistling. Charles continued wading through his mound of letters and blank prescriptions with attached post-it notes. He didn't print scripts on his computer. In truth, I'm not sure he knew how to turn it on. Manager Ellen booted up his machine every morning and had succeeded in badgering him into typing surgery consultations, albeit by laborious one-finger tapping. But while Charles might pretend to be daft, when it came to people, he was shrewd. As Gerry's whistling faded down the corridor, he turned to me. 'You know Beth, if the guy Nancy met is that woman's husband, he's not someone to tackle. She described him as being like an All Black Maori prop forward. Not someone to mess with unless you're very sure of your grounds.'

Though I didn't share Charles's public school passion for rugby, I understood. And this potential spouse must have been something to faze Nancy, a battle-hardened former nursing sister veteran of Glasgow Royal Infirmary's wild Saturday night casualty.

'So, you don't think we should do anything, Charles? Like visit? Or call the police? She was scared.'

Charles looked thoughtful. In his best Midlothian public school accent, he pontificated like an advocate. 'What do we know, Beth? She's odd, quiet, so? Did she have any injuries? No. Did she mention making any police complaints? No. On balance, we've no evidence of any crime. If there were kids, we could have a quiet word with School Health to keep an eye out. Are there?' He took her notes. 'No antenatal stuff.

Nil pregnancies listed on smear request. She's over forty, a grown woman. It's up to her.'

Good old Charles MacTavish: don't get involved. Not the last time he'd give me that advice. Nancy was on holiday out of further quizzing reach. I grabbed a stray custard cream spotted under papers on the coffee table and trotted off to do house calls. On the way back I'd need an Auld's tuna roll or a Spar sandwich.

That night I woke at two. Like I'd told Mary, waking early means something's bothering me. I automatically went to the loo, as you do in the middle of the night when roused. As I sat there, my half-awake brain realised I'd been dreaming about Mary's drawn face. Was Charles MacTavish right? Should I do nothing? Oddly, Ellen hadn't found any telephone numbers for Truscotts in Bearsden or Milngavie. Odder still, the given address and postcode were bogus. The plot thickened. Returning to bed, I met my youngest, Katy, on the landing.

She rubbed sleepy eyes. 'Hi, Mum. You up too? I woke with my heart thumping.'

I took her pulse: normal. She pulled her arm away. 'It's OK now. I just woke with a start. Not done that for years. Remember the Bear in the Wardrobe?'

I laughed. When Katy was small, an innocent bedtime story had resulted in a night light and an open wardrobe door for years. We'd even fixed a wee strip light inside the wardrobe, making it an unattractive place for bear hiding. 'You bet I do! What a lot of electricity that book wasted! I tore your Dad off a strip for buying it.'

'Why are you up?'

'I'm worrying about a patient today who wouldn't talk about what was upsetting her. She's a bit of a puzzle. What's bothering you? Things OK at school?'

As I gave her a hug she started mumbling into my

shoulder. Only weeks ago it would've been my armpit. Growing fast: fourteen in a week. 'Oh, one of the boys said something horrible ...' She shook her head rapidly, looking close to tears.

'What did they say, pet?' Now wide awake, I fetched our dressing gowns and took her downstairs for a chat over hot chocolate. Like two giggling schoolgirls, we pinched big sister Julia's marshmallows from her secret stash and held a conspiratorial discussion about 'sticks and stones' and boys having no right to slag off girls for having 'ginger' hair. Then, after a bit of 'how to survive bullies' and staying 'true to yourself' we headed back to bed. Katy fell asleep quickly. I heard her snoring.

Sleep eluded me, lying preoccupied with the negative thoughts that loom large in the wee small hours, that nadir of existence lying between two and four. I hoped I'd reassured Katy that by next week no one would remember Matt Pearson's hurtful jibes about her ginger hair, especially since it wasn't truly red. But the discussion had brought up my inability to understand why men are so often cruel to women. I'd seen it so much. Like fellow student Conor, a rapist who'd got away with it twenty years ago. I was still angry about his victim's suicide – and guilty I couldn't save Maia. Then those friends who'd stayed in abusive relationships despite warnings. Like my old classmate Wendy, though she'd finally escaped Conor to marry lovely Henry. And best friend Rosie, who'd weathered an uncaring marriage to become a superstar psychiatrist. Fortunately, her James had mellowed with age. That diverted me: I should phone her soon. It'd been too long. Ruminating on my luck with my own happy second marriage, I eventually fell asleep.

Next morning, my mind was centred on finding gym kits, books, homework diaries and socks before corralling a warring Jules and Katy into the car for school. I envied Ralph, doubtless enjoying breakfast in his swanky London Hotel while discussing the 'Future of General Practice' (or more likely, Scotland's chances in the Five Nations), before his academic conference. The girls were arguing about the most fanciable member of East 17, as all nearly 14 and 15-year-olds did then, thus ending up with no time for breakfast. I managed to coax them to take a slug of milk and two Jaffa cakes, consoling myself that this at least provided some calcium (milk), iron (chocolate), Vitamin C (Jaffa orange goo) and energy (cake carbs). I was no better; fighting with them left me no time for anything myself. Dropping off the still-arguing girls at the school gate, I headed for the Spar.

Anila Chaudri's bulky figure bustled about in her orderly corner shop, putting my purchases in a bag, and ringing them up on the till. A cheery woman in a sapphire-blue salwar-kameez, she had a wide laughing mouth, kohl-lined eyes and silvery-streaked black hair bedecked with sparkling combs. Anila always brightened a cold, grey Scottish morning

'This is brunch!' I told her.

'Come at one tomorrow, I have roti for you, Doctor! You're too thin!'

She pretended to look cross, then laughed. A warm, generous, motherly woman whose homemade food was mouth-watering. Picking up my gammon salad roll plus guilty crisps and Kit Kat, I replied, 'I'd love that! Anila, you're a life saver!' How I miss her.

Two

Old Enemies

Hilton Hotel, Edinburgh, Friday 13th November 1992

Surely, she was mistaken – it couldn't be him. At a psychiatric conference? Dr Rosie Hutton suppressed the surge of emotion rising in her chest and closed her eyes. When she opened them, he had gone. It had only been a back view. But the slim, expensively suited figure was of a man probably in his forties standing square-on, legs spread wide and head held high. Was it ridiculous to think she could identify him merely by his arrogant stance, that left hand in his pocket, jiggling car keys? By the way he waved his right one expansively to emphasise a point? He'd been talking to Professor Chaim Marinsky, his head nodding, invading Chaim's personal space, inching closer to his prey. True to form. But why would he be in Edinburgh talking to a world-renowned suicide expert? He, of all people. Rosie knew it could be her mind playing tricks as she was feeling unusually anxious today. Although it wasn't her first presentation at a Royal College of Psychiatrists conference, it was the first time she'd been scheduled last. By 4 p.m. the audience would be tired. As would she.

No, the man in the sharp grey suit couldn't be the one responsible for Maia's suicide twenty-two years ago, the bastard who'd tainted so many lives before Beth finally exposed him. Mind you, they'd never discovered where he'd gone after he was erased from the Medical Register, but it was impossible for him to be back in medicine as a psychiatrist. A sharp elbow in her ribs made her turn to the woman beside her.

'Sorry, I was miles away, Judy. What did you say?'

'I just said let's go and sit down, Dr Dozy! Are you OK, Rosemarie? You look kinda pale.'

Rosie smiled at her Californian friend, the ebullient Professor Judy Diefenbaker, the only person who ever used her full name. 'Sure, Jude, I'm fine. Just thought I saw a ghost, that's all. Conor Towmey – remember him?'

'How could I forget that horror? Say, wasn't his name the cement that bound us two together that first day we met? No way, girl, could I forget him! But isn't he locked up?'

'No. In the end, he wasn't prosecuted on any of the counts.' Rosie ran her right hand through her blonde curls and cradled her heavy bag onto her left hip as they walked through the packed meeting room.

Judy paused, ample chin wobbling as she shook her head in puzzlement. 'But the GMC threw the book at him, right?'

'Well, they only need "balance of probability" unlike, according to my legal-eagle husband, the Law Courts, who require "beyond reasonable doubt" to convict. After the GMC hearing he took sick, then none of the victims successfully pursued him in court. That patient of yours he groped? She refused to stand up in court, as you know. The ex-mistress whose surgery he botched did try, but her case was a cock-up. Towmey's barrister got him off on technicalities over his arrest warrant and missing records or something. The other research-stealing charge wasn't followed up either. My friend Henry said he wasn't wasting time and money going to court. Mind you, he did take Con's wife! Him marrying Wendy must have been punishment of sorts for Con. Henry and Wendy are so happy now and have a cute toddler called Maia.'

'Sweet! After your friend who died, yes? Can't believe he never got time for raping her, you having that DNA evidence.'

Rosie sighed as they sat down in the front row. 'Not

admissible. The Procurator said no victim had formally complained, there was no known date or time for an offence and DNA from knicker semen wasn't proof of rape. Plus Wendy got Conor's DNA sample without permission.' Rosie tailed off. How Conor could get under your skin! Too upsetting to revisit, wouldn't do for a psychiatrist to shed tears, especially one with a high-powered lecture to deliver. Thank God she had a few hours yet to compose herself. Judy patted her arm as the first speaker took the podium.

At 4.30 p.m., the fervent applause after she finished surprised Rosie. Gratifying though. She'd been preparing her presentation for months. The results she'd reported were good, her outcomes for anorexia and depression better than those where kids were treated in adult wards. She'd campaigned hard for her Specialist Adolescent Unit but emphasised that there was still room for improvement in services. Sitting back beside Judy for the summing-up, Rosie allowed herself to relax. But after the President's votes of thanks, when she stood up to gather her bags, papers and brochures, as she turned her back to the podium, she froze.

It was Conor Towmey. Face on, there was absolutely no doubt, even seen through the milling throng of dispersing delegates. Tanned, slim, restored to his old handsome self. And he knew it. His arm rested around the shoulders of a smart young drug rep she'd seen earlier. Rosie's blood curdled as the girl laughed and nudged him flirtatiously. Earlier, Rosie had discussed a new drug from her company, Constella. Wanting to try her new anti-depressant on recalcitrant patients, she'd taken a Drug Data Sheet in order to remember the medication's name. She certainly wouldn't forget it now.

Judy had moved off to talk to London colleagues, but Rosie remained rooted to her spot. As the crowd ahead of her thinned, she watched an all-too-familiar scenario: Conor heading out, ushering the girl along, his hand dropping from back to buttock. But the girl didn't object. That black skirt was short for business. Her striped blouse strained across her assets, the kind of assets that had proved Conor Towmey's downfall. Not that he looked like he'd learned any lessons. With the hall's main doors propped open, Rosie made out the pair crossing the lobby to the street door and kissing before stepping out into the icy Edinburgh twilight. The doorman smiled. Conor gave him a thumbs-up. And a wink? Rosie felt sick.

She couldn't speak when Judy returned and dumped her bag on a seat. 'Watch that, honey, will you? Need a quick trip to the restroom.'

The minute Judy moved off, Rosie slung her own bag over a shoulder, lifted Judy's and headed for the side rooms where the trade stalls were being dismantled. At Constella Pharmaceuticals, a lad in his early twenties was packing up.

'Excuse me, I was speaking earlier to one of your colleagues, Jane, I think?'

'Jane Chancellor? You've just missed her, Doctor. Is there something I can do for you?'

The boy was a typical drug rep: handsome, personable, endearing. Trained in ingratiation. Rosie scolded herself for being so cynical. He was only earning a living.

'No, thanks, I have all the drug data, but I wondered perhaps if Jane could visit me at the Unit to discuss a few things I didn't think of asking earlier – had my mind on my paper.'

'Yes, I heard you. Good stuff, Doc! Sure, I'll ask her. Do you have a card?'

Rosie fumbled, balancing Judy's bag, her own and her heavy acetate presentation folder, before finally fishing out a business card. 'Tell me, do you know who the chap was I saw her with earlier? The tanned one in a grey suit?'

'Oh, Conrad Towie? You not met him? His Eureka

Research Consultancy does trials and regulatory stuff for us. He's a high-flyer. Just back from the States. Works a lot with Jane.'

Rosie thought it more likely he was working on Jane. The leopard hadn't changed his spots: still the sexual predator she'd known from Glasgow Uni. But Conrad? Why bother changing Conor to Conrad? Didn't seem worth the effort. And only dropping the 'm' from Towmey – why not something completely different? The biggest question of all, though, was how did someone who'd been struck off from the Medical Register for, amongst other things, falsifying research, come to be running a research company?

Later, Rosie was in the kitchen rustling up lasagne and salad while James moaned about missing his usual Friday fish and chips. Judy came through to hand him a bottle of wine.

'Sorry, James, my fault. I'm allergic to fish! But here.'

'Oh, well, this is an improvement on our average! Thanks, Judy.' Removing the cork from Judy's claret, he sniffed appreciatively and poured three large glasses.

Rosie kissed him as she passed. 'Shouldn't you let it breathe?'

'Oh, we'll just give it a swirl!' He demonstrated.

'Since you can't have your fish, James, I've made your favourite pud, Eton mess. No mean feat. So hard finding decent raspberries in November!' James blew her a kiss.

It was 9 p.m., with Nathan finally tucked up in bed, before they finally sat down for dinner. Nathan had created chaos the way 15-month-olds do when they have someone new to impress. James praised Rosie's lasagne, poured wine generously and played to his visiting audience. Discretion went out of the window. Judy was astounded by the antics of Scottish barristers: their horse-trading, their 'jiggery-pokery' with evidence, as James put it, and some bizarre Judge's rulings. Having heard it all before, Rosie headed for the kitchen to load the dishwasher. Then she returned with Armagnac.

James jumped up. 'Rosie! You know it gives you a headache. Wouldn't you rather have some more wine? I've got a Barzac for the pudding.'

'Sorry, no. I need the strongest drink I can get. I have to tell you something.'

'Sorry, darling. I forgot to ask about your paper presentation, did something go wrong?'

'No. It was fine. It was bloody Conor Towmey that was the problem.'

James looked puzzled and Judy shook her head. 'But you only thought you saw him, Rosie. He wasn't actually there, was he?'

'Oh, yes he was. I was too upset to tell you in the taxi home, then I didn't want to shout and swear in front of Nathan. But he was there, and worst of all, James, he went off curled round an innocent young lassie who has no idea what she's getting herself into. I've left word asking her to call on me, ostensibly about a new drug she's peddling.'

'What on earth was he doing at a psychiatric conference? He lost his attempt to get back onto the Medical List.' James drained his wineglass. 'Dan said his appeal failed. And he certainly can't have become a psychiatrist – though I suspect he's certifiable by one.' James pushed his silvering dark fringe back off his forehead.

Rosie flushed, eyes wide, and raised her voice. 'You didn't tell me that he'd appealed? Bloody cheek after everything he did! I don't think Beth knows that either. But he was with the pharma crowd. He's running a pharmaceutical consultancy firm!' She thudded the brandy bottle down. James was a whisky drinker but lifted the brandy to pour a generous measure into his barely drained wine glass, usually a heinous crime. Rosie made no comment as she took a large swig from the proper brandy glass she'd brought. Judy hesitated before copying James.

James gulped then coughed. 'How in God's name can someone struck off for incompetence and research fraud run a pharma consultancy? Is it his own? Though how could a stony-broke, gambling, coke addict find money to start any company?'

'Maybe you could look up Companies House and see who's behind Eureka Research Consultancy? Constella Pharma seem very cosy with them.' Rosie slumped back. 'Oh, hell, what can we do? Anyone for Eton mess?'

In the kitchen she realised she hadn't prepared the cream. Violently hand-whipping it, she came to her senses just before it turned to butter. After folding the cream into fruit and crushed meringues in a crystal bowl, she plonked it on the table with its matching dishes: a wedding present from Beth. She sighed. Beth would have to be told Teflon Towmey had bounced back, especially back to Scotland! Hopefully, if he was based here in Edinburgh, Beth would be unlikely to run across him. Poor Beth. How awful it must have been for her having to identify Maia's body all those miles from home on that Sydney scholarship. And poor Wendy, almost driven mental by Con. Thank God she was far away, down in Bristol with Henry. James changed the subject, but all Rosie could think about was the injustice of Conor walking free.

Next morning, Rosie walked Judy from their New Town flat to Waverley for her London train. Driving wasn't an option: the Armagnac bottle had emptied well after three. The stroll on the crisp cold Saturday morning revived her as she chatted about Nat's recent exploits, like flooding the flat by filling the downstairs loo with potatoes dragged from the kitchen.

'Threw out the potatoes, of course. Yuck!'

'Oh, Rosemarie, surely they'd have been OK after cooking? Mind you, I've a colleague so terrified of germs he even wipes doorknobs with antiseptic wipes!'

Rosie didn't join Judy laughing. 'Poor thing. Can't someone help?'

'You worry too much about everyone, girl!' They'd reached the platform turnstile. Judy fished out her ticket and stood back from her old friend. 'And that goes for that young drug rep too. Don't you go barging in – she might not appreciate it.'

'Easier said than done. Anyway, I'll let you know what we find out about his company. It's shocking. He's an untrustworthy rat – shouldn't be doing research!'

Judy looked at the destination board. 'Platform's up. Time to go. Remember, girl, Conor's not your problem!' She pushed through the barrier, blew a kiss, waved and was gone.

Rosie walked slowly home. Beth needed told. In person.

*

The next weekend, Rosie sat with me in the kitchen of our Bearsden house, Rowanlea. Even without make-up, her skin was flawless, and her short, curly bob was immaculate. In contrast, I had a peely-wally face and tangled, dull brown bed-hair. Snow had fallen overnight. We'd slept soundly after a long libation-laden dinner of groaning reminiscences. Nathan was rapturous when Julia and Katy got him up, dressed him in his padded snowsuit and took him out to build a snowman. Snowballs were tricky: his hands were too wee to make them, but he could throw ones Katy made. He was constantly falling over and chuckling loudly. James and Ralph, aided by Julia, were enthusiastically building a horse. Well, they said it was a horse, but when its head repeatedly fell off, it looked more like a hump-backed whale with stumpy legs. Rosie and I opted to cosy up in front of the Rayburn with hot chocolate and croissants, a welcome quiet Saturday morning break for busy medical mums. We watched the happy scene through the window. Then Rosie spoiled it.

'Con's back. Heading a research company. Calls himself Conrad Towie!'

'How? What company? *Conrad*?' I couldn't believe this.

'I saw him at the psych conference last week at the Hilton. He does a lot for Constella Pharma, whose guy said "Conrad" ran Eureka Research Consultancy. James says Eureka lists Dr Conrad Towie as MD, an Alexander Kane as CEO and a Mrs Tuva Kane as Company Secretary.'

'That's that wee surgeon guy from St Jasper's, Sandy Kane, who was Conor's sole character witness at his hearing. Tuva's probably his wife.'

'Yes, I think so. Kane was a surgeon Conor worked for. Think he mentored him into his consultancy. Kane's Harley Street, so I suppose he's minted. Tuva is his fourth wife, by all accounts, a beautiful Swedish heiress who is also a qualified pharmacologist. Her family own Heidrich-Holtz Pharmaceuticals, who in turn own a majority share in Eureka.'

'This Sandy can't be very bright if he's put Conor, or rather Conrad, in charge. Have you told Wendy he's resurfaced?'

'Not yet, Beth. She's flat out just now, what with school health reorganization in Bristol and the two babes. Since she's unlikely to cross his path down there, thought I'd leave it.'

Before I could comment, the phone rang, and Conor's horrifying renaissance faded into secondary importance. The caller was Antar, a young patient. Surprising, for I wasn't on-call and my phone wasn't on divert. I wondered how he knew our ex-directory number, then remembered he was in Julia's class.

'Do you want Julia? She's outside. I'll fetch her.'

'No. It's you, Doctor.' His voice broke. 'Can you come?

It's my mother. She's dead.'

I was stunned. Anila, my generous Spar shop friend, the wonderful cook – dead?

'Oh Antar, that's awful! What happened?'

'I thought she had gone to sleep. I fell asleep in the kitchen, but when I took up her chai at six, she was gone!'

'Have you had the out-of-hours doctor in?' I hoped he didn't think I was trying to get out of visiting, but formalities needed to be observed.

'Yes. We've been given a death certificate, but I'm worried it's not right. I think something bad happened. My uncles are here, they … Oh, Doctor, please come.'

'OK, I'll come round. You're at number two Radley Road, aren't you?'

'Yes. Thank you, Doctor.'

I fetched my medical bag. Not sure why. I was hardly going to be examining or dispensing to a dead woman. Back in the kitchen I told Rosie. 'I'm not sure how long I'll be, can you feed the troops?'

'Sure!' Outside in the garden, our six-foot husbands were now trying to build a sort of crooked igloo while Katy and Julia pelted them with snowballs. I waved Julia to come in. She was upset when I told her about Anila.

'She was lovely. Poor Antar. What's going to happen to them all now?'

Only then I remembered he had lots of younger siblings and his dad had died last year. They'd be orphans now. But I hadn't got the sense the kids were Antar's worry. Plus he'd said uncles were there, so what was wrong, or 'bad' as he'd put it?

Three

The Art of Death

The adjacent small town of Milngavie, the same weekend

Leaning forward, he closes her lids and lifts the lacy edge of the sheet. The daughter stands in the doorway. An occasional shoulder movement and sniff into an embroidered lawn handkerchief is the only betrayal of emotion. She is genteel and restrained, admirable in a woman. Gathering his instruments from the silk eiderdown, he notes she is dabbing her eyes with the handkerchief: unwise, risks conjunctivitis.

'Thanks for coming so promptly, Doctor. I wasn't sure whether to phone you or call 999.'

'It was no bother, Miss Thomas. I'm sorry I couldn't do more for her.'

Saturday morning was earlier than he'd predicted. He'd expected to hear of her demise on Monday, probably a call from Jenny the cleaner. Packing ophthalmoscope and stethoscope into his Gladstone bag, he regards Miss Thomas. She stands breathing in through dilated nostrils, compressing her lips, stretching her long attractive neck, so like her mother's in early photos. Before age wormed into the picture to compress her spine, suck collagen from her skin and atrophy the hair from her scalp. The daughter sighs and meets his gaze.

'Now, you'll have to guide me through the formalities. I'm afraid I couldn't get back from New York till the day before Dad's funeral.'

Always away, this daddy's girl. How Dorcas had mourned the widening gap between them since his death. He knows it's been months since Brighid's last visit.

'I'll be delighted, Miss Thomas. It is fairly straightforward. Perhaps we could discuss it downstairs?'

'Right.' She is twisting the handkerchief round her thumb. 'I'll go and put the kettle on. You will have a cup of tea, won't you?'

'Of course. Milk and two sugars please. I'll just say a prayer before coming down. It's a habit I've developed over the years. I shan't be long.' He inclines his right ear towards his shoulder, smiling with his eyes, a favoured expression. He wonders if Dorcas has told her of his lay preaching? Perhaps not. Dorcas had also mentioned her regret at the brevity of Brighid's weekly calls. Curious how different this closed, cool, confident daughter was from emotional Dorcas. But that tortured hanky betrayed emotion. Inevitably, bereavement moved people, though the emotions elicited varied. Sorrow, of course, for those burdened by compassion. Other reactions depended on your degree of involvement, or the consequences of the death, such as reward. He smiles with his lips.

'Fine, Doctor. I'm not religious but pray if you must. I'll see you downstairs.'

Her lack of religiosity is a bonus, appeasing the flutters he's been experiencing since catching sight of the Sacred Heart picture behind the door. How did he miss that? Dorcas never mentioned Catholicism. He watches Brighid leave. Smart. Crocodile courts, crisp, white cotton shirt unbuttoned to a hint of décolletage. She leaves a lingering whiff of scent which triggers memories: a sweet perfume mingling with stale milk in a corridor, a bell ringing. A transient inner glow from being hugged. More memories drift from years later: the aroma of hot chocolate, *Ticket to Ride* pulsing from a juke box, an encouraging smile, another slender pale neck rising to pearl earrings on delicate lobes. Mrs O'Neill, like Brighid, was a classy woman. The current fashions for those abominable workmen's jeans and sloppy sweaters, or even worse, those intimidating Sue Ellen shoulder pads from that dissolute TV drama he'd stopped Clara watching, *Dallas*, were below Brighid. And all decent women. He knew Brighid to be single, fortyish, Harvard-educated, a banking high-flier like her father. Thinking of those excellent pert breasts, undamaged by suckling, he feels a stirring. In another situation, perhaps. But for now, there is a task to be done.

Rapidly, he searches bedside drawers, dressing table, a tallboy and an en-suite shower room before finding the incriminating pill box and substituting another. Closing the bathroom cabinet, he considers his image, re-adjusts his tie, smooths his difficult hair and converts his satisfied grin into respectful empathy, as advised in his current book on neuro-linguistic programming. So illuminating. He must seek a course in it. Naturally, he'd always been aware that expressions and gestures conveyed more than words, but perhaps in the past he may have been overly theatrical in attempting to give the right impression. NLP shows there are subtler signals of care, compassion and honesty, or of satisfaction and superiority: emotions best not conveyed. Genuine feelings need never be discernible. Life is an act.

He descends the ruby carpeted stairs, touches the damask walls hung with exquisite gilded oils, like this Hornel, *Girl on a Swing*. Dorcas had taste. Pictures were an ideal legacy. He smiles, anticipating his usual self-deprecatory phone call response to the lawyer: 'Oh, how kind, I did admire it, but never expected ...' This will be his fifth painting since coming west. Four he has sold, plus some antiques, in Edinburgh and London. Safety in distance. But he will keep this picture. A fortunate care-free child plays in the sunshine.

In the kitchen, the kettle clicks in completion. Curtains are drawn, the tea tray is laid.

'Shall we go through to the parlour?'

He is not surprised she uses her mother's old-fashioned

term, but is at the sooty rings round her eyes. Tears are unsurprising, but her doubtless expensive mascara should not have run. She should ask for a refund. Her mother would have.

'Oh, please don't trouble carrying things through. We can sort out the paperwork here.' He removes a blue pad from his case. 'I give you this death certificate for the Registrar in Roman Road over in Bearsden. And you'll need to contact undertakers. Whom will you use?'

'I don't know, I haven't thought.'

'Why not Wylie and Lochead? A little further away in town, but highly efficient and professional. I'm sure you'd like your mother cared for by the best.' Spread the load. One to Dawson's last week, two last month.

'Right.' She is gazing into middle distance. 'You know, Doctor, I can't believe it.'

'Shock and denial are the first stages of grief.' He nods. She'll get to pain and guilt soon enough. Then blame, if he's unlucky and she challenges his story. 'It takes time to come to terms with loss.'

'She seemed fine on the phone yesterday.'

'I understand how hard it is. I remember losing my own mother.' In truth, he had experienced no stages of grief then. She'd been lost to him for years.

Brighid sighs. 'I took today off. Said I'd be here by noon. We were going to Daly's for afternoon tea. Mum loved her cream scones!' She blows her nose. 'My plane was late. I expected she'd be pacing in the hall, but when she didn't answer the door, I let myself in. She was lying in her bed, so still.' She sobbed into her crumpled hanky. 'I never had a chance to say goodbye.'

'Console yourself that she slipped away peacefully in her sleep. Best way to go with heart disease.' The palpitations would have been immense. He looks upwards.

'Heart disease? She never said!'

'No? I expect she thought you'd worry. She thought the world of you, you know.'

Brighid relaxes. 'And she thought the world of you. You were so attentive.'

Ah, so he has been mentioned! Had Dorcas told of the Hornel bequest? Inclining his head, he proffers the death certificate before filling in the GP-retained part, like a cheque. He adds name, date, time (a guess), mode and cause of death (a lie). Blotting his spidery writing, he sheaths his shiny red Schaeffer pen before slipping it into into his jacket pocket. He has several. And a Mont Blanc. Patients are so generous. He reaches for the familiar delicate china cup. Insufficient sugar. He doesn't say. Brighid is peering at his certificate. She needs an optician.

'Myocardial infarction? What's that?'

'The medical term for a heart attack. Now, you'll also need a cremation form. I'll do my part one and ask another doctor to sign part two tonight and have all the forms at Wylie's by Monday. There's a legal requirement for two doctors to confirm the circumstances of death before cremation. The other doctor may phone to speak with you.'

'Cremation? Oh, I don't think so. Mother was Roman Catholic.'

Heart quickening and jaw tightening, he pats her manicured hand. Lovely ruby ring. 'Did she not say she wanted cremation? Indeed, she said so often. She'd stopped going to mass but attended Northwood Parish Church up the road.' A gamble worth taking …

'Really?'

'Oh, yes. She attends their Women's Guild with my practice manager, Maureen.' This, at least, is true. He has heard Maureen speak of it in the surgery. 'She finds the Reverend Andrew Stock's church very welcoming.'

Brighid's brow knits. 'She never said.'

He is banking on that. 'Your mother had decided that

cremation was the modern way, and wished her ashes scattered at Luss.' He points to a photo on the kitchen sideboard of a smiling Dorcas, her beloved Edward and a teenage Brighid beside a car. 'I know she loved Loch Lomond. She told me of that day when the car broke down at the Lochside and the AA took hours to come. Wonderful cars, Austin Princesses. My father had one.' He has no idea what car his father had, if any. How easy lying becomes. Brighid looks thoughtful. More empathy should do it. 'Arranging a funeral is hard, isn't it? We are never fully prepared for loss. But when our Lord judges us ...'

Brighid sighs. 'I stopped believing years ago. Dad wasn't Catholic, you know, only paid lip service to converting for Mum. I was confirmed at school, but by uni I was an atheist. Religion's all mumbo jumbo. Actually, on balance, maybe it isn't surprising she changed church. After Dad died, she was cross at her priest who kept turning up looking for money. Trying for a guilt trip I suspect, for her giving Dad the Protestant send-off he'd asked for at the end.'

Reining in his anger at religions being flipped in such a cavalier manner, he manages, 'It was a lovely service, well attended.' A dangerous service, one quite lulling him into assuming Dorcas was also Church of Scotland.

Brighid gathers up the teacups. 'Well, there's only me left and I'm not facing that grasping old lech, Father McAdam. Church of Scotland it is, then. Do I phone the minister now?'

'Wylie's first, I'd suggest. Do let me know when the service is. Maureen and I will wish to pay our respects.'

'You've been so kind, Doctor. I can't thank you enough for everything you've done for my mother.'

'It's been a pleasure. It's what we are paid for, easing our patients through life.'

And out. When it's their time.

Four

Doubt & Acceptance

Rowanlea, 21st November 1992 continued

That Saturday, we'd had the heaviest snowfall we'd seen for years. Snow is fun if you don't have to go anywhere. No snow plough had yet reached our non-bus-route avenue. Digging out the car seemed a waste of time, so Julia and I set off on foot to see Antar. It was a half-hour trudge.

While Julia knew Antar fairly well, I'd only met him a few times outside of the surgery. Once taking him to an inter-school debating competition, once at our door when he'd been in a group collecting Julia for some school function, and a couple of times in his mother's shop at weekends. My recollection was of a smiling, shy boy, young for his age. I did hesitate about going, worrying I was interfering in another doctor's case, but Rosie had shamed me. 'The poor boy's crying out for help and reassurance, you can't refuse!' In full adolescent psychiatrist mode, she'd urged me to take Julia. 'Antar might appreciate talking to someone his own age.'

The sombre, tight-lipped boy who opened the door was unrecognisable as the sunny youngster I'd met previously. He led us past the open door of a lounge full of men in Punjabi traditional dress mingling in a musical hubbub of loud Urdu, to a family sitting room at the rear where his quiet siblings sat looking small amongst the red velvet cushions and fringed throws of an ornately carved Indian sofa. He introduced us to Mannat, a tearful pigtailed teenager who threw herself sobbing on Julia, Nazreen, a late primary beauty with soulful eyes, twisting her long hair round her fingers, and seven-year-old twins, Jasir and sister Sibal, looking bemused but dry-eyed. I wasn't sure they'd taken in what had happened. No one had helped the little Sibal out of her nightdress. She looked at me with her mother's eyes. With a pang of sadness, I remembered visiting a year ago when Mr Chaudri had died while awaiting a kidney transplant.

'How old are you Antar?' I asked.

'Seventeen this month,' he replied. He was agitated, speaking rapidly. 'I am sorry I phoned to trouble you, Dr Semple. My uncles are angry. They say I must accept the Will of Allah, that mother has died of her diabetes and that is an end to it.' He sighed and hung his head. 'I'm sorry I've wasted your time.'

'But what was it that worried you so much that you phoned Mum?' said Julia.

His eyes swivelled out to the hall and back to me. 'I wondered if maybe she needn't have died, could have been saved. Or if something was given to her and it wasn't natural.'

'Natural? What do you mean?' I found myself looking about shiftily. I caught Sibal's unsettling brown-eyed stare.

Antar now looked distracted. 'My mother is in her bedroom. Perhaps you would like to see her?' He headed for the stairs.

I hesitated. This was not a scenario medical school had prepared me for. What did he think had happened? Was this a crime scene? Should I have called the police before coming? My thoughts were all over the place.

'Go on, Mum,' said Julia, sitting down, lifting a hairbrush, and starting to plait Sibal's wild hair. 'I'll stay with the kids.' She nodded at Antar's back and then at me, inclining her head to the door. Her eyes spoke volumes: she looked as scared as I felt. Heart racing, I followed Antar up the red-carpeted stairs towards his mother's bedroom.

Anila lay on her back on the large carved bed, arms folded over her chest, eyes closed, wrapped tightly in a thin, white and silver garment with a scarf encircling her jaw and head. A wizened, elfin lady was about to lift a sheet up and over her but paused, looking to Antar. He dismissed her with an imperious wave as if he had already assumed the mantle of master of the house. How long social services would allow that might be another thing. The woman collected her washbowl and towels and backed out of the room.

I shivered. The radiator was cold to the touch. 'So exactly what happened yesterday Antar?'

'When I went to the shop after school she'd been sick. She said it must have been something she'd eaten, but she was in quite a lot of pain from her tummy, so we closed the shop early at five. At home, she wouldn't eat anything, only drank some water. But still she kept being sick, so about midnight I decided she needed a doctor and called the out-of-hours number. The doctor came out and gave her an injection.'

'What did he say?'

'That she had an infection and needed antibiotics. That I should try and make her drink and eat. That she must have her insulin as usual and I should phone your surgery today if she wasn't better. But at four in the morning I had to phone again. She was raving at me, throwing things, not making sense. I couldn't get her to check her blood sugar, though I gave her the needles and strips. The doctor took a while to come the second time, and by the time he was here she was breathing funny and mumbling. He seemed annoyed.'

'What do you mean? He was angry you'd called him out again?'

'I'm not sure why. He said she was delirious with the infection and high blood sugar. He gave her another injection. I don't know what of, then he left a prescription to get today.'

He showed me it: amoxicillin 500mg three times a day, an antibiotic. Nothing odd about that. Though I did wonder whether, if she'd been delirious, she mightn't have been ill enough to send into hospital for a drip. 'Did he examine her?'

'Yes. He put me out of the room, but I saw him listen to her chest and feel her tummy.'

'Antar, I know it's awful losing your mum, but why were you upset enough to call me too?'

'The blood sugar. I know how important it is when you're diabetic. She wouldn't let me prick her finger, but I don't think he did it either, though he *said* he did after I went to fetch the water he asked for. But I was only away seconds. I grabbed a glass from the bathroom next door. I saw no test strips or little lancets on the bed, only the ones I put there.' He pointed to her bedside table where the equipment still lay. 'I told him she wouldn't let me give her insulin, but I didn't see him draw up any from her bottle and give it. Nor did he try to get her to drink the water. Worse, he also said funny things, like how "Mothers were a trial for a boy, weren't they?" And when he looked at her his lip sort of curled. He pinched her belly, and said, "Hasn't she let herself go?" I didn't think it was very nice.'

I didn't either, it sounded appalling! Being angry at getting called out a second time overnight was no excuse for rudeness. The boy looked exhausted. I asked him to wait outside before carefully unwrapping the shroud-like coverings and reviewing Anila's body like that of any deceased I needed to certify. There was nothing to suggest inflicted injury or anything untoward. Her tummy was scarred from years of insulin injections and a couple of Caesareans. The only finding was slight bruising in the crook of her left arm. Had someone taken a blood sample from her elbow? I brought Antar back. 'Did he take blood?'

'I didn't see any blood bottles on the bed. There was only his stethoscope thingy.'

'Did he give her an injection there?' I pointed to the front of her elbow.

'Not that I saw. He gave her the first injection here.' He

pointed to his left upper arm.

I moved her cap sleeve and saw a bruise there. Not a route I would have normally used for a large-volume antibiotic jab, lateral thighs or buttocks would be less painful, but it might depend what it was. Could the elbow needle-mark be from an intravenous glucose shot, given in Antar's absence? Had the GP thought that her blood sugar was low, not high? But there was no proof from recent prick marks on her fingers that he had actually checked it. Antar let out a sob so I put my arm round him. I would have liked to see the death certificate but didn't have the heart to ask those uncles. Perhaps there were things needing clarified here.

'Look, Antar, as her GP, I can request a post-mortem via the Fiscal's office which might set your mind at rest.' Before he could answer, the door opened.

'Good afternoon, Doctor. Antar told me he had called you. But there is no need for you to be concerned. Anila is now at peace. We can look after her family.' He bowed his head towards me and looked at Antar. 'And all her business. I am her younger brother, Bashir.'

'And I am her eldest son.' Antar stood to his full height which made him substantially taller than this obsequious uncle bearing a malicious smile. My dislike for him intensified as he stepped forward and insinuated himself between me and the bed.

'You will leave now,' Bashir grasped my arm as another less vertically challenged uncle appeared to hold the door open and dismissively gesture me to exit. His expression was contemptuous. I stood my ground for a moment.

'I am sorry for your loss. I knew Anila well and came to pay my respects. She was a lovely woman.' The uncle by the door pulled Antar out of the room. Something told me he'd be 'for it' when we left. Bashir was now pulling my arm. I forcefully removed his hand. 'Please keep your hands off me.'

Bashir hesitated before taking a step back. 'We took the death certificate to the Registrar's before it closed at noon today. There are traditions which must be followed. The Imam is expected. You must leave.' The uncle folded his arms. I saw his jaw tighten.

A dejected Antar sagged against the stair bannister outside on the landing. Feeling awkward and intimidated, I patted his arm then hurried down the stairs to where Julia was sitting with the younger children, who were now smiling. She has a way with kids, does Julia. Some women Antar called 'aunties' were now visible in the kitchen next door, chopping, arguing and banging pots at the stove. The sound of bubbling oil and an aroma of spices filled the air. One aunty by the back door was murdering a ball of dough, slamming it on the table. The beater's gaze was unfriendly. The diminutive shroud-woman from upstairs was sweeping the pristine floor while being loudly berated by another burly, cross aunty in a straining red Kameez and pointy shoes. I wouldn't mess with her. This was a high-tension household: time we left.

Back at home I was angry and couldn't eat Rosie's lunch of tinned tomato soup and cheese rolls. The interlude had been surreal, but I believed Antar was right to be doubtful about what had happened. Something didn't add up. He'd been there. The uncles hadn't. But their attitude angered me. I even wondered whether Uncle Bashir had been there when she'd died. With Antar underage, the uncles had much to gain from Anila's nice little business and substantial detached property. My anger turned towards myself when I realised that I'd forgotten to ask Antar the name of the doctor. What was I thinking?

James snapped, 'For goodness sake, Beth, wasn't that the most important thing to ask?'

Lawyers see life in concrete facts. Doctors sense it in symptoms and signs. 'You weren't there! I felt really on the spot. And the Registrar is shut now so I can't even phone to ask who certified the death or the cause given!'

Worse, I couldn't remember which practice in our out-of-hours rota was on call. But even so, the GP on might have been any one from that practice – or a locum. It would have to wait until Monday. In any case, whoever was on would phone to notify us of any events. Had this death been preventable? Even without evidence of kidney or heart disease at her recent diabetic check-ups, septicaemia from a kidney infection could prove fatal. Sadly, Rosie couldn't comment. She'd been in adolescent psychiatry so long that the intricacies of diabetic complications were out of her sphere. But she agreed hospital admission might've been best.

Outside it was gloomy. Darkness came early and snow fell so heavily the roads became indiscernible from the pavements. The garden was a spectacular white-out punctuated by eerie supernatural lumps of the boys's constructions. Not a night for a long drive. Rosie, James and Nathan stayed over Saturday night. We watched videos and went to bed late. To the kids' annoyance, by noon the next day the ploughs had been busy, and the snow was melting. When Rosie and James set off for Edinburgh at two, Julia decided to visit her bereaved classmate.

'Why not ask him for tea? He might appreciate a bit of time out.'

But when she returned, she was livid. 'There's hundreds more family there, God knows where they'll all sleep! Antar's horrible Uncle Bashir wouldn't let him come out to speak to me. Said "Don't call again." Bloody rude! He said it "wasn't fitting for a young girl to visit a boy alone!"'

Deciding not to chide her swearing, I just gave her a hug. 'Different people have different ideas about what's fitting, darling. According to our customs, you were only being kind.' I kissed the side of her cheek: the top of her head was no longer a place within easy reach. I noticed her hair was almost reaching her waist now. Perhaps she should have it cut: a diverting discussion.

Next morning, the practice rota board showed that the Kilnglass practice had been on. We also share weekends with Drumlea (Drs Baldwin and Blair) and the single-handed Dr Brian Nesbitt. Brian was a colourful character, prone to tweed suits and buggering off to ski in the Cairngorms without a by your leave. Mind you, he'd always put the phone over to ensure we'd cover his patients. Naughtily, he was also prone, on occasion, to ask them to phone after 6 when we were on call. Charles just laughed.

'Isn't Brian a card?'

Ellen thinks Charles's tolerance comes from them being Lodge brothers, but in my view it's an Alma Mater thing, both being Edinburgh Faculty boys. Whilst Charles is senior partner, nothing will change. It is a man's world.

I had spent Sunday convincing myself that poor Antar was merely overwrought and being assertive against his domineering uncles, but by Monday noon I was itching to know who the GP was and what he'd done. Having had no call from Kilnglass, I spoke to Charles who volunteered to phone them. I swiftly agreed since I didn't know any of them well. The practice had had a change of partners over the last year and my contact had been limited to odd chats about terminal patients needing weekend visits. Charles got the youngest partner on the line and chatted amicably, nodding, and taking notes as I poured tea and nibbled a Penguin. Putting down the phone, he relayed the discussion.

'Kevin says the senior partner was on and he'd mentioned Anila's death before going home. He thought it was certified as septicaemia, but the death cert book is in his partner's bag so he can't check.'

'Right. Anything else? Did he mention blood sugar

levels?'

'No. Kevin did know she was diabetic, but oddly not about all the kids. He was a bit out of order though, only worried the Spar shop might close as it's one of the few places you can get booze round here at night! Oh, and he mentioned Brian's done a Part Two. That puzzled me, I thought Muslims were against cremation?'

'I've no idea. So that's it?'

'Yeah, though he couldn't resist a dig about Anila likely having poor diabetic control. Said his guy had mentioned she was obese and must have loved chapatis too much.'

'Charming! Antar was upset the GP mocked her weight. It's not on, you know. It's harder genetically for folk from the Indian sub-continent to keep their weight down. But her diabetic control was good.'

'Still, all fine, Beth. Best leave it be. Fussing won't bring her back.'

'I haven't met any of that lot at any post-grad days, have you? Funny, I mean the senior partner's been there a wee while.'

'He's said to have come from a London teaching hospital, preferring practice for its freedom and autonomy, putting patients before politics.'

'Can't argue with that. But we have a new patient who's left him as he was too abrupt.'

'Well, my next-door neighbour likes him. Don't think the chap's Dr Crippen!'

'I'm not suggesting he is. But it was just all a bit strange.' I left it there, collected my paperwork and went to my room. Charles was happy. I didn't phone the Fiscal. I also didn't look up Muslim views on cremation. After all, why would they have asked for forms if they didn't do it?

The next day, Brian Nesbitt phoned requesting I do a Part Two cremation form for him.

'A quick neat cremmie for you, Beth. Donny Simpson, 78, Lung CA. Wife's been through it the last six weeks. Marie Curie nurses been in giving her a break.

'That's a shame. Poor thing. Right. So where is the body?'

'At Dawson's, complete with death certificate. The daughter's around if you want a chat re death circs. Wife's too distraught. Phone number's 576 8880 ...'

After quick phone chats with the nurse and Donny's daughter about the time and manner of the passing, I drove to Dawson's to view the mortal remains of Donald Simpson, for whom death had been a mercy. His remains would have been a potent warning for smokers: lung cancer is a relentless, voracious consumer of flesh. The pallbearers wouldn't incur muscle strain lifting poor Donny. This being a routine, expected death, seen by a GP the day before, and seeing 'no reason to suspect further examination of the body as necessary', I duly signed my part two form. The youthful and endearing undertaker, Monty, rushed it to the Crematorium Medical Referee, a local pathologist who'd check for a third and final time that there was no reason to doubt the cause of death before permitting cremation.

Driving back, I thought how easy it must have been to bury doctors' mistakes in the old days when no such checks were in place. On the dashboard lay a cheque for the BMA-agreed fee for my part in acknowledging the death 'unsuspicious.' At the surgery it was lodged with Ellen for our Christmas party fund, a tradition that sat ill with me, as I mentioned to Gerry.

'Don't you think we should do something practical with our cremmie fees, like buying equipment? It feels like we're dancing on people's graves.'

Gerry laughed. 'We can't dance on their graves, Bethany – they ain't got any! They've been torched, poof! Ashes to ashes. Lighten up. Why not use ash cash for a knees-up?'

I shook my head. 'You're impossible, Gerry!'

'And speaking of the devil, I've got another at Dawson's for the way home. Good old snow and chill, so many "crumblies" keeling over. Should be a grand party this year!' Throwing his pretentious Tom Smith striped scarf (logo label visibly showing) over his shoulder, he lifted his case with a flourish. 'Bring on the cremmies, I say!'

Not the way I'd have put it, but I did reflect that if Anila's death had been dodgy or Nesbitt had popped off Old Simpson at the end, no one would ever know. No body? No case. Handing my signed letters and scripts to Ellen, I went home for a large glass of Chardonnay with the feet up.

Five

The Diary of Curious Incidents

It's impossible to dwell on your worries when you're being a dog-with-face-up, or indeed, face-down. Since my cancer, I've attended yoga every Wednesday. My husband Ralph doesn't get my enthusiasm for slow breathing and holding my body in poses named after fish, dogs or lions. He laughs, finding my attempts at Vrikshasana, the tree pose (standing on one leg, other foot in crotch and arms arched above the head) especially hilarious and deems my inability to sustain the pose for more than a few seconds evidence of my general imbalance. This from a man who for supper eats Weetabix spread with butter?

It was at yoga I met Jean Radcliffe, a smart, lithe lady in her sixties. I started driving her to classes after she'd fainted a few times and gave up her car. At her home after the session, we'd enjoy a cuppa and chat. She had a Masters in Fine Arts, and taught me a great deal, from knowing my Glasgow Boys to appreciating Degas: basically, the former liked painting cabbages, the latter had an unhealthy fixation with half-dressed pubescent dancers. Jean had led an exciting life, working for Sotheby's in New York before returning to look after ailing parents, now deceased. Her tobacco baron great-grandpa had avidly collected paintings and sculptures. Her home, Grovepark, was more like an art gallery than a house. The collection had continued with her father. He'd even acquired a Dali. It was all worth a fortune and I would have been terrified living there alone. But she didn't even have a burglar alarm.

'Why? I have a guard dog!'

'Winston? He'd mibbe bark at a burglar, but more likely he'd roll over for a tummy rub!'

She'd laughed. 'Oh, Beth, I live quietly. No one knows what's here. An alarm might make people think I have something worth stealing!'

That Wednesday, 9th December 1992 at 6.35 p.m. (such detail being possible as I started a Diary of Curious Incidents soon after), my evening surgery was running late. I phoned Jean to suggest she'd best get a taxi to class. The phone rang out. After my next appointment, I tried again. No answer. I left a message, assuming she'd taken Winston out for a quick walk. My last patient was a DNA, not a chromosome disorder, but a 'Did Not Attend'. Usually they make me cross, but tonight I was delighted. Calling as I went to Ellen to shut down my computer, I dashed home to change. Then in case Jean hadn't got the message, whizzed past her house. It was in darkness. No answer. She'd got it.

The class had started when I arrived. But rolling out my mat, I saw no Jean and assumed she must be unwell. She never missed yoga. It wasn't a good night for harassed, uncoordinated me. The end relaxation didn't send me to sleep as usual (I'm apt to be scolded for not keeping my 'cosmic awareness' – whatever that is). The farewell 'namaste' didn't come fast enough. I drove back via Jean's in case she needed anything.

Grovepark was in darkness as I parked outside. The long red gravel path illuminated by the streetlamps was flanked by spooky large white hellebores and wavering rhododendron bushes. Her usual outside light wasn't on. Before I reached the bottom step, I heard Winston barking. A bell-ring brought no answer. I rang again. The barking became frantic. Negotiating a tangled rose bed, I peered in the window and saw the little Lhasa Apso jumping up, barking, and squealing. And Jean's upturned feet poking from behind the desk. God, how long had she been there?

Hunting under plant pots and mats yielded no key, so I ran next door. Burly Colonel MacArthur answered promptly. As often happens in our locale, I knew him. A nice chap.

'Sorry, Doctor. I don't have a key but come in and we'll phone an ambulance.'

'We'll need the police to break in, too. Unless you know anyone with a key? Doesn't she have a nephew?'

'Doubt he could help. He's in Dorset.' The colonel handed me the phone.

The police were prompt. Or rather, the single police boy was. He took one look at the heavy oak front door and sensibly headed for the rear. Breaking a pane of glass in the back door allowed him to reach in and take the key from the inside lock. 'Hmm, poor security,' he muttered. The colonel and I followed him into the house.

In the study, one look told me we had no need of the ambulance now arriving noisily outside. Jean lay on her back, tweed skirt rumpled, but Pringle cardigan and pearls immaculate, as was her well-lacquered salt-and-pepper hair. Always well-groomed, the soul. Her lips were an odd hue: her signature YSL scarlet lipstick was tinged by cyanotic purple and contrasted starkly with her ashen face, reminding me of a horror film in which shop window dummies came alive. But then followed the realisation that she wasn't in her yoga tracksuit, usually donned well before I picked her up. When I phoned, she may well have been dead for a while.

Assuming professional doctor mode, I knelt to check for pulses. None. She was icy cold. The constable, having shut the excitable Winston in the kitchen, was now stripping off his jacket and kneeling over Jean, hands poised. I stopped him.

'No point in CPR. She's been dead a while.'

The bell rang. I let in the ambulance guys who repeated my checks before sitting back on their heels. The boy policeman nodded towards me.

'The doc says no point in CPR, is that right?'

'Yep. No point. She's well gone.' The ambulance man took out a notebook. 'What do we know about her, Doc? Full name? Family about? Medical history?'

'Sorry, she's not my patient, just a friend. Jean Radcliffe. 63, I think. No family. No siblings. She never married.' I was filling up. Poor Jean, dying here all alone. I wondered who would mourn her? She'd never mentioned friends, living a sheltered life since coming home, seemingly content with her own company, Winston and weekly yoga and hairdresser. She obviously went to the library, for plastic-covered books lay on the desk, and she'd occasionally mentioned the cinema, but never who she'd gone with. The ambulance men sped off to another call. Wonder Boy took out his notepad.

'Miss Jean Radcliffe you say? Can I have your name and address, Doc? And your date of birth? You will be able to give me a death certificate, won't you?' He raised his eyebrows.

'No, sorry. I don't know why she died. She wasn't ill. And she isn't – wasn't – my patient. Before the undertakers take her away, you'll need to find out who her GP was and if he will issue a certificate. If he isn't sure of her cause of death, you'll need to get the police doctor out. Though this doesn't look like a crime scene.'

Not sure why I said this, maybe because he looked so inexperienced. He swallowed and his eyes swivelled alarmingly as if trying to catch thoughts. I hoped he could sort this out pronto as I was suddenly exhausted. And hungry. All I'd had since breakfast was a Kit-Kat. It was now after nine. I needed home.

'Right!' He shot out.

We watched him march down the path. Colonel MacArthur sat down on a Mackintosh chair in the corner. 'I suppose he's gone to phone in from the patrol car. Then he'll want statements from us.' Smoothing down his bushy white moustache, he sighed. 'Might take ages. He's a bit of a dick.'

I had to smile. 'Dick' reappeared, crimson, notebook flapping. 'Sorry, and you are, sir?'

The colonel gruffly recited his name, and then said, 'Widower, over twenty-one, live next door.'

'And how do you know the deceased?'

'As I said, I live next door.'

A woof through the study door reminded me about Winston. I let him in. He scampered over to lick Jean and whimper encouragingly. Wee soul. Dick tried to catch his collar, but he ran off into the hall. I crouched down and called him. He came scampering into my arms.

Dick looked up from his laborious notes. 'Right, Doc, I'll take him to the RSPCA once I've finished. If no one wants him, he'll be put down.'

Winston nuzzled me. I couldn't let him be 'killed' too! My heart raced: why did I say that? There were no signs of a break-in or a struggle – nor surely anyone who might mean Jean harm? I was edgy, needed food, was imagining things. And watched too much Columbo.

'No, don't worry, I'll take him.'

'Right, then I suppose you two can go. I'll wait for the police surgeon.' Dick tentatively stepped over Jean and sat down at her desk. I reflected he didn't look much older than Antar, and wondered that they'd let him out on his own, especially when I'd thought in Scotland you needed two policemen to attend incidents for corroboration or something. 'Don't you have a partner?'

'Sergeant will be here soon, Doc. He was caught short on the way out.'

The colonel snorted at this revelation and walked me out to my car, helpfully carrying my bag since I was carrying Winston.

'She was a real lady, Jean. Kept herself to herself, though. I've only ever seen two visitors, apart from your good self,

43

Doctor.'

'Who were the others?'

'Well, recently there's been that lawyer from the Main Street, Irish name, now, O'Farrell, I think. Yes, Liam, she called him. Said he's been most helpful with changing her will. Hmm, that'll be the day – a helpful lawyer? Now, I can tell you, I've had a run in with a few ...'

'Liam O'Farrell? I know him. And the other visitor?' The dog was struggling in my arms. Perhaps he needed a pee? God knows when he'd last been out.

'Oh, her doc. See him regular, usually Wednesdays. A cheery chap, waves as he leaves. Not that I make a point of looking out the window, you understand. Has a nice big car.'

'Which doctor? Do you know his name?'

'No idea. Tanned. Walks smartly. Middle-aged? Hat. Big coat.'

Could be anyone. Possibly Brian, he was always tanned. Alison spotted him once exiting shiftily from a downtown tanning salon. But before I could describe him for identification, the colonel stood to attention, straightened his tie, and twisted his neck. 'You know, think I'll pop back in and tell Constable Dick about the lawyer. He'll know how to contact the nephew. Otherwise how will they find him? Dorset's a big place!'

Jean's address book by the phone, I thought, but didn't say. The colonel marched briskly back up the path as I let Winston down on to the grass verge, holding on to his collar. From the lengthy stream he produced, he hadn't been out for ages. Jean must have been lying there for hours. Rigor mortis had been setting in. I felt unbearably sad, gave Winston a cuddle and put him in the car.

It was eleven when I got home to find Ralph putting down the phone. He'd found my address book, got Jean's phone number, and called her house.

'I was worried. You're usually well in by now. By the

way, Constable Teviot says he'll have to speak to you again in the morning for a proper statement.'

I groaned. 'I don't care! I need food! I'm starving.'

'Mac and cheese in the oven. Might be a wee bit dried out. Gosh, what the ...' Ralph stepped back in alarm as I opened my coat and dropped down Winston. Ralph hadn't noticed him clutched within my bulky old sheepskin coat. He woofed and galloped off towards the kitchen, where delighted squeals from the girls greeted him. They should be in bed by now on a school night. Ralph was a hopeless disciplinarian.

'Who's this?' Katy appeared with her arms round the wriggling, shaggy cream bundle. She buried her face in his fur as he licked her neck.

'Winston. His mummy's dead,' I said enigmatically. 'Thought we could look after him.'

'Cool!' The girls chorused.

'Please give him some water. And he must be hungry. Not sure when he last ate. Maybe he might like that tin of M&S chicken in white sauce?'

Eating Ralph's offering, I looked enviously at Winston wolfing into his chicken from a cereal bowl. It looked better than my brick-hard macaroni. But hunger is good kitchen, as my gran always said.

It was well past midnight when we went to bed. Katy had rooted out our old dog's bed from under the stairs, along with leads, feeding bowls, toys and doggie paraphernalia I hadn't had the heart to bin when our spaniel had been put down. Ralph had forbidden another dog as the girls had been so devastated when Tiddles died.

I didn't sleep. I had so many unanswered questions. And it was less than three weeks since Anila's troubling death. Winston arrived upstairs to cry, whine and scratch at the door. Ralph eventually let him in to sleep on the bottom of our bed, vowing this wouldn't become a habit. It did. I fell asleep just before the alarm went off.

Morning surgery passed in a haze of forced concentration. Constable Teviot came at eleven, repeated the same questions as the night before, though this time with an audience: a blonde WPC called Lucinda.

'The good news, Doctor, is we've got a death certificate. We've seen Miss Radcliffe's records. She was at her doc's on Monday afternoon. He wasn't surprised at her stroke, what with her blood pressure.'

I was surprised he'd been shown records so freely, but didn't say, being distracted by Lucinda's rapt gaze fixated on PC Dick. She was hanging on every word he uttered.

'And by the way, the colonel's lawyer info was handy. He's got the nephew on his way. Mr O'Farrell knows you from way back. Quite a coincidence.'

Dick relaxed back chattily. He mightn't have better things to do, but I did. I'd been brought up to respect the constabulary, so stood up politely, hoping he'd get the hint. He didn't. Ellen's head appeared round the door. There was a God. 'Patients are getting a bit antsy, Doctor, sorry.' She stood back, holding the door open encouragingly. But Dick doggedly finished reading out my statement and got my signature.

'Thanks for your help, Doctor. Lucinda, shall we …' He ushered her out.

I gave a silent Munch-like scream and closed my eyes. When I opened them, Ellen was at the window. 'Aw, love's young dream!' She pointed out at Dick and Lucinda strolling hand in hand.

'Like Colonel MacArthur says, he is a bit of a dick!' I said. Ellen laughed and left.

My smile soon faded. The first patient was Dermott Green. A hypochondriac who knows more about medicine than I (he thinks) and is always accompanied by his *Family*

Physician, a well-thumbed 1940s home medical almanac which might have been useful for Army wives then, but by 1992 I thought all existing copies needed to be burned. Today I struggled to convince him his ailment wasn't cutaneous leishmaniasis, but psoriasis he'd ulcerated by scratching. He angrily pointed at a coloured plate in his book.

'I'm sorry, Mr Green, but you only get that if you are malnourished and bitten by a sand fly in Africa. We don't have any in Scotland.'

As usual, I had to physically usher him out to the waiting area thrusting on him a steroid cream prescription. 'Now, please use this twice a day and it should clear up. It's not serious.'

He opened his mouth to argue but Charles appeared. He shut it and left. He doesn't like Charles, who doesn't even let him sit down in his room. The waiting room was empty.

'Where did my last two go?'

'I've seen them, Beth. Ellen told me about your friend Jean. Shame. And blethering Dick and the lovely Lucinda. There are only two calls. I'll manage. Why don't you go on home?'

'Great, Charles. I owe you. I'm pooped.' I pecked him on the cheek.

I signed some repeat prescriptions and returned a call while fortified by two paracetamol and a cup of Ellen's strong tea. During the ten-minute drive home, I brooded on Jean, and cursed myself. It seemed I had learned nothing from the Anila debacle and hadn't asked Dick who the GP was. Unbelievable! My brain swirled with the loose ends in Jean's story, but when I opened my front door, Winston's enthusiastic welcome calmed it. We had a quick tuna sandwich together (about which he was ambivalent) then went walkies. The crisp sunny day cheered me. I avoided walking past Grovepark, no point in stressing him. Or me.

We went into Liam's office in the village main street, but

he wasn't in, so I left a message. Winston obviously knew the secretary, who made a fuss of him.

'How lovely you've taken him! By the way, there's been a few enquiries already about the funeral …'

That surprised me. I went home via the Spar for some proper dog food. Another surprise: it was boarded up and bore a 'For Sale' sign. I'd expected the uncles would sell, but thought they'd offer it as a going concern. Anila would have been upset. Worse for her would have been to hear the family was to be split. Boys to the stroppy Uncle Bashir in Manchester, girls to the other uncle in Leicester. Julia said Antar had already left. Appalled at the twins being separated, I'd phoned social work, who appeared unfazed. Having ascertained that these uncles were neither paedophiles nor criminals and that the children were now in England, they said it was completely outside their jurisdiction. When I told Charles, he just scolded me about interfering again. But now I just had to trail off to Asda for dog food.

Leaving a protesting Winston in my car, I rushed round the supermarket grabbing Bonios, Pedigree Chum and a few days' ready meals for us. I was beyond chopping, peeling or recipe-following. After dishing up steak pie and oven chips, I fell asleep in front of *Top of the Pops* till Ralph nudged me for bed.

At 2 a.m., sitting in the loo, I was wide awake and troubled by inconsistencies. One? CVAs – or strokes – are associated with *high* blood pressure. Jean was prone to faint, thus had low. Two? We found her lying flat on her back. I might have expected her to fall forward or crumple onto a weakened side with a stroke. Three? Jean making a Monday GP appointment was odd. Every Monday she went to the hairdresser in Fraser's. She'd only miss it if very unwell, in which case, she'd have phoned me. Four? The colonel said her GP usually visited on Wednesdays. Did that include yesterday? Five? Why had her GP actually shown Teviot her computer records? Unusual. Could we be sure they were accurate? Or might they have been falsified? I stopped counting, but wondered also why would a GP issue a dodgy death certificate? And if she hadn't had a stroke, what did she die of? I'd already considered there was no evidence of a break-in, no obvious injury. Did a police doctor examine her body?

Returning to bed, I came upon Winston who'd padded upstairs from his new bed in the kitchen. As he circled my ankles, I lifted him for a cuddle. 'So, what happened to mummy, Winston?' Pity I didn't know a Dr Doolittle to ask him. Winston was the only one who knew the truth. I took him into bed whereupon he promptly fell asleep. I didn't. Grumbling 'gut feelings' are potent arousers of adrenaline.

Next morning, I decided to speak to Liam. I hadn't seen him since uni, where he'd been an old school pal of our appalling classmate, Conor Towmey. But he was a nice fellow who'd distanced himself from Con years ago. I'd swithered about speaking to Charles about Jean, but after the Anila debacle, felt Liam was a better sounding block – a respected lawyer, sharp and worldly-wise. Plus, he'd likely know who Jean's GP was, and I was reluctant to admit to Charles that I hadn't asked. Again. My guess was Brian Nesbitt, well-known for visiting lonely spinsters and widows. In Ellen's view, he was missing his old mum. One widow had bequeathed him a vintage Triumph in which he zoomed about, hood down, all summer. But his main car was a black Rover coupe. A good bet he was the colonel's GP with a big car?

Six

Lady in a Hat & Happy Families

Next morning, I woke to find myself alone in bed. Well, not quite. Winston lay across my feet. It was only coming out of the shower that I remembered Ralph was already on the Friday 7.30 from Queen Street to Edinburgh. His alarm hadn't roused me as he never sets one, just decides what time he wants to wake, and does. Unnatural, to my mind, but then I'm an owl not a lark. We have other differences. Like committees. His quarterly Primary Care Think Tank at the Scottish Office would drive me to distraction. Endless discussions on NHS policies to make 'the-powers-that-be' look like they're tackling 'the issues', in other words, to provide good media soundbites that are largely cost-neutral. Waiting list 'targets' are a prime example. Hospital administrators run committees to invent methods for delaying putting folk on lists in the first place. For instance, they send letters to referred patients insisting they confirm they want appointments, thus keeping them off the list for a month. Conveniently, postage is a different budget. Consultants like my cardiologist ex-husband, Dan, fear the NHS is degenerating into a war zone between administrators and clinicians, patients always losing out. Anyway, I admire Ralph's efforts, but he's welcome to his committees.

As I cleaned my teeth, shouted at the girls to get moving and tripped over Winston, I decided I'd try to pop into Liam's office before evening surgery. For a moment I couldn't remember what I'd wanted to ask him; my brain was ageing even faster than the gaunt face reflected at me in the mirror. Blasting my hair with the dryer, I slapped on make-up and ran downstairs. The girls were up and dressed. Perhaps the day was improving.

Not so. The kitchen was strewn with dirty laundry. A destroyed wicker basket lay at the door of the utility room. 'Winston!' I groaned, bending to pick up strewn smalls.

'Mum, there's no cornflakes left,' yelled Katy, deafeningly, not realising I was now behind her.

'Well then, who put an empty packet back in the cupboard without telling me?' I crossly took a cup of tea from Julia, slopped in some milk, and tugged at the cutlery drawer for a spoon. It jammed, leaving me clutching a loose drawer handle. Worse, my tea was curdled. My, 'Who left the milk out all night again?' shout fell on deaf ears. There was some not-too-far-out-of-date orange juice in the fridge which I gulped, but zilch ingredients for a lunchtime sandwich. I sighed unhappily, being no longer able to bank on Anila for sustenance. Winston looked up, woofed and pawed the back door. I let him out. He performed and got a treat before ambling back to his bed. Lucky thing. Though maybe not: his new bedfellows were Katy's sweaty gym kit and a curry-besmirched tea towel.

'It's half-past, girls!'

A few shrieks, grabbed coats, scarves, gloves and bags and we were off.

Morning surgery was, thankfully, run-of-the-mill. No Marys, no Dermott Greens. At lunch break (a cracker and a Cup-a-Soup from Ellen) Alison buzzed through.

'There's a Mr Liam Something on for you, Dr S.'

I was delighted – by speaking to him now, I'd manage Asda before evening surgery. Cradling the receiver, I grabbed a post-it and started scribbling a list: milk, Rioja, mince, onions, spag bol sauce, wine, orange juice, gin, cheesecake, wine, tonic, cornflakes …

Liam was breezy. 'Hello stranger! How are you? How

long has it been?'

'A few years anyway. I'm fine, how are you?'

'Grand. You wanted to speak to me?'

'I wondered if Jean Radcliffe's funeral was sorted yet?'

'Friday next, all being well. There's a family crypt at the Necropolis though there's some paperwork confusion that John, her nephew, needs to sort. Likely be resolved today. I'll put funeral details in Monday's *Herald* and *The Scotsman*.'

'So it's a burial?'

'Yes. I think so. Does that matter?'

'It might. I'm a bit unhappy about the cause of death.' I explained about the discrepancy between strokes and Jean's low BP, plus the unlikelihood of her making Monday appointments. 'Funny her GP insisted on showing the police her records, we're usually told not to, unless absolutely necessary. Och, maybe she was just entered for the wrong day.'

'Bit unlikely, that, isn't it? There's not much to go on for querying a death, though. I am surprised, however, given it was a sudden unexpected death, that the police doctor didn't request a post-mortem.'

'Well, her own GP issued a death certificate.'

'There you are then, must be fine! Goodman's a nice chap. By the way, did Jean tell you you're in her will?'

'No! Really?' I put down my pen after scribbling 'Goodman.'

'Yup, she's left you a lovely Cadell painting: a woman in a big black velvet hat. Pretty valuable. Could sub you a nice wee sports car.' Liam's priorities obviously differed from mine. 'We had everything valued when Jean decided to bequeath her collection to Kelvingrove, wanting it kept together as a sort of family memorial. Said her nephew was a philistine who'd only sell it off!'

'Oh, I'd never sell that painting. She knew I loved it.'

'One interesting aside is – and please keep this to yourself

– I had a bigwig Edinburgh lawyer on a minute ago, accusing me of pinching his client. Seems he saw the death notice in *The Scotsman* and contacted the police, saying he had her will. Odd thing to do, I thought. Anyway, he was furious to learn she'd changed to me. No wonder! The probate fees will be substantial. What he didn't realise was that I know that Jean was about to sue them for siphoning off money. I haven't said anything to the bobbies till I get the forensic accountant's report, but Jean said she'd confronted the senior partner a few months ago about discrepancies which he, of course, denied. Surprised he'd the cheek to contact me! If you think she's been murdered, then my number one suspect would be Lawrence Spencer from Spencer, Larkin and Dibbs!'

'Oh, Liam, I don't think she was murdered, just maybe got the wrong treatment or her GP mixed her up with someone else.'

'Where's your evidence, Beth? Forget it. But she's left you this nice pic. Do you want to meet me tomorrow at her house and get it? Police gave me the keys to get the broken glass fixed. Probate's not finished obviously, but I'd be happier if you took the pic and signed for it in case it gets swept up with the gallery stuff. Why not bring Ralph and the girls along and come back to our house for lunch to meet Jan and my terrible trio? Teenage triplets are a nightmare!'

'Triplets! Gosh! That'd be great, Liam. By the way, did you know Conor's back?'

'No. I did not. Hell mend him. He's a bloody embarrassment.' Pausing to clear his throat, he asked, 'So, what's he up to?'

Same old Liam. Loved a gossip.

'Changed his name. Running a pharma regulatory company.'

'Jesus H. Christ! After being convicted for research fraud? He's testing drugs?'

'Well, he wasn't formally convicted in court, only "erased" from the Medical Register. We think an old friend in high places got him the job. And changing his name must have helped keep his background quiet.'

'What's he calling himself?'

'Conrad Towie.'

'Eh? That's pathetic. Though enough of a tweak to prevent an internet search throwing up his murky past. Where did you meet him?'

'I haven't, Rosie saw him. Remember Rosie? Married James?'

'Petite, blonde, gorgeous Rosie?'

'That's her! She's a psychiatrist now, saw Con at an Edinburgh conference.'

Liam laughed. 'A psychiatrist? As I recall, at uni she could have done with one herself! But what a brass neck Con has. Hope I don't bump into him when I'm through at the Festival. Sorry, Beth, a client's arrived. Shall we say eleven tomorrow at Jean's?'

'Fine, see you then.'

I made it to Asda before surgery and home in good time. Flinging the front mat mail pile onto the kitchen dresser, I rustled up a Bolognese sauce before tackling the mix of journals and letters, mostly rubbish. Then I squealed in fright.

'God, I didn't hear you come in! Ralph, you're freezing!' He had flung his arms round me and planted a kiss on the back of my neck.

'It's cold outside!'

'Do you hear that?' I pointed upstairs.

Ralph cocked his head. A moody saxophone jazz solo wafted down. 'Katy's pretty good for fourteen, isn't she?'

'Yep. And by the way, the Christmas concert is a week tonight at seven. We mustn't miss it.'

'I'll cross the afternoon off to be sure.'

'And I'll get Ellen to push Friday evening extras to Saturday morning since I'm on then.'

'Busy day?' Ralph leaned against the Rayburn, warming up.

'Had my first Christmas emergency, "Wee Johnnie's singing solo in the school nativity and has a sore throat!" Understandable, unlike my last extra, a real lulu. "Flying to Barbados tomorrow, Doc. Need a script for antihistamines in case I get prickly heat." The things folk think are urgent!'

'Ridiculous! If you can afford to fly there, you can afford to buy your own. You should've told her to sod off and buy some.'

'It was a guy.'

'Thought you said it was a Lulu?'

'Idiot!' I flicked a tea towel at his ear but missed. Winston sprang up to join the game.

'Patients, eh? Who needs them, Winston?' Ralph wrestled on the floor with the wee dog and rolled onto spilled tomato sauce, but I didn't say, just pointedly handed him a corkscrew and the Rioja. With my back to him, I managed to quietly manoeuvre the handle-less cutlery drawer open with a knife: no point in spoiling an evening by adding to the already long list of jobs-needing-doing. Gershwin's *Summertime* wafted into the kitchen. Ralph swept me into a whirl for a few bars.

'I love this. And I love you too.' With a lingering kiss, he pulled me down onto the old kitchen sofa from which the girls watched TV when we had visitors.

I fought him off. 'I need to check the dinner!'

'No romance in your soul, girl!'

'We mustn't have burnt Bolognese.' My stirring intensified the lovely aroma of basil and oregano. Ralph handed me a glass of wine and pulled me back down to the sofa, clinking glasses. I sipped my wine, feeling warm and happy, having become unashamedly more sentimental since my cancer. Lying back on Ralph's shoulder I asked, 'Where did Katy get her musical genes from, do you think? Not from me – or Dan. The only thing he ever played was me – for a fool!'

'Now, now, he may not be a model dad, but he has been more in contact with the girls lately. Hasn't he even been remembering birthdays and stuff?'

'Oh, sure. Plus, it wasn't all his fault. I married too impulsively after finals.'

'Still, if you hadn't, you wouldn't have Jules and Katy, would you? No, the fool around here was me, chucking you at the end of first.'

'Och, all's well that ends well, as they say.'

A complex modern jazz piece wafted in. Ralph made a face. 'Not sure I like this.'

Feeling similarly, I rose to rummage in the cupboard for pasta. None. Rice would have to do. 'Did you play anything at school, Ralph?'

'The violin at primary, pretty dire. Then piano at boarding school where my teacher was a gorgeous Audrey Hepburn lookalike! Did you?'

'No money for lessons. Oh, by the way, Katy has a boy on the go.'

'A boy? She's a bit young for that, surely?'

'No, she isn't! I dated first year secondary, she's in second. It's all quite innocent. He's new and shy. She's trying to make him feel welcome.'

'Ah! Katy loves an underdog. Not the first waif and stray she's brought home, is it?'

We laughed. 'Remember that mangy stray cat in primary six? Well, at least this boy doesn't have fleas! His family have been renting in West Chapelton Drive but are moving to that big house, Westhaven, in Roman Road. He was boarding in Edinburgh till recently. Quiet, nice lad, bit monosyllabic. Come to think of it, a normal teenager!'

'Did you give the poor boy the third degree? At that age I wouldn't speak to a girl, never mind her mother. I was fifteen before I asked one out, though turned out she was eighteen. Scathing about my novice kissing technique. Damaging.'

'Ah, a misspent youth, lusting after piano teachers and older women, eh? Anyway, Katy's lad is OK. And she talks enough for two. Gosh, is that the time?'

'No. Remember I put it ten minutes fast to speed up the girls in the morning!'

'Like that works! Go easy on that wine please. You'll need to get Julia from Netball Club. Tea will be ready at half past. While you're out, I'll proofread the blurb for that stupid New Contract Practice Leaflet thingy. Don't want to spoil Sunday night.'

'It's not stupid. Leaflets show patients where and when their doctors graduated, and the services practices provide. It's good for people moving into an area, as they'll be available in libraries. Plus, they're a good vehicle for health advice, not to mention great practice PR.'

'Public Relations? We're not selling beans! And all us GPs do the same thing, don't we?'

'You'd be surprised. Research is showing even some training practices need to buck up. Not all patients are getting the service they deserve.'

'A poxy leaflet's not going to stop charlatans – they'll just make stuff up. Maybe I will too. What might be good propaganda?'

'OK, Goebbels, go and do your leaflet. I'll empty the sink, load the dishwasher, bring you a coffee to the study and then go get Julia.'

'Good man!'

As I heard the car reverse out of the drive, I realised I'd forgotten to tell him about Liam and the painting. My brain was overloaded.

*

West Chapelton Drive

She removed their empty plates from the table and put them in the sink.

'Perhaps you'd like to invite her for tea, Neil?'

'I don't think so, Mum, not yet. But she's nice. Hardly anyone else speaks to me.'

'Give them time. New schools are always tricky at first.'

'I know, I've been to enough! I hope we stay here for a bit, at least till after Highers. The teachers are better than Gillespie's, especially the music ones. I hated it there, everyone trying to be posh. But Bristol wasn't too bad.'

'I really liked it there too, but you know your father.' She tied her apron tightly round her waist and smoothed it down. 'I think he will settle here. He's put money into the surgery and likes it being his own practice now. He's tetchy in this little house, but it'll be fine once we move to Westhaven. That basement might take a table tennis table for you to have friends in.'

'Not sure Dad would like that.' Neil was sitting at the table lining up cutlery. 'I've often wondered. Why did we move so often? I mean, why did it take so long for Dad to become a GP partner? Couldn't he just put up a plate and open his door?'

'Doesn't work like that. You need a patient list and contract from the Health Board which means another GP has to move or retire or die.'

Neil sighed. 'It's funny. One of the boys in the class saw Dad for his acne and thought he was great. Patients like him, don't they? I think he's different at work. In the surgery he had the girls laughing.'

'When were you there?'

'Yesterday. He needed a patient's records to do a house call after dropping me off.' He sighed. 'You know I'd rather walk to school, but he won't listen.'

'I'll have a word. Have you much homework this weekend?'

'Lots. I'm behind in Latin especially. Nearly said to Dad he wasted his money paying for Gillespie's.' His mother looked stricken. 'Don't worry, I didn't! When's he due in?'

'Oh, late as always.'

'By the way, Katy's mum's a doctor too. And her dad's a GP professor at Glasgow Uni. I didn't know they had professors of general practice. Her mum works full time.'

'Really? That must be hard. Three days a week's enough for me.' She started stacking plates back in the cupboard, thinking about how nice the new house would be, with its modern kitchen and dishwasher. Though it would have been nice to see it before buying. She'd only learned about it when she saw the mortgage papers on the sideboard: signed, supposedly, by her. Witnessed too.

Neil watched his mother at the sink. She looked paler than ever, her hair more silver than blonde. Thin, quiet, kind of merging into the periphery of anywhere she inhabited, like a wood nymph or sprite. He'd considered her one since reading *The Water Babies* in primary six. The tale had stirred him: the idea of escaping to 'a magical world', as Mrs Clark had put it. He'd identified with its hero, Tom. Pity he couldn't spirit his mother away. Still, recently he'd felt more confident, assertive, probably capable of managing things better for himself. Yet he was anxious he couldn't do more for his mother.

What an ill-matched pair his parents were. In looks: she so pale, he so dark. Italian forebears, he said. While in personality Mum was warm, eager to please; Dad strict, bossy, reserved. He only talked at mealtimes, never about anything much, was never encouraging. Only once had he paid Neil a compliment. He'd been very small.

'How pale and beautiful you are, so like your mother. So lucky.'

That night had also been the only time he recalled his father touching him. He'd stroked his hair and kissed his head while he'd knelt for bedside prayers after his story. That had been the last bedtime story. Nightly supervised prayers continued, but instead of stories came short Bible sayings, like, 'Remember the Lord helps them that help themselves.' Sometimes late on, his mother would creep in for a hug and kiss. Sometimes. He watched her basting roast potatoes and moved to give her a cuddle from behind. Drying her hands, she turned to hug him fiercely. Now towering over her, he prayed that as he got bigger, she'd feel safer.

'Best go up and practise before Dad gets in.'

He went up to his room with his new music. Noise annoyed his father. A lot of things annoyed him. As Neil's fingers flew over the clarinet keys, calm flowed through his veins. And satisfaction. He was well ahead in music which had replaced Kingsley as his salvation. His *Water Babies* book had kept disappearing: how often his mother had retrieved it from the bin and re-hid it. His first clarinet had completely vanished. But this one was safe, for it belonged to the school. As he changed the music on the stand for his last piece, he heard the front door opening then banging shut.

His mother's cheerful greeting was met by, 'No! I have not had a good day …'

The rest of the tirade was lost in the slam of the study door. Who had annoyed him today? What made him so horrible, so difficult to live with? If only there were relatives he could ask. Everyone else had at least one grandparent or some cousins or aunties. The last music piece he played as quietly as he could. *Stranger on the Shore* matched his mood.

*

That Saturday, I collected the Cadell and we all had a lovely lunch with Liam, wife Jan and their girls: Ingrid, Imogen and Isabelle. It was bedlam with five teenage girls talking over one another, but we resolved to do it again. Sleepovers were discussed. Liam's wife Jan pronounced me brave.

At home, I propped the picture up on the dining room sideboard until I could get strong picture hooks. It was a restful portrait of a woman in a large hat sitting serenely in a sunlit blue drawing room. Although it was a kind thought, I already worried that every time I looked at it, I'd feel guilty that I might have let Jean down.

Seven

Rum & Rats

Kilburn, London, 1965, 27 years earlier

His mother doesn't like him taking so many baths.

'Why do you need one every day? Hot water costs money, you know. We're not loaded like your fancy friends.'

'Would you rather I smelled like you?' He knows his lip is curling into a snarl. But he knows it always sets her off and tries to practise it in the mirror every day now.

She screams, clutching her throat. So predictable, so Bette Davis. 'What an ungrateful son you are – after all I've sacrificed for you!' The back of the hand is now on the forehead. The swaying has started, making her look even more like a bloody ham actress. 'I was destined for great things, you know. If your father hadn't died ...'

She withdraws her hand from her face and leans on the mantelpiece, gazing at a fading photo in a tarnished silver frame. It sits in its usual shrine amidst red plastic carnations and other hellish keepsakes. A dance hall ticket. A bottle of Evening in Paris. A tatty Dior lipstick. A broken tortoiseshell clasp. A West End theatre programme from a venue long closed. The only fresh colour in the room comes from jewel-like Quality Street sweet wrappers scattered on the chairs and hearth. Fraying firelighters spill from a tattered overturned basket beside the fire which has not been lit for some time. He wrinkles his nose. The flat stinks. No window is ever opened. No rug ever hoovered. She is not allowed in his room. It may be spartan, but it is clean.

He is losing patience. 'Why don't you just go to bed, Winnie?' She does. After a few minutes of wailing, he hears a clink. She's found the stash he'd 'hidden.' Peace soon.

He clears space on the table by piling the free junk magazines and newspapers on to a nearby cracked leatherette chair. A squidgy banana skin he drops in the bin: as usual, overflowing. He'll take it out later. Working at the table makes a change from lying on the cold lino of his bedroom floor or the lumpy, ink-stained candlewick of his bed. From his bedroom he fetches his Dettol and two cloths – one for cleaning, one for drying – before laying out homework books and jotters in the usual order. He lifts his pen, a primary seven gift from Mrs O'Neill. 'Parkers last a lifetime,' she'd said. She still provides refills.

Mrs O is the only woman who has visited here in the past seven years. Lucky he'd known she was coming that day. He'd done his best to clean up. Hearing the bell click, it being broken like everything else, he'd rushed out to bring her straight here into the sitting room through the passageway he'd cleared in the hall. The room had almost looked like a parlour after his efforts. God knows how many bags he'd filled with rubbish. He'd put books on the mantelpiece, and Gran's old lace cloth on the table, cleaned the window, dusted and even borrowed Mrs Baker's hoover. But he'd dreaded Mrs O saying she wanted to go to the bathroom. He hadn't had the gall to ask Mrs Baker for her brush thing and definitely couldn't put his hand into the pan to clean the brown stains with a cloth. Now he had a loo brush. And bleach as well as Dettol. Mrs B next door told him about Dettol. It killed all germs.

But Margaret O'Neill has taught him everything else. She told Mother he was the cleverest boy she'd ever taught. Mother was astonished, but she'd nearly ruined the day with that stupid sob story about his 'war hero' father, killed in action before he was born. Mrs O would have seen through that, known the photo Mother waved was of some random wartime Air Force guy who bore him no resemblance. In any case, the war ended four years before he was born. The stupid cow should have told Mrs O his father had been killed in Malaya. We had forces there in 1948. But she only knew about movies and dance music, ignorant bitch. His brains must have come from his grandmother.

Sad Gran didn't live to see him start the Grammar. She'd have been so proud. It had been due to Mrs O. Though with his IQ – 150, she'd said – he'd found the work pretty easy. Mrs O had done everything: found him a second-hand uniform, sourced books, gave him extra tuition in the summer holidays to ensure he didn't struggle. But, importantly, she'd explained 'how things were done' there. And she'd carried on meeting him monthly in the Ivy opposite the Grammar gate. Those lovely chats. Squash and cakes. Bakewell tarts. No one else had ever bought him cakes. He knew he held a place in Margaret O'Neill's heart, she being a childless widow. A genuine war widow. Listening, supporting, advising, cheering up. She did everything his hopeless mother didn't. She didn't obsess about old lovers, ignoring her only son.

The current mantelpiece photo catches his eye. A more recent fable, it shows a 'father' who'd died trying to save a drowning boy in the Thames. A Woolworth's frame. A cut-out filched from a stolen library newspaper. Pathetic how she continually tries to convince him, oblivious to his sneers. Does she simply fancy this one more than the last? When he's pointed out the guy has a different surname, she maintains she kept her maiden name for the stage. He isn't fooled: she's never been married. She is a whore. He's rummaged for hours while she languishes in bed like a dying duck, but he's never found a marriage certificate. On the mantelpiece he's put up Mrs O's birthday card. His only birthday card. Today he is sixteen, a man. From this day, he vows he'll never pretend to listen to her delusional rambles. Fuck her. But he will find out the truth about his father.

For a long time, he'd imagined he'd been born without

a father. Sunday School had been confusing, talking about Immaculate Conceptions. Even after all these years, he feels his face suffusing. He'd actually asked Pastor Graham if he might be another Jesus. He must have been about six. The pastor had looked sad and ruffled his long hair.

'When did you last have a haircut, Stan?'

'Gran took me last Christmas,' he'd said. Like she'd taken him to school to enrol. And collected him every day first term till she got ill and went, just before New Year. Since then, he'd walked home himself. He could still see Pastor Graham's shocked expression. 'That's almost a year! You poor boy. The school should have got the Social in a long time ago.'

The Pastor had taken him to a barber who'd laughed. 'So, who's this little girl?'

It was the first and only time he ever cried in public. Pastor Graham had been angry at the barber and told him Stan's story. Mr Singh has cut his hair for a shilling ever since. Wanker.

The 'Father' question has dominated his life since his grandmother's hints just before she went that he was 'coloured.' But he isn't black like the Nigerian Ngomos up the road. Gran had become too delirious to elaborate, but next night she'd muttered another odd thing. 'She put your poor daddy away, you know. He wasn't a bad lad.' There had been no sense out of her after that, apart from mumbles about the 'wind rushing' and 'she drove him to it.' He could now well believe his mother had driven someone mad. Perhaps his father is still in a mental hospital.

When Gran had stopped breathing, he'd cried. Afterwards, only once had he asked his mother where his father had been 'put' and why. He got a slap and never asked again.

But this brooding isn't getting his studying done. Looking round the room, he's saddened how fast the mess has re-gathered since his last clear out. Oh, why should he give a fuck about it? No one visits now. Apart from Pastor Graham, he only has a vague memory of one other man being in the old house. After Gran's death came a man in a shiny suit and moustache. He'd been a few times. There'd been grunting from behind his mother's closed bedroom door. She'd said she was paying her rent.

The old Pastor had always stayed in the kitchen. That last time, he'd put Stan into his room while he spoke to his mother. They'd had a terrible row. Must've been the year after they'd moved here to Kilburn, the year after Gran died. Mother and Gran had screaming arguments all the time, like when Mother was sacked from the laundry for pilfering and Gran had cried, 'What are we going to do for money now, Winnie?' But the shindig with the Pastor had been a biggie. Graham had threatened Mother with Social Services.

'This house is a dump unfit for a child! And you need to see a doctor, Winnie. You're killing yourself with drink. Think on that wee lad.'

He remembered the yelling, a bottle being smashed against a wall and shouts of 'get the fuck out!' It had taken ages to sweep up the broken glass. On the way out, as the pastor had patted Stan's head, Mother had hurled a shoe at his back. He'd never returned.

The house had looked normal to him then. It was only later, when he saw his school friend's houses, that he'd learned homes could be cosy, clean. Have curtains, fungus-free fridges and uncluttered sideboards. Proper homes had proper fathers. And other things he'd missed out on, like pocket money. In primary four he'd learned about Social Services and benefits. Seeing his elbows sticking out of his jumper and his shoes with holes, Mrs O had brought Mother forms to fill in for money. It was years before he knew where her previous money had come from, understood why he'd spent nights alone while Winnie went out dressed up. After the giros came, she went out less. She liked the giros, but not the weekly lady home help advising on housework and budgeting. When Mother had moved them to this house in the middle of the night, she'd continued the giros, but refused the home help. Stan had been sad, missing Mrs Cox with her sweets and comics. House chaos had resumed. Since then, he'd fetched bread, milk and tins of food from the corner shop. The off-licence delivered.

After Pastor Graham's 'nosey-parkering', they'd stopped going to church. He'd missed Sundays, the happy singing. But once his reading was good enough, he read his Bible every night as Gran had. Her death ended so much. Instead of order, there'd been chaos, dirt, mail piles and newspapers. Instead of hot stews and soups, there'd been spam sandwiches or cereal with curdled milk. Gran had brought brightness, lemonade, company and laughter to life. Her absence left it grey in every way.

But now he is in control. Having perfected Winnie's scrawl, he collects the benefits. The chap in the post office doesn't query him. He buys his own food as his mother is too drunk to bother. He gives Winnie her giro money, but keeps the Child Allowance, his by right.

Enough daydreaming. He must study. But concentrating is difficult. Becoming sixteen is such a landmark. Fetching a glass of milk, he sits back down. No point in dwelling on his problems: they aren't new. Reminiscing won't help him escape. Work will. He charges through algebra and, comforted by bedroom snores, rapidly finishes chemistry and English. Biology is last, his favourite. Anger rises as his world of amoebae and fungi is disturbed by a slurred voice from the bedroom.

'Sweetheart boy, how about a cup of tea for your poor mother?'

He obliges. Otherwise she'll get up. As the kettle whistles, he hears her sing Danny Boy. She might have a talent for tall stories, but she has none for singing; God knows why *anyone paid her money for it. She'd never have made it in the shows. Her only talent lay in sinning. He suspects his absent father was a married man. He's learned from Oscar at school that prostitutes met 'punters' and called their sex acts 'tricks.' He doesn't like to think he is the result of a quick fuck from a one-nighter, but why else has he no relatives on his father's side? Winnie might be his only family, but he'll be better off without her. Taking the kettle off the stove, he turns off the burner. He debates on gas – it can kill. But then leaving a gas tap on will affect him too.*

Patience. In two years' time he will escape. The headmaster is confident of a university bursary. A life without obligation and tyranny is in sight, but for now, he needs peace. Reaching for the teabags he makes two decisions. One, step up the booze. Library research shows him alcohol can kill, especially in women. The human liver only takes so much before the body gets yellow, swollen, twitchy and dies. So, no more hiding the rum and gin. And if she's permanently sozzled, there'll be the bonus of a reduction in her disgusting demands. He always refuses now. Plus she'll stop smashing plates and chucking things because he's hidden the Morgan's. He pours a generous measure into her tea. He has a stockpile in a padlocked cupboard in his room. The mug isn't too clean. He sniggers. Germs are unlikely to get her: she must have buckets of immunity after living like a pig since Gran's death. Poor Gran. Winnie should have got a doctor earlier. People can recover from pneumonia. Oscar's mum did. But she went to hospital.

The extra granules he adds dissolve slowly. Stirring, he thinks about Decision Two: find his birth certificate. Winnie must have it. Mrs O said she'd have needed one to register him for school. There is still one well-guarded suitcase under his mother's bed. Oscar says his father's name should be on the certificate, which will help trace his father, and make him pay for condemning a son to a life like this. Jimmy up the road says his Dad pays 'maintenance' for him and his sisters even though he's left to start another family. Once he gets a name, Oscar will help find him. Oscar's father is an underworld king, they say, can put 'frighteners' on anyone. Must be grand. Or Mrs O will help. Perhaps he might find the certificate before meeting her next week at the Ivy Tearoom? Like clockwork, she's there, first Wednesday of the month, always on time despite her now being a head teacher. Never lets him down.

He takes his mother the tea, setting it down amongst the tissues and debris at the bedside. She's dozed off again. She looks like a disgusting tramp: matted grey-brown hair, sallow yellow skin, purple puffy nose. Needs a bath. The bath was another potential idea. Jimmy's old granda drowned in one, had a 'stroke', whatever that was. Jimmy said he'd slipped under, couldn't get out or call for help. But using the bath wasn't a good idea for Winnie. He'd need to lift her into it and hold her under. She was heavy, and if he got her rat-arsed, she'd be even more of a dead weight. Rats. He grins. His current inspiration.

They'd been overrun by them at the back of the terrace. Two days ago, he'd clobbered one with a broom. Huge, it was. He'd watched it twitching till he'd become bored and finished it off with a kitchen knife, slitting it open after donning rubber gloves. All he'd found inside were slimy stinky tubes. He'd scrubbed himself with Dettol afterwards since he'd read rats were dirty feeders, carried plague. After the council men had put down blue poison, he'd scooped up some to plug the bathroom skirting where a rat had poked its head out. But he's kept some back. Pity he isn't sure what kind of poison it is. Rat poisons haven't figured in any of his library murder books. But why not experiment?

Smiling, he shakes her awake and lifts the teacup to her mouth. The poison granules have dissolved. Helpfully, the mug is dark blue, and anyway, colours are indistinguishable *in her murky bedroom: the only light comes from a tatty red-shaded lamp. Last week he'd put in a lower watt bulb so he wouldn't have to see her face properly. And she likes the curtains drawn in the daytime. The room smells. Like the bins. Like waste. And life passing. Given time he'll be free.*

Eight

The Hippocratic Oath

Glasgow, Friday 18th December 1992

Driving away from the Necropolis, he relishes the usual wave of satisfaction he experiences on completion. This latest triumph is a little younger than his usual, but no less warranted. The experimental cocktail in her tea had worked splendidly, affording just enough time for her to remove the treasure from her safe and place it in his hands. How gratifying that the object had come in its own little velvet lined box with its Sotheby's receipt. And how useful that it was not yet in her probate list for Kelvingrove. It had arrived by special courier from New York. She had not even had time to tell her nephew. Now he would never know.

The icon will be his oldest and most expensive work to date: 15th Century, Russian, very rare. As a Baptist, he has no spiritual need for religious iconography, but this little wooden Virgin and Child had captivated him last week when she'd shown him it in the brochure. Unusually etched in silver instead of gold, its figures had pale blue robes. The contrast with the dark skin of the mother and child had made him think. Jesus was not white. And how conveniently the icon had fitted into his Gladstone bag. One must beware curtain twitchers.

He thought the Radcliffe woman had made a splendid figure when he'd laid her out in the study. The dog had been a dratted nuisance round his feet as he'd carefully washed the cups in the kitchen. Why would anyone keep such a pathetic excuse for a dog? But his plan had gone splendidly, apart from that idiot policeman hinting that the 'friend' who had found her was that Semple woman. She'd suggested calling the police surgeon! But no matter. His immaculate records had satisfied the constable.

As he leaves Cathedral Square and drives down Castle Street heading for the M8, he gives thanks for the way society is changing. Amazing how many rich old ducks have few relatives and need home visits, which he feels are key for his purpose, promoting intimacy and confidences. What's also helpful is the modern trend for offspring to scatter far and wide. The trivia of doctor's visits fades to routine, unworthy of mention during infrequent phone calls. Offspring become embroiled in their own insignificant lives. Selfish. Undeserving of beneficence. And as one ages, friends die off. Fewer and fewer people visit or question your demise. Basically, aged citizens contribute little to society and are largely superfluous.

As he leaves the motorway, he glances in the mirror. Time is a relentless enemy. His reflection is a reminder of his own mortality: a few new wrinkles. And his hair needs a treatment. Once on the Clydeside Expressway, he squeezes more power from his Jaguar. The dashboard clock shows scant time is left before evening surgery. He is unfazed. No computer amendments are required today.

His most satisfying case recently had to be Dorcas Thomas. Ah, that clever hospital ECG referral form he'd slipped into the kitchen mail pile while Brighid fetched biscuits! When one fell out of his bag with the death certificate book, he'd seized the chance to scribble a request for a hospital exercise ECG appointment for 'discomfort on walking up stairs.' So useful at her funeral. 'Such a pity Mrs Thomas didn't manage to take her form up to the clinic for a cardiograph test.' Of course, he'd logged an extra appointment at which she'd 'reported' such symptoms. Belt and braces had come from the successful replacement of the toxic thyroid tablets with angina ones, a tablet popped out for each day since the

'Monday' surgery appointment. His community pharmacy access for drugs, labelling and amending dispensing records is excellent. And personal delivery of tablets is always appreciated: Dorcas had been quite unaware that no chemist would have dispensed her high dose.

As he drives through Bearsden, he passes Dorcas' house. The daughter had phoned with thanks before returning to London. How malleable she'd been, how easily charmed into cremation and Wylie's! Dawson's have received a lot of custom from him these last few months. Best exercise restraint: over-enthusiasm risks errors. The Catholic devotional in Dorcas's bedroom was a lesson learned: not all Catholics display hall crucifixes.

Outside his Milngavie surgery, he is enraged to find a beat-up B-reg Vauxhall in his space, clearly marked 'Doctors Only.' After being forced to park his new R-reg Jaguar at the far side of the carpark, he sits to compose himself and admire his modern, purpose-built surgery. Smart. Now all his. Poor William, dying so suddenly. Shocked everyone. Except him. And Jack, taking early retirement soon after. Everyone thought that Willie's heart attack in his early fifties had precipitated Jack's decision to leave. How easily ideas are seeded. Only he knew Jack was an odious lecher: that affair with a girl half his age – and him an elder in the Church! He'd been lucky to get a fair share of the surgery valuation, never mind be allowed to retire to Fife with his unsuspecting wife. Minus a substantive blackmail sum now accumulating nicely in Switzerland, of course.

While reaching back for his doctor's bag, he lifts a Bonham's catalogue. He wonders if it is worth bidding for that Bessie MacNicol on Saturday? Associated with the Glasgow Boys, she'd died young, making her work rare. An advantage, dying young. Not just for artists. Can set others free. Three score and ten is plenty for a woman. He, however, expects to reach one hundred. Quite attainable with his exercise and diet regime. He is exceptionally fit for 43. And hobbies are known to promote longevity: he has many projects planned.

Striding across the car park in the horizontal rain, he tosses the catalogue into a waste-bin. Why waste money on art he can acquire gratis? Perhaps a better use of money might be a holiday in the sunshine? It will need to be after his Christmas church commitments. Somewhere warm. Jamaica, perhaps, for New Year? He retains curiosity. Or might Barbados be more stylish? Tomorrow is Saturday. Ideal for a visit to Thomas Cook after morning emergency surgery. A last minute bargain villa perhaps?

The new boys will grumble at the short notice for finding a locum. Any strop and he'll play the 'comply or forget partnership and references' card. Not that he has any intention of making them partners. Why cede patient lists and profit shares when he can pay lower fixed salaries? They are tied up anyway, their contracts stipulating they can't set up within ten miles and steal away patients. As for Kevin, he should think himself fortunate to have got any job at all after his six-month GMC suspension! Losing his Sheffield partnership, marriage, and house after two patient affairs and having to return to his harridan of a mother? Careless. If his mother was a patient, she might be tempting … But she isn't.

In the waiting room, a girl is turning up the heater. As she leaves, he turns it back down. Phones are ringing, patients queuing at the desk. His well-chosen staff look good in their mandatory high heels, navy suits and white blouses.

His manager comes out of her office. 'Good evening, Doctor, shall I take your coat?'

She knows he will never leave his expensive Abercrombie in the consulting room. Even in this well-heeled locality, patients have light fingers: toilet rolls, waiting-room toys, magazines, even prescription pads, have wandered. The police are useless.

'Thank you. And, by the way, please put a strongly worded note on that disgusting car in my space. I'd like it towed away.'

'Sorry, but the police were adamant last time – you can't get people towed away in Scotland, not even that lecturer who left his car over the weekend.'

'Pshaw! But we put him off the list, didn't we? See if you can find out who owns it, a hideous old Vauxhall.'

While she scurries off, he checks his hair in the mirror for wind damage before sitting down. By the time his computer boots up, his manager is back with his tea: milk, two sugars, two Hobnobs. The rain is battering the windows. A night for the study, for planning. He recalls a notion he had earlier.

'Thank you. Could you add a notebook to the stationery order? Something sturdy, please, Maureen. Leather and lockable if possible.'

The woman takes a large rubber-banded bundle of tattered case notes from under her arm and places it on the desk. 'Life will be much easier, won't it, Doctor, when the computers take over at New Year? I am glad the new doctors agreed.'

'Indeed, old Dr Willie was a Luddite.' He doubts she understands the term. Weather is a safer topic. 'Dreadful day, isn't it? Thinking of taking the family away at New Year for some sun. Put feelers out for a locum, will you?'

'Sure, Doctor.' She nods. Her boss appreciates her departing size twelve figure, a reminder you don't need to let yourself go at forty. Clara is slipping.

Drinking his tea, he gazes at the gilt-framed manuscript on the facing wall. Has he given a return appointment to the Heidrich-Holtz drug rep who brought it? Their new asthma study promises to be more lucrative than the last psychiatric one: more patients, more follow-ups, more money - especially if enhanced by fictional patients and beefed up by positive outcomes or early completion. Speedier reimbursement!

Moving around funds will be easier with the New Contract Fundholding, a gift for his 'double book' system. Large sums should flood in from the Health Board to buy hospital services for patients. And they couldn't possibly monitor every penny. Siphoning should be easier. Luckily, Harry and Kevin show no interest in the accounts. Not that he's offered. They don't see reps either. They'll never enjoy golf at Turnberry, or need Swiss bank accounts! The manuscript is hanging crookedly. He rises to correct this Vatican version of the Hippocratic Oath. It is set out in the form of a cross. He smiles as he reads its first line. 'First do no harm.' Yet the Greeks had poisoning down to a fine art!

Buzzing for his first patient, he assumes his standard avuncular expression for 'caring.'

'Good evening, Mrs Munro, how nice to see you. Do take a seat.'

Nine

Teenage Angst & Jigsaws

Balgrove Academy, Milngavie, three months later

Last period Wednesday was Latin. Katy hated it. All that tense stuff? Future-perfect-pluperfect twaddle! She sighed. Ralph said she couldn't chuck it if she wanted to get into Medicine. Neil needed Latin too, not to follow his Dad's career as a doctor, but for Law. His aim was to earn 'shedloads' to look after his mother. Looking across the classroom at Neil, studiously concentrating, Katy wondered if she was wasting her time with him. His life centred so much round his blooming mother. Did he even consider her as his girlfriend? He'd never kissed her. Andy Baxter had. God, there was Andy now, looking back, winking at her. So immature!

The minute she'd seen Neil, she'd fancied him. Across the church aisle on his first day, he'd stood out, not just because of his height. Blue eyed, blonde wavy hair, chiselled features. Maybe a tad skinny, but she loved his kind smile. It must have been tough to come into term half-way through, yet he didn't show it. He took everything in his stride. He wasn't a cocky show-off, constantly 'on the make' like the others. That first day he'd bumped into her as she was packing up her books at break time, he'd apologised. Sweet. Wouldn't catch the other boys apologising! She'd plucked up the courage to ask him to walk over to the Ref for lunch: bold for her. Susan had muscled in with her usual fluttery lashes and pout, but Neil had only laughed. 'Your friend's a character, isn't she?' But it was Katy he'd walked out with.

She'd been 'seeing' him for two months, though

annoyingly, felt she still knew little about him. She did know he'd hated his private Edinburgh boarding school, Robert Gillespie's. He'd felt most boys had been 'up-themselves' and was delighted his Mum had persuaded his Dad to let him leave and come to a day school. She'd also gathered that he'd moved about the UK a bit. And they had a few things in common: both from medical families, both rubbish at sport, both loving music. He played clarinet. She'd taken him to band practice. Mr Stephens had been pleased.

'A clarinet? Great! We're a bit thin on the ground for clarinets. Why not stay and listen today, then bring your instrument next week?'

She'd been surprised when Neil said he didn't have one, but Mr Stephens gave him a school instrument and sheet music for the pieces they were working on. Neil sat out at the side and smiled at her. But fifteen minutes later, she looked up and he'd gone. That was the first time she'd had that odd tummy thing, not like colic nor the time of the month, more an uneasiness she got when thinking of or waiting on him. Was this falling in love? She couldn't exactly say she *always* felt happy when with him, but there was *something* about him. That first Tuesday, she'd been so upset after he'd shot off that Mr Stephen had rapped on her stand.

'You've missed the intro, Katy, pay attention! Where's your head? We're in Gershwin's! Keep up with the other saxes!' She hadn't known where her head was, but her eyes had been on the empty chair.

Next day, Neil didn't say why he'd left. She didn't ask, having quickly realised he wasn't keen on questions. Over the last few weeks they'd lunched together, walked home side by side, and after band practice on Tuesdays, stopped at Fanconi's for ice cream. Or frothy coffee if it was cold. She'd always paid, saying it didn't matter he'd no cash. But she thought that weird. His family can't have been poor.

The final bell ended Latin. By the time she'd filled her

bag, Neil had gone. Katy decided she needed to know where she stood. Next day was the last day before the Easter holidays. She'd force a proper chat at Fanconi's on the way home.

In the café next day, Neil was quiet, looking so tired and pale that Katy chickened out of asking her burning question. Instead she asked about his holiday plans.

'My stepdad's father is ninety on Easter Sunday, so we're going to Bristol to see him. Lionel's great fun, but he's had to move into a wee sheltered house, so we can't stay with him now. Going to friends. Where do your grandparents live, Neil?'

'I don't have any. I don't have any relatives.' His spoon circled in his melting ice cream.

Katy licked raspberry sauce off hers. 'What, no aunties or cousins?' Neil shook his head. 'That's a pity.' She'd never met anyone without relatives. Neil was looking flushed. 'Well then, you doing anything much in the holidays?'

Neil shrugged. 'No.'

'You not going away for a break? We've got two weeks off.'

'Dad doesn't go for holidays much, though we've done some cruises.'

'Sounds fab. I've only been abroad once, to California, after mum's chemotherapy.'

'Your mum looks well. I didn't know she'd been ill.'

'Och, she's fine now! I don't like to think about it.'

'Why California?'

'Mum has a friend there, Uncle Yousef. He's amazing, and so's his house. It's got a swimming pool! Anyway, where did you cruise to?'

'Oh, the Med and the Caribbean. Dunno why Dad loves it, all that getting dressed up for stupid dinners. Mum liked it, mostly 'cos she didn't have to cook or clean. But the food's too fancy for me – and there's hardly anyone my age. Would prefer a hotel mibbe, but Dad hates them. Stupid. Aren't cruise ships just floating hotels? By the way, have I told you he's mad?'

Katy was surprised at his sudden outburst and decided to change tack again. 'My mum's dad built liners you know. He was a carpenter in the shipyards.'

Neil wasn't listening, just sitting slumped, staring at a faded photo on the wall of a jolly Italian family eating dinner alfresco. Katy waited for Neil to speak. He didn't.

'You know, I haven't met your parents, Neil. Maybe I should pop round, say "hi" to them?'

Neil sat up immediately. 'No. I don't think that's a good idea. Dad doesn't like visitors.'

Katy was shocked: a doctor who disliked visitors, and hotels, though liked cruise ships? Neil looked completely down in the dumps. With a sinking feeling she realised this relationship was doomed if he wouldn't even take her home. No wonder, she was so skinny and spotty. Today's new throbbing chin visitor had refused to be concealed by make-up. Draining her remaining melted vanilla ice, she stood up.

'Oh, forget it. Let's go home.'

They didn't speak on the way. She didn't ask him in when they reached her house.

'See you.' He walked off, flicking his hand from the end of a drooping arm.

Heading to her room, she decided she'd return to sit beside Susan in the band after Easter. Thomson wouldn't care where she sat amongst the saxes. Neil certainly wouldn't.

*

Next week, Bristol

I'm not prone to jealousy, but I do envy my old friend Wendy for her house, or rather, mansion. Granted, she inherited a fortune from her earl grandpa, but she has class and an eye for style I'll never match. Her Wiltshire home is *Country House & Garden* standard, but she'd been a generous host since Ralph's father moved into a tiny cottage and couldn't put us up on our visits to see him. On a surprisingly warm, blue-skied, late April morning, we sat having breakfast in her conservatory surrounded by potted palms.

'Another croissant, Beth?'

'No thanks,' I leaned over to wipe Roland's mouth. Wendy's youngest sat in his highchair gurgling eggy dribbles and gazing hypnotically at a spoon, the way you do at seven months old. Big sister Maia was solemnly spreading toast, more with her fingers than her Tommee Tippee knife, the way you do at two. Her jumper cuffs sported more butter than her bread as she eyed the marmalade dish. Wendy moved it out of harm's way, taking a piece of kitchen roll to degrease her daughter.

'When are you heading over to Lionel's? Haven't heard the girls stir yet.'

'Och, I've left them for a long lie. They're exhausted. I'm a bit worried about Katy.'

'Is she coming down with something? I thought she was unusually quiet last night when you arrived. She's usually right in there, scooping up cats, straight off to the horses. '

'It's not medical, I suspect. More a moody thing. Fourteen's a funny age.'

'It'll be boy trouble. I remember myself at fourteen.' Wendy feigned a swoon, eyes closed, hand clutching her breast. Unfortunately, she'd forgotten about holding the greasy kitchen roll. I refrained from pointing out the stain now marring her silk blouse.

'Thought you didn't have any boyfriends till Conor?'

'Ah, well, true. Might've been more discerning if I'd had! But there were some *in principle*, so to speak. In my head. Like Paul McCartney or dreamy Scott from the tennis club – such a hunk! But father would've had a fit if I'd gone out with anyone, so I didn't.'

'Katy's brought home a boy recently. Nice lad. Maybe they've fallen out. Might be for the best. I'd die if she got pregnant. Or eloped!'

'Don't be ridiculous, Beth – what a worrier you are! That kind of thing only happens in books. You mustn't read so much into everything!'

'That's what I'm always telling her.' Ralph strolled in with Henry through the open patio doors from the terrace. They'd already breakfasted and had gone down to the village for the papers.

'What's up, girls?' Henry stooped to give me a kiss, but my darling husband strolled round the table to sit opposite and grab an almond croissant.

Ralph waved the croissant at Wendy before biting into it. 'You know, Wendy, your friend has a very active imagination. She thinks there's a GP bumping off folk in our area.'

'What?' Henry poured coffee while looking at me, not his cup. A dark spreading stain appeared on the table.

Wendy shouted, 'Hoi, that's a clean cloth!'

Henry laughed. 'It'll wash. So, Beth, who's been bumped off? How? Why?'

'Oh, I don't know. It's just some odd things about the deaths of two women. One Indian lady whose son, Antar, a friend of Julia's, felt the attending GP was rude and didn't check her blood sugar. Even the boy knew that was important since she was diabetic. The other one was Jean, my yoga friend. She often fainted, yet her GP, the same one, said she died of a stroke due to high BP. Doesn't add up.'

'Now, why would he lie?' Henry looked quizzical. As he stretched back in his small chair, I heard an ominous creak. Henry not being a small chap, Wendy looked alarmed. He immediately sat forward, making a face at her.

Ralph reached for a second pastry. 'No one else thought

the deaths were dodgy, Henry. Not sure why Beth's become so aerated about them.' Ralph poured a coffee and stirred in two sugars, obviously thinking I wasn't watching. I wasn't pleased: he'd gone up two trouser sizes and was risking a third.

'Did you speak to the police, Beth?' Wendy picked a cranky Roland out of his chair for a cuddle. The spoon had lost its charm.

'No, I'd nothing to go on, really. Looking at it now, maybe I was overreacting.'

'You know, I worked with a Dr Death once,' said Henry, dipping his damp spoon in the sugar and sucking it. He also had a sweet tooth, worse than Ralph: he'd spent years exercising and trying to lose weight.

'Did he get jailed?' I asked.

'No. Odd bloke, Truscott. A surgical Senior Registrar here in Bristol when I was a skin SR. I was asked to see a rash on one of his patients, but when I went back to do a biopsy the following day, the old boy had suddenly snuffed it overnight. The staff nurse whispered about funny inexplicable deaths when Truscott was on. She thought him creepy, always hanging about, keen to certify any deaths. None of the docs made anything of it, but she reported him. Melanie, her name was. Such a nice girl.' Henry looked to middle distance.

Ralph laughed. 'Ah, do I detect an old flame? I see that look!'

Wendy raised an eyebrow. Henry flushed, shaking his head. 'Doesn't matter, old story.'

'Never mind him, Henry. So, Melanie blew the whistle and ...?' I was curious.

'Well, the hospital admin brought in the police. Think they reviewed the cases and interviewed him but found nothing untoward. In fact, they reported him as a charming chap who'd been very upset by her allegations. He made a complaint about her and I think there was to be a disciplinary thing.'

'That's hardly fair if she was expressing genuine concern about patients!'

'She moved away. Truscott left too, went to be a GP, I heard.'

'Maybe he's moved to Milngavie to continue his murderous ways!'

I didn't think this was funny, but Henry joined Ralph's laughter. Maia comically aped him, throwing her head back and almost falling off her chair.

'Heaven forbid!' I said. 'We've already got Conor Towmey prowling around Scotland.'

Wendy looked tight-lipped at the mention of her abusive ex-husband and stood to clear the table. I left to dig Katy and Julia out of bed. Time to visit Grandpa Lionel.

We had a lovely week in Somerset. I forgot all about dodgy GPs and Henry's Dr Death. After days feasting on cream teas, we watched hilarious old home movies Lionel had discovered in a box. Ralph, age seven, trying to teach an uninterested family dog tricks by jumping through a hula hoop himself, was a classic. As were his knitted, green 1950s holiday swim shorts. The girls will never let him forget those.

A few months later, we were in a restaurant and I was distracting myself from work worries by musing on the notion you might guess a person's personality type by which curry they chose. It wasn't an original idea; my friend Ailsa had started classifying people by food metaphors at school. I still noted how many crème puffs, dry tea biscuits and the odd fruitcake came into my surgery! I do love curry, and I love the Shish Mahal. Originally situated near our old stamping grounds at the university, it moved to new premises due to subsidence or something, but still retained the same luxury feel: red silk walls, gilded mirrors, plush carpets, spicy aromas and atmospheric Indian music with sitars. In complete contrast to our old café haunts with Formica tables, chrome chairs and jukebox pop, the new Shish was a velvet-chaired, flickering-candled oasis. We went whenever possible. Curries held a special place in my heart. For ages after chemotherapy they were the only food not tasting of cardboard.

We were dining with old classmate Gordon Tindall and his teacher wife, Heather. Having four kids, the Tindalls didn't often get out, but that evening my mother was hosting their kids at our house for videos and a sleepover. We'd left six kids covered in flour, coconut and cinnamon making doughnuts for their TV movie. As my ex, Dan, was on his monthly visit, he was in our party.

I kicked off my curry diagnostic test by pointing to my plate. 'So, what does this prawn korma say about me? Creamy, not so spicy. So, am I over-cautious, unadventurous and keen to avoid the heat?'

Everyone laughed.

'Now, I have lamb rogan josh,' said Heather. 'Menu says it's strong and rich with tangy tomato. How does that sound, eh, Gordon?'

Her husband wagged a finger at her. 'Yet sparky and spicy when stirred! My beef madras is hot and daring. Pretty macho. Perfect for me!'

'There my theory falls down, Gordon. You're the least macho person I know!'

Feigning offence, Gordon turned to Dan. 'You've ordered whole chilli pakora and vindaloo. Hot, strong, definitely flamboyant – bit aggressive? Made for a tough, hard-pressed London cardiologist battling for research funds?'

Dan flexed his biceps, pretending to look tough, then pointed at Ralph's plate. 'What does veggie sag aloo and dahl say about Ralph, then? Suppose sort of calm, maybe becomes heated under extreme pressure, like his intestinal gas will be after all those lentils and onions!'

'Enough!' cried Heather.

I went to the loo. On my return, they were talking about death. I'd have preferred flatulence. Influenced by his fourth pint, Gordon was waxing eloquent on the subject of death certification whilst scraping blood-red sauce off his plate with naan bread. As he moved on to cremations, Heather rolled her eyes, drained her wine and called a waiter for another bottle.

'Now, part two cremation certificates can be tricky things. This week I had a request for one from a practice seven miles away from Kirkintilloch who've never asked us before.'

'Who? And why?' I coughed as a deceptively innocuous-looking pink onion side-dish made my eyes water.

'Chap at Kilnglass. Kinda vague on reasons, implied your lot, Beth, were too busy, some "Brian" was away, and he couldn't get through to Drumlea.'

'When was this?'

'Wednesday afternoon.'

'Practice half day. But I was on, Gordon, and not busy, mostly just catching up on paperwork. And I had several telephone consultations, so there was zilch wrong with our phones.'

'You know, I'd a feeling it was a bit of a fudge.'

'Which GP?' I wasn't repeating my usual mistake in not asking names.

'Kerr? No, Kevin Nixon. But when I got to the undertaker, it was his partner waiting, a Goodman chap, who said Kevin had gone home with a migraine. Goodman gave me the same story as Kevin. Had an odd accent, Goodman.' His brow knitted. 'East coast maybe? Or southern? Did ask him where he was from, but he didn't answer, just hovered till I'd done. Didn't care for him. Bit too smooth. Hard to put a finger on it.'

'Like Bodkin Adams?' Dan interjected. 'The serial killer?' He opened wide googly eyes.

'Och, no, course not! And he never actually looked me in the eye. Kind of peculiar for a colleague, don't you think? Anyway, to be honest, it was almost three and I wanted home to watch the tennis, so I did the needful and scooted.'

'It was an OK death, was it?' I had to ask.

'Sure. Ancient biddy, classic MI. Been on angina treatment. He'd come along, he said, to get her sister on the phone to speak to me. She confirmed the story. Nothing about it that didn't ring true, though oddly, the sister sounded English. Suppose she might've lived down south for a bit. Anyway, first time I've met Goodman. Never seen him at any post-grad education sessions or anything. Have you, Beth?'

'No, but funnily enough I was talking to Charles about him. He became senior partner at Kilnglass very swiftly. Willie Reid died last year in the surgery. MI, poor chap. Then the other guy there, Jack Young, suddenly upped sticks and retired early to Fife. Goodman took on Harry Tait and Kevin Nixon. I've met Kevin at the Health Board Local Medical Committee where he just doodles and yawns, but I've never physically met Harry or Goodman. Charles thinks Goodman's OK, if a bit cocky. He's heard he was a London high-flyer before becoming a GP. Charles met him at LMC meetings before Harry arrived. Goodman's a fundholding enthusiast, I believe.'

'I'm fed up with the Local Medical Committee stuff, Beth. Going to demand one of my partners takes a turn. Wednesday half days are for golf!' Gordon turned to Ralph with whom he occasionally played. 'I'm playing off six now, did I say?'

I countered with 'Six what – beers?' Only Heather laughed. 'I tried playing, you know, Gordon, at Douglas

Park with Charles, but it's just so slow and boring. Isn't there something daft about grown men strutting about waving sticks and whacking a ball?'

Gordon bristled. 'Rubbish, Beth! It's good physical exercise with enjoyable banter!'

'Gossiping, more like,' said Heather. 'Beth's right about strutting. I mean, have you seen those lurid pullovers and checked pants at the Open? Hilarious!'

Before Gordon could protest, Dan sprang to our defence. 'The girls have a point. It is a kind of ritual showing off, isn't it?' He winked at me, blue eyes twinkling: still the looker, even though flushed by his chilli-laden dinner. 'Think it's a bit of a poncy game, myself.' He grinned. 'Now tennis, that's a game for real men. Takes brawn, power and skill!' I knew Dan was playing several times a week, and squash in winter. He added, 'Isn't golf mainly an excuse for GPs to get away from the phones – and wives – on their afternoons off? Beth's partner, Gerry, uses sailing out of Rhu for the same reason!'

Ralph wasn't having it. 'Come on, there's more than GPs up the course too, Dan. Lawyers, surgeons. I agree with Gordon, it's a good safety valve – exercise with psychotherapy from mates!'

'Och, I'd rather have a G&T and a good book than whack balls around in the rain!'

Ralph laughed at me. 'Ha! I heard you did a lot more ball-hunting than whacking! But Beth, maybe tennis is an idea? We could join Westerlands again. It's near uni and on the way home. We need to get fit.'

Watching my husband say this with a mouthful of gooey sweet gulab jamun, I didn't take it seriously.

'On that subject,' said Dan, 'who d'you reckon'll win Wimbledon tomorrow, Sampras or Courier?'

By the time I'd consumed my three thousand plus calories of ghee-laden curry and reached home in a taxi,

I'd forgotten about dodgy cremation requests and worries giving me uneasy gut feelings. But in the middle of the night the gut feelings which transpired made me vow to lay off curries for a bit.

Ten

Reunions

Edinburgh, June 1993

He'd forgotten how light Scottish midsummer evenings
were compared to London. But he wasn't embarrassed
about leaving here while it was still light. Conor strolled
down the broad curving Edwardian staircase, hands in
pockets, whistling. A nice sky was forming. Weak flares of
orange already tinged the undersides of the ever-present,
wind-whipped clouds over the Firth of Forth. The large hall
windows offered a panorama over Edinburgh's Georgian
roofline. Grand, huge windows, each pane larger than the
sum of the windows in his pokey attic flat. But give it a
month or two and he'd be able to move on. Early completion
of his latest project meant a bonus was now on the way.
Completion of his statistics Master's from Heriot Watt had
helped greatly. He'd surprised himself, and after him vowing
no more exams *ever* after Surgery Part Two!

Skipping down and out, Conor winked at the door
girl. He'd had her: a quickie – no foreplay – after a night
in the Scotsman Bar. This evening, however, had been a
professional occasion with Zara, taking his time, paying for
it. Flexing his shoulders, he strode out. During the evening,
he'd decided he'd skip next month's graduation ceremony.
No point. No one to invite, not even Aisling. Too busy with
her three kids and nursing home. Silly ass, that husband of
hers earned enough to keep them both. Certainly was no
point inviting his dad, now off the planet. Wouldn't be long
before his body joined his mind and packed in. Served the
drunken, whoring bastard right. Aisling was too soft, taking

him in. He didn't deserve it after the way he'd treated them and their poor mother.

Out on the pavement, he lit up and lounged against the railings, watching a guy coming up the hill with turned-up collar and pulled-down hat. Who was he kidding? Everyone would know why he was here. Edinburgh looked genteel and ultra-civilised on the surface, but plenty took advantage of its underbelly. It had almost as many dark spots of iniquity as London. Waterfront Leith had the most action, according to local boy Gavin in the office, who'd warned Con to look at arms and ankles before indulging. Teaching his grandmother egg-sucking! All medics knew the desperate ones soon ran out of easy arm veins for a fix. Risky, too, needle-sharing. But unlikely in this parlour. High-end. He knew the VD guy who regularly checked the girls for Hepatitis and HIV. Bloody AIDS. Took poor old Frank. Must be three years now. Such a crazy oddball, a risk taker. Maybe he could have been kinder latterly, for he, of all people, knew how hard appetites were to resist. Poor Frank's bisexual or homosexual or whatever carry-on, that can't have been easy. He smiled, remembering a wild student Sauchiehall Street Saturday night with Frank chucking beer cans at the polis. God, they'd tried a lot of stuff then; that might've been the night he snorted his first coke!

Drugs had always been part of his life. Once ruled by recreational chemicals, now he ruled them. Fancy him taking the bloody things to market! A subtler kind of power than that from a scalpel, but still, life versus death. God bless Sandy, making him CEO of Eureka, his wife's company. Wife number four! Mad to have a kid on the way at his age, with all that screaming and baby poo. Sandy was a big wean himself, a bumptious snob in raised golf shoes. But a Lloyd's name, Sandy, minted from years of nipping and tucking the stars and manoeuvring within his old boy network. Pity Conor's own had shrunk drastically overnight.

Getting erased from the Medical Register meant 'friends' vanished.

He was glad Eureka's head office had moved to Edinburgh. Less folk knew him up here than in London. Well, there was Frank's brother James and his wife, Rosie, but the chances of running into a barrister and child psychiatrist weren't high. The name change should help. Life went on. He still had his vices, his fags and sex, but did the gym stuff now too. He'd noticed the sex 'itch' had diminished somewhat; his needs had changed. He preferred to pay professionals for what he wanted. Scots girls liked it more conventional. This parlour was top end. Zara serviced a judge, an assistant chief constable, MPs and actors. Of course, he also had Jane – not as stacked or compliant as Zara, but still a goer. Mid-twenties, admirably ambitious, well versed in using her long limbs and curvy body, she'd go far in pharmaceuticals. He knew he was but one in a line of work conquests, but non-exclusivity worked both ways.

In no rush to move off, he enjoyed the smoke he'd been gasping for, but hadn't wanted to waste paid 'bedtime' on. Cupping his hands in the breeze, he lit a second Lambert and Butler. The hill climber drew level.

'I'll be damned, Stan Truscott! God, it must be what, twelve, thirteen years ago since St Jasper's?' He remembered this guy well: ambitious, studious, a bit humourless, but a friend of a sort. Yet Stan didn't look particularly pleased to see him.

'I'm going in for a massage.' Stan's face was bland.

Con smiled and restrained from joking about what he wanted massaged. Stan wouldn't appreciate it. But he noticed the boy looked different. Better groomed? Bespoke suit, heavy Raymond Weil watch.

'Say, you've had your nose fixed, haven't you?'

'Yes. The old rugby injury became problematic.'

Con chuckled inwardly: he was sure Stan had never played

rugby. Not after that time he'd taken him to Twickenham and tried to discuss tactics. He trawled his memory banks for something to say.

'You went off to Bristol, didn't you? Do you know after you went, one of your old Unit guys topped himself? Quite a scandal.'

Stan looked straight at him. 'I know. Such a shame.'

'So, you a consultant up here now?'

'No. I'm here for a conference.'

'Oh, right. You still vascular? Here or in Dundee?'

'No. I now lead a large fundholding practice. Surgery was a dead loss. Too many backstabbers, too much administrative interference. I prefer being my own boss.'

'Too right.' Con took a deep drag from his cigarette, expelling smoke upwards. 'I'm out too. Perhaps you read about it?' He gave a short, mocking laugh. 'All a conspiracy led by my ex-wife, the bitch Wendy. Don't think you ever met her? Took me to the cleaners. And her lover took me to the GMC, said I'd stolen his bloody research. Bastards the lot of them.'

'I did see it. Very unfortunate. The press was most unkind.'

'Jackals!'

'You should have appealed. One of my practice associates had GMC trouble, but got reinstated.'

'I tried. Useless barrister bastard was a bloody waste of money. Gave up, not waiting five years to pay the GMC a fortune to be "assessed" to see if I'd dealt with their bloody issues. Fuck that! It was green cheese too, you know. I was a threat to the London establishment. You've no idea how ruthless these boys can be.'

'Oh, I do. Sometimes you have to back off, rise above it, seek revenge when you can, don't you?' He declined a cigarette but mirrored Conor's stance, leaning on the railings. 'So, what do you do now?'

'Oh, I manage a research company, Eureka. Owned by old Sandy Kane – you remember him? It's his wife Tove's company. Bride number four, a Scandinavian goddess, all boobs but not inconsiderable brain. Wouldn't mind giving her one but hey, mustn't shit in the backyard, eh? We do pharma regulatory stuff, phase three trials and so on. Patient data sheets, licence lobbying, result massaging as necessary.' He laughed. 'Pays the bills. Better than all-nighters up to your elbows in bellies full of gore. My nights are my own now! Say, you might like to put some patients into one of our trials. Cash payments.' Conor noted Stan stopped fidgeting and looked around before he turned to face him.

'Oh? What kind of trials? And how much?'

Blunt as ever. Stan hadn't changed. 'Psychotropics like a new anti-depressant this month, a tranquilliser and an asthma drug soon. It's fifty a patient on enrolment and fifty for follow up. Twenty or so guinea pigs each time. Here's a card, bell me!'

Stan took it. 'Thank you, Conor.'

'It's Conrad now, by the way. Been nice meeting you after all these years.'

Con watched Stan mount the steps to ring the bell and be admitted by Tania. She kissed him: not his first time, then.

Tossing his cigarette stub, Con walked off. A watch glance showed he'd missed last orders at ten. No matter. There was the back door of that Rose Street place. Knock three times …

While drinking his first pint, he remembered about Stan's wife. Shame. Drowned returning from honeymoon in France. Didn't he go all religious afterwards? Or was he mixing him up with Frank who went pious before AIDs got him? Yeah. Couldn't have been Stan or he wouldn't have been heading into a brothel, for God's sake. Or rather his dick's sake! He chuckled. And he hadn't thought about that guy at Jasper's who topped himself for years. Bit superior, Kenneth Stewart. A gossip. It was Ken who'd told him about Stan's psycho heiress wife. Hadn't Ken's suicide rocked the hospital just a few months after Stan had buggered off to Bristol with some new bird? Bristol: he shuddered. Home to that bitch Wendy who'd ruined him.

Anyway, come more trial patients off Stan, he'd be even nearer a new flat deposit. Stan wouldn't mind fudging a few results to speed things up. Wasn't it suggested he'd fudged a drug prescription Kardex at Jasper's? He couldn't remember why.

For some reason, meeting Stan had perked him up, albeit made him nostalgic. Soon it'd be twenty years since graduation. Time for a Theta Club reunion. He doubted he'd be notified, not after being 'de-frocked.' Wendy would be there.

The juke box in the smoke-filled, crowded Black Cat was playing *Nothing's Gonna Stop Us Now*. He turned to a slim, leggy girl next to him. 'You want a drink?' She took a Bacardi and Coke. He ordered another pint of Special with a Grouse chaser.

*

Rowanlea, Bearsden

On the last Friday of June, I hosted our final Theta committee meeting before the September reunion. The kids were being pests, 'demob happy', as my dad would've said: the summer break was only days away. As teenagers, Julia and Katy should have known better than to run in and out interrupting. I regretted not asking Mum over, but felt she was already doing me big favours by child-minding for the whole school holidays.

We had a full house. Henry had arrived from Bristol and it was Dan's routine weekend. They were sharing Katy's twin-bedded room. Rosie had come through but would have to make do with the study sofa-bed. Gordon had come over, as had Stella. Luckily, she didn't need a bed, living only twenty minutes away. Now a Glasgow consultant surgeon, and always very organised, she handed us each an agenda.

Every medical year at Glasgow has a social committee designated by a Greek letter. Our Theta Club had already held a Tenth Reunion. I hoped the Twentieth would be better: the last one had been marred by an exhausting, explosive mix of affairs, declarations of unrequited love and illegal body disposal admissions. Hopefully, this time it would involve socialising with old friends without clandestine trysts or murders.

'One hundred rooms booked so far,' said Stella. 'The hotel's showing more bookings than I thought, but they're a bit vague on how many are single occupancy which makes estimating numbers for the gala dinner difficult.'

'Why don't we send another mailshot, requesting folk confirm by 31st July that they're coming? I'm off next week so I can do letters and send them.' Rosie's suggestion was quickly accepted.

'Ask who wants Saturday morning golf, too. I have to pay a deposit at the Old Course and don't want to be out of pocket or disappoint folk.' Typical Gordon: golf has priority.

The menu choices for the dinner were agreed, Stella confirmed the ceilidh band booking, and Dan the speakers for the Sunday morning.

'Must we have them?' asked Rosie. 'I mean, old codgers droning on?'

'Well, the overseas folk can claim tax back if we have a teaching element,' said Dan. 'The guys will keep it light. I haven't asked any known windbags! You can stay in bed if you want. It's not compulsory.'

'Fair enough. Do you think we could claim tax too?' said Henry. 'Must ask my accountant.'

Just as I was saying, 'Is it worth the bother?' Katy stormed in to object she wasn't being allowed to watch her favourite TV programme. Ralph went to arbitrate. In the lull, Stella dropped a bombshell.

'Mrs Jacobsen at the Faculty Office said she'd had an enquiry from a year member who was no longer practising, asking if he would still be considered a member of the Theta Club.'

'Who?' I demanded. 'And what did she say?'

'She was very coy about who, but said she told him it depended on our Constitution.'

'Do we have one?' Stella sat back, making a face.

'Not that I know of.' I looked round the room to head shakes and shrugs.

'Should we draw one up so that anyone struck off, for example, or convicted of anything awful, can no longer be a member of the Theta Club?'

Rosie's eyes locked on mine. 'Maybe James could rustle something up?'

'Good idea. Ask him, Rosie. As soon as possible. Don't think Wendy could take it if you-know-who turned up to this one.' Henry was being discreet.

I wasn't. 'Conor shouldn't get within a mile of this.'

'We can't book the whole hotel though, Beth,' Rosie shook her head. 'We can't prevent them from taking other guest bookings.'

Ralph returned with coffee plus the cakes and sandwiches I'd made earlier. Sensing the tension, he fetched wine. Amazing how mentioning Con could put such a dampener on a previously jovial evening. We sipped, drafted a letter for Rosie to send, and made a checklist of outstanding questions for the hotel staff re Friday's buffet menus, the Saturday gala dinner and dance timings. Gradually, tension eased. Whisky was opened. It was almost midnight when Gordon and Stella left.

Rosie loaded the dishwasher. 'I keep thinking about that lassie, Jane, I saw with Conor. She never did come to see me, Beth. Constella sent a young guy.'

'Perhaps she's moved on. Reps do. Hopefully away from him. But you can't save everyone from themselves, Rosie. You know that.'

I gave her a hug and went to bed. By the time I reached bed, Ralph was snoring loudly. He shouldn't drink MacAllan. But otherwise, he has few faults.

*

Gordon thought drug reps were improving. Currently, he saw two per week, mostly personable young men in white shirts, old boy ties, smart suits and polished shoes. This leggy lass was white-shirted and suited, but lacking a tie, offered more cleavage than necessary. She was recruiting for a drug trial needing ten patients enrolled for final testing of an asthma drug to be taken for a month on top of their inhaler. All that was required was a weekly peak flow measurement and the patient's sliding scale estimation of symptom severity on exertion, coughing or sleep, plus a note of any side effects. Few had been reported, she said. Gordon was a bit cross she kept repeating the fees payable, he was more interested in the drug and improving patients. With a lot of asthmatics, he wouldn't have trouble recruiting cases.

The girl pointed at her papers. 'As you see, Dr Tindall, the form's very straightforward – why, even your practice nurse could do it!' She leaned forward and licked her fuchsia pink lips, flashing a wide smile.

'Fine. Leave me the pro-formas and I'll be in touch when it's done.'

'Super!' She bounced up. For a moment, he thought she was about to fling her arms round him and was fleetingly disappointed when she only gathered her folders and left.

Doubtless she'd assume it was her force of personality and attractiveness that had recruited him, but the money would buy a spirometer to save his patients trailing to hospital for further asthma tests. He looked at her calling card. Jane Chancellor didn't look old enough to have a Pharma Science BSc and a master's. He sighed. It wasn't just policemen looking younger as you got older, as Beth had laughed about last week.

Heather would think it hilarious a 'dolly bird' had flirted with him. She was always teasing that with his protruding ears and gangly frame, no one else would have him, cheeky besom! Mind you, Jane wasn't after his body, only ticks in her wee boxes. Just like the NHS. He returned to logging the 'MOT' check-ups for over seventy-five-year-olds that his nurse had completed. Pointless, since only the 'worried well' answered the invites, making this unlikely to save lives. Which was the aim of being a good GP, wasn't it?

Eleven

Plans, Inconsistencies & Green Pens

Westhaven, Bearsden

On balance, he feels it is probably not worth taking time to encrypt the notebook. It is always locked out of sight. Opening it up, he notes four possibilities are listed for this month.

Mrs Mac is a good choice. Foolish woman, leaving a financial balance sheet in full public view on a sideboard. No family of note nearby. Her filthy little dog had left teeth marks on his ankle. Suki. Such a ridiculous name. Its food dish always lies in the kitchen, but she is a better target. And due a visit this week.

Selecting the correct paper, he feeds it into the printer before he starts typing. Nigel has obliged, not only with the stationery, but the required official wording. What a pathetic specimen Nigel Warnock is. So pitifully grateful for his prescriptions, even lapping up the higher dosage despite its risk of increased dependency. Hopefully, he'll obey instructions and vary the chemists he uses. With frequent trips to see clients in Edinburgh, he has many options. If only Nigel's high-powered clients knew how weak their solicitor was.

He pauses to consider the amount. Five thousand? The usual. Not excessive. After reading over his missive, he hits *print*. Mrs Mac favours those cheap blue Bic pens when signing the back of her prescriptions. Plenty of those in the practice office. Then he'll be set. He has the pills from Simon. And different pens for the 'witness' signatures.

Next morning, his first patient is a shoo-in for the Heidrich-Holtz trial.

'Perhaps, Mrs Lester, you would like to try this new tablet for your asthma?'

'It isn't bothering me too much just now. My eczema is.' She exhibits a forearm.

'But the tablets may mean you could stop your inhalers.'

'Really?'

'It's being used a lot in the States.'

As she takes the packet, he wonders whether he should have read the protocol. Time later. No point in mentioning it's a drug trial, or that these tablets might be placebo. It's all the same to her.

After she leaves with pills and hydrocortisone cream, he fills out the H-H forms with today's date, initials, date of birth and gender. Then, for years on asthma treatment, he puts down '20', and scores symptom severity for her at 8/9. Under 'other medication' he writes 'Becotide inhaler b.d.' Finally, taking a return visit slip, he dates it for four weeks hence, records an improved symptom score of 3/9 and gives patient satisfaction as 9/9. One hundred pounds down. If he doesn't find enough cases in the next fortnight, he'll just take names off the asthma clinic list. No one will ever know. He dislikes the Lester woman, an irritating asthma campaigner. Divorced. No wonder. Butch and pushy. He buzzes. God, it's a tedious old moaner. He smiles. 'Sorry to keep you waiting, Mr Gillen.'

'Oh, no problem, Doctor, I'm only pleased I managed to get this appointment.'

So he should be. 'So, what can I do for you today?'

'It's the knees, Doctor, they're giving me gyp!'

He leans forward. It shows concern.

*

Oakfield Surgery, 2 weeks later

A warm July afternoon had not daunted Mr Dermott Green from coming into the surgery. He was even more agitated than usual. Having acquired a computer, his medical research had escalated beyond the confines of his tattered *Family Physician*. Today's self-diagnosis was 'prostrate' cancer.

I was feeling prostrate myself. Last week we'd had his testicle drama: he found his right one was bigger than his left. It wasn't, but his right did sit slightly higher than the other, a common finding. Today I helped his shaking hand roll up his sleeve and took blood before asking him to pop onto the couch. He almost knocked me over in his eagerness to submit to the indignity of a rectal examination. I reassured him he didn't have an enlarged prostate and binned his brandished print-out urging 'Find out before it's too late!'

'It's definitely not cancer, Mr Green.' Seeing him relax a little, but still exuding stress, I said, 'Would you like me to give you something to stop you worrying so much? Just to take when you get very anxious?'

He shook his head indignantly. 'When will the blood result be back?'

'I expect it'll be normal, but phone on Tuesday.' Then, perhaps because I was off on holiday to Jersey within hours and feeling magnanimous, I gave him a specimen bottle. 'If you like, we could check your urine too.'

He beamed. 'A first thing sample, Doctor?'

Checking for infection, it didn't matter what time of day, but I nodded. 'Perfect, Mr Green. Hand it in on Monday.' Poor soul, loving tests, welded to his inner workings. Where would his anxiety focus next? As he closed the door, I buzzed through. 'Any more customers, Alison?'

'No more emergencies, Doctor. Only one call left in the book, that terminal patient of Dr MacTavish's. Oh, and a chap from Kilnglass was on. I said you'd phone him back.'

I groaned. 'Thought I was getting off too lightly. Can

you get him for me?' I signed some scripts and speed read some hospital letters, marking them, 'normal', or, 'collect a script', or 'phone patient to come in for discussion'. But they'd have to see one of the boys. I'd be on the beach! My spirits lifting, I answered the phone on first ring.

'Hello?'

'Good afternoon, Dr Semple, how are you?'

'I'm fine, thank you. Sorry, to whom am I speaking?'

'Dr David Goodman here.'

'What can I do for you?'

'I wondered if you'd be kind enough to do a part two cremation form today.'

My heart lurched, not just because of the extra hour's work. 'For?'

'A lady in her eighties, a Mrs Isabel Mackintosh, passed away yesterday. Sudden, so sad. We tried CPR but by the time the ambulance came, she was gone. Distressing for the staff.'

'What was wrong with her?'

'Angina, arthritis and a hiatus hernia. She came in complaining of tiredness. I was taking blood from her myself, to save her coming back to the nurse, when she collapsed on the floor.'

He sounded charming and very sincere. How had I doubted this man?

'So it was a sudden death outside the home? Have the police been told?'

'Oh, of course. And I phoned her daughter, Mrs Johnstone. She came over from Strathaven straight away. Poor woman was distraught. There can be no doubt Mrs Mackintosh had a heart attack. I witnessed her clutching her arm and gasping with chest pain. Anyway, we all decided it would be too traumatic for her family not to issue a death certificate, the cause of death was obvious. And of course, we could hardly hold the body in the surgery with a full waiting room.

Besides, Mrs Johnstone insists her mother had a horror of post-mortems. I couldn't do it to her.'

'But surely a sudden death outside of home merits Procurator Fiscal notification?'

'Ah, I've checked that before. If you're young and normally fit, certainly. But these circumstances were textbook. My partner Kevin had increased her beta blockers and angina tablets only last week. Pity she refused referral to a consultant. A lovely lady, but stubborn.'

'I don't know, Dr Goodman. Perhaps you should ask someone else. I'm off on holiday tonight.'

'But now I've explained it all to you!'

He sounded sincere and caring. I felt obliged. 'OK. I've one call to do and I'll be there.'

'Splendid, Doctor. I will be waiting.'

The Kilnglass practice was a modern purpose-built facility, unlike our inter-war converted bungalow. Dr Goodman ushered me into his smart consulting room. Tidy, a neat bookcase of up-to-date medical books, the Hippocratic Oath and Ben Lomond on the walls.

'Maureen, a quick cup of tea and a biscuit while I take Dr Semple through this?' His girl beamed and left. 'These are her consultation entries.' He scrolled down the screen.

As a fund-holder, he used a different computer programme from my GPass one, but I grasped entries going back months, all confirming his story. As did her prescription history. Maureen returned with tea in matching gold-rimmed porcelain cups. At Oakfield we used random freebie drug company mugs.

He relaxed back in his chair. 'Right, I'll get Mrs Mac's daughter on the phone, then you can pop round to Dawson's and tie this up before you jet off. Going somewhere nice?'

'Jersey.'

'Delightful. But you should try a cruise. Treat you like

kings, you know.'

His accent was intriguing. I asked where he was from.

'I trained in London but have worked all over the UK, until I fell in love with Scotland. Quiet roads, friendly people. Please excuse me for one moment, I've something to attend to in reception. Finish your tea.'

As he left, I relaxed. There was nothing suspicious about this death. Goodman was perfectly nice. I picked up a practice leaflet – very professional. This man couldn't have said what Antar had alleged. The door opened. Maureen came in to remove the tray.

'Must have been awful, that lady dying in here yesterday.'

'Terrible! When Dr Goodman came out to phone for an ambulance, I rushed in and couldn't believe it, her lying there on the couch, so white, blue lips and everything. He rushed back in to start CPR. The practice nurse wasn't in, but she thinks we should get a bicarbonate drip in case it happens again and Dr Goodman's considering a de-fibrillator.'

Goodman came in. 'Come along, Maureen, no time for chatting. The doctor's got a flight to catch! When you've packed up, don't forget to put the phones over to Drumlea.'

'Of course, Doctor.' Maureen bustled off.

Dr Goodman dialled a number. 'Mrs Johnstone? Right, here is a doctor who has to ask you a few questions for legal purposes, a Dr Semple.' He handed me the phone.

'Good morning, Mrs Johnstone, I'm sorry for your loss. Can I just ask about your mother's health recently?' Goodman sat nodding and smiling at me while she gave an account of her mother's angina and how it'd meant she'd recently had to ask her neighbour to walk her dog. She ended with a tribute to Dr Goodman.

'I don't know what they'd have done without him, Doctor.' She spoke softly, sounded muffled. Maybe she had a cold? 'I do hope things can be tied up today. I'd like to arrange the funeral as soon as possible.'

I couldn't think why she'd say that, but didn't feel I could ask. As I hung up, Goodman looked at his watch.

'Time marches on, Doctor. Shall we?' He gestured to the door.

'Yes, of course.'

I left him standing at reception, head tilted to the side and smiling that smile which was permanently on show. Gordon's comments in the Shish came back to me. Was there an edge of ... something? Insincerity? I chided myself for being paranoid and headed for Dawson's.

A chirpy Monty exposed the sad remains of Mrs Isabel Mackintosh, a healthy looking eighty-year-old woman with good skin and a fine head of professionally dyed brown hair. But of course, sadly, stone cold with indigo lips. Fresh puncture wounds were visible in both antecubital fossae. Why both? And why did one show extensive bruising? Poor veins necessitating repeated blood-letting attempts? Goodman hadn't mentioned that. My brain rolled over possible scenarios. And why had Goodman gone out to reception to phone an ambulance? We all had desk phones. Curious.

Monty was hovering, fidgeting and smoothing his wavy hair. Giving a small cough, he nodded down at the corpse. 'Glad I'm not with Kilnglass, Doc.'

'What do you mean?'

'Well, two deaths this month actually *in* the surgery? Wee bitty careless, if you ask me!'

'Really?' My stomach churned to match my brain. I mulled over two oddities in the story I'd been given. Maureen had said she saw her on the couch, but Goodman had said she'd collapsed on the floor. She was a big lady. How had he got her back up unaided? Then the daughter. Hadn't her story sounded a bit pat? She had used practically the same phraseology as Goodman! I'd have preferred to speak to her alone, without him looming. And had she sounded odd, scared even? Or just upset and grieving? I made a snap decision.

'Monty, I'm not signing part two. I can't say on soul and conscience that further examination of this body isn't necessary, sorry.'

Monty carefully pulled the cotton sheet back over Isabel. 'Good on ye, Doctor. He's a funny chap, that Goodman. Comes in here to pray over his patients. Have you heard the like?'

I shivered. Who'd come into a freezing morgue unless they had to, never mind to pray?

'Shall you give him the good news, or shall I?' Monty shuffled from one foot to the other.

I sighed. 'Oh, it's my responsibility, but thanks for offering.'

Monty smiled. 'I'd like to be a fly on the wall when you do.'

I phoned the local police station as we are instructed to do for sudden deaths when the Fiscal's office is closed and got Constable Teviot. Just my luck. As I told him the story of the death in the surgery and discrepancies in the stories of the practice manager and doctor, I could visualise him laboriously writing it all down. He found no record of them being informed, which made me realise Goodman had lied about notifying the authorities. I pointed out that I wasn't accusing anyone of anything, but wasn't sure this woman had died of a heart attack. 'I'd like the police surgeon to look into it and maybe get a post-mortem done. You know, I've heard this is the second death in his surgery in a month. In all my years as a GP, we haven't had one.'

I heard Teviot breathe heavily then repeat all my words slowly. Eventually he finished.

'Leave it to me, Doctor. I'll get on it.'

Perhaps naughtily, I didn't mention I was going off on holiday. Taking a deep breath, I phoned Kilnglass.

Thankfully, their line was already on divert. I left an answer machine message. 'I am sorry, Dr Goodman, but I've asked the police to arrange a post-mortem as I cannot say with certainty how Mrs Mackintosh died.' I then dashed off home to change.

We were on the plane before I told Ralph.

'That'll be the cat amongst the pigeons now!' was his reply. 'I hope you're right doing this, Beth. It's a pretty big thing to call into doubt another doctor's professional opinion. The Defence Unions discourage it.'

On his other side, in her window seat, my mother looked alarmed. 'Will this cause trouble for Beth, Ralph?'

'Well, Beth has to follow her conscience. No one should sign anything if they are in any doubt.' He took my hand. I could have kissed him. But I knew this time I'd crossed the Rubicon.

The Jersey holiday was fine for everyone bar me, brooding on Mrs Mackintosh. First thing on the Monday, I'd phoned the Medical Defence Society from the hotel. Their advisor had fully supported my actions and promised a visit on my return. Despite this reassurance, whenever I wasn't fully occupied, I'd see Goodman's face, head cocked to the side, nodding and smiling as I'd left him. God, I didn't know whether to hope I was right or completely wrong.

Shortly after we arrived home on the Sunday night, Charles appeared at the door. From his grim expression, it wasn't a social call. I'd never seen him so apoplectic.

'I hope you're pleased with yourself!'

I sat on the sofa. He remained towering over me. 'What do you mean, Charles?'

'Well, it appears that instead of a 1-in-9 rota for weekends, we are now a 1-in-5. Kilnglass and Nesbitt are forming their own co-operative for out-of-hours cover. In fact, Nesbitt's joining Goodman full tilt and going fundholding with him.'

'What? I'd heard Brian couldn't stand him!'

'Looks like that's another of your fantasies, Beth. This carry on over the Mackintosh woman, what were you thinking of? You'll have to see Goodman and apologise. Say you weren't well or harassed going off on holiday and not thinking straight or something!'

Ralph came out from behind the *Sunday Times* in the corner, put it down and was on his feet. 'Wait a minute, Charles, Beth acted in good faith. The Defence Society says she was quite right. The story didn't add up.'

Charles shook his head vigorously, causing even more dandruff than usual on his collar – not a time to mention Head & Shoulders. How my brain whirls out of control under duress.

'Goodman says the police surgeon accepted his evidence without question and Brian Nesbitt signed part two without quibble. He says he has no confidence in your clinical judgement, thinks you have a vendetta against him, so wants nothing more to do with us. So, no holiday or weekend cover from them. I think the least you can do is offer to take extra weekend slots.'

'I don't think so, Charles. We have a contract stipulating equal out-of-hours shares. It's not my fault his practice manager gave a completely different account of Mrs Mackintosh's demise. Anyone would have asked for confirmation of cause of death.'

'My God, Beth, you have an overactive imagination. This has to stop. NOW!'

'But ...'

'No buts. The way I feel today, if I could sack you, I would, but I've been advised this isn't sufficient grounds to terminate a partnership. So we'll have to work together and make the best of it. Just keep your mouth shut and don't go off half tilt to the police or anyone else without speaking to me first.'

My mother came in at that point with tea and biscuits, her prescription for stressful situations. Charles brushed past her and stormed out, banging the front door.

'What a rude man! That's no way for a doctor to behave!'

Ralph shook his head at her to say nothing. I was on the verge of tears. Or, in truth, screaming. I went upstairs, ran a bath and nursed my emotional wounds with Chanel No 5 bubbles and a scented candle. I lay back thinking of Henry's Bristol nurse friend, Melanie. I knew how she'd felt. The door opened. The lock needed fixed. Ralph sat on the end of the bath and handed me a glass.

'Vouvray. We were keeping it for a special occasion. I reckon this is one.'

'What?' His logic escaped me.

'You stood up for what you believed to be right, I'm proud of you. Charles will come around – he's just been stewing for a week till you came back. And in the long run, I suspect you'll be better off not working with Kilnglass. Or Nesbitt, from what I've heard.'

He bent to kiss me and left. I didn't ask what he meant. I had enough trouble processing what I suspected already.

Thankfully, most of the next week went quietly. Concentrating on diagnosing and treating disease is a strong antidote to self-pity. I kept out of Charles's way. On the Friday though, I had to speak to him. My mail contained a shock.

It was a short note which Charles read out: '*We no you are selling prescripshuns to the boys on the skeme. We have prufe and are goin to the polis. Youse better be carefool!*' Green felt tip, a childish scrawl and, to my mind, exaggerated illiteracy.

Charles was neither cross nor did he laugh. 'Is this the first one you've had?' I nodded. 'It's childish stuff. You annoyed any of the junkies from the estate? Refused someone codeine linctus or anything?'

'No. Anyway, we don't have many. They're mostly with Kilnglass.'

'Bin it. Forget it. I had something similar years ago.'

'Shouldn't I tell the police? What if it's Goodman trying to put the wind up me?'

'For God's sake, Beth, give it a break! And stay away from the police – please!'

I threw it in his waste basket but logged it in my Diary of Curious Incidents. I was amassing several. Anila. Jean. Mrs Mac. Now poison pen letters.

Twelve

The Visitation

After evening surgery, Ellen caught me back in Charles's room, rifling through his bin. She didn't query it, looking upset.

'What's wrong, Ellen?' I retrieved my crumpled green-inked missive.

'It's my friend Senga. Her son Martin just phoned. They found her dead in bed today.'

'Oh, dear!' I hugged her before leading her back to my room. 'Have you been friends long?'

'Since school. She got divorced about the same time as my Ian left. Since then we've gone to the pictures every week. We'd planned on seeing *The Fugitive* tomorrow. She loves – loved – Harrison Ford.'

I handed the now sobbing Ellen a tissue from my ever-ready desk box. 'Has she been ill?'

'No. Well, she had asthma, but it didn't bother her much. And she was fine last night. Mind you, she mentioned some new tablets.' She caught her breath. 'I can't believe she's gone!'

'Sadly, people still do die of asthma.' Ellen started weeping uncontrollably. I couldn't let her go home alone like this. 'Listen, Ellen – why don't you come home for tea? Give me five minutes.'

I phoned Ralph to ask him to thaw another steak. 'I'm bringing Ellen home, her friend's died.'

'Oh, shame. Who was her GP?'

'I didn't ask. Don't be funny!'

He apologised, but after we'd listened to Ellen over tea,

my little red Diary of Curious Incidents had another new entry.

The summer was poor. Without usual tennis and cycle exercise, the girls were stir-crazy by August. Mum tried hard, but outings to Kelvingrove Art Gallery and the Transport Museum proved 'boring.' Swimming was KO'd as apparently 'chlorine wrecks your hair.' My reading suggestions were swiftly rebuffed. 'For heaven's sake, Mum, we get enough of books at school!'

One Thursday, Katy suggested we invite Liam's brood for a sleepover. The last one had been a roaring success, though we'd had to replace a mangled Twister mat. Liam and Jan agreed they'd come a week on the Saturday. The girls were a bit miffed it wasn't that weekend, but the O'Farrells were away. Patience has never been a strong point for my two. Persuading them that it gave them time to plan a special feast, they sat down with my long-suffering mother and cookery books.

Next morning, as I left early, Mum handed me a packed lunch: someone cared. I parked outside the surgery, steeling myself for a hectic day. Gerry was in Portugal and we hadn't found a locum. The week proved bearable, however, and by Saturday the rain stopped. We went walking in the Campsies for a pub lunch.

Next week was downhill all the way: Sunday night on call was hectic, Monday horrendous. I didn't get home till eight after dealing with a collapsed miscarriage lady and a domestic assault requiring police intervention. The woman wouldn't go to casualty. I had to stitch her head wound. Then the police fumed as she wouldn't charge her partner. I prayed next time it wouldn't be something worse. On Tuesday, Charles took pity on my exhaustion and awarded me an extra few hours off. At least professional relations in Oakfield practice had thawed: he'd eventually accepted I'd only followed my conscience over the Kilnglass death. No apology, but a truce.

On Thursday, my mail mountain looked especially challenging. My mood darkened. *Relax* blasted from the waiting area. 'Alison, can't you turn that down? There's enough deaf folk in the practice already without Frankie Goes to Hollywood!'

Alison glared. Ellen appeared from her office to switch over to subtler Radio 2. She was looking better. I'd persuaded her to take a few days off.

'You OK, Ellen? How was Senga's funeral yesterday?'

'Yes, thanks, Doctor. The funeral went fine. How's Sheba? Has she settled in?'

'Grand. In fact, Winston lets her sleep in his bed. Katy's convinced he doesn't think she's a cat – too fluffy!'

Ellen laughed and returned to her den. Senga's son had asked her to take Sheba, but her flat complex didn't allow pets, so we'd taken the Persian cat. Once in my room, I scanned my mail, selecting first a brown envelope stamped 'Personal' and bearing a type-written label. I slit it open and sighed. Another one.

You want to watch that Practiss Manager of yures ... I no stuff about her that would make yer hare stand on end! She's a whore – and a murderer. Pink felt tip this time, postmarked Edinburgh. I phoned through to Ellen.

'Can you spare a moment?'

She turned white when she read it.

'Ellen, is there something I should know about?'

'No, nothing!' A tear fell down her cheek. Poor soul. I shouldn't have said anything.

'Sorry, Ellen, forget it, it's spiteful rubbish.' I threw it in the bin. 'Gosh, it's ten past nine already! I better get started. Let's chat later.'

The thing about poison pen letters is they do unnerve

you, make you wonder if there isn't some substance to their allegations. But mostly, my worry was who'd sent it and why. But my anxiety turned towards myself when Alison put through an insistent caller who wouldn't wait until the end of surgery.

'Good afternoon, Dr Semple. This is Dr Robin Butler of the Area Pharmaceutical Committee. I wondered if it would be convenient for us to visit tomorrow at 12.30?'

'Well, actually, tomorrow isn't convenient. We're a partner down and I'll have house calls plus the Friday antenatal clinic at one. Couldn't it wait till Monday?'

'I am afraid not. Serious allegations have been made.'

'What allegations? By whom?'

'That, I am not at liberty to divulge. We will see you at noon tomorrow for a preliminary chat then make further arrangements as necessary. Dr Morgan from the LMC will accompany me.'

Well, that was something. Morgan was a nice chap. This Butler sounded pompous and officious. I phoned Ralph, who was indignant.

'What's so urgent they can't leave till Monday? And why the Area Pharmaceutical Committee – shouldn't it be the Area Medical Committee for complaints? Best, pet, if you phone the Medical Defence Union. Get them on board in case you need them.'

This time I didn't hesitate in phoning. They advised 'say as little as possible and phone us back when you know what it's about.' I didn't sleep, endlessly trying to think of any disgruntled patients who might have complained. And as for drugs? None had gone missing and our drug records were immaculate.

Friday was a long morning. I managed to run to time and speed through the post-surgery business. I'd asked Ellen to bring in tea when the inquisition came and to hover. On the dot, they appeared. Tubby Morgan shook my hand as he said hello. He looked uncomfortable. Not good.

Thin, suave Butler sat down without being asked, adjusted his gold-rimmed glasses and regarded me as if I were a pathological specimen. I dived in. 'So, gentlemen, what can I do for you?'

'There has been a complaint that you have been supplying controlled drugs for money.' Butler pursed his lips. He looked like Frankie Howard. But this was no comedy.

'What? That's ridiculous!'

Ellen arrived with tea, poured and stood back. Butler barked. 'Please leave!' She looked hesitant as Butler dismissively waved his hand.

'Please stay, Ellen. This man has made a serious allegation. I want a witness to my categorical denial and demand to know who has made this complaint!'

'We had this letter.' From his inside pocket, Morgan produced a folded polythene bag containing a type-written letter without date, address or signature alleging I was 'making a mint' from selling dangerous drugs. Two patients were named.

'These are my patients. Both get analgesics for legitimate conditions. Who are these "many others" I'm supposed to be supplying? It's preposterous! Why are you giving this the time of day?'

'Ah, well, Doctor, so many drugs on the street nowadays, you know, the police insist on vigilance. We have initiated a search to pull every prescription you have written for opiates and Valium over the last few years to check their validity.'

I was speechless.

Ellen interjected. 'I am sorry, but if Dr Semple is being accused of criminality, you should desist until she has a lawyer present.'

'Madam, we are merely trying to ascertain the facts before we bring in the police. We have to inform you that there will be an operative in here over the weekend analysing your computer drug entries. Please give us a key.' Butler smirked. Morgan looked down and shifted in his seat.

I took a deep breath. 'I am giving you nothing until I have consulted the MDDUS Union. You will return only when I have someone here to ensure my interests are represented.'

The door opened and Ellen entered. I hadn't noticed her slip out whilst Butler was pontificating. She folded her arms. 'Dr Semple's lawyer is on his way. Perhaps you would care to return to the waiting room and let her get on with tending sick patients until he arrives?'

Morgan looked relieved and rose. Butler flared his nostrils, but reluctantly followed. Ellen escorted them out to return, smiling. 'They've gone, flea in their ear! What a lot of nonsense!'

'Who did you phone? Jim Jenkins is golfing in Vilamoura with Gerry.'

'I phoned that nice Mr Liam O'Farrell from the High Street, the one you said you'd known from university? He didn't hesitate ...'

Minutes later, the door opened wide as Liam marched in. 'Jumped a couple of lights – but I'm here! So, what's the emergency? Where are these Health Board clowns?'

'Ellen saw them off. But they'll be back. This is what it's about.' I proffered the letter in its bag. In their abrupt departure, they'd forgotten to take it, though I was sure they'd have another copy.

'Poison pen kinda thing, isn't it? Bit high-handed, guys strolling in like the FBI just for this!'

'They wanted the surgery keys to search the computers over the weekend, but I said no.'

I was beginning to shake. Tears welled. Ellen patted my hand. 'Time for hot sweet tea and a plan. Tell him about the other letters Beth. I think they're linked.'

I produced the old green and the new pink one I'd retrieved from my bin.

'Now, who have you pissed off?' Liam smiled as I sniffed into a hanky.

'No one. Well, maybe Dr Goodman at Kilnglass. I refused to sign a cremation form for him as I thought his story didn't add up. I've also queried some things before.'

'But another GP wouldn't do this, surely – send illiterate notes? Not awfully likely, mmm?'

'Well, you never know. He is pretty cocky.'

Liam frowned. 'Whatever you do, don't make any accusations without evidence. My advice is to get the Medical Defence team here on Monday. I'd happily help, but you're paying for them and they're the medical experts. I'd doubt you are legally obliged to give these bully boys the keys to come in when you're not here. They're not the police. But it might look bad if you don't.'

'Yes. OK. Thanks for coming, Liam.'

He stood up to give me a bear hug. 'You still on for tomorrow night? You could come to us if you don't feel up to it?'

'Oh no, I'd not hear the end of it from Katy. It's the highlight of their holidays! See you at seven? The girls are cooking. But if it all goes pear-shaped, we can send out for pizzas!'

I took the letters home to Ralph who said little till we were getting into bed.

'A couple of things strike me, Beth. The complaint letter was addressed to 'Chair of the Area Pharmaceutical Committee.' Now who outside medical circles knows he exists? And talking about drugs, in one place it refers to 'DDAs.' That's a professional term. It must be someone who's a doctor or nurse. Or have you annoyed any pharmacists lately?'

'No!' I said indignantly. But Ralph just smiled, gave me a whisky kiss, lay down and went straight to sleep. I didn't.

On Sunday, we went bowling at Clydebank with Liam's

triplets before taking them home. I usually manage a couple of strikes, but that afternoon I was rubbish. Katy won one game, Julia the next: a recipe for peace. Back at Liam's house, dropping off the girls, I brought up Ralph's comments.

'Sorry, but a few phrases aren't much help in identifying the culprit, Beth. Often, you never find out who's sent poison pens. Just don't let it get you down. You've a reputation as a good doctor and this lunatic will likely soon move on to someone else.'

Sleep came after a large dinner, a half bottle of Californian red, a giant bar of Cadbury's and a couple of Armagnacs. Not to be recommended if you've to be up and out by eight next morning. My cerebral arteries complained. I had a migraine.

At Oakfield, two young IT guys lived with us for a fortnight. The Medical Defence forbade removal of computers as being too disruptive to patient care. All our computer drives were scrutinised: reception, those of Charles, Gerry and Ellen as well as mine. The only saving grace was that Dougie and Colin were nice lads. The staff didn't query Ellen's explanation of their presence being a Health Board audit. Alison underwent a personality transformation, swooning over blonde Dougie, pandering to his every need, rocketing our coffee and biscuit bills. The IT boys didn't speak to me, nor I to them, as advised by the Medical Defence.

By the first week of September, there was still no word of me being off the hook. I tried to carry on normally and was looking forward to a post-grad weekend education thing I'd booked on, one of five study days we needed to do each year to get our 'educational allowance', basically a bribe to encourage GPs to stay up to date. Gordon was also going to the Neuro-linguistic Programming course trumpeted as the key to 'knowing our strengths to improve consultation skills'. As usual, I arrived late and was forced to sit at the back. It being too dark to take notes, I hoped there'd be a handout provided. It seemed complex neuroscience. After an hour, the lights went up, and we were divided into pairs. Spotting me, Gordon came over to be my partner. It was my first ever 'role play'. Pretending to be a difficult patient for Gordon, I channelled Mr Green. Gordon coped well, according to the assessor who crept round us all individually, eavesdropping. It wasn't till the coffee break I saw *him*.

I nudged Gordon. 'There's Goodman.'

'Really? Oh, that looks like the guy who left Bishopbriggs under a cloud, though he's got a beard now. I'd forgotten about him. Saw him at a party just before the fuss. Was with his wife, nice-looking lass. Punching above his weight!'

'Whose party?'

'Duncan Pearson, my old GP trainer. Goodman was his "assistant with a view," I think.'

'What was the fuss?'

'Damned if I can remember. He left at short notice, Dunky was furious. Wait, maybe a receptionist accused him of something? I thought he was called Goodall. Should have twigged! You meet so many people in this game, don't you?'

The organiser came in, clapping to usher us back in for the next session. This was a multi-choice exam paper, designed to diagnose what kind of person we were in 'Neuro-Linguistic Programming' terms. We scored one another's papers (obviously not being trusted to do our own). I scored highly (65%) on comprehending the world visually, but my aural capabilities were poor, being liable to recall only ten percent of what I heard (thus I'd wasted my time for years at lectures!). Gordon was high on sensitivity score, i.e. being in tune with what others were feeling and was equal for visual and aural information processing. The lecturer reassured me that my score meant I was an excellent observer, but I was upset to have only half of Gordon's sensitivity. Gordon pronounced it all 'bollocks.' His whispered, 'Wanna bet Goodman cheated to a hundred percent for sensitivity?'

cheered me on the way to lunch.

The sun shone warmly through the large windows of the Lancaster Crescent Post-grad Centre. It was a bright September day. I was sitting in an uncomfortable wooden chair with a rakish side-swinging table on which I'd perched my plate of chicken curry, when I felt a sudden chill. My sunshine had been eclipsed by a large muscular figure. Standing very close.

'Good afternoon, Dr Semple. How are we?'

'I am fine, Dr Goodman. How are you?'

'Never better!' As he walked off to sit on the opposite side of the room, I noticed his plate held only rice. He was even weirder than I'd thought.

Gordon came over in consternation. 'What did he say? Can't believe he spoke to you after all the things he said to Charles!'

'What things?'

Biting into a chunk of naan bread, Gordon shook his head.' Oh, you know, after ... Och, water under the bridge. D'you think he's trying to mend fences?'

Goodman was now smiling over at me while listening to an animated woman in a short red skirt with high black patent heels. I looked away, but swivelling my eyes, caught a flash of such hostility from him that it made me gasp. Or did I imagine it? When I next looked over, he was taking the woman's empty plate from her lap. Walking back to the buffet, he reminded me of a panther: slow, deliberate. As he stood in the pudding queue, he straightened his tie and brushed his hair flat while joking with the serving ladies who were laughing. I didn't need neuro-linguistic programming to know he was flirting. Though he appeared charming, and indeed was reasonably attractive, I thought the reaction of his stilettoed companion - profusely thanking him for her highly heaped dessert plate - was over-the-top. For himself, he'd taken some fresh fruit salad without cream.

'Who's the woman with Goodman, Gordon?'

Gordon looked across. 'Oh, that's the new Area Medical Committee Chairman, Culshaw. A GP in Pollokshields, I think. Rumoured man-eater.' He wolfed sticky toffee pudding. I'd lost my appetite.

The afternoon session was thankfully non-participatory, with the lights out. If I hadn't been spooked by Goodman, I might have fallen asleep. I often do at courses. But it was interesting. We were shown consultation videos accompanied by commentaries explaining how to detect from body language and eye movements when someone was lying, or just thinking or looking back to the past. By the break, however, I'd had enough and slunk off. I'd still get my 'brownie points' since at lunch I'd signed for the afternoon. I was copying Gerry, who was worse. He often left at morning coffee after smooching up to the wee lassie left in charge of the register who would sign him in for the afternoon so he could get in a game of golf. Not sure if she ever got anything in return.

I decided to pass on the next day's proceedings, so on the Sunday went with Ralph and the girls to Drymen for a walk and lunch in the Buchanan Arms. By 9 p.m., I was enjoying a glass of wine on the sofa with *The House of Eliott* when the phone rang. Ralph was snoozing. The girls were upstairs. I picked up the receiver and answered, 'Hello, Mum?' She was a bit later than usual.

No one spoke, but I could hear breathing. Was it someone in distress? But I wasn't on call.'

'Hello! Anyone there?' I must have shouted. Ralph woke up to appear at my side.

'What's up?'

'There's only heavy breathing …'

He took the phone and listened before replacing it.

'Wrong number, I expect. Cup of tea, pet?'

'Fine.' I returned to my sofa and the 1920s.

In bed by 10.30 p.m., I fell into a deep sleep. Too deep. One minute I heard a fire engine clanging past, the next I was awake with a start and realised I'd been dreaming. There was no fire, but the phone was ringing. Wearily, I picked it up.

'Hello?' No answer. 'Hello?' Heavy breathing. Again. This was no wrong number. 'Who is this? Do you realise the time? This isn't funny!' It was 2.30 a.m., the worst time to wake anyone: cortisol levels at their lowest, energy levels and good humour at their nadir. I slammed down the phone.

Ralph sat up. 'What the hell?'

'Another heavy breathing call. These are nuisance calls. It's deliberate.'

Ralph walked round to pull the phone from its socket. 'If it happens again, the police can trace calls.' He gave me a hug and we lay down. But we didn't go back to sleep straight away. Ralph knows ways to defuse me. I think he enjoyed it too.

But when I did fall asleep, it was fitful. I dreamed I was in Central Station, but couldn't find my train platform so had to ask a policeman who was herding sheep up the concourse. Then, without getting on a train, I seemed to be at a country church which looked like the one in Drymen. Its bells were ringing. There was a happy couple kissing. When I finally woke, I had a pounding headache. The groom had been Goodman. Bloody man was even appearing in my dreams! Getting up at six, I wondered if it might have been more profitable to have taken a course on dream interpretation, instead of NLP. Must be Gordon's fault, him wondering how Goodman had bagged such a beautiful wife. Frankly, I didn't care. All I wanted was for that creep to stay out of my subconscious.

Thirteen

Elimination of Obstacles

St Jasper's Hospital, London, June 1977, 16 years earlier

It isn't fair. He's worked just as hard as Kenneth Stewart and he deserves the Senior Registrar job. Overnight he's revisited his interview: faultless, textbook answers. And, unlike Stewart, he passed the surgical primary exam first time and has published research papers. Criminal to have been passed over for a second time at St Jasper's, especially being knocked back for that jumped-up, blue-eyed, public school boy from a medical family. The familiar throat tightening starts. He mightn't be one of them, but he is smarter.

There's the smug bastard now, coming out of the prof's room, walking with even more of a swagger than usual, taking up far more of this narrow corridor than he deserves. Should he be magnanimous and congratulate him? Swallowing hard, he balances the pros and cons, but decides to stand firm, silent. With a trolley here beside him, Kenneth Stewart will have to move round him to pass. But the bastard doesn't deviate, just pushes past, digging him in the ribs. 'Tough call, Sambo. Better luck next time!'

Staring after the strutting fool, he decides there won't be a next time. He is going. No more hanging around London being demeaned and mocked. With glowing references from previous posts, he isn't dependent solely on the prof, that snooty tosser. Why, you could drive a bus up his conk! He snorts and laughs so loudly that Kenneth turns back, calling out 'What?' Turning away, Stan heads for the canteen.

Interviews in Bristol and Leeds next week. Mother has been weeping. Doesn't want to move. She needn't. The biggest mistake of his life has been moving back home after Magda's death, done purely for appearances as a bereft young husband. But enough is enough.

In the canteen he selects fish and chips and custard pudding. No point in expecting dinner on the table at home. Things need to change. First, grooming. He'll try the place up town that Josh from the Church recommends for new permanent hair-straightening. Second, he must catch up with Oscar and Jimmy. They're doing well, in cahoots with the big East End boys since leaving school, proper gangsters! Worth keeping in with. Never knew when you might need some of that. Third, the Mother Question. Needs urgent attention.

The second he's in the door, the familiar smell assails him. Still, with professional help, the musty aroma should be easily eliminated, the place cleaned up for selling. They should never have bought this house; there'd be no profit in selling after such a short time. Stupid Magda.

'Come on,' she'd said, 'I'll buy it, give your old mum security so she won't have to worry when we marry and move away.' Silly bitch. Still, it was her money. For all the good it did her.

'Hello, Mother.' He gives her the Daily Express and blows a kiss past her left ear.

'Hello, my sweetheart boy. Had a good day?'

'Not really.'

'Good, good. The doctor says I've to rest. You'll have to make supper. But first there's a shopping list on the table. Make me a cup of tea before you go, won't you?' Winnie is lying on the sofa in standard 'dying-duck' pose, tartan mohair wrap over shoulders, fingerless gloves on her hands. The fire is stacked and lit, so she hasn't been at death's door all day, though swollen ankles testify she hasn't moved much. Or might they indicate something inside that carcass is failing? Perhaps heart or liver, he lives in hope.

'I can't do Tesco's, I have a date, but I'll make you cheese on toast before I go.'

'A date? How can you be so callous, leaving me all evening? When I think of everything that I've done for you!'

'I know, but I'm a big boy now. I have a life.'

He goes into the kitchen passing a picture of the latest 'father' on the dresser. He's resigned to the fact he's unlikely to ever find out now who his real father was. The birth certificate that Mrs O got him for uni matriculation listed Father as 'Unknown.' So much for Gran's last ramblings about his father being put away. But if he had been, where? Well, if the guy is locked up in a loony bin, he can stay there. Winnie can fantasise all she likes about the man who deserted her, the war hero, TB victim, drowned-in-the-Thames hero or whoever she currently had trumped up, but chips down, he's finally decided he doesn't care. Though he'll never forgive him for his legacy of dirty skin and matted hair. Mother's fixation with the old bastard's memory is pathological. What did the bugger ever do for her? Nothing he hasn't had to. More things than any boy should ever be asked to do.

Slicing cheese, he grips the knife so tightly it imprints his palm. He likes knives, remembers the first time he incised flesh. Chopping up rats and mice never taught him much, but he'd got that first rush of ... what? pleasure? No, power! Now, with his scalpel he is recognised as having skill. The power of life and death. He toasts her cheese, fills a cup with boiling water, adding something extra with the teabag for peace and quiet. Once he's dressed for the off, he'll lift her into bed. There'll be no time for any funny business. He uses her 'Best Mother in the World' mug. Who was she kidding?

The tack has changed. She smiles, pats his arm. 'Such a good boy. Where would I be without you? Of course you must go out. I don't want to be a burden. You must bring this girl home. I'd like to meet her.'

That'll be the day. He leans over. 'She's better than

Magda. You know she slipped off the ferry, don't you? You've no idea how easy it was. I'd had enough. And it's the same with you, a clinging tart whinging at me, the only worthwhile thing you ever did. Now, I'm in charge. And I know what to do.'

He sees fear in her eyes for the first time. Lifting the cup to her lips, he forces her to drink. Time to end it soon.

The first time he'd tried had been his sixteenth birthday, St David's Day. The second, had been at seventeen, after she'd turned up at the school prize-giving drunk and dressed like a whore. That time he hadn't known the dose needed, so she'd only vomited, bled, been hospitalised and returned home in forty-eight hours. Mrs O had said that if she'd died, they wouldn't give him tenancy since he was under eighteen. He hadn't realised. No way he'd go to one of those awful hostels they sent boys to, so he hadn't tried again. But this time, he's planned it all, spoken to the neighbours about her drinking, even had a GP in and reported her worsening clumsiness, or ataxia as it's medically called, and twitching. Soon, she'd fit, maybe go blind. Weekend after next was his target. He'll ask Mrs Fellowes to come in and sit as he has to be on call and will be 'worried about leaving her.' Fellow Baptist Constance Fellowes is a burly Jamaican neighbour of little brain but large tongue, a gossiper. 'Winnie's poor son! On call in the hospital on Saturday night when it happened.' She'd likely lead his mother in prayers. Mother would like that, bloody hypocritical harlot. She should suffer Hell and Damnation for making his life such a misery.

He wasn't sure how long the thallium would take. Certainly longer than Ngaio Marsh's victim in Final Curtain. Marsh was quite wrong: it didn't cause sudden death, not like cyanide.

Today's career setback has galvanised him into action. Using thallium is genius, it so mimics the end trajectory of ethanol abuse. His stuff is ten years old but should still be OK.

Would have to be, no chance of getting more since the law changed after that Graham Young murdered his workmates. Stupid prat. He could so have gotten away with it if he'd kept his mouth shut. He sighs. For now, toasted cheese and tea with two barbiturates and a slug of rum will have to suffice. In his room he irons a pristine white shirt and sponges a vague suggestion of a mark on his suit, before buffing his shoes to a mirrored shine. Carefully, he replaces the iron, its board and the cleaning materials in the hall cupboard. It's been a slow process trying to make this dingy ex-council terrace semi-tolerable. Roll on fumigating and selling up. How right he'd been to insist it was in his name, despite his mother's protestations. She'd thought he'd bought it, having no idea about Magda's huge inheritance, now nestling in a Swiss bank. By the time he lifts his car keys she's snoring.

In case she wakes, he leaves rum by her bed.

Clara is sitting in the corner of The Griffin with a Martini and lemonade. She's had the gall to order at the bar! Quite forward, out of character. Best let it go for now. More important things need said.

'Sorry I'm late. My mother wasn't well. Again.'

'What a shame. Doesn't matter, Stan. I just got here.'

She is like a beautiful swan. Long neck, porcelain skin, short blonde wavy hair, blue-grey eyes, slim legs in sheer nylons crossed demurely at the ankle. Her shoes are patent high heels. He likes high heels, elegant, feminine. She's had many suitors, including Kenneth, though that was a sham. Kenneth is a faggot. Clara has been very sheltered by her religious parents. She's admitted it's his old-fashioned ways which appeal to her. So mannerly, a gentleman – not 'trying it on' at every opportunity like most. She tells everyone he even visited the hospital pharmacy four times before asking her out.

He covers her hand with his. 'Any advance on the work

front, darling?' She doesn't know she's the first woman he's ever called darling. Magda hadn't merited that.

'I didn't get the St George's job, Stan, but there'll be others. No rush, I've still got three months of contract left at Jasper's, remember.'

'I feel it's time for me to move on as well. The vascular unit isn't stretching me enough. I have a good feeling about the Bristol interview. If I do move, I'd love you to come with me.'

'Why, Dr Goodman, is that a proposition?'

'No. It's a proposal. Clara, will you marry me?'

'Oh, darling, yes!' She throws her arms around him then rests her head on his shoulder. At two inches shorter, she is the perfect height for him. After giving him an affectionate squeeze, she kisses him passionately. 'So now you'll take me home to meet your mother?'

She claps her hands like a child, an embarrassing trait of over-exuberance. But he knows she is biddable. It's been easy enough to get her to drop her Catholic double moniker. He couldn't marry a Marie Claire. Sounded like a nun.

'Soon, when she's better.' *Hardly worth it. Winnie won't be at the wedding.*

'Where shall we marry – the cathedral? Daddy knows the bishop.'

'Let's think about it, no hurry.' *Never the cathedral! But a registry office might be problematic. As they have records on site, he may have to declare himself as 'widower.' But he has no intention of telling Clara about Magda. His mother's Baptist church know about her, which is why he's moved to a new congregation. Fortunately, Magda's 'accident' wasn't widely publicised, being conveniently pushed out of the press by a string of IRA atrocities that weekend. No relatives appeared after she 'fell' off the ferry. Her few friends had already distanced themselves after she'd become an erratic, disinhibited and frequently sectioned embarrassment. But*

God, he still recalled the thrill of seeing her for the first time at Ronnie Scott's during final year. Oscar always took him out on his birthday. Great boy, Oscar. His grammar school friend now worked for the Krays.

'You look miles away, darling! Shall we have another drink?'

'Sure!' Stan goes to the bar. 'A pint of bitter and a Martini and lemonade, please.'

The barmaid flutters lashes as she pulls the pint. Coarse features, tight curly hair – she'd have to be kidding! He thinks of the last time with Magda: a fuck in the cabin, then a romantic kiss under the stars, which had disappeared as they hit fog on the Channel, conveniently at its deepest, half-way between Caen and Portsmouth. A deserted deck. Easy. Around four he'd emerged from his cabin to report his 'sleepwalker' wife missing. It was a week before her body had washed up on the south coast. The police had been sympathetic. Such a poor distraught new husband. A disturbed young wife with psychiatric problems. Her lawyer, McAdam, had been a booze-addled lecher. He'd handed over everything. New husband, new will. The idiot had wept, 'Poor Magda, losing her parents in a car crash at sixteen and now her life just two weeks into marriage. Tragic!' He'd asked irritating questions. McAdam had to go.

Suddenly, he notices the barmaid has her hand out. 'Please sir, if you could? A queue's forming!' He gives her a tip and she wiggles off. He returns to Clara.

'I'm off this weekend, why don't we go ring shopping in Bond Street?' Clara claps her hands again: he must stop her doing that. She launches into a list of potential wedding venues. Though nodding in appropriate places, his mind is elsewhere. With the acquisition of someone to look after the cooking, laundering, and cleaning, all for the 'one-off' price of a wedding licence, he'll have more time free. And with no further exams on the horizon, he'll need new challenges.

Perhaps they might come from his recent experiences? There is sport to be had from 'pulling the wool' over authorities' eyes.

'Coooeee, Stan! You're miles away, again. What are you thinking?' Clara kisses him.

'Not in public, darling! I was thinking about our wedding, of course. I'm not keen on the cathedral. It will have to be a small wedding because of Mum. Perhaps my new Baptist church? They are lovely people. I'm hoping to become a deacon there soon.'

Clara looks blank. 'A deacon? But why not my marry in my church?' She pouts.

'But you don't go to church, I do.' He squeezes her hand hard. She shouldn't imagine he would ever become Catholic! Her parents may be arriviste bog Irish, but she hasn't been to mass since that old goat of a priest came on to her. Helpful in distancing her from her interfering family, though she's never told them why she stopped going. A Baptist wedding should distance her even further. Her 'virgin-till-marriage' mentality may be a legacy of her faith but isn't a problem. It's not the main reason he's marrying. Always other outlets.

'And Clara, don't worry that I'll be pushing you to go further now we're engaged. I'm quite willing to wait.' She looks pleased. 'Let's concentrate on finding new jobs before setting the date. You might even consider part-time posts now?' She'll need time for housework. As he adds, 'I do love you, you know,' there are tears in her eyes. She blows her nose delicately. So predictable: like playing a musical instrument. He knows exactly which strings to pluck. One should never show emotion like that, it makes you vulnerable. He never does.

Three months later, Stan is on the M4 driving home to Bristol wondering when they'll discover Kenneth. The typed suicide note he'd put in the boy's white coat pocket bore an authentic-

looking signature: he'd faked it often enough in the past on request forms or records when trying to land his 'mate' in the shit. In any case, doctors' harassed signatures tended to the indecipherable. And suicides were not uncommon in young doctors. Or homosexuals.

Since Jimmy had 'come out' at school, Stan had been expert at spotting closet gays a mile off. Before he'd left St Jasper's he'd paved the way for his plan, ramping up friendly overtures, taking Kenneth's teasing in the neck and indulging in brief bits of bodily contact: a lingering arm pat in conversation, a hand on a shoulder when departing. Tonight, Kenneth had completely bought the story that he was up in London to visit a dying East End uncle and only nipped into Jasper's on the way home for a convenient, cheap, late-night bite. Such a creature of habit, Kenneth. Canteen every night around 10.45 p.m. unless trapped in theatre. Stan couldn't believe his luck at finding him alone. In preparation for his plan, he'd grown a beard, lightened his hair, and lost weight. But with so many jobs changing over on the first of August, many staff would be new and not recognise him anyway.

Predictably, he had found Kenneth depressed, ripe for a willing ear. The usual gripes: staff shortages, workload, the prof's disintegrating marriage and temper. Stan had put his arm round Kenneth, stirring sugar into his coffee. His plan had been for one thing to lead to another. It did, quicker than expected. That part of the plan had been of slight concern.

When Stan had suggested a spot of relief in a quiet room where he knew there was a mattress, Kenneth had laughed. 'You old devil! I always said that marriage of yours was a bloody sham!'

Stan had kept his second marriage to Clara quiet. And once he'd formulated his plan, had stopped countering the jibes about him being gay. He'd also cultivated the notion that he respected Mr Kenneth Stewart, didn't resent his promotion, was eager to move over to Bristol. Hearing someone comment 'Queers stick together' had been gratifying.

Going arm in arm down the corridor, Stan had chatted with his prey. It had been so late they'd met no one. The barbiturates kicked in on the way. He'd barely managed to get Kenneth to the disused basement storeroom, where he'd been too far gone to notice the absence of a mattress. Or the rope already looped over the roof pipes. An ideal spot, chosen months ago, prepared earlier in the day. Organisation and detail. Donning surgical gloves, Stan had pressed the empty barbiturate bottle into Stewart's hand then tossed it on the floor. It was properly labelled, with Kenneth's name, dated a few weeks previously. He'd taken a hospital prescription up to London, pretended it was for his own epilepsy to the pharmacist. Planning was all. Wiping Stewart's pager, he had tossed it into a pre-filled fire bucket. A nice touch: the boy's last act of despair when unable to face work pressures and his homosexuality. Pulling Kenneth up had been harder than envisaged, but he'd soon been rewarded by a muted gurgle and bulging eyes. He'd had to wipe the sweat from his face with a tissue which he'd stuffed into his pocket along with his gloves. Detail. Like checking with switchboard before he set out that Kenneth was on-call this evening.

This plan has been complex, fraught with difficulties, making its success all the sweeter. He savours each moment again as he cruises along the M4 nudging eighty. When he reaches Bristol, Clara is still up.

'You're awfully late, darling. I'm surprised your lawyer sees clients on a Sunday.'

'Oh, he's Jewish.' Clara looks unconvinced. 'There's so much paperwork for settling the house sale. Then he insisted on taking me out for dinner. You know how men get talking.'

'But it's two in the morning!'

'Oh, the rain was heavy and there are roadworks everywhere.' As he bends to kiss her forehead, he pulls a cheque from his pocket. 'Let's have dinner to celebrate tomorrow night. We haven't been out since Mum's funeral.'

'A double celebration, darling. I've been offered that part-time job in Boots.'

'Excellent!'

So convenient having a pharmacist in the house.

Fourteen

Secrets, Snares & Snakes

Maynard's Pharmacy, September 1993

Toby Maynard was a nice man, kind and obliging. His coat was white, not red, but with his high-coloured cheeks, expansive middle and white moustache he looked like Santa, especially when doling out sugar-free lollies to kids. He'd recently sacrificed his beard but had kept his hair long as befitted a former seventies rock star. I'd heard his band then in a club, and felt it was probably just as well that he'd finished his pharmacy degree. He had done well professionally, now having his own independent Bearsden pharmacy near my surgery.

Being on-call for the weekend, I checked my bag and found some vital emergency drugs were out of date, so I hurried over to Toby clutching a stock order form. He was in a good mood, having found a locum to let him go off for the weekend.

'Hello, Beth, haven't seen you for yonks. Good holiday?'

'Gosh, has it been that long? Ancient history now! Jersey was great. I'm on this weekend, can you do this?'

He took the list. 'I've got everything except the Valium jabs, they'll need to be Monday.'

'No bother, I've got one left. It's pethidine injections and tabs I'm most needing. You never know when a renal colic will pop up!'

He smiled, handing the list to his young dispenser. 'Carol, can you get this together for the doctor? I want to have a word with her.' He led me into the tiny kitchen behind his dispensary. It was a bit of a squash.

'So, why this intimate little tête-à-tête, Toby?' I laughed.

His brows furrowed. 'It's a bit delicate, Beth. It's about Dr Nesbitt.'

'Brian? What's he been up to?'

'Well, getting pethidine, mostly, though also some dihydrocodeine and oromorph too.'

'What?'

'How often do you pick up scripts for patients?'

'Occasionally. Housebound old ladies with no neighbours, maybe, or someone I want to start on antibiotics asap who isn't well enough to go out. Why?'

'As I thought. Well, Brian's taken to popping in fairly often with scripts. And his stock orders are a bit heavy on painkillers and benzodiazepines, especially Valium. Tablets, mostly, not the injections you might need in emergencies.'

'Have you spoken to him?'

'No. I wondered if you might?'

'Ooh, not sure I could, Toby, sorry. We've fallen out with Kilnglass and he's joined them.'

'That was a surprise, wasn't it? Thought he wasn't a fan – and Goodman keeps his boys on a tight leash. Would've thought Brian was more of a free spirit, all fast cars and fast women!'

'Yes, I'd say! But also, Toby, I think it would be particularly *not apt* for me to criticise him with a DDA accusation pending against myself ...'

'Really? I hadn't heard. What a thing!'

That was encouraging: if Toby didn't know, it wasn't yet common knowledge.

'Oh, they had an anonymous letter saying I was selling scripts. It's been a right hassle. Anyway, I can't speak to Brian.'

'Not sure what's best to do. I've spoken to other pharmacies. Boots and Collins haven't seen him, but Phil in Drummonds thinks he's personally collected some DDA scripts there, albeit for bona fide patients on his list. It's the pethidine that worries me. My last monthly return showed a rise. I might end up with a Home Office inspection.'

'Then you must say something. Or report him.' Poor Toby looked upset. This wasn't the 'peace, light and love' he'd always aimed for. I patted his arm. 'Why not have a quiet word yourself? If nothing else, he might stop. Anyway, I'll take the stuff you've got to hand and come back for the diazepam, Monday.'

'Och, I'll hand it in. There'll be dressings in by then for your treatment room anyway.'

I returned to Oakfield Surgery and entered into my controlled drug register the names, dosage and amount of my replacement medicines and where I'd obtained them. The rules for controlling drugs liable to addiction were tight, difficult to circumvent. If Brian needed drugs, he'd have to be pretty devious. I heard a knock.

'Hi!' Charles popped his head round the door. 'Beth, could you swap next Wednesday afternoon with me? I've had an invite to Turnberry.'

I laughed. 'Drug company jaunt, I suppose?'

He nodded. 'Constella.'

I wondered if Rosie's rep 'Jane' would be playing, but just replied, 'Sure.' Cooperation was the name of the game now. 'On the subject of drugs, Charles, have you ever thought Brian was a user? Or could be selling on?'

'What? No way. Straight as a die, he's an Edinburgh man! Why?'

'Toby Maynard says Brian's been personally collecting patient scripts, mostly opiates or benzodiazepines. And ordering high Stock Order amounts. Wanted me to speak to him.'

'I hope you kept out of it!' He looked sternly over his tortoiseshell glasses.

'Of course. He hinted other chemists report seeing him.'

'That's a bit worrying. I wonder if he might have started on opiates after that skiing accident last winter? He was badly laid up in St Mungo's with his back and knee after some black run tumble. We covered him remember?'

'Well, he should get legit scripts then, silly boy. Could cost him his job.'

'Think I'll ask him out for a drink and see how he is. If he's got a problem, the BMA has a set-up to help now, I think.'

I left it with Charles and suggested he let Toby know he was doing something. I was anxious his livelihood shouldn't suffer for Brian's idiocy.

*

In nearby Milngavie, another Stock Order is being proffered in Reid's Pharmacy.

'Right, thanks, David. I'll drop this lot in for you tomorrow.'

'That's kind, Simon. Are you well? You're looking tired.'

'Things are tough, don't mind admitting it. Counter's down since the supermarket opened. Folk aren't buying shampoos, nappies and toilet rolls here anymore. And the on-cost profit for scripts has been cut again. The more you dispense, the less you get paid for each, crazy and unfair. Means that though we're busy, our margins are down. Bank still comes for its monthly mortgage whack, though.'

'Oh dear, what a worry.'

Simon holds up the stock form. 'Your GP stock orders are worth more to me than ordinary prescriptions. We get twenty-five percent on-cost for these. So give us as many as you can!'

David picks up his case and opens it on the bench before extracting a pad of forms and tearing off a pair of sheets.

Signing the top copy, he hands them over. 'So, Simon, how about I leave this with you?' He looks round to ensure the assistant is out in the front shop. 'You can add things when I phone, and of course, maybe anything else you *think* we might need. If a few expensive things weren't delivered, well who'd know?'

A risky strategy. And illegal. But risk can pay off. Simon Reid has previously mentioned his precarious finances: arch stupidity taking a second wife when the first one's still alive.

Simon grins. 'Right, great – every little helps! If there's ever anything I can do for you.'

David signs a few more and hands them over. 'Don't overdo it though, Simon. Just send me the carbon copies each month so I can keep track.' Best to have proof.

'Of course.' Simon puts the forms in a drawer.

On the way out, David buys toiletries and sundries from the front shop, declining the proffered professional discount. He does, however, accept a perfume gift for his wife.

Driving his Jaguar away at speed, loot stashed in the well of the passenger seat, David decides Simon Reid really is a fool. Pharmacists are struck off far more quickly than medics, perhaps because they are, obviously, less valuable people in the NHS's scheme of things. By falsifying drug records like stock orders, Simon risks a jail term. But it did make him another useful patsy. He glances at the dashboard clock. Time for a cup of tea before surgery.

*

It was 7.30 p.m.. Time for *Coronation Street*. Pure unchallenging escapism which Ralph loathes. My compulsion is inherited from my mother. Julia is the only other family devotee. We sit curled up on the sofa, watching it together. At the commercial break, I fetched our usual hot chocolate and biscuits and noticed she was twirling her hair.

A sign of anxiety.

'Mum, do you think that saying is true, "Like father, like son?"'

'That's an odd question!' I dunked my digestive and put my feet up on the pouffe.

'Well, I was thinking, you suspect Dr Goodman is creepy, maybe up to no good, like he's careless with lives or maybe even a murderer or whatever ...'

'Oh, I said no such thing, Julia! Where did you hear that?' She blushed. I vowed to ensure closed doors during discussions with Ralph. 'But why should that matter to you?'

'It doesn't, but it might to Katy. Didn't you realise that her Neil is Goodman's son?'

'Really?' I'd never asked his surname. I held my breath for a few seconds. 'But surely Katy and he don't go about together now, do they? They fell out at Easter. She hasn't mentioned him since.'

'They're back. I saw them at lunchtime. I think he's probably OK, if a bit quiet and dull, but I reckon she likes that in men.' Heavens, she sounded about twenty-five! 'I wondered if you should speak to her? I mean, is she safe hanging about with his family? But also, if you wanted, you could pump her for more info about Neil's old man.'

'Julia, I am not Miss Marple! And I haven't any ongoing case to prove against Dr Goodman. The things I queried were all just misunderstandings.'

I couldn't possibly tell her about the deadly look Goodman had shot me at that study day, or my suspicion he was behind the letters and calls. We'd seen no sense in worrying the girls about them. Taking a deep breath and utilising my newly acquired NLP signifiers of lying, I smiled while looking straight into Julia's eyes. 'I'm sure if Katy likes him, he's fine.'

Inwardly, I was churning. I'd have to speak to Katy, say Neil's welcome, but I'd prefer she didn't go to their house.

And I'd need to invent a logical, non-judgemental reason. God, parenting was so hard. As *Coronation Street*'s families were showing. I threw Julia a distraction. 'Don't forget I need you two to come Saturday morning to help me choose a dress for the reunion. And you two will need new swimsuits. There's a pool at the Old Course.'

'Cool! Is Uncle Yousef coming?'

'As far as I know. Shhh ...' I'd missed a heated argument in The Rover's Return. As the cheesy 'Daaa, da, da, da-da-da ...' brass music finally marked the end of the programme, I thought things could be worse. Tracy Barlow could be my daughter.

Next day was my unscheduled half day as reward for allowing Charles off for golf. I was in the kitchen reading the BMJ, Winston across my feet, the post-school squash and snacks at my elbow, when Katy arrived. She looked round.

'Where's Gran?'

'Gone home. I forgot to tell you I'm off today.'

A figure emerged from behind her. Katy's eyes swivelled from me to Neil and back.

'Is it OK if Neil stays for a bit?'

'Of course,' I said. 'How's school?'

'Fine,' Katy slung her bag into the corner whereupon Winston leaped to growl and attack it. Katy sat down laughing. 'Nothing edible left in there, boy! I'm starving.' She attacked the plate of sandwiches and fed him a half when he abandoned the bag.

'And how are you, Neil?'

'I'm fine, Dr Semple. Thank you for having me.'

He was politely nibbling his first gammon sandwich. Katy was on her third and now feeding Winston forbidden crisps. I felt like a nervous teenager. My brain wanted to say, 'So, do you think your father is a rude and callous doctor who does away with women?' but it didn't seem quite the thing. This boy was nice. Quite good-looking, though stick-thin wrists like long-necked bowling pins poked from his cuffs. More refined in features – and manner – than his father. Must be more like his mother. 'What does your mother do now you've moved here, does she work?'

'Yes. A few days a week at Collin's Pharmacy in Anniesland. She used to be in Boots.'

'As an assistant?

'No, she's a pharmacist. That's how she met my father.'

'And he's a GP?'

'Yes. I expect you know of him.'

How innocent and open he was.

'He runs the Kilnglass practice, though he used to be a vascular surgeon in London. He was top in his year and won gold medals.'

Proud of his dad. I couldn't fault that.

Katy made eyes at me, nodding towards the door. 'Don't let us keep you back, Mum. I'm sure you've got a lot to get on with.' She now raised an eyebrow at me and turned to Neil. 'I suppose we could go up to my room?'

Message received, I stood up. She swigged from a bottle of usually weekday-forbidden Coke she'd opened while I was chatting to Neil.

'No need, darling. You two stay in here and have your chinwag. Put on the radio, if you like. It won't disturb me in the study. Tea will be late, by the way. Ralph's examining. Neil's welcome to stay, there's plenty. He could phone his mum.'

I left. That boy looked undernourished. If he was to become a regular, I'd tell Mum to feed him up. I doubted he was any threat to my lovely Katy and thought Julia was worrying needlessly.

However, by 2.30 a.m. I had a different worry. Another breathy call from Mr No One. There had been one earlier that evening while Ralph was at Rotary, but otherwise my phantom caller had been inactive for a few weeks. I now hung up immediately without comment.

Ralph hugged me as I lay back down. 'You'll have to report these calls.'

But I was busy. Mr No One didn't call again that week.

I worked the following Wednesday afternoon, my usual half-day, to earn an early Friday finish for the Reunion. No such luck. Friday saw me flat out in the surgery then rushing around like a loony when I got home. The girls hadn't packed the night before as promised, no one had clean knickers and Winston was in a skittish mood, jumping and tripping me up. Katy had suggested we take him to St Andrews. I didn't bother asking whether the Old Course Hotel welcomed wild animals but asked Mum to dog-sit. She came willingly, saying she'd gone up a dress size and needed dog-walking exercise.

The car was eventually crammed with girls, bags, tennis rackets and everything Katy could think of which involved multiple dashes up and down stairs. The girls were high, delighted I'd begged them off their last two periods of school. Katy especially, as she was missing double Latin. Despite leaving later than planned and the 'tractor-factor' on Fife's narrow roads, Ralph got us there in time for a pre-dinner swim. Well, they swam. I opted for a G&T.

The waiter brought my drink with some nuts, but before I could start on them, Wendy appeared, still looking like the Tatler cover girl she'd once been. Long legs encased in fashionable wide-legged wool trousers, eyeshadow matching her purple fluffy cardigan, hair perfectly styled. My M&S jeans and frizzy hair couldn't compete.

'Beth! Great to see you!'

Henry came behind and pulled me up for a bear hug as Wendy sat down. They looked so happy. I banished an image from the last reunion: a bruised, drunk, and distressed Wendy with Conor. A happy ending, good old Henry Galahad. He set off to fetch drinks.

'So where are the kids?' I asked her.

'In the pool with our au pair. She's the daughter of a French friend, taking time out before uni. Roly's babbling Franglais already. Maia's favourite word is "Non!" Wee madam.'

Henry returned with three glasses of champagne. 'Let's start as if we mean business! Cheers! Here's to us and happy families!' He chinked my glass. 'Where's Ralph?'

'With the girls in the pool. He's been on a fitness kick and lost a stone. Aiming for lean and mean, he says!'

'He'll never be mean.' Wendy sneezed. 'Oh, the bubbles - must be getting old!'

I didn't know which drink to have first, but decided since I'd had nothing since breakfast, I'd do nuts, then the champagne, then the gin. 'I am really celebrating, Henry. I had a letter from the Health Board this morning.'

'Saying what?'

'It would appear they no longer consider your good friend Beth is a drug runner.'

'I should think so too! I hope you got grovelling apologies.'

'Not exactly, just "We are pleased to inform you we found no evidence …"'

'Have you no redress? It was defamatory.'

'Och, the blame lies with the letter writer. I've asked for the original to give to the police along with the other two, but it'll have been contaminated by God-knows-who's DNA. Not sure if you get fingerprints from paper. Must ask my forensic sister-in-law. Ralph wants to go to the police on Monday anyway over the nuisance phone calls.'

'Phone calls?' Henry blew a sigh like a raspberry, one of his specialities.

'Hi, you lot! On the sauce already?' Gordon strolled up, windswept and flushed. 'We've been along the front.' Heather followed with her teenage trio clad in identical black Doc Martens, cuffed jeans and leather jackets. They threw themselves onto an adjacent sofa demanding hot chocolate and marshmallows. Henry, as ever, rose to oblige.

'Thanks Henry, we'll have coffees!' Gordon sat. 'What was that about nuisance calls?'

'Oh, I've been getting heavy breathing ones. Didn't I say? Started not long after I refused that Goodman chap's Part Two, but the Defence folk cautioned me against accusing him. No evidence and all that.'

'How often have you had them?'

'There was a lull, then one a week last Tuesday, about nine and a couple the next night. Two in the morning is his favourite time. '

'Don't know about the Wednesday, but week last Tuesday, Goodman was in Rogano's a few tables from us with a teenage boy. Definitely Tuesday - it was Heather's birthday. He didn't acknowledge me, nor I him. But it makes him unlikely to be your phantom caller that night. He was there till ten anyway.' Gordon nodded.

For some reason, that felt like a blow. If not him, then who the hell was my mystery caller? Henry returned, as did my glowing, if dishevelled girls. So much for them suggesting they mightn't swim since chlorine ruined your hair: Katy's hadn't seen a brush and Julia's was wet and scraped back in a rubber band. Ralph looked knackered as he flopped down. New faces arrived. Katy stood up to throw her arms round Uncle Yousef, exclaiming at his pretty dark-eyed daughters, Iris and Iolanthe, now eight and ten. Rosie then came running into the room pursuing little Nathan, while Dad James sauntered in after her. Everyone talked over one another in 'how-are-yous', 'how-was-your-journeys', 'what-room-are-you-ins' and 'what-time's-this-buffet-dinners?'

Some adjacent 'non-reunion' people left. I didn't blame them. We pulled their seats into an ever-expanding circle. My girls went off to form a separate group at the window with Gordon's tribe and other youngsters. I looked at my watch. Only half an hour till dinner!

'Let's go girls – party time!' I went over to pull Katy up but stopped abruptly. Strolling into the lounge, woman on his arm, was a figure in a sharp pin-striped suit shouting Savile Row, a watch shouting money to burn and a swagger of pure conceit. The woman exuded sex: cleavage, short skirt, exaggerated sashay and gravity-defying shoes. Conrad Towie – or Conor Towmey – had arrived. His model's clinging red dress left nothing to the imagination.

Rosie whispered, 'That's the Constella girl, Jane. But why is she dressed so tarty?'

My brain didn't register an opinion at first, being pre-occupied with the worry that my washed-at-the-last-minute knickers on the radiator upstairs might not be dry enough to wear to dinner under my white trousers. Serious. The ones I was wearing were black so would show through. In fury, I grabbed both my girls by the hand and tore off, not daring to look at Wendy. How dare he slither in here after being sent a copy of our new Constitution and a letter stating he was no longer eligible to be a member of Glasgow University Theta Club?

Fifteen

The Way

Westhaven

The study was not what he'd expected, but more opulent and less ascetic. Con wandered round. It was unusually spacious for a study, larger than the living room across the hall. Its walls were covered in a textile of racing green, quite restful. The lighting was subdued: a corner standard lamp and a brass desk light. Heavy green and black brocade curtains were retained by gold cords. Three walls held large, gallery quality oil paintings in heavy gilt frames. One depicted children playing on a beach, one a reclining pubic, pale, and provocative Rubenesque nude and another was of a hunting scene sporting entrails. Not to his taste.

The fourth wall was given up entirely to purpose-built mahogany bookcases rising from floor to ceiling. The titles were a mixed bag. Low down sat medical and surgical books, no surprise there, but two rows above held pristine sets of murder mystery books arranged alphabetically by author's names. Some, like Christie he recognised, but Ngaio Marsh? From their stylised covers, he reckoned many were from the fifties. Above them were heavy tomes, some bristling with little bookmarks. These volumes were less pristine and ordered by descending size: a fat *APBI Medicines Compendium*, a *Materia Medica*, an *Introduction to Toxicology*, a copy of the *Birth of Forensic Medicine* and some Jurisprudence titles including the seminal one by the famous Glasgow police surgeon, John Glaister. The very top shelves held books Conor would have displayed more prominently. Leather-bound, gold-tooled volumes. One he pulled out was an Edgar Allan Poe first edition. Impressed, he replaced it gently.

The substantial mahogany desk was splendid. The only personal item visible in this curiously theatrical study, was a silver-framed photo of a schoolboy alongside a smartly-dressed woman in a velvet-trimmed 'pancake' straw hat à la Grace Kelly, a full-skirted, dated, dress and white gloves. Goodman's mother?

Con couldn't get used to Stan as 'David Goodman', though he couldn't talk, having changed his own name to Conrad Towie. He'd hoped this would make it less likely researchers might discover his GMC past. But when Stan told him he was now 'David', he'd only shrugged when asked why. Con didn't pursue it. Not worth it.

Con tried pulling the brass-handled desk drawers, but they were both locked, as had been the room when Goodman had ushered him in, calling it his 'inner sanctum'. Bizarrely, a box of latex gloves lay next to the photo, alongside a new Dell computer and two very neat piles of stapled papers stacked typeface-down. One pile was weighed down by a paper knife with a heavy silver and amber handle, the other by a Perspex dome encasing the Eiffel Tower. He was shaking this as his host returned.

'Sorry, Con, I had to take that call. My practice manager is hysterical about some missing accounts. Women do fuss so.' Removing the snowing globe from Conor's hand, he replaced it, then looked at it and turned it round. 'Not sure why I've kept that. Silly honeymoon memento of my wife's.' He gestured to the armchairs either side of the ornate fireplace. 'Please do sit. Whisky?'

He was slurred. No wonder, Con had watched him swallow double his own intake over the evening. It had been a good night at the Grosvenor. Constella's latest product launch had gone well, but he'd had to help Goodman into the taxi. And up the path and steps into the house. The pale little wife who'd let them in had wordlessly scurried off upstairs.

The whisky was a good Islay malt. Conor noted his host had poured himself a larger double compared to his, but he wasn't bothered. He had to be up early in the morning to collect the hire car. Jane would be ready and waiting by twelve, with his new clubs, if she remembered to collect them. Would be a shame to go to St Andrews and not play golf. The drive through to Fife should be pleasant and, if the weather held, he'd arrive with the top down, show Wendy he was uncowed by her punishing settlement.

'Slanj! Good of you to put me up for the night, David. Wouldn't have liked driving through to Edinburgh after all that wine. Great presentation of Jane's, eh? Rubeniclast is on track for spring release. Should corner the market. Heinrich's is a goer. You bought any shares? If not, now's the time. I've taken a few.'

'Certainly not. The stock market is but sinful gambling. A shure shtep on the road to perdition.' He wrinkled his nose. 'Like immoral women!'

Conor watched David's eyelids droop after this slurred pronouncement. Was that a joke? As usual with David, he wasn't sure. He laughed lightly. 'Morals are a nuisance, aren't they? Always get in the way of fun.'

At this, his companion sat bolt upright, opened his eyes and snorted. 'Life isn't about fun, it's about survival. And an eye for an eye!' He lurched forward, flushed, eyes bulging so much that Conor feared he was having a stroke.

'I couldn't agree more. In fact, I'm about to exert a bit of revenge on my ex-wife and her cronies at our reunion. They should pay for what they did to me! That bitch Wendy and her sidekick Beth Semple. I'm going to thoroughly spoil their weekend!'

'Why not fix them properly?' David cackled, jerking his arm, spilling whisky on the silk Chinese rug. He didn't notice.

Con leaned on his chair arm. 'So, how d'you suggest fixing them? The courts are useless.'

'Oh, there are many ways.' David looked at the ceiling then at Con. 'Potassium chloride is good, more-or-less undetectable at post-mortem, but needs injecting. A bit tricky out of a clinical situation. Still.'

Con couldn't fathom his expression. Another joke? What an odd cove David was. Yet earlier, so full of bonhomie. His host continued.

'Then there's insulin. Depends if you want disposal to be slow or swift and painful. Best nothing too acutely poisonous, like cyanide. Not good, attracts attention. Then again, for people who get in the way, sometimes it's worth taking a chance.' His mouth lolled open and he looked miles away. Con was becoming uncomfortable, regretting he'd egged David on.

Suddenly David leaned forward to speak un-slurred. 'If they tip me over, Con, I feel compelled.' His eyes narrowed as his shaking hand raised his glass. He drained it in one gulp.

Conor was unnerved. This wasn't funny. He didn't want to hear any more. 'Sorry, think I'll go up to bed, if you don't mind, David. Early start. Don't let me forget to give you the papers for the new anti-depressant trial in the morning.'

'And remind me to give you Nesbitt's last Rubeniclast forms. Fool abandoned recruiting after that Lester woman died. But don't worry, I've fixed the lot.' Goodman nodded.

Cold crawled up Conor's back. Fiddling the odd result was one thing, but had he blatantly made up a whole trial cohort? Turning to stand up, he found himself eye to eye with a super-sized hunter presiding triumphantly over bloodied guts spilling into his lap from an indeterminate dead, shaggy, horned animal. In the distance, dogs looked to be howling while nearby a wild-eyed, rearing horse foamed at the mouth. A discarded Stetson lay in the dust. The dead animal must be a bison. He jumped as he felt his arm patted.

David pointed at the painting. 'Great, isn't it?' Got it off an old American in Bristol in lieu of fees. This painting can teach us a lot you know, Conrad. Life, death and power – it's all there! Wife hates it.' He gave a throaty chuckle.

Suddenly, Conor felt sober. At the door, he nodded. 'See you in the morning, then.'

David rose to sway unsteadily towards his drinks trolley. 'Think I'll just have one more nightcap while I check tomorrow's sermon.' He burped loudly as he reached for the whisky bottle. 'They love me at the church, you know.' He sat back down to rock back and forth like a child, smiling to himself. 'Use my old name there. Best of both worlds.'

As Conor quietly closed the door behind him, he heard a clatter. A glass falling on the hearth, maybe? But he didn't go back in to see. He practically ran upstairs, heart pounding.

He was regretting that he'd helped massage the bold boy's fundholding stats and books, for David looked like he had flipped. What if he slipped up, was found out? David might shift the blame on him! And from David's hints, he'd likely faked most of his trial stats. They must be omitted from the final returns. Vigorously cleaning his teeth in the bathroom, Conor felt uneasy that he'd admitted a few 'peccadillos' to David in the past. The last hour had demonstrated David's frightening instability, if not insanity. That had been more than just drink talking. He couldn't be trusted.

Returning to his bedroom, Conor noticed every door he passed had a key in the lock. Goodman was paranoid. He already knew Goodman had a Dettol obsession and germ phobia, but Christ, who kept latex gloves in their *study*? After rapidly undressing, Conor strode over to turn the key in the door. David was crackers, but shit, it was catching! As he clicked off the light, one of the many clocks in the corridor dinged 3 a.m.. A short while later, so did another. And another. Con didn't sleep.

Next morning, he was up and dressed by 6 a.m., helped himself to a glass of milk from the fridge and left a brief note thanking his hostess. He wasn't waiting around to say goodbye.

*

Clara found the note while making Neil's breakfast and put it in her apron pocket. Nice to be appreciated. She enjoyed her Sunday mornings sitting alone with her son in peace and quiet. At 10 a.m. she wakened her husband. He was due at his town centre church by noon. Why he couldn't attend a nearer one, she'd no idea. She'd never asked.

He came down the stairs no better than usual after a Saturday night blow-out. His absent house guest wasn't referred to. She didn't mention the note. Wordlessly, she drove them to church in the big car. She preferred driving the small one, but he wouldn't be seen dead exiting a tiny Fiesta at church. It was only to get her to drive him on Sunday mornings that he'd allowed her to take driving lessons. After twelve years of persuasion.

Sitting at the back of the meeting hall with Neil, she listened to his sermon. 'Loving thy neighbour like thyself', with a touch of 'The Way, the Truth and the Life'. He loved preaching. He was good at it. If a trifle overdramatic. The congregation always lapped it up. But she no longer had faith. God hadn't shown her any way forward. Her truth was unpalatable. Life offered no solutions to her predicament. Neil took her hand and squeezed it. Not long till he'd be off to university. Then she hoped to leave.

She'd thought of building a medical history of depression due to her unhappy marriage with that nice woman GP at Oakfield but had changed her mind. Too dangerous. He might find out. For now, her duty lay in providing a home for Neil to study and grow. She was growing something herself: a building society account. Its passbook was locked up at work. Asking to be paid in cash had caused comment, but her boss complied, which meant she could hide exactly what she was earning from David and salt some away, safely stowing her payslips beside her 'work-name' passbook. Tax implications worried her slightly, but she paid PAYE. Why HMRC hadn't caught up with David was a mystery. He didn't file returns. Perhaps not having an accountant helped. Anyway, she'd heard as self-employed, he might not be registered with the local tax office. And hopefully, with her keeping her maiden name for work, she wouldn't be linked to him.

It was a long hour and a half. As with gripes and rows, he liked to spin things out. His chosen hymns were dreary. Outside the sky was blue. Birds wheeled and swooped. Free. In her head she was elsewhere by the amens.

The drive home was silent. Neil in the back, David in the front wearing his Sunday piety face, one worthy of a Baptist deacon professing wisdom, faith, honesty and sincerity, who 'manages a household well and drinks alcohol sparingly' as she'd given witness to for his ordination in London in the early days. She wouldn't now.

She spent the rest of the day in the kitchen. He was in the study, typing away. She moved some old foolscap parchment paper off the dining room table. God knows what that was for. She covered the table with a white cloth. She'd have preferred to have given it a good polish first, but she couldn't find the Pledge. Doubtless, he had it in the study. But she wouldn't ask. It might provoke a row. Compliance was the way forward. Though some recent commands had troubled her: those phone calls pretending to be someone else, the deletions of dispensary computer entries. She hadn't asked for explanations. In truth, she was beyond caring. Returning to the kitchen, she heard the familiar whizz, clunk, whizz from the basement which meant a welcome half-hour respite. Keeping fit on his rowing machine, vain bugger. Like his hair treatments, pure narcissism. She opened the oven to check on the roast.

*

He checks his pulse. Still low. Fit despite last night's whisky binge. Speeding up for twenty minutes on the rower, he then moves on to the treadmill, increasing the incline and target speed. His fitness is exceptional for forty-four. Con needs to watch it, though the paunchy boy was good company last night.

He's finding attending drug dinners and medical functions easier now. They are important, increase his network, demonstrate his worth, show he's part of the community. Coming off the treadmill, he lifts his weights. Today he feels powerful, in control. Although, some of last night is hazy. Did he indiscreetly mention some 'methods' to Con? No matter, he was drunk too. And Con is no angel, partly why he likes him. Admirable how he's bounced back after being struck off. He showed them! Con is the first person he's taken into the study. It had impressed him, he could see. Con's sounding off about vengeance on his ex-wife was intriguing. As was his revelation that Beth Semple had been involved in his downfall. Going for her would help them both. He is loath to just eliminate her, surely more satisfying to engineer targeted mayhem, ruin her reputation, cause lasting damage? What might be her most tender Achilles heel? For pharmacist Simon, it is money. For Brian Nesbitt, codeine. But Beth Semple? Her vulnerability surely lay in her reputation. And, of course, her family.

He showers and retires to his study.

Sixteen

Pretty Woman & Lamborghini Man

St Andrews

I decided Katy was right. As I watched Uncle Gordon unwinding his very long legs from the low sofa on the Saturday morning of our reunion, he looked every inch Roald Dahl's Big Friendly Giant. Opposite him, Dan was muttering while angrily flicking at the *Scottish Daily Mail* sports section. As I approached to sit, he folded up the offending paper.

'Morning, Beth. Good buffet last night, wasn't it? Where are the girls?'

'Off out with Henry and little Nathan to find some amazing Italian ice cream shop the receptionist recommended.'

Gordon joined in. 'Heather and the girls are out too. You're looking well, today. In fact you've got a glow on you!' He pretended to warm his hands either side of my face.

'I've just had a rejuvenating facial. They've told me not to apply any make-up for a few hours, so I feel a bit naked. Didn't expect to find anyone in here. Still, nice to see you two. Is there a waiter about? Thought I'd just creep in for a drink!'

'Let me get you something – a wee G&T, hair of the dog? We're on the Belhaven.' Dan waved towards their beers.

'No, it's only gone 11.30! By drink I mean tea, a proper pot of the stuff, not a "dooked" teabag from the wee room kettle. And maybe a sultana scone – with jam and cream!'

A waiter had arrived and heard me. 'Sure, madam!'

With a big grin and a thumbs up, he dashed off. Sweet young lad, probably new. As yet unjaded by demanding five-star hotel customers, he dashed about like an eager spaniel while other staff languidly strolled about like slightly snooty borzois.

'Didn't see Wendy at breakfast,' said Dan, taking a slug of his beer by the neck though they'd given him a glass. His mother would have been appalled.

'No, she had it in her room.'

'That's a shame. Conor, eh?' Gordon pursed his lips. 'He's got a brass neck, coming here. Maybe we shouldn't have sent him that note?'

'But it only said, 'We regret you are no longer a member of the Theta Club.' It didn't mention the reunion or that it was here. Not sure how he got to know.'

'It'll be the Faculty Office. Con was very cosy with one of the girls there who's now the boss.' Gordon tapped the side of his nose suggestively.

Rubbing his stubbly chin, Dan moved forward to sit on the edge of his sofa. With elbows on thighs, hands clasped, he opened his mouth as if about to say something, then shut it. His hands clenched and unclenched before finally, he took a deep breath. 'On the subject of Conor, Beth,' he looked me in the eye, 'Gordon has something to tell you.' He made wide eyes at his friend while tilting his head sideways towards me.

My curiosity was piqued. 'What?'

Gordon swallowed. 'I was at a drug dinner in the Grosvenor last week.'

'So?'

'Guess who were sitting together, knocking it back, thick as thieves?'

'Oh, come on, who?'

'Conor and David Goodman.' Gordon's face was impassive.

My stomach started churning. But why should this be disturbing? I couldn't pinpoint any specific reason, but it was. 'Coincidence. Just met, surely, Gordon?'

Gordon shook his head. 'They didn't look like new acquaintances. Pretty familiar. Back slapping, glass clinking etcetera.'

I had a sinking feeling and hoped the weekend was not going to be ruined. 'Dan, do you think they knew one another down in London?'

Dan looked to the heavens. 'Couldn't say for sure, but I don't remember any surgeon called Goodman in St Jasper's or George's where Conor worked. Unless the gossip's false, and Goodman wasn't a surgeon? I mean if he'd been in a minor speciality like Eyes or ENT, I might not have come across him.' Dan sat back.

Gordon sighed. 'So, where did they meet then? What else d'you know about Goodman, Beth?'

I shrugged. 'Och, not much. Anyway, does it matter? Goodman's entitled to be friends with anyone he likes. Conor's the immediate bugbear. I'm more worried about getting Wendy out of her room. After my treatment, I went up to change and knocked her door. When I told her I wasn't taking no for an answer, she agreed to get dressed and come down here for a cuppa. So, when she comes, let's keep off the Conor subject. And frankly, I'd quite like a weekend without the bloody Goodman subject too.'

'The last thing I'll say, Beth, is that the girl Con's with is a drug rep who got me to try a new asthma drug. '

'I know, Gordon. Rosie says she's called Jane Chancellor. She saw her with Con in Edinburgh last autumn when she was with Constella Pharma pushing psychiatric drugs.'

'Well, she's with Heidrich-Holtz now, marketing asthma ones. This one's a turkey. The first two patients I tried with it became very unwell and I know of other GPs who've pulled out of the drug trial after severe side effects in some patients. One girl collapsed with anaphylaxis needing adrenaline and a lad got palpitations so severe he was admitted. Yet at Thursday's dinner they were promoting this Rubiwhatsit drug like a panacea for all ills, maintaining it'll pass by the Safety of Medicines Committee on a nod. I only went to the meeting because the speaker, Prof Paterson from Edinburgh, is a leading asthma guy. God knows why he was on their platform endorsing the drug.'

I shook my head. This dangerous game of drug marketing was beyond me. I turned to concentrate on my scone, now in two halves, each with the regulatory layers of cream and strawberry jam necessary for maximum enjoyment. Dan wouldn't let it go though.

'I'm sorry for the girl though, if she thinks Conor's a catch.'

Gordon uncharacteristically erupted, swearing loudly. 'Don't be sorry for her. Christ, she's a callous, unethical bitch. When she came to collect my trial results and I challenged her about the adverse effects, d'you know what she said?'

I shook my head. My mouth was otherwise engaged.

'"Your patients must be rare anomalies – just omit them!" I threw her out. Scandalous!'

I wiped cream from my lip with a napkin. 'You should report that to someone.'

'Thought about it, Beth, but to whom? No point in a yellow warning card to the Safety of Medicines Committee, it isn't a licensed product yet.'

'You could phone the Medical & Dental Defence Union and ask their advice?' Dan's suggestion was sound. 'I mean, anaphylaxis can be fatal.'

'So, what's this little serious pow-wow about?' Wendy stood over us looking great: red sweater, matching lipstick, black jeans and perfect hair. My spaniel waiter whizzed up and whizzed off as she pointed to my snack. 'One of those please!'

Putting down my cream-laden napkin, I patted an

adjacent chair for Wendy. 'I was just saying how dreadful it must be if you're allergic to strawberries. Imagine having to carry around an epi-pen and face life without strawberry jam?' Gordon laughed awkwardly. I glared at him.

Wendy sat down with her back to the lobby and asked about my facial as she'd made an appointment for the afternoon. Dan retreated behind his sports section. I was pouring myself more tea when Gordon nudged me, nodding towards the door.

'Has he been lurking, waiting for her to appear?'

Conor Towmey filled the doorway with his six-foot rugby frame and advanced into the lounge swinging a large key fob. Looking beyond me, he waved at someone. As he drew level, he paused. Whizzy boy waiter had just laid a scone before Wendy. Mine was half finished.

'Not counting the calories anymore girls? Stopped watching those waistlines?'

The waiter stood transfixed by the vision of Jane, sashaying into view to take Conor's arm. The poor boy's jaw was almost on the floor. Eyes wide, head lolling, he looked like a dog regarding his dinner, though fortunately without salivation. I frowned and he shot off.

'This is my fiancée, Jane.' Conor lifted her left hand, exposing an obscenely large solitaire. She beamed at our little group, even Gordon, whom she can't have recognised out of context as a GP who'd flung her out of his surgery. Conor squeezed her waist. 'Taking Janey for a spin up the coast in the Lamborghini, guys. See you later.' They left.

Ah, that's what the key-fob-swinging was about! As if any of us cared he had an Italian sports car. I saw Wendy wilt momentarily, then sit up straight, face taut, expressionless. I was proud of her as she said emphatically, 'What a bloody prat he is!'

'He's not going to spoil this weekend, Wendy,' I lifted her scone plate. 'Have this, here's some extra jam and cream.'

'That poor girl, Beth, she's no idea what she's taking on.' Wendy's hand trembled as she lifted her knife.

I glared at Gordon in case he added to the stress with another invective on Jane. We needed to let this incident pass as quickly as possible. Wendy may have divorced Conor, but the years of manipulative abuse she'd suffered had taken their toll. Gordon met my eye in understanding. He rose and stretched. 'Right, I'm off for a swim. Coming, Dan?' He bent to kiss Wendy and left. Dan followed, muttering sotto voce at me as he passed, 'He'll get his comeuppance eventually. As will she!'

Sadly, experience had taught me life wasn't that simple. Despite Conor having been GMC censured and losing his job, here he was, back, testing drugs and causing mayhem as usual. Returning to our cream teas, Wendy and I enjoyed the short period of calm before our husbands and kids noisily returned. My cry to Henry not to buy the girls sugary drinks on the grounds of excitability had fallen on deaf ears. The girls gulped Cokes. Henry and Ralph talked rugby. Wendy and I resorted to discussing Roly's potty training. It was preferable to other subjects.

At the evening reception before the gala dinner, everyone brushed up well. Looking round, I felt the girls had aged better than the lads. Amazing how well-cut clothes, haircuts and make up can cover a multitude of sins. The guys couldn't just have aged faster from career pressures; most girls worked too. I decided the biggest ageing factor was creeping baldness.

'I wonder, Rosie, do you think a lot of the boys have grown beards as a sort of compensation for going bald, like a need to prove they can produce hair *somewhere*?'

Rosie chuckled as James arrived. She kissed him. 'Thank God you shaved your beard off.'

'What?' James looked from Rosie to me, puzzled.

'That ghastly, prickly, holiday beard you grew, yuk!'
Rosie stuck out her tongue. James looked hurt.

'But James has lovely hair!' I said.

He proudly patted his thick dark thatch. 'Thank you,
Beth! Pity it's under a wig in court most of the time.'

'Don't encourage him, he's vain enough already. Pity the
wig doesn't stop his head getting bigger!'

'That's unfair, Rosie! But you can't mock beards now,
they're a big legal issue in the US. Domino's Pizza are
defending their right to ban beards in employees, but staff
say a beard is a human right.'

'I still say, yuk!' Rosie screwed up her face. 'I wouldn't
want a waiter's beardy hairs on my pizza!'

Gordon and Heather arrived, along with my charming
whizzy waiter with a tray of fizz. He blushed. I thought he'd
overheard Rosie's 'beardy waiters' comment. His was ginger,
short and neat. 'Beards are fine!' I said lamely, offering a big
smile as I swapped my empty glass for a full one. He winked
and I giggled. A passing Lurch-like maître d' materialised
to whisk him away, scolding him about 'over-familiarity.' I
almost followed to defend his right to wink. Such a nice boy.
I stopped myself, feeling the effect of three glasses of fizz on
an empty stomach.

Yousef appeared at my side and became embroiled in
the end of the beard thread in his capacity as a US plastic
surgeon. He confidently launched into a scientific discourse
on testosterone expression and its effect on male hair
patterns. Seemed you could easily have a beard and be bald.

'Too technical,' said Rosie, hiccupping. 'Can you put it
more simply?' She'd drained her third glass.

'Well, to ensure a full head of hair, the only real answer is
castration.' Conversations died around us. Everyone turned
to stare. Gordon snorted and trailed Heather off to chat to
one of our old professors.

I spotted my beloved Professor Killin with his wife and

was about to go over when I caught a flash of red in the doorway. God, did she only own red *Pretty Woman* dresses? It was a different shade from yesterday's, more claret than scarlet, but no more generously cut. Slinking across the room, she lifted a glass from whizzy waiter's tray. He must have been allowed back in after a pep talk, but now stood mesmerised, rooted to his spot, eyes following Jane's progress. I caught up with her.

'What do you think you are doing?'

'Well, it looked a lovely party. I can't understand why Conor isn't in joining you all here when he's said you were at university together. Seems daft. He came back from the gym and went into the shower. Since I was dressed already, I thought I'd come take a peek.'

My brain was in freefall calculating algorithms of possibility. Was she playing some calculated game at the behest of her fiancé? Or just ignorant, even totally naïve? I'd previously deterred Rosie from contacting her, but deciding her smile did seem artlessly genuine, I made a snap decision. Taking her arm, I steered her to the Ladies' - the only place women can talk in private.

'Look, Jane, I don't know what Conor's told you.'

'Conor? You mean Conrad?'

'No, he's Conor. Conrad's a name he's adopted to try to hide his past.'

Prof Killin's wife came in, hugged me warmly and went into a cubicle. I ran a tap. God, too many movies! I whispered forcefully, 'Jane, he isn't who you think he is. His name is Conor Towmey. He was struck off years ago for research fraud, incompetence and affairs with patients.' No point in beating around the bush.

'No! What are you saying?' She scanned my face. 'Why are you doing this?'

'Sorry, on my kids' lives, it's true.'

Her brows knitted together. She started slumping and

clutched at the wash handbasin.

'What's more, Jane, the girl you saw with me in the bar, Wendy, is his ex-wife, whom he abused abominably – emotionally and physically. Why would I make this up?'

Jane covered her mouth and nose with her hand as I continued. 'He is a rat and ...'

Dorothy Killin came out of the toilet and was about to speak, but instead, took one look at the stricken girl I was now supporting, rapidly washed her hands and left.

'... and worst of all, I lost a dear friend who committed suicide after he raped her.' Jane's eyes were filling. 'We had DNA proof, but for several reasons, it never went to court.' I was getting teary myself now. 'Anyway, for your own sake, leave him and get another job quickly.'

'But he's been so attentive, so romantic! So full of plans! Why should I believe you?'

'That's exactly what Wendy said when I tried to stop her marrying him. Why would I make this up? You'll have to trust me, I'm a doctor!' Christ, had I really said that? I was agitated, desperate and starting to feel light-headed. I needed my dinner.

The girl sucked hard on her lower lip, leaving it six shades paler than her crimson upper. 'I'll need to think about this.' Pulling a paper towel, she dampened it to wipe the blurry mascara smudges on her cheeks before pulling down the hem of her clinging jersey dress. 'He buys me dresses, you know. He bought me this.' That explained the wardrobe.

'That's his style. Controlling, manipulative. You don't even see it coming.'

'I've got two degrees, I'm not a fool. How could I be so taken in by him?'

I sighed in relief: she believed me. 'Love does mad things to us, Jane, as I know. But look up Towmey's GMC case if you've any doubts. It'll be on file and it was all over the papers.'

'I will!' She abruptly scurried out.

Outside, the reception room was empty apart from Dan and Ralph.

'Come on! Where have you been? Gordon's about to start. He's doing his speech with the starters for some reason.' Dan walked swiftly ahead into the ballroom.

Ralph took my arm. 'What's up, Beth? You're very pale. You feeling all right?'

'Bit dizzy to be honest, think I need to eat. But happy. I think I've saved someone a lot of grief. Tell you later.' I gave him a kiss on the cheek.

He kissed me swiftly on the mouth. 'I love you, Beth. You look beautiful in that red dress.'

Nice as it was to bask in his compliment, I had seen enough red dresses for a while and vowed I'd buy no more. I sat down opposite Wendy, looking great in full-length blue chiffon, Henry's arm across her shoulders.

Gordon made a good opening speech, reading out the list of those who were no longer with us, omitting to say two of them were suicides. Then he announced the achievements of people in our year – present and afar. Dan received a round of applause for his professorship. My memory gets a bit jumbled after that. I felt shaky but was relieved to see my hand looked steady as a I raised my wineglass. My thoughts were in turmoil. Though pleased Jane hadn't asked my name, I knew if she told Con she'd met 'one of those girls from this morning', he'd guess. I started to feel sick.

Ralph nudged me. 'If you don't want that smoked salmon, I'll have it.'

I wolfed it down. To my other side was Stella, my old friend who'd finally made it to surgical consultant. Though we'd met on and off at the reunion committee meetings, we'd never had enough time for a proper catch up. I think I was asking the usual rote things about work and kids. I remember hearing laughter, not sure if it was mine, then I felt I was hovering over the table looking down. I'd heard of such 'out of body experiences'. How curious.

The next thing I knew, voices were talking to me through water. I was lying on a couch in the reception room and a paramedic was taking my blood pressure.

'Ouch! That's too tight.' I found my voice.

She smiled. 'Hello, glad you could join us! You passed out. Any chest pain or anything?'

'No.' I mentally checked round my body and felt nothing, except a hand round mine. It was Wendy. Ralph was kneeling beside me.

'What a fright you gave us, you just keeled over!'

I sat up. 'Are you dizzy sitting up?' asked the ambulance lady.

'No, I'm fine now, thanks. I'd like to finish my dinner.'

'It'll be cold.' Wendy shook her head. 'You've been out for a bit. Maybe it was the heat? Or was that scone the only thing you've had all day? Hypoglycaemia might be a contributor.'

Ralph looked concerned. 'She's never fainted before.'

'Hey, I'm here! Who's this "she" you're talking about? The cat's mother?' I suddenly felt flushed. What an exhibition I'd made of myself, flaking out in public! Embarrassment was taking blood back to my brain. As I stood up, Ralph grabbed my arm. 'Sit here for a minute.'

'I'm really thirsty.'

Wendy went for a glass of water. The onlookers and paramedics left.

'A room full of doctors and they called an ambulance?' I laughed, nudging Ralph, who now sat beside me, his arm round my shoulders.

He smiled. 'They probably have a protocol that must be followed!'

'Sounds like a Royal College! You know, Ralph, I think I fainted from emotional stress. I never thought that was really possible, thought all those swooning Victorian women in novels were just hysterics!' I broke off as I saw Wendy in the doorway, followed by a concerned-looking Mr Whizzy Waiter with a glass of water grandly placed on a tray.

'You've got a fan there, Doctor!' Ralph whispered, winking at me like a silly schoolboy. The world was going mad. People kept winking at me. I graciously thanked Whizzy for the tumbler, reassuring him I was fine, and gulped down the water. We made our way back in. The big ballroom was now dark as some visiting professor was showing slides on the wall about India or something. The pudding plates were being cleared. At Ralph's command, two main courses appeared. I wolfed into mine, and the big meringue dessert following, mindful of Wendy's dig about blood sugar.

Still feeling a trifle wobbly, I didn't dance at the ceilidh, but did take a couple of glasses of wine, despite Ralph's misgivings. Finally, I began to relax. It was such a joy to see Wendy's blue chiffon swirling alongside Henry in *The Dashing White Sergeant*. She was strong now. And so was I. Conor and his stupid mate Goodman could go hang.

Seventeen

Bone of Contention

I left the ceilidh at midnight. Next morning, I left Ralph snoring at eight. The aroma of whisky in the bedroom spurred me on: I hate peaty malts. Obviously, copious amounts had been consumed by the boys as 'nightcaps'. Downstairs, few of the boys were visible at breakfast. Neither were my girls, who reneged on our arranged 8 a.m. breakfast to retreat groaning under the duvet. Roistering in Gordon's triplets' room had obviously gone on late, though I noted his girls had made it down with their mum and could be seen hoovering up pancakes and syrup. Heather waved me over.

'How are you feeling, Beth? Any idea what caused your faint?'

'Much better.' I decided not to share my suspicion it was the stress of my dramatic confrontation with Jane. 'Och, I was probably too hot and hadn't eaten enough. Is Gordon like Ralph, sleeping it off?'

Heather laughed. 'It was three when he came up, still rambling about Conor's fiancée.'

'What about her?'

'After midnight, Gordon said he'd seen the girl get in a taxi, sobbing. I just said, "It'll be all Conor's fault and who cares?" but he went on and on, saying they deserved each other and were both just unethical shites!' Her kids aped horror at this swearing, then sniggered behind their hands. 'And did he tell you about that ridiculous red Lamborghini Con came in?' I shook my head. 'No? Guess what? When Conor insisted Gordy sit in it yesterday, he saw a hire agreement in the door pocket! Who did Conor think he was kidding?'

'Ah, so that explains how he could afford a car costing more than my house!'

'He's gone, thank God. Saw him from the lobby this morning, belting off up the drive, tyres screaming. Poor Wendy. Think his main aim was spoiling her weekend. Is she OK?'

'Oh, she's fine.'

I collected some breakfast and sat with Heather. After a while, my sleepy girls appeared: hunger had succeeded where maternal nagging hadn't. They took off to graze at the buffet. On their return, I wasn't pleased. Despite having doctor parents and my healthy fruit and muesli example, their plates were piled high with cholesterol-rich fried eggs, bacon, sausage, haggis, black pudding, beans, potato scones- and maple syrup! Seeing my face, Julia feigned indignation.

'Well, beans and tomatoes are healthy.'

They could forget lunch. Anyway, it was now 10.30, and with no sign of Ralph, likely I'd be the one driving home. Even by late morning, he'd still be liable to fail a breathalyser. At this rate it might be well into Sunday afternoon before we'd set off. The smell of the bacon forced me to capitulate. I headed for the buffet. Shame to waste food already cooked for us.

It was noon when Ralph appeared and five when we got home. A good drive: no tractor delays, only a few stray sheep. Winston greeted us exuberantly. I drove Mum home to Govan. By the time I got back, Ralph was snoozing upstairs. The hotel bar must be re-stocking today. Julia and Katy disappeared to do homework which, on Friday, they'd denied having.

Winston was particularly frisky and bouncy after having had the sole company of my mother all weekend. He was a real part of the family now. The girls adored him, at least one of them usually coming on his walks. But tonight, the pleasure fell solely to me.

In our turn round the park, Winston made a new friend, a cocker spaniel called Spot whose owner looked vaguely familiar. I asked her if she was an Oakfield patient. She wasn't. As the dogs chased one another's tails, she ventured that she worked in a doctor's surgery, Kilnglass. I realised then that she was Goodman's practice manager. We'd met that fateful day of the cremation form fiasco. She'd changed her hair colour and was in casual clothes – amazing the difference that made. Ye Gods! I couldn't even walk the dogs without him coming up! As she extolled his virtues, I pointedly consulted my watch. 'Gracious! Is that the time? Must dash!'

'Nice meeting you.' I didn't think she remembered me. Probably just as well. She walked away.

I know Neuro-linguistic Programming classes highlighted me as visually aware, but maybe I over-analyse signs. Glancing at her back, I detected sadness. And had that been a spark in her eye as she'd talked about Goodman? No wedding ring. Did she hold a torch for him, perhaps an unrequited crush? Or was he another Conor, taking advantage? I got angry at myself: not my problem. But I vowed to change my walking route.

The rest of the week was normal. Mr Green self-diagnosed bowel cancer. He did have a wee bleeding pile, but I sent him for proctoscopy anyway. He was delighted. Not sure he'd feel the same having a camera shoved up his rectum.

Not normal, was our Alison. The 'audit' boys had gone, but Dougie had transformed our Alison from truculent madam to amiable, willing assistant, exuding bonhomie and prattling, mainly about Dougie's virtues. But her boss, Ellen, was subdued. Martin Lester, her friend Senga's son, had sought her help in clearing out her flat, full of poignant memories of their friendship. And other things. Thursday morning, Ellen came into my room clutching a polythene bag.

'Doctor, d'you have a minute?'

'Sure.' My last patient had gone.

She placed her bag on the desk. 'This was in Senga's tea caddy.'

I picked it up. It held a plain white box of pills sporting a Heinrich-Holtz label saying 'Patient no 266' and 'Expiry date March 1996.' The drug was Rubeniclast: Gordon's bad trial medicine. Unease crept up my back.

'Why've you put this in a bag, Ellen? Or did you find it in one?'

'No. I thought it might be evidence and needed bagged. What if these killed Senga?'

'Oh, Ellen, we mustn't read too much into things.' I hesitated from telling her about Gordon's experience with Rubeniclast. 'But, why were they in the caddy, of all places?'

'Well, she told me once if she was on an antibiotic or on anything not her usual, she'd put them there so at least she'd remember to take them when she made a cuppa.'

Sounded a good idea for suggesting to some of my erratic patients! I opened the sealed freezer bag, took out the packet and inspected the bubble pack inside: three tablets had been pushed out. The box didn't contain the usual side effect data sheet, only a note stating that 'this medication should be taken only by the named patient. In case of problems contact the prescriber.'

'You know, Ellen, these mightn't even be actual drugs, they could be placebo. Only half of trial patients get the real medicine.' I thought of the time I'd assumed I'd been given a drug trial placebo, but hadn't. That drug, Navdidolol, never got licensed. From the sound of it, neither should Rubeniclast. But though Ellen knew nothing of Gordon's worries, she was very upset.

'Come on, Ellen, is there something else?'

'Oh, it's just, well, Senga liked Dr Nesbitt. You know he was single-handed before he joined Kilnglass? Martin said Senga told him that last time she had to see Dr Goodman instead. She'd thought him perfectly nice, but Andrew was mad, said he must have given her these trial pills, was using her as a guinea pig. Might be an explanation, but I thought you'd want to know, what with the other things that have happened.'

Goodman again. If it wasn't him, it was Conor stressing me out. No respite. I closed my eyes and sighed, stretching back in my chair. 'Leave it with me, Ellen. I'll have a cup of tea and a think.' After she left, I replaced the pills in the polythene bag and locked them in the cupboard where I kept drugs for out-of-hours.

In the practice sitting room, Charles was grumpy. He'd had a complaint letter, so I didn't bring up Senga. Anyway, I knew what he'd say: 'She's not our patient.' Or 'Bloody Goodman again, give it a rest!' I was tired. Thank God the next day was Friday. The Senga Question would wait. Nothing would bring her back.

Saturday morning was very stressful. Deciding what to wear for teenage parties is hell. They have odd ideas about appropriate clothes. In my view, gluteal-revealing shorts and skimpy crop tops are *never* appropriate except on a beach. After hysterical heaping of discarded outfits on the bed, a compromise was achieved: dark tights would be worn under the hot pants. At seven we dropped them at their friend's birthday party and headed to the Shish for a curry. First proper chance all week for Ralph and me to talk.

When I outlined the story of Senga, Goodman and the tea caddy pills, he simply said, 'phone the Defence Society.'

'Oh Ralph, I can't phone them again. They'll think I'm a paranoid nutcase.'

'But someone needs to tell the pharmaceutical authorities about Gordon's info and Senga's death.'

'Well, I'm not telling Robin Butler at the Pharmaceutical Committee. The man's an ass!'

'No, Beth, I mean the *regulatory* people. OK, let me look into it. And I'll speak to Gordon. Now, what are you having? I fancy a paneer korma.'

I was grateful for Ralph's assertiveness. What would I do without him to bounce things off? Poor Ellen and that Kilnglass woman in the park, both all alone. How terrible to have no confidante in times of stress.

When we got home, the house was in uproar. Mum stood in the hall with Dettol in one hand and a cloth in the other. Winston had vomited there, and in the kitchen and in the utility room. Ralph returned from fetching the girls from their party to find me stuffing the dog's bed into a bin bag: it was beyond salvation. As Katy cradled the wee soul in a blanket, he started twitching. I grabbed the phone and called the vet. John, a patient, was also a friend. He told us to bring Winston over immediately. We drove in a fury to his house and surgery, where the whimpering dog was examined and given an injection to calm him down.

John took blood samples. 'What's he been eating?

'Nothing unusual,' said Julia. 'He gets the diet you suggested when we got him.' She was stroking Winston's head. It was pitiful.

I was fighting tears. 'So, what do you think is wrong with him? I thought he was having seizures on the way here.'

'Frankly, it looks like poisoning. Vomiting as much so suddenly is unusual with anything else. Mind you, its violence may save his bacon. But he's pretty dehydrated, Beth. I'll put up a drip and keep him overnight. If he worsens, I'll take him to the vet hospital. Is that OK? You've got insurance, I know.'

'Of course, anything that needs done.'

'And even though it's Sunday tomorrow, I'll take the bloods over to the hospital for urgent toxicology screening. Did your mum say what he'd eaten tonight?'

'Usual Pedigree stuff. A new packet.' I said.

'Gran says she let him out at ten and he ran around a bit, but when she called him in, he was coughing and minutes later started throwing up everywhere.' Katy was sobbing. 'Is there something poisonous in chicken nuggets dogs shouldn't have, like chocolate? I gave him one at tea-time.'

John put his arm round her. 'No, it's nothing to do with nuggets. Why don't you go home, have a look round the garden, see if there's any clues as to what he might have eaten?'

Winston was quieter, breathing easier as John inserted a drip cannula and attached saline. He gently put him into a cage on the bench, hanging the drip above. 'He's stable. I think he's vomited up the worst of it. Do you have any of the vomit?'

'There's plenty on his bed. It's in a bin bag.'

He handed me a specimen bottle. 'Might help solve the mystery, Beth. Get it to me by ten tomorrow if you can?'

We left feeling a bit happier about Winston, especially as John said he'd check on him regularly during the night. A hissing cat in a cage had spat at me as I'd passed, making me remember Sheba. I hoped she was all right.

Thankfully, she was sleeping peacefully on her bed where mum said she'd flopped after a sortie into the garden when we'd left. I taped the cat flap securely and exhorted everyone not to let her out till we'd searched the garden. No point doing it in the dark. Exhausted, we went to bed.

Next morning started with the delightful task of extracting vomit from the smelly bin bag. Then Katy and I trawled the garden. It's quite a big garden: a patio beside the house, a lawn surrounded by flower beds, some prickly roses Winston steers clear of and a kind of wild bit at the end backing onto the path leading to the golf course. We found two well-chewed balls of Winston's, a sock of Ralph's and a mangled toy mouse.

'Do you think Winston ate a poisonous plant?' asked Katy.

'I don't think we have any. There's nothing like belladonna or aconite here.'

Julia had emerged wearing my yellow rubber gloves from under the sink and her wellies. She was clutching a couple of bin-bags and the shaft of my kitchen brush. Ralph might be right: Julie was a forensic scientist in-the-making. Just like his sister Cressida.

'I'm going to look down the end. Winston loves that long grass.' She disappeared into the undergrowth of tall seed-headed grasses, nettles, weigela and forsythia bushes, poking about with the brush handle. After a few minutes she emerged holding up a bag.

'This was over near the fence. When did Winston last have a big bone?'

'He doesn't get big bones like that.' I looked in the torn-open bag which held a large, gelatinous knuckle bone flecked with raw flesh. Fairly fresh and clean, so unlikely he'd dug it up. Someone could have thrown it over the fence, but why? I took the bag gingerly.

'Go and wash your hands in hot soapy water, Julia. Throw the gloves out in a bag without touching the outside of them with your bare hands. There's another pair in the cupboard if we need them.'

I was relieved she'd the sense to come out wearing gloves. I hadn't. Poisons could be absorbed through the skin as well as the gut. I put the bone down on top of newspaper in the utility room and washed my hands. My anxiety was mounting. I cornered Ralph in the kitchen making coffee.

'Should we take the bone to the police? It must be

deliberate.'

'Steady, we don't know for sure it was poison – nor if that bone is linked, however odd its presence may be at the bottom of our garden. Let's get the sick sample to John, see how Winston is, and keep the fuss to a minimum. Best not alarm the girls.' He fetched the bone bag, lifting it using another carrier bag, and locked it in the shed.

Next day at John's surgery, we heard Winston before we saw him. He was barking at the cat in the cage and scratching furiously at a plastic collar. John was laughing and rubbing him behind the ears. 'He's stopped vomiting and slavered on my hand, so I've taken down the drip.' John cut the collar off. 'He's a resilient wee bugger – you can take him home.'

To my surprise, Katy gave John a cuddle. John looked very pleased. Ralph asked the girls to take Winston for a 'wee' before going in the car. Though not his usual exuberant bouncy self, his tail was wagging slowly, a good sign. John handed me a note and a small box.

'Here's suggested things to feed him and some charcoal tablets. Make sure he has plenty of water. Any twitching, vomiting or whatever, phone me straight away. Thanks.' He took the vomit specimen from Ralph, who, I realised in horror, had brought it, un-bagged, in his jacket pocket. I bit my tongue but spoke to John.

'We found a strange big bone in the garden near the fence adjoining the golf club path. Not like ones we give to Winston, but he could have gnawed it. Should we bring it in to see if it was the culprit?'

John looked shocked. 'I've never seen any, but I've heard of cases where some nutter goes around poisoning dogs. They go in spates. Let's hope there aren't any more. Still, maybe wait till we get the toxicology results, shall we? If it's poison, it'll be for the police.'

'I've bagged it and locked it up.' Ralph sounded like a

TV cop. God, we were all playing amateur detective. And there was Ellen's 'evidence' about her friend's odd death, the poly bag of pills locked in my surgery. What should I do with that?

On the way home, we stopped for another dog bed at the new superstore, which sold everything you could ever imagine. Julia bought a cat lead: she wasn't letting Sheba out of her sight until we were sure the garden was safe. I wasn't sure Sheba would be appreciative. Back home, I had to open all the windows. Whatever Winston had vomited up was unbelievably whiffy. Julia produced air freshener from the shopping bag. Way ahead of me, clever girl, she'd slipped it into the trolley.

It was a night for wine. We had a bottle of some German stuff we'd been given. Riesling. Not my favourite, but acceptable. Katy took Winston to her bed. I accepted that too.

Things reverted to normal for a few days. The cat lead was abandoned. There were no unwelcome notes, anonymous calls nor animal vomiting. Winston was fine. We delayed seeing the police till we had the toxicology report. Then Tuesday lunch time Alison put through John.

He was blunt. 'There's no doubt Winston ate something poisonous. His vomit contained high levels of two insecticides and rhubarb leaves, toxic due to oxalic acid. Do you grow it?'

'No, we all hate it. And I don't use insecticides as you'd see if you ever came to look at my roses. I breed greenfly. My mum sprays them with soapy water.'

'A novel idea ...'

'Oh, she saw it in the *Sunday Post*, so it must be right! But poison? That's shocking. Does this mean we should take the bone to the police?'

'I think so. It's hard to see how Winston would get such

a high dose from eating a plant sprayed with insecticide. If he's doing OK, stop the charcoal tabs and bring him in for a blood check. Unfortunately, kidney failure can be a late sequela of oxalic acid poisoning.'

'So, we're not out of the woods yet? Oh dear. But thanks, John.'

Ralph and I got home early from work on the Tuesday and had a council of war. So many questions arose now that we knew Winston had been poisoned. Most likely by this bone. Had it been tossed into our garden on purpose? If so, by whom? Ralph looked serious.

'I'm going to the police station in the morning. I'll want those letters. I think you can get good fingerprints from paper, not sure about bone. Let's phone Cressida tonight.'

The big bone lay between us on the table. I'd brought it in again to look at it carefully, rubber-gloved. To my horror I noticed the marrow in the cut end showed tiny flecks of dark green vegetable matter poked into it. Rhubarb leaf?

'And then there's the calls.' Ralph started making a list of when we'd received them from my detailed diary. I was pleased he was taking the initiative. I didn't like to admit it, but I was scared.

'Not a word of this to the girls in the meantime. From now till this is sorted, I'll do a circuit of the garden every night. And we must get Katy and Jules from everything they're at. They must stick together and wait at school to get picked up.'

'If you're going to insist that they do that, Ralph, you're going to have to tell them why. They're almost adults.'

He sighed but nodded, leaving to collect them from art club. It was only as the door shut, I realised that while we'd sorted out what to do about the bone and our harassment, there was also the problem of Senga's tablets. I shivered. It was becoming too much.

*

Next week, Neil was looking pleased with himself as he carried over the tray in Fanconi's.

'Gosh, Neil – what are we celebrating?'

'Well, Katy, I told Mum how you were always buying me ice cream or coffee on the way home after band practice and I felt bad having no money, so she gave me some to buy you a wee treat! She's going to try to give me some each week. Dad says kids shouldn't get any till they've earned it.' He handed Katy a long-handled spoon and put a large banana split between them. She was already sucking on her chocolate milk shake.

'Yum! Thank your mum!'

'She doesn't have an easy time, you know. Dad's so fussy about everything. I'd hoped he'd get less cross when we moved to the new house or then when he took in Dr Nesbitt, but he's no better and still hardly takes any time off. Sorry, Katy, I heard that Dad fell out with your mum and quit the rotas his practice shared with her, but I don't know why – do you?'

'Not sure, something to do with her refusing to sign some paper for him. He got mad. Thought she was accusing him of something. Mum's usually pretty fair, to be honest, but she's a bit *do-it-by-the-book*.'

'They're well matched then! But at least she lets you do your own thing.'

'Up to a point. I mean, I'm not meant to walk home alone anymore in case someone kidnaps me!'

'You are joking?'

'Well, I exaggerate, but she'll be here to pick me up in a minute. It's worse since poor Winston got poisoned. Anyway, what d'you think of today's new piece? Pretty tricky, I think, almost Tommy Smith stuff. How's the clarinet part?'

Katy was itching to tell him about the letters and calls, but she'd sworn to Ralph she wouldn't tell anyone. So she didn't. Seeing her mother's car pull up outside, she rose. 'Bye, Neil.'

Eighteen

The Inspiration of Teeth

Milngavie

It was a tricky time for gardening, October. A month to clear the old and make way for the new. Like life really. In his Milngavie garden, Brian Nesbitt gingerly bent forward to rake fallen leaves from under the shrubs. Progress: he couldn't have done that a few months ago. He had decided however, that he'd best get someone in to do the hedges and heavy stuff his back wasn't up to. Those gladioli and dahlias needed lifting. Perhaps he could ask Jimmie, the surgery gardener?

Brian noticed the shaking had started again as sweat trickled from his forehead. But it was getting less, and the cramps and itch had gone. Down to only six a day this week. Well, eight yesterday with Buggerlugs stressing him out with more odd orders. He was sick of it. But he was hoping that if he could keep to bringing home only enough tablets for a bedtime and breakfast dose and leave the rest locked up at work, he could keep on track. Pulling himself up, he breathed in. He was a professional. He could do it.

The veg patch was a sorry sight. His mother would be horrified to see these canes of grey and yellowing stems hung with shrivelled, rotten and blackened beans. Compost heap material. Much like himself a few months ago. The grass had been a challenge as the mower had packed up at the first push and he'd had to strim it all, but he'd been careful not to twist his back again. The last thing he needed was to get more pain and need more analgesics.

Since Jenny's wedding in June he'd done zilch in the

garden. Just as well his sister was now in South Shields. Nagging about his habit hadn't helped it. He'd thought the only other folk who'd known of his addiction were Buggerlugs and Charlie MacTavish, but Charlie had said Toby and Beth Semple knew. He hadn't twigged Charlie's intention when he'd asked him out for a drink, but he'd been glad in the end: it'd been a relief to be able to confess, spilling it all out after a few whiskies. He'd cried. Embarrassing. If Charles had spilled the beans it would have been career curtains, but he wasn't like Buggerlugs Goodman, he'd wanted to help, got the counsellor. Pity the wake-up call had come too late to avoid him being shackled under Goodman. Charles didn't know the half of it. But his confidential counsellor had been a great support. He had worried that Beth might 'shop' him. Perhaps involving the Health Board had been petty, but he'd found it satisfying to have her hassled. Pity they'd found nothing untoward on her computers. His own 'cleaned' patient records now graced Kilnglass's computer system. And his old smashed hard drive was in the municipal dump in Possil.

It had been a relief to be able to join Charles's list for legit, gradually reducing scripts to wean him off. Goodman hadn't been pleased, knowing he could no longer add lies in his records as fuel for more blackmail. Difficult to predict what he'd do when he discovered his victim was becoming clean and less malleable. A flower bed beside the road caught his eye. The roses looked awful: tatty, mildewed and black-spotted. Was it worth spraying them this time of year? Bollocks, he didn't have any insecticide left. Bloody Goodman.

'Afternoon, Doctor!'

Brian paused, annoyed. That blithering idiot from Number 2 was standing at the gate with his ludicrous bloody dachshund that dug up his tulips last year. Shit, it had slipped its lead and was running up his path, barking and scampering.

'Stop!' As the low-slung dog dived for his ankles, he aimed a kick at it. 'Get this fucking dog off me!' He hated dogs.

'Leave my dog alone, you bastard!' yelled Torquil McLeod, adding an aside in Gaelic before rushing in to pick up his dog.

Brian shouted after him 'You should keep that little rat under control!'

It was only three weeks since he was last bitten. A bloody Rottweiler in the high flats. Geronimo, stupid name for a dog. Definitely the largest and scariest he'd encountered as a GP. He'd begun wondering if dogs like that were actually allowed in those flats? Might be worth a letter to the council. Surprising how much notice was taken of anonymous complaints. He'd heard the Social caught most benefit fraud wasters from tip-offs. His ankle still ached. The Geronimo wound had turned septic. Dogs were a health hazard. If he had his way, they'd all be put down. Those bones were a good idea. Cheap from the butcher's, too.

His phone rang.

'Hello, Jackie! No, I'm not busy tonight.' He listened, laughing. 'Great, see you at eight then.' He'd been neglecting her. Time to get back in the social swing. A night in town boozing would perk him up. No point in becoming a monk. He headed in for a shower.

*

I was dashing out of the supermarket in heavy rain, and she was a couple of parking lanes away, but it was definitely Mary. She was getting into a Fiesta driving seat as a tall thin male climbed into the passenger side. If that was her controlling, abusive husband, he wasn't the rugby-like bloke from Charles's story. But as I know from Wendy, bullying doesn't need to be physical. Mary couldn't have seen me and was well away by the time I'd struggled out to my Escort, filled my boot and returned the wonky trolley back to its bay. Squelching to the car, I wondered whether indeed that loose-limbed figure hadn't been younger than a husband. A son or nephew perhaps? I drove off.

At the surgery, I hung up my dripping coat and went for a cuppa before evening surgery.

'All right, Beth?'

'Yes, Charles.' I sat with my tea, the last bourbon biccie, and a pile of letters for signing.

'By the way, Beth, without elaborating too much, I think I'm on top of your Brian problem. He's on a programme. Doing well.' Charles seemed pleased with himself and in a particularly good mood. 'And another thing. That son of Senga Lester, Martin, has joined Rotary. He's a probationer solicitor with Jim Jenkins who brought him along. Nice lad. He mentioned how he'd thought Goodman kind when he came to the house after Senga died to take away her old pills and inhalers to save him the trouble of disposing of them, but now he's incandescent as he thinks Goodman gave her some experimental drug. Do you know anything about that? He's thinking about suing.'

I told him about the tea caddy pills now in my cupboard, which I suspected was what Goodman had really been after. 'Never got around to telling you about them with everything that's been going on. They are a drug called Rubeniclast, and I've heard they can cause serious side effects. Ralph's looking into it.'

'Heavens, is there no end to the problems connected with Goodman? Maybe it's as well we're not in a rota with him after all!'

I couldn't believe what I was hearing: such a change of tune! I told him also about Gordon's patients, the Jane 'fake-the-form' carry-on, Conor's involvement, and the reunion debacle. He looked amazed.

'By God, Beth, you don't half know some rum folk!' He took out a cigarette and lit it.

'Charles, what are you doing? You know you can't smoke in here!' I'd never seen him with a cigarette.

'Sorry, I keep some in here to remind me I've kicked it.' He patted his inside pocket. I smothered a giggle as he blushed like a shame-faced schoolboy, though he still took quite a few heavy draughts before stubbing it out in the sink and burying it in the bin under paper towels. I opened the window.

'Should I get you some patches?'

'Oh, it's just been some day. There's another Goodman problem.'

'Oh Lord, not sure I can take any more.'

'There's a friend of Gwen's from the Church.'

I sipped my tepid tea. 'How is Gwen?' I loved his wife, a stalwart of Northwood Parish Church, its first woman elder, its Sunday School manager and Women's Guild secretary.

'Gwen's not so good. The Saturday morning of your reunion weekend, she went to see her friend Olive Crawford – a lady well into her seventies – about some Sunday School stuff and found her looking terrible. Olive said she had flu and that Dr Goodman had given her an injection the night before, then came back again that morning and gave her another. Gwen went to make her a cup of tea but when she returned, Olive was unconscious. She phoned an ambulance, but Olive stopped breathing so she gave her CPR. She was upset that she mightn't have done it properly since she'd been away from nursing for ten years, but I'm sure she did her best. As the ambulance guys pronounced Olive dead, Goodman arrived. He bustled Gwen on with her coat, practically pushed her out of the house, saying not to worry, he'd phone the daughter and the undertaker. Then, at the door, he suddenly stopped and said, 'Sorry for your loss,' and 'Wasn't she a lovely woman?' Gwen said he was totally weird. She hasn't shut up about it since. I don't know what to make of it. We've known Olive for years. She used to babysit for us. We're both cut up, but I'm baffled. I mean, what drug would you inject for flu – and twice?'

'I can't think of anything. Did she say what symptoms Olive had?'

'She'd been tired, had a bit of a cough when she went to the surgery. On the way home on Friday she'd felt dizzy and had palpitations. After Goodman's second early morning jab, she'd felt anxious and nauseous. Gwen said she looked ashen, sweaty and trembling. She'd thought Olive was hypoglycaemic and needed hot, sweet tea.'

'Could it have been a coronary?'

'Exactly what I said, but Gwen says she didn't have chest or jaw pain and didn't 'look' like an MI. Remember, she was a coronary care sister for years. But it's been thinking about Goodman's actions and manner which has upset her most.'

'Why exactly?'

'She thought he didn't look fazed, like he'd expected to find Olive dead. And she saw no reason for him to have come that Saturday morning without being called. Olive thought it nice he'd come to check on her, but I agree with Gwen. There was no clinical rationale for it. She hadn't been ill enough to merit another house call. And most of all, if I'd found a patient dead, I'd have been a bit upset, wouldn't you?'

'Sure.' It made no sense to me, either. Like so many other current questions.

'Also, Olive's daughter Angela, who lives in London, has come up. She phoned Gwen yesterday about the funeral. Angela said that Olive had been so taken with Goodman's services that she'd changed her will. On Olive's dressing table, she found a codicil benefiting him. Her family lawyer says it's kosher, though Angela thinks it's funny her mother never mentioned it. Seems Olive was minted.'

'So how much does Goodman get?'

'Five thousand pounds, apparently. How much have you ever been left by a patient?'

'Nothing, apart from grateful thanks in a press death acknowledgement! But I thought we weren't meant to accept bequests, especially if there's a cremation. Doesn't the form ask if you have any pecuniary interest in the death of the deceased?'

'Yes, of course. Well, the only good thing, as far as I'm concerned, is that Angela isn't having Olive cremated. It's a burial in Maryhill in the family plot.'

'Did he try to push cremation?'

'No idea. I have been dithering all week about phoning the Fiscal, it's a big step.'

'Charles, I think maybe you should. You could mention the Senga thing too.'

'The funeral's tomorrow. Beth, I know it's your half day, but Gwen wondered if you'd go with her? Her two best friends are away, and she's scared of seeing Goodman again on her own. Think she's worrying unnecessarily. It'll be a big funeral. All the great and good of the Kirk will be there.'

'Don't think I'll be much help – I'm not keen on seeing him either! But OK.'

'Thanks. It's at two. Gwen phoned Dawson's to check, but I see it's in the *Evening Times* tonight. I owe you one, Beth. I'd go but the auditors are coming.'

As I left, he was lifting the phone. If the funeral was tomorrow, a death certificate must have been issued. I wondered what Goodman had put? Consumed by curiosity as usual, I decided that after the funeral, I'd pop into Dawson's. Monty would know.

*

It was so busy we had to sit at the front behind the seats

reserved for the funeral party. Northwood was a large parish church, its rich carpet and pew cushions testimony to its well-heeled congregation. Being Church of Scotland, the décor was simple, but the carving was beautiful, as were the stained-glass windows, the brass lightshades with filigree crosses and the sparkling embroidered altar linen.

We arrived late as Gwen had faffed about anxiously looking for her specs, purse and hanky, all of which she knew she'd had a minute before. Eventually, I got her into her coat and out. We'd had to park well along the road as the church car park was full. Olive had obviously touched a lot of lives. Gwen steadied up as we walked in.

Going down the central aisle, I scanned the assembled throng and was pleased to see no sign of Goodman. Gwen smiled and nodded when I told her. I was dying to hear her version of what happened to Olive, but this wasn't the time. A coffee next day was my plan. I felt an annoying twinge in my left upper jaw. This wasn't the time for toothache. And I'd no paracetamol with me. The organ started playing *I to the Hills Will Lift Mine Eyes* as the coffin entered draped in creamy lilies offering a beautiful scent as it passed. Six strong men bore it and family members walked behind. A tear-stained young woman touched Gwen's arm in passing: Angela?

The service was touching. The minister spoke at length about how much Olive would be missed. The readings were about love and service. We sang the 23rd Psalm. One of her grandsons delivered an emotional tribute, mentioning her generosity, her Land Army days, her tireless work for the church and overseas mission charities. The sermon exhorted us to 'Fear no evil' and then the organist played *By Cool Siloam's Shady Rill*. Surely a christening hymn? I felt it was fine singing about how 'fair the lily grows' but thought 'the lily must decay' wasn't a good metaphor for a funeral, though Gwen later explained it was Olive's favourite. As the last organ chord faded, I looked up above the altar at the blue stained-glass Jesus, arms outstretched, hovering over Galilee like Dali's *Christ of St John of the Cross* in Kelvingrove. At that precise moment, the lowering winter sun pulsed a flash of light through the prism of a lower clear glass pane into my eyes and I had to turn away as the congregation bowed heads for the benediction. That was when I saw him. Across the aisle at the end of the row behind, Goodman sat erect, eyes wide open, staring ahead, a satisfied smile upon his face. At the low cadence of the final 'A-a-a-a-men,' he bowed his head briefly to synchronise lifting it with the rest of the congregation. I knew he'd killed her.

Fortunately, by the time Gwen had blown her nose and collected her bag, brolly and order of service, he'd gone. I didn't mention him as we filed out. At the greeting line in the vestibule, Angela insisted we go back to the house for the wake. We walked up the road to it, fearful there'd be nowhere else to park.

This was another lovely house, like Jean's, but with less high-end art. The two ground floor reception rooms had been made into one by rolling back folding wooden doors. Waitresses handed out alcohol and sausage rolls. I found a seat for Gwen, who was feeling shaky, and sought out a cup of tea for her rather than the proffered sherry or whisky. On the way, I met many people I knew. Patients, parents of the girls' friends, the bank manager. Turned out the late Mr Crawford had been a bigwig at Royal Bank headquarters. I fought my way to the dining room where staff bustled and Angela was talking to her lawyer, also our practice one, Jim Jenkins. As a girl went to fetch the tea, Jim beckoned me out into the hall and spoke softly.

'What do you think of this chap Goodman, Beth?'

The pain worsened in my throbbing upper left molar. 'I don't really know him, why?'

'Angela gave me a codicil. It's all a bit delicate, but d'you think you could ask Gwen if Olive ever mentioned signing it? I feel I can't ask Gwen just now. She looks really upset.'

The girl came with the tea and I sent her off in search of Gwen, describing where I'd left her. Jim was looking at me expectantly. He picked a silver-handled walking stick from the umbrella stand beside us in the hall and regarded it before he put it back.

'Widows living alone, Beth. Vulnerable, especially if wealthy.'

'I'll ask Gwen and let you know. In all honesty, quite confidentially, I'm not sure about Goodman, Jim. He's done some funny things. A friend of mine died and left him a painting. She'd never said anything about it, even though it was a picture we'd discussed. It isn't common to leave your GP stuff.' I shrugged and tailed off. There was going to be a lot to put into my Diary of Curious Incidents tonight.

Jim looked deep in thought. In his old-fashioned, long black jacket and pinstriped trousers, he looked positively Dickensian, a bit Uriah Heep. I needed to get a grip. As I manoeuvred past the umbrella stand, I had a thought. 'Tell me, Jim, was it Mr O'Farrell in the village who did the codicil? That's where my friend Jean went.' Surely to God, Liam had no part to play in all this?

'No, it was a firm in the city.' He took papers out of his inside pocket. 'Warnock and Tait. You know them?'

'No, sorry. Right. I'd better go and see how Gwen is. She'll be wanting to get home. I'll phone you if I find out anything of interest.'

He went to look for Angela. I found Gwen and took her to the car. My tooth was throbbing. I'd need to try and call the dentist before they closed at six for the weekend. I wasn't good with dentists. In fact, a couple of times I'd passed out, though I'd not told Ralph, being embarrassed. I was driving round the big roundabout at Milngavie when it hit me. Not a car, but a thundering revelation. I knew how he'd killed her.

Nineteen

Memento Mori

As I turned into the Oakfield car park the following Monday, my heart sank. A police patrol car was parked right at the front door. If it had been any other vehicle without a disabled sign, I'd have been straight back out with our 'DO NOT PARK HERE. THIS SPACE IS RESERVED FOR DISABLED PATIENTS' notice. Inside, Constable Teviot stood perusing the patients' noticeboard. Alison was chatting animatedly with another officer.

'Oh, morning, Doctor! Sergeant MacPherson would like a word.' The sergeant tucked his hat under his arm and nodded affably. He was well-known to me as a patient.

'Come on in, Sergeant. Alison, when we're done could you bring me in the mail from my dooket, please?'

'Of course, Doctor.' She beamed. Three days till her Tenerife holiday with IT Dougie. Rumour had it she had expectations of a proposal. Early days, perhaps, but I feared the consequences if she didn't get one.

Lobbing my doctor's bag onto the worktop, I sat down, waving towards the patient's seat. 'So, what can I do for you, Sergeant?' Constable Teviot hovered. He was sporting a fuzzy brown line indicative of a nascent beard, though if he was aiming for the gravitas of his silver-haired sergeant, it was unlikely to confer maturity. MacPherson sat with notebook poised.

'Right then. I had a chat with your husband about the wee doggie.'

I'd almost forgotten about Winston's ordeal. So much had happened since. 'The bone?'

'Seems it was covered with poisonous ...' he squinted down to read, '"di-hydroxy-tetra-methyl-penta-cosa," a nasty insecticide. Comes in several brands. D'you keep any yourself?'

'No. I don't use pesticides in my garden.'

'So, we can safely assume you didn't dip the wee bone in it for any reason at all?'

'No. Why on earth would I?'

'Your husband says it was found it at the bottom of the garden, is that right?'

My hackles were rising. 'Yes, that's why he said so! It might've been thrown over the wall from the golf course path. The garden's wild and overgrown there, so we didn't see it until my daughter searched. We've cleared it out now and are paving it over.'

'My next question is, who would want to poison the wee doggie?'

'Oh, who knows? The vet said sometimes you get spates of these incidents. Perhaps you could ask other vets in the area to see if there's been any other poisonings?'

'Good idea, Doc!' The sergeant scribbled.

Praying he wasn't going to read it out slowly and ask me to sign it, I looked at my watch.

'However, Sergeant, isn't it possible the malicious calls and letters I've had may be connected? Have forensics looked at those poison pen letters, especially the one sent to the Health Board?'

'Oh, I wouldn't fash about them, Doc – ten a penny! If I'd a fiver for every one of them I've seen ...'

'But have they been sent to people who are *also* getting nuisance phone calls? Or had their dogs poisoned?' I put my hand to my cheek: my molar felt ready to explode. 'Right, I'm worried about my family. I think we should monitor my house phone, dust the letters for fingerprints and get a handwriting expert to look at them.' I wasn't sure if my suggestions were feasible, but I'd be on the phone to my forensic sister-in-law tonight to find out.

MacPherson shifted in his seat, looking surprised. 'You don't want much, Doctor! I mean, resources are limited.'

My tooth was on fire. I decided enough was enough. 'If I tell you whom I suspect, I hope you'll look into it, but don't directly say I named them. I don't want to find a daughter lying in a pool of vomit like Winston. Or worse.'

The sergeant blanched and wrote feverishly in his little book. I went for broke. 'You may not be aware, but I have an Assistant Chief Constable in my immediate family whom I aim to consult on what should be done here. Please let me know if you need access to the house for the phone screening. In fact, don't you have officers advising on home security? Perhaps you'd be kind enough to get one to call. Thank you, Sergeant. I have sick people to attend to.'

Constable Teviot was suppressing a grin as he watched his perspiring sergeant rise to his feet with a final question. 'Right, Doc, so who d'you think might be behind this?'

'A GP colleague whom my partner has had cause to report to the Fiscal. I've also had cause to doubt his veracity. Dr David Goodman at Kilnglass. I can't think of any other potential enemy. Perhaps you could liaise with the Fiscal? Good morning. Thank you for coming.'

As they exited, I shut the door and sat down to get my breath. I was buzzing. God, I'd been rude to a policeman just doing his job! But in my defence, I knew it was because, for the first time in my life, I was properly scared. It had taken a lot for me to say Goodman's name outright. After letting my heart rate normalise, I buzzed for a patient. For once I didn't walk out to greet them. A girl in her late twenties came in, sobbing.

'I've lost a baby again, Doctor. That's three!'

I handed her the first tissue of the day. Maybe there were worse worries than mine.

I made it till 3 p.m. with two more doses of paracetamol before heading for the dentist. She was new. Old McKenzie had retired. Mrs Jay was charming.

'I see you had some reaction before to the usual lignocaine and adrenaline jab, Doctor. What happened?'

'The first time, I was just light-headed with palpitations. The second time, I flaked out.'

'Right, so it'll be plain lignocaine then!' She smiled and filled her syringe.

I closed my eyes. She worked fast drilling and filling the molar. I didn't feel a thing. Adrenaline is included in the standard jab, I believe, to constrict the arteries and thus prolong anaesthetic effect while reducing bleeding. Dentistry isn't my field, but I knew my adrenaline symptoms. I suspected someone else had experienced them but not lived to tell the tale: Gwen's poor friend Olive. But what to do? And how to prove it? Post-mortem blood sampling wouldn't necessarily show anything amiss: adrenaline occurs naturally in the body. Was that why it had been used? When I was done, I saw there was half an hour left till evening surgery, so quickly headed over to Dawson's.

Monty was pleased to see me and offered a cup of tea. Fearing my crooked mouth would mean dribbling and ruining my professional standing, I declined. We sat in his office.

'What can I do you for, Doc?'

'What kind of records do you keep?'

'For what?'

'Like, d'you record each body with its death diagnosis?'

'Yes, there's a big ledger. My dad was a stickler for it.'

'Can you do me a favour and let me see it, Monty?'

Gary Montgomery scratched his chin as though he was weighing up the proprieties, but soon said, 'I don't see why not. Hang on.'

He returned with a giant old book with a cover of lovely

watermarked Florentine print. With its pink tooled edges and cream pages of long inked columns, it was like ledgers I'd seen as a small child on the bank counter while my granny did her business. Instead of deposit and withdrawal columns of figures, here sections across the two pages listed name, date of birth and death, address, GP, certificated cause of death, next of kin, disposal destination (C for cremation, B for burial) plus ceremony locus (parlour, church or crematorium). The last three columns named GP signatories for cremation certificates and total funeral fees due, a few in red, possibly outstanding? It was detailed and thorough. I gave a silent prayer of thanks to Monty's father. It was all here, easy to see in one go, unlike on computers. Turning the pages slowly, Monty looked over my shoulder.

'There, there and there.' He pointed.

I looked up at him. 'How do you know what I'm looking for?'

'Stands to reason, dunnit? It's Dr Death. You're the only one who's twigged at his shenanigans.'

'Why do you say that?'

'I think Goodman's rubbish. He's had more deaths than he should have. I checked up his practice numbers and compared his numbers of deaths to your Oakfield lot and Drumlea. You know my wife, Evelyn, Doc? She works at the Health Board and got me the patient numbers. She even spoke to her boss, who didn't want to know, said it was just chance. "Unlucky," he said. I don't think Goodman's "unlucky" – but his patients are. Got my mum-in-law to shift to your lot. He has a name for liking old ducks living alone, so he does.'

I was taken aback but ran my finger down the lists. 'Let's look at the ones I know about.'

He sat down, head on his hand, looking glum. 'I wondered if he wasn't really qualified. You hear about that sometimes, don't you? Like someone pretends they are a doc using faked papers. But Evelyn says the Board checks everyone's kosher before they're allowed on the practitioner's list.'

I looked at Monty with new eyes. I'd valued him as being perfect for his job: kind, quiet-spoken, considerate to the bereaved and a dutiful follower in his late father's footsteps. I hadn't credited him with such astuteness. I felt humbled.

'So, what d'ya think, Doc?' As he scratched his neck under his collar, I noticed a patch of eczema. I should give him a prescription for it.

'Right. Here's the entry for Olive Crawford: cerebrovascular accident secondary to hypertension. Part one cremation, Goodman. Part two, Nesbitt. But she was buried – there's a B. You don't need cremation certificates for burial.'

'Yup, that's happened a couple of times. Like that Spar lady.'

Anila! I turned back a couple of pages. Beside her name were cremation form entries: Part one, Dr G. Part two, Dr N. Disposal: Muslim Burial. Locus, Mosque. Fees, in red.

'Caused a right rumpus that one. When I presented the bill, it included cremation form fees and Mrs Chaudri's brother nearly took my head off. I blamed my assistant for the muddle, but Dr Goodman had told us it would be a cremation. The old guy wouldn't pay up for anything, accused us of cheating him because of the colour of his skin. They've buggered off back down to the Midlands, but I've got his address and we're looking into a small claims court thing there. Trouble was, we'd paid the docs already. I didn't have the balls to ask for the money back, but since last month I've told Kilnglass they'll need to wait till the family's paid before they are. Haven't seen any of them for a bit.'

'Were there other ones he tried pushing into cremation?'

'Well there was that lady whose daughter lived in London.' He flicked back. 'There, Jean Radcliffe, daughter lives in Kensington. Goodman got the cremmie paperwork up and running, but daughter was horrified. He should ask first.'

I nodded sadly. 'Jean was a friend. I wasn't happy about her given cause of death. Oh, and here it gives MI, a heart attack, plus hypertension – but his partner said Goodman certified a CVA, a stroke or cerebrovascular accident. I see he is definitely keen on cremation. Destroys evidence, I suppose. Disturbing, isn't it?'

Monty whistled out long and low through pursed lips. 'What should we do, Doc?'

'In the meantime, could you make a list of the dates, names, ages and causes of death of Goodman's patients? He's been up here three years, I think. Was in Bishopbriggs too. And asterisk the ones he did cremation papers for, but which ended up burials. Keep it to yourself. I'm going to talk to a few people. Heavens, is that the time? I've got a surgery in ten minutes.'

Monty stood up, shook my hand with his right, then put his left one over the top and squeezed. He was emotional. 'It's good to know I'm not daft, Doc.'

I gave him a quick script for his rash. He gave me a hug. Gracious! But it was reassuring for me too: someone else doubted Goodman. I drove back on autopilot. It was too much to take in. A thought popped up. What about the other undertakers within shouting distance? I didn't know them well. Should I ask Monty to speer about?

Back at the surgery, a woman broke her waters in the waiting room and went into labour. My mind had to focus on the living.

After tea, I opened a bottle of red wine. Ralph raised an eyebrow: we don't drink on weeknights. Well, rarely. When I told him about the chat with Monty, he poured himself a large glass. He'd already agreed with my adrenaline theory for Mrs Crawford.

'Wine won't help your toothache,' said Ralph.

'It's fine. Great new dentist! By the way, Sergeant MacPherson came in to check your story.'

'Good. I thought he wasn't much bothered. What did you say?'

'Oh, I lost it! Threatened him with ACC Tim. Not my finest hour, but I had toothache and patients waiting. All in, I felt he just wanted to make notes and file them.'

'My impression too. I might phone Cressie and ask her advice.'

'Sure. I mentioned her too, though didn't say she was the forensics prof at Dundee. I actually named Goodman, said Charles was reporting another case to the Fiscal and told him to check with them. Bit cheeky, I know. Here's hoping the Fiscal gets the police to investigate Charles's one'

'Which one was that?'

I laughed. 'Sorry, it isn't funny really, but there's quite a few now, aren't there? Charles and Gwen doubt Goodman's explanation for her friend Olive Crawford's death, where Goodman acted oddly. And Charles also told the Fiscal about Goodman coming to Ellen's friend Senga's house after she died to collect tablets, and about the ones Ellen found that he missed, the tea-caddy, possibly dodgy drug trial ones.'

Just then, the girls appeared, and the subject swiftly changed to dresses for the Christmas dance. Ralph filled his glass and went to the study to phone Cressie. After draining my wine rather too quickly, I made hot chocolates for the girls and tea for me. In the tea caddy, I found two paracetamol I'd brought down at breakfast for my toothache but then lost. My mind was going. I dissolved them in the sink then wrote up my Diary of Curious Incidents. It was filling up.

At bedtime, Ralph reported Cressie's info that fingerprints might be possible on a clean bone. I didn't get a good night's sleep, being pursued by an unknown foe down a dark lane. Exhausting.

Neil was half-way up the stairs when his father called him down.

'Mother says you've been seeing a girl.'

'She's only a friend. She's in the wind band.'

'What's her name?

'Katy.'

'Katy who?

'Sheehan, why?' He saw his father's jaw relax as he smiled that smile that never warmed him like his mother's.

'No reason. That's fine. Go on up. By the way, your clarinet playing is improving.'

Neil was dumbstruck. A compliment! But he was also worried. Why did his father want to know Katy's surname? He shivered. The heating had gone off at ten as usual: too early on such a freezing night. He heard rockets. Guy Fawkes. Mother had said she'd ask if he could go to Katy's birthday party tonight, but she hadn't found a suitable moment. He was sure her family would give her a lovely time. From the landing, he saw his father stand staring at the front door before going into his study. The lock clicked. Why did he always lock the study door? What did he have to hide? And what did he do in there for hours on end? He'd love a quick peek in that room.

*

On her way to bed, Clara paused at the study door and heard faint strains of Doris Day. A drawer shutting. A loud creak. A chair moving! She jerked back in fright and ran upstairs. Pulling up the blankets, she tried to remember the last time she and David had made love. She couldn't. Sad. Not that she suspected affairs. Still, men had their needs, she knew.

Was he 'seeing to himself', as her late brother referred to masturbation? Did he sit watching those blue movies on that VHS player she'd found when she'd sneaked in after the decorators left the door open? Sighing, she put out the light and turned over.

*

Neil's father swivels from side to side in his padded leather chair. He is unperturbed by the failure of the dog plan. Maureen had given him the idea, telling him she'd met Semple in the park with a dog. She'd also unwittingly informed him that he'd failed, for she'd seen the animal again last night. Had Brian put the bone in the right garden? If so, all was not yet lost.

He wonders exactly what the police want tomorrow. Maureen said the two detectives had requested half an hour but wouldn't say why. Annoying. But even if it concerns a case, he is not concerned. All records are in order and he has had no complaints from relatives. In any circumstance, by design, he chooses cases with few. And incriminating physical evidence is unlikely. Even un-cremated remains are usually embalmed, precluding blood toxicity testing. He smiles, sipping his Bruichladdich. Nectar. He considers watching one of his Dutch movies but decides instead on a journal browse before bed. Unlocking the top desk drawer, he lifts out the leather book along with its little companion Asprey bundle and carefully opens at the latest page.

Case No 35 - Dorcas T: Death Cert: Heart Failure. Ah, Dorcas, a woman of taste! He gazes towards the *Girl on a Swing* painting. From the jewellery roll, he lifts his loupe to inspect a ring labelled *D.T.*, taken when switching those decoy angina pills for the fatal thyroid ones. Having no emotional connotations, this ruby and diamond ring could be sold soon. Twenty-two carat gold. London perhaps?

Case No 36 - Senga L: Death Cert: Asthma. The irritating campaigning woman! Pity he hadn't been present at this one. A lovely memento here of an Art Deco bracelet similar to one owned by Mrs O. The Lester son, Martin, wouldn't miss it. Totally dim. Hadn't followed him upstairs while he'd scouted for medicines. Unfortunate about the tea caddy, but that loose end had been safely secured.

Case No 37 - Percy G: Death Cert: Cardiac Arrest. In truth, death by air embolism. Daft, constantly complaining old man, almost not worth the effort. Ninny didn't flinch at the intravenous injection by empty syringe! Ironic that even air was fatal in the wrong place.

He replaces the jewellery in the roll, and the roll in the drawer. Removing his latex gloves, he places them in the under-desk dispenser and resumes reading his notebook.

Case No 38 - Isabel Mac: Death Cert: MI. He stiffens. Best glossed over, that bloody Semple bitch doubting his word!

The following cases he has listed are provisional.

Case No 39 - Nigel W. He may not pursue this; tame lawyers are useful unless they develop a conscience. The jury is out on Warnock.

Case No 40 - Janet W. Death cert will probably be MI. Mode will be collapse following insulin. The will is ready, in the drawer. There is some very nice jewellery on her dressing table. On balance, best left till New Year when influenza is in full swing. Good cover.

In view of his forthcoming flight, he should get a flu jab himself. He's surprised himself by booking Klosters. The blue-skied Switzerland poster in Thomas Cook's had looked most attractive, quite diverted him from booking a cruise. Though he's never skied, it looks easy. The boy should learn. Useful socially. Klosters hosts royals and the famous. The private chalet comes with a maid. He'll tell Clara and Neil about the holiday tomorrow. They will be pleased.

His finger traces the winding pattern on his crystal glass. He would rather not speak to the police. Doubtless, any concerns raised will have come from inferior minds, but he will be on attack, always the best form of defence. With the increased network and prestige he plans to cultivate, in future, few will challenge him. He can already count on many, but more associates of probity will strengthen his aims. Picking up his Schaeffer, he starts a new list and considers his options.

1: Local Medical Committee. He shall start attending personally, not leave it to Kevin. The LMC is the hub of all Heath Board and practice information. And gossip.

2: Area Medical Committee. Membership here is prestigious. He must book lunch with that flighty Dr Culshaw from the NLP course. A good potential ally, being AMC Chair.

3: Post Graduate Education Days. Book more. Meet, mingle, charm.

4: Apply for Training Practice Status. Shows integrity.

5: Charity Work. Increases community standing. Rotary? Round Table? Perhaps the Masons? Police said to be rife with the latter. Masons look after their own.

6: Police Benevolent Fund. Donate, ensuring no newspaper publicity.

7: Oakfield Surgery. A spy there should be useful. Maureen of course attends practice manager meetings and may be a good source of information. The Semple woman is a thorn in the flesh. Querying that Spar woman's death. And refusing his cremation form. How dare she!

8: Engage a new local lawyer for patients. Seeing O'Farrell talking to Semple in the High Street makes him risky.

9: Ramp up campaign against B.S. No more prevarication!

Adding her as *Case No 41*, he blots his journal, replaces it in its locked drawer and heads for bed.

Twenty

Fireworks

The girls were cross they weren't allowed to light the rockets themselves, but Ralph and Gordon were in charge. They'd been down the bottom of the garden planting them in milk bottles embedded in the earth round our new terrace, and sticking exploding candles in the old sandpit. They'd also tacked Catherine wheels to our newly exposed brick boundary wall. When I'd arrived clutching a new fire extinguisher, Ralph laughingly asked why I hadn't bought him a fireproof suit and goggles too.

'Not such a bad idea. You boys have no conception of health and safety!' I retorted. They might mock, but I'd been scarred by past Guy Fawkes casualty duties. All those poor youngsters agonisingly burned. I had Burneeze at the ready.

Both Gordon's and Liam's lot had come early. Katy's school friends were arriving. Katy was upset Neil wasn't coming to her birthday party, but he'd said his dad forbade late nights during the week. My mum had been cooking all day but was now out in the garden, wielding a sherry, all wrapped up in her fur-hooded coat. In the kitchen, I administered Lemsip and sympathy to a snuffling and sneezing Liam.

'Thanks Beth, you're an angel. I get no sympathy at home!'

'Och, that's a very red throat. Best stay in here and watch. We'll eat inside too. It's bitter. Rain's on the way. They'll be lucky to get through the fireworks.' I made tea and sat with him. 'You should take tomorrow off.'

He noisily blew his nose. 'You're a great doc, Beth.

Everyone says so.'

'Doubt that. Mind you, most patients like their docs, even Goodman's.' He was never far from my thoughts.

'I know you don't like him, but folk do sing his praises. Last month he drove in a pensioner to me who said she'd never had such a caring GP who'd go beyond the call of duty.'

'Hmm, was she making a will?' I grimaced at Liam's nod. 'Wonder how many women have left him stuff?'

'Well, funnily enough, that occurred to me today while doing a probate. Looking back, I estimate he's had two paintings, a silver Georgian clock and two bequests of five thousand pounds in the last year. And that's just from clients in our practice – but you can't repeat that.'

'Any grumbles about him, like from relatives?'

'No. Most deceased had no kids or just distant offspring wanting everything settled asap so they could return home.'

'Monty from Dawson's and I discussed whether in fact Goodman might be,' I paused, searching for the right words, 'actually hastening ends?'

Liam whistled. 'Big jump, that. What did the police say about Charles's case?'

'No idea. Probably same as my complaint about the letters, calls and poor Winston's drama: note and file.'

Katy came in squashing her hands into her armpits. Despite her new thick-padded birthday parka, she was frozen. Mind you, gloves might have helped. The other girls followed. Gordon's Gregor, the only boy present, had tagged on to his dad and Ralph. A double of his dad, he was now a first year medic at Glasgow. How time flew. The boys clumped in trailing muddy footprints. I was glad I hadn't wasted energy cleaning the floor. Winston went from pat to pat, tail wagging, unfazed by the bangs. He hadn't needed John's 'Guy Fawkes' doggy sedatives. Sheba snoozed in the corner.

'Coats, Julia, please!'

She gathered armfuls of anoraks, gloves, scarves and hats, before speeding upstairs. Liam's triplets, unbidden, carried trays through to the dining room laden with plates, napkins, cutlery and glasses, following Katy cradling the tablecloth and heat resistant mats. The food was as ordered by the birthday girl: baked potatoes with sour cream, crusty sausages in barbecue sauce, lamb cutlets, chicken legs with garlic crumb, onion rings and, as a sop to healthy eating, salad and coleslaw. I unloaded the oven contents onto serving dishes which Heather whisked off. Mum piled up garlic bread in a basket and took it through with her salad. I shoved the apple and blackberry crumbles in the oven and poured custard in a pot to heat later. The wind and rain started rattling the windows. The fireworks had finished just in time. Dinner on the terrace would have been suicide. Hustling a sniffling Liam through to the fire in the lounge, I gave him a throw to snuggle into. 'I'll get you some food – what would you like?'

'A wee bit of everything, please.' He smiled ruefully.

'Not dead yet, then?'

Before pudding, Katy insisted on opening her presents in the lounge. Julia had given her a polo-neck jumper. Liam's lot, Nina Ricci perfume. Gordon handed over a box with pink ribbon. Opening it, she blushed. Gordon stooped to kiss her.

'Thought you can never have enough Roald Dahl, even at fifteen. Of course, I've included *The BFG* ...'

Her hand covered a pink face. 'How did you know?'

'Well, I have got big ears!'

Everyone laughed. Susan and the girls selected some of Katy's new CDs. I was relieved they put on East 17: Iron Maiden isn't my bag. Neil's present lay unopened on the piano. Mum called 'Pudding's up!' so everyone trailed back next door. I sat where I was. Katy, realising I was exhausted, brought me crumble. I hoped this was what she wanted: a noisy, happy, hugging and presents night. She started singing along. 'It's alright. It's OK. Don't let your troubles get in the way' while squashing up wrapping paper for the bin. I stopped her. 'Leave that, pet. I'll get it. Go to your friends.'

She hugged me and joined the others. I noticed Neil's flat, brown-paper-wrapped present lay unopened. Shame he hadn't been allowed to come. Before bed, Katy opened his gift. It was *The Water Babies*, obviously second-hand. She smiled. Curious.

*

During the early hours in the second week of November, a warmly wrapped figure parks in Anniesland. It is silent apart from the periodic howls of the wind. He hurries along in the lashing rain, keeping close to the buildings till he reaches the door and glances up and down the street. Thankfully, it is empty at this time of night. He is pleased there are no noisy metal shutters as with London pharmacies.

Turning the key, he enters and punches in the alarm code, silencing it after two bleeps. No point in waking the flat above. Inside, he pulls over the curtain at the dispensary to prevent the computer screen being visible from the front shop, then boots up the computer using the password: *ClockworkOrange1993*. Obviously not one chosen by Clara. Familiar with the operating system, he rapidly finds the target patient record with its unwise 'not dispensed' still clearly visible. It was dispensed, of course, albeit not with a script for the Health Board. He deletes the whole drug entry and checks one other record before shutting everything down. The screen blanks. When Clara had casually mentioned at tea-time that even a label could leave a record, he had to remove it, and all reference to Dorcas. Parting the curtain, he delays re-setting the alarm as he sees two police patrolmen across the road. They pass. Back in the car the clock shows that it's 3 a.m.. Peeling off his gloves, he starts up. It's a foul night. The windscreen wipers can barely cope. He speeds home.

*

Kilnglass Surgery

Next morning, Goodman regards the figure opposite him. DCI Maitland is florid, bull-necked and arrogant, with a pitted, puffy nose he suspects is incipient rhinophyma, likely due to alcohol misuse. The side-kick Sergeant Digby seems wiry, edgy, with busy eyes. Unpredictable. One to beware.

'Tea, Chief Inspector?'

'No, if you don't mind, Doctor, best get on.'

'As you like, but it would be no trouble.' Casual clasping of hands on desk. Relaxed pose.

'Well, we would like to know about a patient of yours, a Mrs Crawford.'

'Yes?'

'Can you show us her records, Doctor? Mrs Olive Anne Crawford.'

'I don't usually …'

'I would suggest, Doctor, that as she is dead and we have her daughter's permission, indeed we are here at her specific request, it would be wise to allow us access to her records.'

'Of course. It's only that we have Hippocratic rules, you know, on confidentiality …' Meeting a glare, he starts typing. 'Let me see, to which Mrs Olive Crawford are you referring? The one in Westland Drive?'

'Westland Drive.'

'Here we are. Date of birth 10.7.10. And what would you like to know?'

'Can you print out her history for us? Every contact detail, all medications prescribed, acute and repeats, in its entirety.' The Chief Inspector meets his eyes.

'You're well informed on medical records, Inspector. What exactly is this about?' He keys in instructions. The printer whirs. Keeping his voice light, quizzical, he knits his brow and looks steadily at Maitland: two can play at that game. He smiles. Nothing to hide.

'There are some questions to be answered about her death.'

'Has there been a complaint about her care?' His left forefinger gently rubs his lower lip.

'We have spoken to a number of people, including a Mrs Gwen MacTavish.'

'And she is? That's not her daughter's name, she's an Angela Smith, I believe. Is Mrs MacTavish another relative?'

'No. Mrs MacTavish informs us she was present at the death. She maintains you arrived unbidden to the house and ejected her.'

Goodman laughs. 'Oh, no, no! I did no such thing! The woman was obviously distressed at finding her friend dead, so I merely suggested she'd best go home and have a cup of tea, and that I'd see to everything, contact the daughter and so on.'

'But tell me, Doctor, why exactly *were* you there? We have testimony that says Mrs Crawford never mentioned calling for you that afternoon.'

'I was worried about her. She was a sweet soul, living alone. She'd called me out first thing with dizziness and I was concerned she might be developing something more than flu, so I went back to check on her on my way home.'

'And the injections? What was in them?'

'What injections?'

'She told a witness you gave her an injection on the Friday evening in the surgery and again at nine on the Saturday morning at home.'

He scrolls down the computer screen. 'Ah, yes, I

remember. On the Friday, I gave her an injection of hydroxocobalamin, vitamin B12. Her blood test showed she was deficient. It can't be absorbed by mouth, you know, requires parenteral administration. Lack of it causes pernicious anaemia, requires a few starter doses, then three monthly top-ups.'

'And Mrs Crawford had this kind of anaemia?

'Oh, yes. Diagnosed that week. Here is the blood result.' He turns the screen towards the detective, pointing out a slightly distorted, scanned-in photocopy. 'We put everything on to the computer now.'

'And the injection on Saturday morning?'

'I gave no injection on Saturday morning.'

'And you are sure this lady died of a heart attack?'

'Indeed. She'd already experienced chest pains. I'd wanted to refer her for assessment, but she declined. Perhaps if I had been more insistent, we might not be sitting here having this discussion. Does her daughter query my diagnosis?'

'Dr Goodman, may I be blunt? Mrs MacTavish, who was present at the death, was a coronary care nurse. She doubts the clinical picture was that of a coronary. Her husband, a GP, is also sceptical.'

MacTavish! The woman must be the wife of that Oakfield GP. Goodman sits up in his chair. 'I am confident that my diagnosis was correct. Mrs MacTavish was highly emotional, hardly able to form a value judgement. And with due respect, Inspector, *Dr* MacTavish was not there.'

'It's Chief Inspector.' His eyes were cold. 'Let's leave that case to one side. Our medical expert will review it.' Handing the printout sheets to the sergeant, he turns back. 'Can you pull up the records, please, for,' he consults his notebook. 'Mrs Senga Lester, age forty-five.'

Goodman's fingers fly over the keys. 'Willowbank, Roman Road?'

'That's the one. Please print everything you have for her in the same way as the last case.'

He complies.

'Now, the problem with this patient is that tablets for a drug trial were found in her home, a drug for which serious side effects have been alleged. We are anxious to ascertain whether it could have been a factor in her death.'

His ribcage is enlarging to accommodate increased pounding of his heart, though he is sure he appears perfectly calm. He offers a perplexed smile. 'Sorry, what drug trial?'

The inspector consults his book again. 'Rubeniclast.'

'Oh, the Heidrich-Holtz asthma drug? Yes, I recall asking Mrs Lester if she would like to try it for her asthma, which was severe, you know. Indeed it was responsible for her death. But she was not entered on the trial.'

'So how come the drug was found in her tea caddy?'

'Ah, that I may have an explanation for!'

'Yes?' Maitland's pen hovers above his notebook.

'There was a missing trial packet.'

'A missing packet of drugs? When did it go missing?'

'I used to keep trial drugs and paperwork laid out on the bench over there, probably unwise, but still.' He shrugged. 'Each pack is numbered, you know, and neither the patients nor we know which contain the active drug or the placebo. While enrolling a patient the next day, I noticed a packet, let me see, perhaps number 266, was missing, yet I still had a blank form to go with it. I was puzzled as to where the pills might have gone. Thank you, Inspector, for solving my conundrum! Now I think on it, I did leave the room when Senga was here. A patient became unwell in the treatment room.'

'What? Are you saying Mrs Lester stole it? A rum do, surely? Why do that and forego proper supervision?'

'Oh, you know women, Chief Inspector, a law unto themselves at times. Unfathomable.'

Chief Inspector Maitland is frowning heavily. Diversion may help.

'I sincerely doubt those pills had anything to do with Mrs Lester's death. And in any case, packet 266 may well have been placebo. Such a sad loss, you know. Mrs Lester was a tireless advocate for patients with her asthma support group.' Who continually criticised doctors. Intolerable.

'So, your story is that she took the tablets unbeknown to you?

'It is not a story, Chief Inspector, it is the truth. I have no idea why she decided to try them without entering in the Heidrich-Holtz trial, but as you will see,' he points at the printed sheets of Senga's records, 'if she'd been enrolled, it would be documented. It isn't. '

'And how can we get in touch with this Heidrich-Holtz company?'

He copies down contact details from his diary. They take them and leave. No word of thanks. How rude.

As soon as they leave, he lifts the phone.

'Conrad, we have a problem. Can you pull patient 266 and destroy that record?'

'What do you mean, "destroy"?'

'Well, the return appointment you have logging improvement ... That's actually a week after she died. Just report 266 as lost. You never received any data.'

'Christ! What's going on? Lost? How?'

'That's of no consequence, but you may expect an imminent visit from two CID plods. All that you are required to do Conrad, is to show them that there is no entry for patient no 266. It should be registered void, as the drugs went missing.'

He replaces the receiver ignoring the barrage of expletives coming down the line. This was a close call. Perhaps he might give trials a miss for a bit.

Twenty-One

Meryl Streep & Jaguars

Next morning in Edinburgh, Conor was regretting that he'd ever got embroiled with Goodman. Nonetheless, he'd fiddled the computer last night. Patient 266 was no longer listed as Mrs Senga Lester. He hoped Goodman was grateful for the hassle he'd gone to. What a fuss. Fudging the paperwork, photocopying a duplicate form in colour, covering the original writing and inserting a 'void for technical reasons' entry. Faking that idiot's spidery writing was risky, but better than chancing Lester being reported as 'symptoms ameliorated' when in fact she'd been six feet under for a week. He was worried Goodman might have falsified other patients, skewing the trial results. And after Jane had demanded Gordon Tindall's Kirkintilloch patients be re-instated with their adverse effects, the results were now a mess. Jane was the limit. It'd been her idea to leave them out in the first place, arguing they were just exceptions! He'd never understand women. After that fracas at the reunion, he'd thought he'd patched things up, convinced her the GMC thing was a stitch-up, but now she knew all about this data stuff and his past, he was uneasy. She wouldn't tell him who'd spoken to her at St Andrews, but he suspected Wendy or Beth. Bitches. The phone rang: his secretary with more 'good' news.

'The police are here to see you, Mr Towie.'

The door opened to admit Laurel and Hardy. Flashing warrant cards, they sat down and nodded. Hardy pointed to himself then skinny Laurel.

'Chief Inspector Harold Maitland and Detective Sergeant

Digby from Glasgow CID.'

'Glasgow? What's brought you all the way through to Edinburgh?'

As if he didn't know.

*

On St Andrew's Day, the last day of November, Ralph informed me over breakfast that Scotland shares its patron saint with Cyprus, Greece, Romania, Russia, Ukraine, Bulgaria, Colombia and Barbados.

'Is that a fact? Now aren't you a fount of all knowledge?'

'No, but *The Herald* is! I'll take haggis for tea, if you like.'

I promised him a freshly shot one, not frozen. He's English, thinks it's an animal. On the way into the surgery I got the haggis, neeps and tatties but not the booze. Too early for Scotland's restricted alcohol laws. I hoped I'd get away early enough to buy it on the way home. But today no patient was simple.

Mrs Sadie Nuttall was well-named, a female Mr Green. Tired, I gave in to her requested laxatives for 'severe bowel blockage'. She didn't have blocked bowels, but coincidentally, half an hour later I saw someone who did and needed admission. Then came a sprained ankle needing strapping and a spotty teen needing a long reassuring chat that acne wasn't the end of the world. Afternoon surgery ran late. Finally, as I clicked 'save' on the last patient record, Alison rang through.

'Sorry, Doc, there's an extra. A temporary resident. Says she knows you.'

I sighed. TRs usually take longer. 'Send her in. '

I was packing my bag, back to the door, when a voice stopped me.

'Sorry, Beth. I'm not really a patient, but I didn't know

how else to get to see you.'

I turned and sat down abruptly. 'Jane? What are you doing here?' She looked different: smart navy suit, white shirt, mid-heel courts. Less Julia Roberts, more Meryl Streep.

'I'm off to a new job with Pfizer in Kent, but I wanted to come and thank you.'

'Thank me?'

'For being so brutally honest. When you grabbed me in St Andrews, I was about to make the worst decision of my life.'

I stared at her. 'It's his day today, St Andrew.' Hardly relevant, but I was tired.

'Is it? Well, anyway, I checked up and found Conor was as bad as you said. Worse – that botched surgery, the womanising! And what he's up to now with drug trials is nothing short of criminal. I've copied as many computer files as I could and photocopied some of the proformas.'

'What are you going to do with it?'

'I think I'll go to the Safety of Medicines Committee, but the police may need involved. I intend taking advice from my brother who's a lawyer in London. It's tricky. I've worked hard to get where I am, and I don't want to ruin my career completely,' she sighed, 'but I'll probably have to admit to a few things I'm not proud of.'

'I'm sure whistle-blowing will go in your favour.'

'I hope so. But I just had to thank you.'

'I'm glad you are free of Conor now. He's toxic.'

'And that asthma drug mustn't go to market. I won't hang about, don't worry. But so far, all I've done is tried to appeal to Con's conscience to stop him quashing the bad results.'

'Good luck with that. I don't think he has one!'

'Anyway, I mustn't keep you. It's awful, all this, isn't it?' She stood up and started sobbing, I gave her a hug and a hanky, my stock in trade. She left. Ralph wasn't going to believe this.

Ellen finished the day by coming in to plonk down an official letter of complaint from Mr Green, irate he'd being kept waiting for 'hours' and refused 'essential medication' last week. I left it and headed for Asda where booze would now be legally on sale. It might be Tuesday night, but mine was a bottle of red. At this rate, I'd be heading for alcoholism any time soon. Anyway, what wine went best with haggis?

Christmas was rushing towards us, and on Thursday 9th December, the school was looking very festive. I'm normally not a fan of *In the Deep Midwinter*, but Katy's sax solo at the Christmas concert was pure, controlled, and sweet. So proud. Julia's vocal solo during the choir finale of *White Christmas* was terrific, earning thunderous applause. Mum, Ralph and I were 'dead chuffed', as they'd have said in my Govan childhood. Out in the lobby, Julia appeared within minutes but there was no sign of Katy.

'What is she doing? How long does it take to put an instrument in a case and grab your coat?'

Ralph was pacing, anxious to be home as it had started snowing. And he had an early start for Edinburgh in the morning. Julia went to see where Katy had got to.

Some kids with instrument cases appeared. The waiting parent crowd thinned. I finally spied Julia shepherding Katy down the corridor with her singing, smiling, laughing gang. Neil give her a chaste peck on the cheek and detached himself to head towards the side playground door where he joined a woman looking pleased to see him. As she patted his back and stroked his cheek, I realised I knew her. Mary! It must have been Neil I'd seen her with in the supermarket car park. But as she had a different surname, she couldn't be his mother. Aunt perhaps? Or nanny? A pity his father hadn't come to support him, but at least someone appreciated his hard work. Neil's clarinet solo had been splendid. By the time we'd done our congratulatory hugs with Katy's lot, Neil and his companion had gone. We ran, heads down, through the blizzard to the car.

Next morning, the girls piled into the car for school. The snow had dissolved to mild slush, making me worry about Ralph getting safely to Edinburgh. When the radio had announced the train service to the capital was subject to delays, he'd decided to drive. Switching on my engine, I started backing out of the drive, turning on the gravel to face the right way. There was more resistance than usual, so I checked I hadn't partially left on the handbrake, an occasional failing of mine. Could the brakes have seized? I tried accelerating to swing around out onto the road and got a flop, flop sound followed by scraping metal screech as I hit tarmac. I managed to 'sort-of' park and got out. My front tyre was completely deflated with the alloy wheel rim resting on the road. I gave a silent scream. Julia had got out of the passenger seat and came round.

'You've got a flat, Mum.'

'I know, I can see it!'

She walked round the back of the car. 'Oh, they're all flat! How did that happen?'

'Well, something tells me it wasn't an accident.' Slamming the car door, I marched back up the path.

Mum was polishing the hall table. 'What's wrong, you forgotten something?'

'No. Some bloody moron has slashed my tyres!'

She went back to the kitchen and put on the kettle. Standard mum.

I phoned for a taxi, then Reg Anderson at the local garage. 'I've had all my tyres slashed, Reg. Can you replace them at the house and leave the buggered ones in the garden so I can have the police look at them?'

'Sure thing, Doc. You do know your insurance probably won't pay?'

'Really? Shit! Sorry, but thanks. I'll leave you a cheque for the tyres.'

He insisted it would do later, but I headed into the kitchen, miraculously located the cheque book in the kitchen paper mountain, signed a blank one, gave it to mum with the keys and went out to the shivering girls on the pavement. As the taxi drew up, Gertie next door passed with Spencer, her bully mastiff, as Katy calls him. Winston keeps well out of his way, sensing that he's just about the right size as a snack for Spencer. The bulldog growled as usual. Gertie doesn't often stop to chat when she's being taken for a walk by Spencer, but today she had gossip to impart. I could see it in her eyes and quivering smile.

'You had a visitor while you were out last night, Doctor. Did he get you? Or leave a note?'

'No, but someone slashed my tyres.'

'Gracious me! Oh, I don't think it would have been that man, he looked very respectable. Nice big car, silver. A Mercedes? Shiny animal on the bonnet. Parked at Professor Glen's.'

I was disappointed: Goodman's car was black. And she was clueless: Mercs didn't have bonnet animals. But why would someone park three doors up? It wasn't as if there were many cars left out on this road. Everyone had a driveway.

'Sorry, no idea who that was, but I'm reporting the vandalism to the police. They'll probably want to speak to you if you were at home.'

'The Police? Oh dear!' She stepped back as if she'd been stabbed. A great witness she'd be! As she scurried off, Bully Mastiff growled, farting loudly as he went. Thankfully, at that point our taxi arrived.

After dropping off the girls, I arrived at the surgery twenty minutes late. The waiting room exuded mumbling grumbles, disapproving glares, and some pointed looks at the clock and then me. There could have been many reasons beyond my control for being late, like an emergency, but then, everyone's time is precious. Ellen followed me into my room with the mail and reports. Dumping my bag, I switched on the computer before taking off my big coat.

'Morning, Doctor. Not like you to be late. Everything all right? I was just about to phone.'

'No, it bloody isn't. Some maniac slashed all my tyres and I had to get a taxi.'

'Oh dear! That's odd. Dr Charles has just told me Mrs MacTavish found the same thing this morning. She's had to swap her Meals on Wheels run with Betty Harper.'

'Gwen too? Now, isn't that a coincidence! By the way, Ellen, could you phone Anderson's and ask Reg to please bring the car here once they've put on new tyres? I wasn't thinking straight. Obviously, I'll need it at lunchtime for calls.'

'Certainly, Doctor.' She glanced at my screen. 'You up and running? Right, first one in.'

Reg brought the keys back at 11.30 a.m. and confirmed my tyres had been well and truly slashed, each in at least two places: a proper job. More annoying was his news about a fresh deep, gouge in the paintwork running the length of the passenger side which I hadn't noticed in my fury to get to work. Suggesting it needed bodywork repair asap, he offered to pick up the car at the house later and fix it over the weekend.

'Are you sure? We could leave it till next week. I could borrow Ralph's car, drop him off before work.'

'It's a deep and vindictive key job, Doc, best get it done. Besides, I'm on call for breakdowns in the snow at the weekend anyway, so it's no bother. Especially when I think what you did for my Jenny!'

In reality, admitting Jenny to hospital was what any doctor would've done. Late pregnancy pre-eclampsia is a life-threatening emergency needing immediate delivery. But nice to be appreciated. 'I'm delighted everything turned out well.'

He produced a picture of a plump, smiley babe in a pram piled so high with fluffy be-ribboned pink pillows that I worried there was a risk of smothering. But I admired Lucinda Anderson, thinking how lucky she was to have such a proud and loving dad.

It was becoming a regular thing, practising with two heads on: one on the patient and one on other, usually Goodman-related problems. Over lunch, Charles told me he was worried too. Gwen's car and mine would mend, but what might happen next? With twenty minutes till the first evening appointment, I telephoned the local police and got an old friend.

'Oh, hello, Doctor, how are you?'

'Fine, Sergeant MacPherson. Well, not really. Someone slashed all my tyres overnight. Anderson's confirmed it was deliberate. My partner's wife, Mrs Gwen MacTavish, was targeted too. I think it may be related to the previous problems we've had. Too much of a coincidence.'

'Well, we had a spate of them before. Usually on a Friday night. Lads up for a lark on the way home from the pub.'

'Oh no. This is different. It was last night, a Thursday, with a blizzard and a gale blowing a hooly. Don't know what youngster would go out larking in that.'

'OK, Doc. I'll send someone to the house in the morning for a chat. You kept the tyres?

'They should be in my front garden.'

'Right, oh.'

'And another thing, there's criminal damage to my car paintwork, a nasty gouge needing bodywork repair. '

'Leave it with me.'

As I went in to tell Charles I'd reported the tyres, I realised that the efficient sergeant hadn't asked for his address. Charles wasn't surprised. 'Typical! I'll phone them too, make it official. Gwen's really upset. We were out at that drug dinner in the Grosvenor all evening. Thought you and Ralph might have gone?'

'School concert. Kids were great.'

'Came back half eleven, but never looked at Gwen's Astra then. Could have been done anytime in the evening or wee small hours. It's bloody annoying!'

'Yes, such a hassle. My neighbour saw someone go up our drive. Didn't find any note though. Weirdly, they parked along the road. Big silver car, animal on bonnet – ring any bells?'

Charles frowned. 'Brian's just bought himself a silver Jag. Said he'd had a windfall.'

'Jags have bonnet mascots, don't they? But why would it be him? He's surely not the vindictive type to key a car. Bit of a wuss, I think.'

'No, can't imagine it.' Charles shook his head decisively. 'Right, patients waiting. The show must go on! Enjoy your day off tomorrow.'

*

Charles didn't let it lie. Once he was home, he phoned Brian. 'Were you in your car near Cedar Drive last night?

'No – why would I be?'

'A silver Jag was seen near where Beth Semple lives and cars got vandalised.'

'Come on, me? As if! Actually, David asked me to lend it to Nigel Warnock, the lawyer, to take his wife for a spin. He's thinking of buying one. Stupid night to try it out. But shouldn't think vandalism's much in his line!'

Charles felt no further on. If it hadn't been for Beth's neighbour, he'd have assumed it was Dr G in his jag. But it was black.

Twenty-Two

What's in a Name?

I was looking forward to a weekend with Henry and Wendy. Since he was to be up for a dermatology symposium in Glasgow as key speaker, Wendy had decided to take a few days leave and come too with Maia and Roly. I took Friday off to blitz the house and change beds. The girls were hoping for snow. It was cold enough. In the morning, I had a leisurely bath and then breakfast with Mum who'd stayed over due to the weather. We were discussing a housework battle plan when the doorbell rang. Mum ended up 'setting to' herself with the duster and hoover. MacPherson and Teviot had come about the tyres. The boy's beard was looking better. I presumed his romance was going well, judging by his cheery demeanour.

'The beard's looking good,' I said. Teviot grinned.

'It's only allowed if you've got a skin condition,' grunted MacPherson. 'He's got eczema.'

To spare Teviot more blushes, I launched into the story of my tyres and paintwork. The gouge out of my lovely Escort Ghia Sport was photographed from several angles by Teviot, wielding a professional-looking camera. The tyres were put in the patrol car boot; I wasn't sure what for. Don't think they knew either. The merits of getting 'fingerprints' in was discussed, but as I pointed out, loads of folk had touched the car and the 'perp' (blame *Columbo*) probably wore gloves. I sent the boys next door to see Gertie.

'Watch out for Spencer,' I felt obliged to add.

'Who's Spencer?' Teviot had his pen poised.

'You'll hear him before she opens the door. He growls.

Big teeth.'

Teviot laughed. He wasn't so bad. I had to relax about the police. They were like us GPs: a front line, demand-led service with limited resources, doing their best.

Wendy and Henry arrived early at 4 p.m.. It's a long drive from Bristol but Roly had slept all the way. Ralph was home early, and the boys volunteered to do an Asda run with my list as the police had wiped out my allotted 10-11 a.m. 'supermarket slot' and I'd had to spend ages mopping up the flood from the washing machine outlet thingy getting blocked by a sock. In the end, Mum did most of the housework, especially eliminating teetering-toddler dangers which I'd forgotten about, being a bit out of practice. The garage took my 'poisonous-if-eaten' dieffenbachia plant, the top shelf received the bleach and soap powder, and the tea caddy the paracetamol. Mightn't have thought of that, pre-Senga.

Mum hugged Henry, her favourite amongst my friends, admired the kids and exclaimed at Wendy's slender form. She then headed off for her bus, declining a lift. She had an evening of bingo at the bowling club. Sometimes I forgot she had her own life, she so selflessly supported mine. I resolved to send her and Aunty Pat to Pitlochry for a weekend. Something else to organise before Christmas. Three weeks to go and no presents bought!

I gave Wendy a cuppa, left her in the lounge with a magazine and the kids playing at her feet, and went to change the spare room bed. The travel cots were already assembled in Katy's room. The boys had taken the cases upstairs and the girls would be back from their new regular Friday café session any minute. From the spare room I heard the front door open, then a commotion downstairs in the kitchen.

I rushed down to find Henry had dropped shopping bags willy-nilly. Apples and lemons tumbled on the kitchen floor amongst paper, catalogues, receipts, carry-out menus and slippery medical journals in plastic wrappers. Up on the work top, formerly the site of my usual kitchen paper pile, sat a triumphant Roly, face and hands covered in chocolate. He'd been hand-printing the tiles and chocolate brownie-ing his hair and was now trying to wipe his hands, bless him, on the tea towel mum had left over her Friday 'treat tray' for the girls. Henry was shouting at him. I suspected Roly's platform for ascent must have been a chair, now on its side.

I picked it up as Julia entered to snatch Roly. 'Right, bath time for you, you wee monster! Nothing else for it.' She tickled him on his sticky tummy. He giggled. 'Might as well get you into your jammies now. Let's go find them while your bath's running.' She swung him onto her hip and was gone.

Henry was clucking about like a mad thing picking up papers, piling them back on the worktop. 'What is this stuff?'

'It's Beth's "I'll get around to it" pile,' Ralph muttered as he filled the fridge.

'I usually do, eventually, get around to it, but lately there's been so much going on. And anyway, you could help. Like, why can't you file the bank stuff? I don't know where it all goes.'

A bleary-eyed Wendy came to the door holding little Maia by the hand. 'What's up, guys? Sorry, I fell asleep. I've been on late all week. Where's Roly?'

'Your son has demolished the kitchen and Julia has taken ...' Henry froze, looking down at his hand.

'Where did you get this, Beth?'

I was spraying kitchen cleaner on the tiles. 'Where did I get what?' I took the crumpled paper from him. It was the outer page of a practice leaflet, the inner pages presumably being in the chaotic chocolatey pile on the floor. 'What about it?'

Henry flattened it on the table, roughly pushing aside

Ralph's neat piles of biscuit and oatcake packets assembled ready for the larder. 'Dr Death, that's him.' He put a finger on the leaflet front page. There were three photos, each with a name, place, and year of graduation underneath.

'Think I picked it up in Kilnglass Surgery the day Goodman asked me to do that fateful cremmie. Must've been kicking about in my bag and got emptied one day into the pile. But it can't be Harry Tait, he's too young, an Aberdeen grad and never been a surgeon.'

'No, this one!' His finger moved to tap more centrally on Goodman's photo.

I was shocked. 'Are you sure?'

'Well, he's giving a different name and looks a bit different, but I'd swear on my father's grave that he is Stanley David Truscott, M.B.B.S., FRCS.'

Ralph, Henry and I sat down at the table. Wendy had taken Maia upstairs.

'How is he different?' I took the leaflet.

'Well, I think he's had work done on his nose. And his hair is less kinky and lighter. Skin too, maybe. There are cosmetic salons now who do hair straightening and skin whitening.'

'Are you sure it's him?' Ralph peered at the leaflet.

'It may well be,' I said quietly. 'You know, now I think on it, that woman Mary I was worried about? She was called Truscott. My God, I'm a complete idiot. When I saw her with Neil at the school concert, I assumed she was his aunt or something! Though Katy said Neil's mum was called Clara. No wonder we couldn't find a phone number for Truscott – she used their old name to register.'

Ralph was pale. 'Surely everyone can't have changed *all* their names!'

Katy came in. She looked down at the leaflet. 'Why have you got Neil's dad's leaflet?'

Ralph spoke quietly. 'He used to be called Truscott.

Uncle Henry knew him.'

'Neil's never mentioned being a Truscott. He did say his dad was weird. And that once he asked about my surname, seemed pleased it was Sheehan. Neil thinks he watches us outside school, sometimes. It makes him nervous. Think lots of things about his dad worry him.'

My heart chilled. 'Think it's just as well, Katy, that you still have your dad's name.'

Katy was on the verge of tears. 'What does all this mean?'

'It means we'll be having a long chat with your Uncle Tim, who's coming on Sunday with Aunt Cressie for lunch. It was meant to be a pre-Christmas surprise, but now I think it will be a godsend.'

Katy nodded at a puzzled looking Henry. 'Uncle Tim's the Chief Constable in Edinburgh now, you know.'

'Assistant Chief Constable, Katy.' Ralph spoke firmly. 'Now, there may be a perfectly simple explanation for all this, but in the meantime, we'll make doubly sure Susan's mum picks you up from school and brings you here if Gran's in or I'll pick you up from their house. Also, probably best that you only see Neil in the school grounds, Katy. And don't say we know his father changed his name. We don't know if he knows and don't want him asking. Might make his dad angry.'

Katy was white. 'OK. I'm going up to read a story to Roly.' She left.

Ralph looked serious. 'It's all very well that Bristol nurse suspecting him of foul play years ago, and us now, but we have absolutely no proof he's done anything.'

Henry bit his lip. 'It's devastating. What about that poor boy if his father is a murderer?'

I was filled with dread. Not just for us, but for Neil and Mary, or should I say Clara? Contemplating Goodman as a killer who, like Conor, had changed his name to conceal his past, was horrifying. I opened one of the bottles of wine the boys had bought. It was the only thing to do. We finished several that night once the kids were in bed.

Twenty-Three

Roots

August 1978, London, 15 years earlier

The baby is a tiny miracle. He finds himself strangely emotional as he looks at the child now regarding him unblinkingly with the pale grey-blue eyes which had so attracted him to his mother. She now lies opposite, exhausted, sleeping soundly. He has no idea how the birth has been. He'd left them to it. Women's work. He is pleased she didn't insist he be there. Unwrapping the child, he lays him in the small Perspex cot, lifts his stethoscope and listens to his heart before turning him over in search of any small imperfections. There are none. His weight is good for gestation, despite arriving two weeks early. As the baby yawns, he marvels at the pinkness of his tongue against the paleness of his skin. No unnecessary pigment. His life will be so very different. Re-dressing the infant, he swaddles him tightly in his blanket before laying him on his side. Feeling satisfied, he quietly leaves the room without disturbing Clara.

At home, he heats some lasagne and prepares a salad. Naming the child is problematic; they cannot decide. But first things first. He must clear out the spare room and assemble the cot. The room is still cluttered with stuff from the old house, boxes thrown together in haste when they'd sold Kilburn. This Clapham flat is not much bigger in overall floor space, but it is a much better address and in a superior school catchment area. He could have bought something bigger, but as yet, he has not disclosed his wealth to Clara.

He washes, dries and replaces his plate and cutlery. Would be wasteful to use the new dishwasher for one person's meal. He wipes the worktops with Dettol. With a baby coming home, hygiene is more imperative than ever. Indications are for discharge in 48 hours. Everything must be ready.

The spare room contains an assortment of neglected articles and cardboard cartons stacked in some sort of formerly decided order. Boxes, lamps, a bookcase and various items of bric-a-brac lie along the far wall. Most of the box contents will be rubbish, but best to check; there might be something of value. He has brought home a shredder from the ward office which must be returned early Monday before any secretary notices. Sitting on the floor, he pulls over the first box. It holds old welfare paperwork, yellowing newspaper pages kept for no reason that he can discern, bank statements (mainly in red), utility bills (ditto) and receipts. All for the shredding pile, not for the dustbin. He imagines foxes knocking over a bin and personal information floating around and shivers. The neighbours are nosy enough.

The second box holds a surprise. A big brown envelope contains school reports, pictures and stories he'd brought home from primary, plus a programme for a nativity play listing his name as playing Joseph. At the dress rehearsal a teacher had mocked, 'Well, I suppose Jesus was brown.' Even now, his cheeks burn at the insult. The contents of these early memento envelopes are catalogued on the outside in his gran's old-fashioned writing. The later ones are less full, more scantily annotated in his mother's haphazard, childish script. A St Alfred's school magazine falls out, opening to a photo of him in a line-up of fifth year prefects. He remembers giving it to Mother. She had barely glanced at it before asking what was for tea. But she'd kept it.

The next box contains Gran's books: Penguins and other paperbacks. Ngaio Marsh and Christie he'd especially loved. And The Talented Mr. Ripley *had been a revelation. How he'd admired that US conman, Ripley. Someone with a taste for fine living and no conscience about how to attain it! There are a few hardbacks and some never-returned library books, complete with their polythene jackets and rubber date-stamps.* Real Cool Killers *he doesn't recognise, but* The Killer Inside Me *by J. Thompson, he does. Oh, and that book's outwardly genial but privately murderous Texas sheriff. Such a lesson in deceit and cleverness! He keeps back* Real Cool Killers *and consigns the rest to the dumping pile.*

At the bottom of the box lies a curling, black, leather-bound book. He lifts it with reverence. It is his gran's Bible, read by her every night of her life. Underneath it lies a plump white envelope, sealed, but un-addressed. He slits it open with the knife that he's brought for slashing sealing tape. Several letters fall out. As he reads, his hand starts shaking.

Parkhurst Prison
Isle of Wight
6th February 1952

Dear Elsie,

Well, here I am now. Fully sentenced. What a kettle of fish. They say with good behaviour the earliest I can even apply for parole will be January '77. The boy will be a man by then.

I've lots of regrets, and to tell the truth, one is that I didn't take the boy back to Jamaica when I had the chance. I just hoped we could make a go of it, Winnie and me. But you can't imagine how it was when you were in hospital and I'd come back from work to her lying drunk and snoring, the pickney in a right state. Nappy stinking, starving, eating stuff out of the bin. She didn't care. I am glad you are there now. I can rest a bit easier knowing someone's looking out for him.

I don't want no visits. I don't want the child to know his da's inside for attempted murder of his mother. That could muck up a man for life. Mind you, he might think that being done for armed robbery too was a cool thing, but that guard that got shot wasn't me. I'm the patsy. I wasn't even carrying. I've never fired a gun in my life. You know, I never even got the dosh, Elsie. But I'm no nark.

They've got me signed up for more schooling. You know I did well at school in Kingston, had a good job in a bank - so that's how I knew how they worked. Ha! I wish I was still back in the sun and never set foot on that Windrush. All Clint's fault, my stupid cousin. 'Passport to a big future!' he said. Hear he's banged up somewhere too, now. He's got a lot to answer for. Like Winnie. Nothing was ever enough. Thought that one robbery and some big money would help. I know she's your daughter, but it's not your fault. There was no dealing with her when she was under the drink.

So, that's it. I'd be glad if you could send me some letters, maybe even some photos, about the boy now and again. I'd be grateful.

God bless you, Elsie. Keep that boy on the road with Jesus.

Your faithful 'son-in-law' (pity, never did manage to make that legal, did we?),

David Stanley Goodman.

He folds over the letter and replaces it with its later-dated companions. He can't face reading more today. Laying them in the small 'keep' pile, he dumps the old books into a bin liner and twists it shut. He shreds the collected papers before cramming their ribbons into another bin bag. Collecting the assorted useless household items and the refuse bags, he makes several trips to the bin. It's full, so he piles a few into someone else's. Back in the flat, he stacks the remaining unopened, smaller boxes at the back of the hall press; he's done with reminiscing for now. Vigorously, he then Dettols and Pledges the room: skirting board, light switches, ceiling fittings, before carefully hoovering the floor, re-tracing half a hoover width each time he moves back and forth. A carpet stain needs Bex-Bissell, a greasy window streak, newspaper and vinegar, like Gran showed him. Replacing everything in the hall press, he fetches his toolbox and reads the cot assembly instructions. A troubling thought lingers: is his father still alive?

Clara looks exhausted as she gets out of the car but insists on lifting the carrycot from the back seat herself. Always pale, today tiny, blue thread veins mar her temples and lend her skin a transparent quality. Her pale tea-rose lips match her thin duster coat. He suspects she is anaemic, though she's just told him no one has checked her blood since delivery: sheer incompetence! He'll bring home a syringe and do it himself. She'll need plenty of iron for breast-feeding. Though she hadn't been keen, he's insisted on that. She'll soon get the hang of it. Breast milk gives extra immunoglobulins against infection and is perfectly balanced for human development. As a pharmacist, she should know. It also means she'll be tied to the infant. He won't be getting up at night to take a turn.

The nursery pleases her. He's been to Oxford Street, fetched circus pictures for the walls and a colourful woven rug. A mobile of little elephants dangles over the cot. A blue teddy bear lies on the special smother-proof pillow and the bedding sports giraffes. The new chest of drawers is full of things he's bought. She's been so unwell in the last few months. The Mothercare girl had assembled everything they'd need, not just clothes, but changing mats, bags, a *bath, white towels. So much that he couldn't carry it all. He'd had to take the car to the back of the shop for loading. The girl had loved his instant Polaroid photo of the baby.*

'How wonderful, such a bundle of joy!' she had exclaimed.

Though thinking this over-sentimental, he had to quietly acknowledge he feels a warmth towards this tiny form that he's never experienced for any other living thing. Something of his own. He leads his wife and child into the newly prepared room.

She sobs. 'Oh, it's lovely, darling. How extravagant!'

It wasn't, of course: there was still plenty dosh left from Magda. Clara was properly crying now. Hormones. He'll have to ride the storm. All will be calm by six weeks.

'Oh, there's a single bed in here too. Who's that for?'

'I thought it would be more convenient, my love, for you when you're getting up in the middle of the night.'

'Right. I see. Well, perhaps for a little while.' She sits on the bed. He lifts the baby from the carrycot on the floor, and places him into the big cot.

'Why don't you have a lie down and I'll make you a cup of tea?'

'Thank you. You are a great husband, you know.'

'Nonsense. You've become a mother, you need spoiled.'

As he sets a tray, he thinks on his own upbringing. Defective mothering. No fathering. Though at least now he knows his father's name. Yet, he means nothing to him. The only person who ever cared was Gran. And Mrs O'Neill. How thrilled she will be to see his new prize!

He carries the tea through to find Clara already asleep. Drinking his own, he regards the sleeping child. What name should he have? His wife's suggested John or James are mundane. No doubt Mrs O would have ideas. He'll let her pick. She'll like that.

It is ten days later when he pulls up outside a smart terrace

house with scalloped blinds and a blooming rose garden.
Some people are leaving. They look very smartly dressed.
Mrs O is on the step, closing the door. He lifts the baby out
and makes his way up the path. He's never been here. They'd
always met in a café or gallery. But this is the address on her
letters. Having no phone number, however, he hasn't been
able to warn her he's coming. She will love the surprise.
He hopes she's better. Her last letter had hinted at possible
surgery. It can't have been necessary in the end. She'd have
told him.

Mrs O opens the door. No. It is not her, but someone
looking similar. She is looking at him in surprise and then
down at the baby. He is tongue-tied.

'Yes?' She smiles Mrs O's smile. But she is not Mrs O.

'Is Mrs O'Neill in?'

'No, I'm sorry – who are you?'

'My name is Stanley Truscott. I am an ex-pupil of Mrs
O'Neill's. She has been very kind to me, and I thought she
would like to see my son.'

The woman bites her lip and catches a sob. 'You poor
boy, come in!'

The house is colourfully furnished, if dated: chintz sofas,
little tables crowded with photos. Stan sits on a sofa and
looks round. 'So, doesn't she live here anymore?'

'No, I'm sorry Stan – that's what she called you, wasn't
it? She didn't make it. The funeral was this morning.'

'Oh, I'm so sorry. I wouldn't have dreamed of intruding
if I'd known.'

'Not at all. And who is this, then? May I?' She stoops to
lift the baby from his carrycot. 'A boy, I take it, from the blue
suit?' She smiles as Stan nods. 'What's his name?'

'That was one of the reasons I came. We can't make up
our minds on a name. He has to be registered by the end of
the week. I'd hoped Mrs O might help. She was always good
at decisions.'

'Well, I'm her sister and I think Margaret would be delighted if you called him Neil. It was her husband's name, Neil O'Neill. She thought his parents had a warped sense of humour.'

Stan takes the baby back as she rises and crosses over to the piano to return with a photo. 'This is Neil.' The sepia print shows a handsome moustached man in RAF Uniform.

'He was killed in the Battle of Britain. Tragic. Such a shame they never had kids, she loved them. You're one of many she helped. There's a rogue's gallery over there.'

From the sideboard she selects, from a dozen or so, a photo in silver frame which she hands to him. 'Perhaps you'd like this as a memento? I think that's you?'

The day comes flooding back. First day at St Alfred's Grammar. Scholarship boy. Mrs O turning up to see him in, giving him money in an envelope.

'I would like that very much, thank you. I'm sorry, I don't know your name?'

'I'm Dulcie, Margaret's twin. Perhaps you'd care to come again? I'd like that. It will be lonely here without her. We are, sorry, were, both war widows.'

'Thank you.' He is on his feet; the baby is stirring. He hopes he'll make it home in time for the next feed.

Clara is looking out of the window as they arrive, a big smile on her face. The door opens.

'How are my favourite boys? I've had a lovely rest.' She takes the baby from him. 'Now, what did Mrs O think of you, my precious?' She kisses his forehead and looks at her husband expectantly. 'Perhaps you could take me next time you go to see her.'

'You can't see her. She's dead. But we'll be calling him Neil.' He goes to shut himself in the small spare room that has become his study. He notices her eyes register that he is carrying the silver photo, but the baby is crying, so she turns to sit and feed him.

*

Even with their connections, it takes Oscar and Jimmy some months to track down his father, now out of prison and in a hostel in Pimlico. The meeting is brief. He looks ill, terminal.

'It's lung cancer,' he coughs. 'Do you smoke, boy? Best stop it now, if you do.'

'Only occasionally, but I know the dangers. I'm a doctor. A surgeon actually.'

'My, you've turned out well. Bless your gran! I'm sorry I wasn't there for you. Made some bad decisions. Now, I don't want you to think I didn't love your mother when you were born. But later, well, I admit I went for her that day. But there were, let's say, extraneous circumstances. You look surprised – not expecting an old lag to use big words like that, eh? I'm educated now, I tell you! BA in English, Open University. Hoped it'd help me get a job on the outside, but no one'll have me in this state. My family have sent me money. Going back to Jamaica to die.'

'I'm sorry.'

'I'm real glad you've tracked me down, Son, so's I can see the man you've become.'

Stan looks at the big man, sees what he might have been without the dilution of English blood: the thickened lips, wide nose, high cheek bones, the tight curly hair streaked with silver. It'd been a strong face, but now it is hollowing, wasting. He shudders at those hands: large and coarse with dirty extra melanin over the knuckles in marked contrast to pale pink palms. Surely, he does not share genes with this man? It may be a mistake.

'If you don't mind, I'd like a swab and hairs for DNA testing.'

The old man looks hurt. 'I know you're mine, no question. But if it'll help you, boy, then go ahead.'

Stan swabs inside the hollow cheeks. Inexperienced in this, he'd asked the pathologist at the hospital what to do. Ted had got him the swabs and instructions for the analysis. As he plucks a few hairs for good measure, his father doesn't flinch. He looks much older than fifty-two years. How cancer ages bodies. As does a hard life.

'And by the way, you're a grandfather. His name's Neil.' He takes out a photo and hands it over. 'Perhaps you'd like this?'

'Bless the Lord! Well done, Stan. Our name goes on! You've no idea how much that pleases me.' He looks as though he is going to cry. Time to leave. As Stan rises, his father catches his arm. 'I'm off next week. Don't suppose you could come again, bring the baby?' There's a hint of pleading. Memories of his mother flood back.

He pauses. Should he acknowledge that this man may have sacrificed contact for years for altruistic reasons? And he has demanded nothing of him. Stan forces a smile and says softly, 'I don't expect so, no. Good luck, then – Father.' He almost offers a hand but restrains himself.

'Bye, Son.'

As he goes down the stairs, he hears a plaintive cry, 'Memba me, Stan!'

In the tube on the way home, Stan is confused. This must be sadness. It is likely that he's found his father. But found and lost. Soon Stanley David Goodman will be gone. But his name wasn't living on – should it? Later, he looks up the meaning of David. Beloved. How apt. Whereas Stanley meant a dweller beside the stones. How mundane.

Twenty-Four

Cups, Catalogues & Karaoke

Glasgow, Saturday 11th December 1993

The teacup ride was a tonic. Watching a giggling Maia spin round in the twirling teacup of the fairground ride in George Square, I almost forgot my troubles. Three and a half is a marvellous age; everyone loves you, no one hates you, the world has endless possibilities and evil is unimaginable.

The Saturday morning following Henry's startling identification of my bête noire, Wendy and I had decided we had to get out. Ralph was in the study, finishing an overdue paper, Henry was off to his conference, so I suggested the rest of us went downtown for the afternoon to Glasgow's George Square with its massive Christmas tree, nativity scene and amusements. My plan was an hour there, then a decamp to nearby Fraser's store for Santa and coffee. Though the amusements weren't a patch on the old Kelvin Hall circus and carnival ones I'd adored with Dad, there was a Ferris wheel. Wendy and the girls waved from on high as I stayed grounded with Maia and Roly. Afterwards, we all rode the carousel, though its jaundiced, freaky, bug-eyed horses looked like they needed treatment for thyroid disease.

We walked round to the sparkly grotto at Frasers, where a solemn Roly accepted a popgun with silent glare. I didn't think it was the real Santa either, too loose a beard and whisky-tinged breath. A laughing Maia got a doll.

Wendy and I sat in the tearoom while the girls browsed the dress department seeking inspiration for school party outfits. Maia was talking to her doll, Roland slept in his push chair.

'You OK, Beth? You're very quiet.'

'Och, I'm anxious. Bit frustrated that there's nothing we can do.'

'You've always worried about everyone, Beth. But let's see what Tim thinks tomorrow.'

'It's just so terrible.'

Wendy stood up. 'Come on, let's go and find out what the girls have found!'

I hoped it was something affordable.

As if by some non-verbal agreement, the evening's conversation was Goodman-free. After dinner we reminisced about university, our first encounters as naive teenagers, our tutors, the great and the not so great. Henry impersonated some. We were laughing and rolling about as Ralph left to answer the phone.

'That was Cressie. They'll be here about noon.'

'How is Cressida?' Wendy crossed her long ski-pant clad legs and sipped her Coke. Two glasses of wine were her limit these days. 'Did she marry Tim?'

'Yes. And just yesterday he became Chief Constable of Lothian! We're doing a Christmas tomorrow with them, by the way, since they'll be in Bristol with Ralph's dad then'.

'Great news about his promotion! And how is Lionel? You know, you could all have stayed with us if you'd wanted and we could have had him over on Christmas Day.'

'He's frail, Wendy. That's kind of you, but Tim and Cressie have booked into the Royal. We arranged tomorrow's Christmas dinner before you phoned to say you were coming up. The girls were meant to put up the tree this morning, but it's still in the garage. Maybe you could help them with it tomorrow?'

Wendy nodded. 'Hot chocolate anyone?'

Ralph waved the wine bottle, but I put a hand over my glass to stop a re-fill. 'No, thanks. Nor chocolate. I'm off to bed.'

When I went over to kiss Ralph, the concern in his eyes didn't help the heaviness in my chest and anxious jittering in my stomach, nor my brain swirling around so many incidents, facts and conversations. I felt as if the weight of the world was on my shoulders; a cliché I never appreciated until then. Collapsing into bed without teeth-cleaning or make-up removal, I didn't wake till 7 a.m., when I crawled out to muster the girls. Thank God I'd already wrapped the presents and pre-prepared the turkey.

My two grumbly daughters donned tracksuits and set to work. By the time the doorbell rang at noon, the living room was Christmassy (despite Winston running off with the tinsel) and the presents for Cressie, Tim and Lionel lay under the tree. Tantalizing aromas wafted from the kitchen. The dining room bore festive red napkins, crystal glasses and silver candles entwined with garden holly (courtesy of Julia). The roasts, carrots and parsnips were in the oven (Katy) and the trifle (Ralph, his mum's recipe) was in the fridge. The soup, cooked and pre-frozen, slowly melted in a big pot on the Rayburn.

After lots of happy hugs, Cressida went into the lounge followed by small people anxious to follow this new person of interest. Tim held back.

'Right Beth, when would you like to discuss this little problem Cressie's told me about?'

'If you don't mind, let's do it after lunch, when the tinies can play in the lounge with the girls and we'll have the dining room to ourselves.'

'OK, good plan.' Taking a glass of orange juice from Henry, he joined Cressida on the sofa, trapped by Roly on her knee and Maia on her feet prattling about teacups. Ralph gave Cressida a Buck's Fizz. I declined. A clear head was called for.

It was after two when Katy slouched in her chair. 'I'm

stuffed. Let's have two Christmases every year!' She'd scraped her trifle dish clean but as usual, had christened her jumper.

'We might be able to organise that,' said Tim. 'But there's one condition.'

'What's that?' Julia turned her eyes to meet his as he held up his watch.

'You two have to clear the dining room table in 10 minutes – starting now!' He looked down at his watch. It's a pity Tim and Cressida can't have kids. Tim would be a splendid father. I couldn't believe how fast the girls moved. Trays vanished, the dishwasher clinked and cries of 'What shall I do with this – clingfilm or a Tupperware?' rent the air.

'Obviously, they're capable of much more than I give them credit for!' I said.

Cressida laughed. 'They're 15 and 16 now, Beth. I mean, Julia could get married …'

'Oh, God. But she's not the one going out with anyone, it's Katy. And the boy's father is the GP I'm worried about. I can't believe out of all the kids at the school she's chosen him!'

As Cressida looked concerned, the doorbell rang. Minutes later, Katy ushered in Liam. 'I didn't know Uncle Liam was coming.' She turned to him. 'Where are the girls?'

'Sorry, Katy, they're at their gran's today. They'll come next time.'

As Katy closed the door, Ralph rose. 'Tim, this is Liam, an old friend of ours and a solicitor in the High Street.' They shook hands. 'Liam, my sister Cressida.' She smiled at him as he sat down beside me. Ralph fetched a blank A4 pad and a pen from the study to set in front of Tim. Wendy returned from changing Roly. 'They're watching *Lion King*. Roly's already out for the count on the sofa. So are Winston and Sheba, though they're on the rug!'

I laughed, though worried Winston might be sick on the

new Chinese carpet after all the titbits he'd successfully bagged at the table.

'Right then, Beth. Fire away. First problem you came across?' Tim had pen poised.

'November last year, Anila Chaudri. Mid-fifties, five kids. My patient. Seen by Goodman one weekend he was covering for us. A Muslim lady whose son, Antar, was a friend of Julia's. Antar was upset at Goodman saying mothers were 'a nuisance for a boy' and mocked her weight, but mainly he was concerned Goodman didn't check her sugar levels though she was diabetic. My partner spoke to Goodman's partner, Kevin, who thought everything had been done that should have been. Then the boy was silenced by horrible pushy uncles who sold up and returned south without questioning the death. But they didn't pay the funeral bill. Seems Goodman had done unnecessary cremation forms which annoyed them.'

Tim was rapidly writing in a neat, tight script. 'Now, there were others?'

'Yes. Jean Radcliffe, my yoga friend. Lived alone. In her sixties. Very fit. Very rich. Known low BP, gave up driving after blackouts. I found her dead, suggested the police surgeon be called, but next thing I knew, her GP, Goodman, had issued a death certificate and showed the police computer records to prove his diagnosis of high –not low – BP!'

'Records may be faked, you know. We have skilled IT departments now who specialise in unravelling such things. And anything else?'

'Then there was my practice manager Ellen's best friend, Senga Lester. Divorced lady. Not sure of her age. Asthmatic. Found dead at her cornflakes with an inhaler on the floor at her side. Ellen found drug trial medicines in her tea caddy when helping her son Martin empty the house. He told her Goodman arrived unbidden after the death and went around the house collecting old medicines – ostensibly to save

Martin himself having to dispose of them.'

'That isn't usual?'

'No. I've never done it, except for dangerous drugs like morphine needing returned to the chemist or locked up at weekends.'

'So, three deaths you think odd?'

'Yes. Then a gap, seven months, I think. Hang on.' I sped to my bag in the kitchen and returned with my red book and flicked through it.

'Your work diary?' Tim asked.

'No, my Diary of Curious Incidents I started after Jean's death. Here it is – July 16th, 1993, Mrs Isabel Mackintosh. Wealthy widow. Died in the surgery. Goodman asked me to do a Part Two cremation form, his first with me. I spoke to her daughter on the phone who sounded, well, a bit rehearsed, maybe? Or perhaps I imagined that?'

'Are you sure it was the daughter you spoke to?'

'Well, no, he dialled her. Anyway, Isabel had a needle mark in her antecubital fossa ...'

'Come again?' Tim's pen had stopped.

'Sorry, front of elbow, here.' I pointed to mine. 'But Goodman never mentioned any blood tests or injections. Monty, the undertaker, said the number of deaths from Goodman's surgery were excessive for his practice numbers, and several died in the actual consulting room. One such death is rare, several suspicious. I felt very pressurized by Goodman to get on and sign the form, but with the receptionist having said the body was on the couch, and Goodman saying she was on the floor, I phoned the police as the Fiscal's Office was closed. Then I went on holiday to Jersey that night. When I came back, I found no post-mortem had been done and someone else had signed the part two. It was after Jersey the phone calls and poison pen letters started.'

'If you don't mind, Beth, I'd like to leave those aside for

now and stick to the deaths?'

'Right.' I flicked my diary pages back and forth. 'Sorry, Senga was the September *after* Mrs Mac.'

'Right. So, Anila, Jean, Mrs Mac and Senga – that it?'

'No, there was another case, a Mrs Olive Crawford, widowed, in her eighties, who died one Saturday morning in the presence of my partner's wife, Gwen MacTavish. Olive had been to see Goodman at surgery the night before with fluey symptoms. She told Gwen he gave her an injection, but she felt worse overnight. He came to see her again on that Saturday morning and gave her another jab, though she didn't know what. Afterwards, she felt terrible and was pleased to see Gwen, who's a former coronary nurse. Gwen said Olive was deathly pale, having palpitations, and in fact had all the signs I get with adrenaline jabs at the dentist, only worse. Olive collapsed, Gwen called 999 and tried CPR to no avail. Goodman turned up unbidden and practically shoved her out of the house, behaving weirdly. Next day, her daughter –' I looked in my diary, '– an Angela Smith from London, told Gwen the death certificate said, "myocardial infarction," which is a heart attack, but Gwen is adamant that wasn't what Olive had. It was this case plus Senga and the tablets that made my partner Charles speak to the Fiscal.'

'And what action was taken?

'We were interviewed by a CID Inspector who said he'd get back to us. He hasn't.'

'OK. So if this guy is bumping off ladies, what's his motive?'

'Ah, that's why I asked Liam along.' I looked up at *The Lady in the Black Hat* now gracing my dining room wall. 'Jean very kindly left me that picture and Liam was her lawyer. In the course of conversation, I mentioned my misgivings about Goodman, though couldn't see any motive. Liam told me Goodman has enjoyed several lucrative bequests.' I waved my hand at Liam who consulted some notes he'd brought.

'I looked up our records. As far as I can see, we've taken to probate five estates he's benefited from. Two bequeathed expensive paintings, one a Georgian silver clock and two more involved five-thousand-pound sums. A couple of these were via a codicil filed at other solicitors which the family found in their houses and brought to me as the family's usual lawyer. All the women I dealt with were elderly, lived alone and had few or distant relatives. One son grumbled about the codicils to "non-family" but the other women's relatives didn't quibble much, usually being independently wealthy individuals keen to return to their lives. Oh, by the way, once he brought a woman in himself to make a will. Sat outside in his car and waited on her.'

Tim now had a deeply knitted brow. 'Do you have a list of these bequests?'

'I'll type up this scribble for you.'

I took over. 'Also, I think Goodman often pushes cremations, like he did for Anila.'

'What do you mean, Beth?' Tim put down his pen.

'Well he did cremation forms for her – but Muslims don't cremate, and as I said, the family are still in dispute with the undertakers about fees charged for forms they hadn't requested. He did forms too for Jean. It's one way to ensure there's no body for forensics.'

'It's beginning to look like we need to study all his deaths and the paperwork. Who are your local undertakers?'

'Dawson's Funeral Parlour do most. I have someone there making a list of the causes of death, disposal destinations of Goodman's patients and cases where the family hadn't asked for cremation forms, but they got them anyway. There's a few, Tim.'

Tim sat back and looked at Liam and then at me. 'You certainly don't do things by halves, Beth, do you?' He shook his head, shuffling his notes.

'And then there's Henry's Dr Death story.'

'My God, Beth, what else?'

'Henry?' I waved a hand to give him the floor.

'I know of two suspicious deaths in the Bristol vascular surgical ward where Goodman worked in 1981. He was Stanley Truscott then, as I'll explain later. I was asked to see one of the men but when I returned the next day to do a biopsy, he'd died overnight. At that time, I was going out with a staff nurse, Melanie Jones, who said some nurses were suspicious of Truscott, wondered if there weren't some unexplained deaths when he was on – or hanging about like he often did. She reported him, but moved on after her complaint was rejected. I managed to trace her as she's kept her maiden name. She's now on the General Nursing Council and I aim to contact her.'

Tim nodded. 'Good idea. Now, do we have any idea how, when and why he changed his name?'

'No,' said Henry. 'But he's changed more than his name. It's my professional view he's also had plastic work on his nose, possibly also a reduction in his lips and definitely lightened and straightened his hair. All done very professionally.'

'Sorry, Henry, what do you do?'

'I'm Lead Dermatologist for the Bristol Hospital Group.'

Tim nodded, writing that down. He stretched back, elbows out, took off his little rimless reading glasses, closed his eyes and pinched his nose. Putting them back on, he sat up.

'Right. My mind is well and truly boggled. Here we have a catalogue of deaths which appear irregular to a professor, a lead clinician, a solicitor, a GP, and an undertaker. We have a scenario of a man closeted daily with multiple trusting patients, a GP who may not have all their interests at heart. This needs a long think, some background checks on him and maybe a quiet call to the GMC in case there have been any other complaints. As a final thing, Beth, do you have any idea where else he's worked?'

'Well, worryingly, Katy is a pal of his son, Neil, who's told me his dad was a university gold medallist and surgeon in London, then Bristol. His practice leaflet says he graduated from St George's Medical School in London. Neil told Katy he knew his dad had changed the family name before he started school in Bristol, though he's no idea why, and apparently you don't ask questions in his house. They then moved to Edinburgh where his dad did locums before going to Bishopbriggs. My GP friend, Dr Gordon Tindall, says he left there under some shadow. Next, he appeared at Kilnglass and became senior partner within a year. The senior partner Dr William Reid died in the surgery with a heart attack and soon after, the younger, Jack Young, took early retirement. Odd, don't you think?'

'Jesus, Beth, no more! Right. I'll collate this and go see my friend Gary, now the Chief in Glasgow. Thank God this will be his baby. There are so many alarm bells going on here, not to mention the possible body count!'

'Oh, and he might have been at St Jaspers in London too, for he's very pally with our old friend Conor Towmey who wasn't at St George's, but *was* at St Jaspers.'

Tim scribbled this down too. 'OK. Let's keep this between ourselves at present. I'd like Liam's bequest list and your funeral chap's list of death causes and disposals, Beth, when you get it. If anything else occurs, feel free.' He passed out cards. 'I think CID will be on to you all for statements, too. Please also send me a list of the harassment stuff, like letters, calls and so on with dates for them as well.' He shook his head ruefully. 'Well, Merry Christmas one and all! I think I need a drink after all that, Beth, but since I'm driving it'll have to be a big mug of strong coffee before we hit the road. On a lighter note, I've got something in the boot for the girls. Can you give me a hand, Ralph?'

I went to put on the percolator with a spring in my step: the burden was shared. As I returned with the hot drinks, the boys staggered in with a huge box encased in gold foil paper. Tim insisted they open it.

'Don't leave it till Christmas morning – I want to hear what you think of it now!'

It was a karaoke machine. The girls were ecstatic. I have never forgiven him.

Twenty-Five

Whiter than Snow

I approached the week with a lighter heart, knowing Tim was now in possession of all the facts – and vague misgivings – about the questionable deaths. I felt confident he'd do everything in his power to get to the truth. All I had to do was keep calm, treat my patients, and prevent my staff from Christmas insanity.

The surgery was a frazzle of tinsel and Christmas paraphernalia. Cheery carols were an improvement on Alison's usual radio rock, but there was a surfeit of glitter and an excess of nativity scenes. One in the loo was, surely, a step too far. The patients would expect a tree, but I thought we shouldn't overdo it. It is no surprise to me that suicides rise at Christmas: the whole world appears to be one big jolly party, and if you're feeling down or live alone, life can become unbearable. I vetoed some over-exuberant flashing lights as a nightmare for epileptics and migraineurs like me; however, Charles, by way of concession, did allow the wearing of flashing reindeer hats and Santa badges on Christmas Eve. Our staff were a great lot, working tirelessly all year round. I didn't begrudge them their long break this year, lasting from Friday till Wednesday, as Christmas Day fell on a Saturday. There would be a huge backlog of patients by the 29th, which Charles dubbed Black Wednesday, but we'd cope.

That Monday before Christmas brought some good news: Neil and his family had gone to Switzerland for two weeks. I cancelled Susan's mum for the week and was grateful there was no chance of bumping into Goodman at Friday's school carol service.

Tuesday morning, I hadn't even taken my coat off when Ellen appeared.

'A Chief Inspector Maitland insists on speaking to you and Dr Charles today, so I've put all the emergencies on to Dr Gerry at eleven. The Inspector wants Gwen too. I'm off to phone her.'

We met in Charles's room. It would have been like the denouement of a *Poirot* episode, except we weren't suspects, but accusers. Charles, Gwen, the Chief Inspector and I bagged the four chairs, leaving Ellen and Detective Sergeant Digby to lounge against the sink unit. My forearms prickled with pins and needles. If our suspicions did prove correct, and we had to testify in court, the disruption to our patients would be great. And for Goodman's patients, the distress and anxiety about any treatment he had given would be incalculable.

The room was warm. The Chief Inspector removed his coat, looking flushed and perspiring. I gave him a glass of water which he drained. His collar was much too tight: veins bulged in his neck. Poor soul. I suspected hypertension or a potential cardiac problem. He needed to lose weight …

Charles was nudging me. Maitland was talking.

'Well folks, thanks for coming together. The situation is, having looked into the cases you brought to our attention, Dr MacTavish, investigations to date don't give the Procurator Fiscal enough evidence of wrongdoing in either case for proceeding further.'

'But Inspector, I am positive Mrs Olive Crawford did not die of a heart attack. I would swear it on the Bible!' She looked fierce.

'That's as may be, Mrs MacTavish, but we've found no evidence to prove otherwise. A medical referee appointed by the Fiscal looked at the patient's records and believes Goodman's explanation. And after all, he's a well-qualified and experienced GP. He was, I believe, a gold medallist at a prestigious university.'

'But the trial drugs at Senga's? Surely that needs looked at? We know they nearly killed some other patients.'

'The doctor insists he informed the trial people of a missing packet of drugs and paperwork confirms this.' Maitland consulted his notebook. 'A Mr Towie at Heidrich-Holtz showed evidence that Mrs Lester was not included in the drug trial.'

I winced at Con's name. In every muddy puddle ...

'Dr Goodman alleges she took the pills herself, while he was out of the room. Her records clearly show that her asthma had been deteriorating, with falling "peak flow" tests – if that's a correct term? We've no proof Dr Goodman prescribed anything other than inhalers.'

We sat silently until Charles exhaled audibly. 'So what you're telling us, Chief Inspector, is that we've been wasting our time?'

'I'm saying that your concerns have been looked into and we've found no evidence of wrongdoing against a well-respected and, from what we heard in the waiting room, a well-liked GP.'

Gwen stood up, and left, slamming the door. Ellen followed. Gangly Sergeant Digby fidgeted uncomfortably.

I was very unhappy. 'Well, I have news for you, Chief Inspector. The Chief Constable of Edinburgh is now in possession of the facts concerning these cases, and others, which he'll be communicating to your bosses in Glasgow. We are sure there have been an excessive number of deaths in that practice for its list size. And pecuniary gain from some deaths.'

To my surprise, Maitland remained impassive. He now stood square, squat and strong in front of Charles's desk. 'Dr Semple, believe me, if there's something to find, we'll find it. But as of now we have nothing. I'd suggest you let the force work through any evidence which comes to light. I expect we may meet again.' He extended a hand which I shook, a very firm reassuring hand. I suspected he, too, had doubts, though was too professional to say more.

'Come on, Digby!' Like a faithful puppy, the sergeant followed him out to the car.

Charles put on his jacket. 'Seems it's up to Tim, now. Enjoy your afternoon off, Beth.'

*

After waiting an age on an ambulance for a patient, I made the Friday school concert as the first carol started: *Once in Royal David's City.* There is a psychotic symptom called 'ideas of reference' where you think every TV or radio programme is aimed personally at you. If this happens and you hear voices, then you likely have schizophrenia. I didn't hear any voices (apart from the heavenly school choir) but decided I now understood how paranoid schizophrenics felt. Everywhere, all I seemed to hear was 'David.' The carol, Royal David's City, the minister, David Airth, the organist, a David Jamieson. Was the Lord trying to tell me something? I felt increasingly anxious that David Goodman knew I'd complained again about him and was terrified he might come after me. My jangled nerves were reflected in my high-pitched singing. My David-itis at an end, I gathered myself together and swept the girls home.

The weekend went by in a blur. School dance Saturday involves lots of shouting, like at your mother who's complaining about the length of your skirt and excess eye-makeup. Then some grovelling, to get her to mend a hem and camouflage a nightmare spot which has exploded on your nose thus making you an object of pity or worse, liable to be *unfanciable.* Julia was fine. She had a particular target of fancy in mind, though he was, unbelievably, a *David*

McGregor. Katy wasn't showing signs of missing Neil while he was away, but then, the acne drama eclipsed all else. Friend Susan was supportive when dropped off early to allow her parents time to get to a law dinner in Edinburgh. Ralph drove off with the three girls all looking gorgeous and very grown up.

With Ralph valiantly offering to stay sober for the later 'taxi' home, I had a wee glass of wine (courtesy of Susan's dad) as we enjoyed a cosy night in front of the telly. The gaggle of giggling girls, as Ralph called them, were extricated from the school and home by midnight, but it was two before we got to bed. The debrief included who got off with whom and who'd tried to snog weedy Mr Tech-Drawing-Dickson for a bet.

'I mean, Mum, how could anyone?' Katy said.

Someone had hidden a bottle of vodka in a ladies' loo cistern. Some unexplained knickers were found in the boys' toilet. It was racier than a US frat house film, yet these were sixteen-year-old schoolgirls!

Finally putting out the bedside light, Ralph turned to me.

'Aren't you blessed with these girls?'

'If they let us get any sleep, I suppose so.' Shrieks of laughter came through the wall. Not the best idea I'd had, letting them all bunk down in Katy's room next door.

'They're great, you know, and adore you. It's a fantastic relationship you all have. I could never have told my mother about vodka smugglers and teacher-snogging pacts!'

'Well, I have told them about things from my schooldays, like the girl who got drunk and pregnant and how ill I was after my first night of drinking in a pub, hoping warnings will stick.'

'And I hope they're always as honest and open with you as they were tonight.' Ralph kissed me and turned over.

Lying listening to his snores, I worried about protecting them. So many unsavoury people about.

As if to remind me, Sunday morning I woke to a phone call from Tim, off to Glasgow on Tuesday to see senior officers and asking if I could get the undertaker's list to hand in to Maryhill CID. Dawson's would have to be added to my house call list first thing Monday.

Monday morning was mostly well-kent faces with well-kent problems. But the last patient was timely. A young blonde woman I knew well.

'Hello, Evelyn. How's Gareth? And where's the baby today?'

'Mum has him. They're grand, Doctor. Oh, and before I forget, this is for you. Gareth says you're expecting it.' She handed over a large brown envelope which I put into my bag. Good old Monty. I might manage home for lunch.

'Thanks, Evelyn. What can I do for you?'

'Well, it's probably nothing, Doctor, but since the baby I've been really tired. Gary helps, so does my mum – even Gary's tries. But actually, she's more, well, trying!'

We laughed. I knew Mrs Montgomery Senior, a fusspot. But on examining Evelyn my amusement faded. She was pale, inside her lower eyelids looked bloodless. This was more than post-baby iron deficiency. There were lumps in her neck. She was a bit short of breath. Taking blood, I prayed I was wrong. Maybe she just needed B12 or iron, and didn't have leukaemia.

I managed a few calls, had a chat with a Maryhill station desk sergeant and dashed back for a cuppa and biscuit before evening surgery. Charles was sitting hunched and drawn.

'What's wrong? Gerry wanting more time off?' A common source of annoyance.

'No. I've just been at the Braidwoods.'

'That nice couple with the wee boy called Maxwell?'

'Yes. He's dead. Been there all afternoon. Sarah found him cold when she went to lift him for a feed. She was a paeds nurse and tried CPR – as did the ambulance guys.' He shook his head. 'Poor girl. Such a long-awaited baby. And the bloody police? Clumped in asking tom-fool questions. I sedated her, told them to come back tomorrow. It's not her fault. Warm room, no pillows, not overfed, both parents non-smokers. It's a cot death. Adds perspective to this though.' He took a letter from his pocket. 'Read that.'

Warnock and Tait, Solicitors,
31 West George Street, Glasgow,
14th December 1993

Dear Mr MacTavish,

We wish to advise you that our client Doctor David Goodman of the Kilnglass Practice, Milngavie, has taken exception to recent allegations you have brought before the police which have been proven unfounded. I am instructed to inform you that if you do not desist forthwith, he will have no choice but to invoke the force of the law and sue you for slander.

Signed,
On soul and conscience,

Nigel Warnock, LLB, MA, Hon

'Oh, Charles.' I gave him a hug. 'You best get on to the Medical Defence guys. I expect I'll get a letter too.'

On the way home I popped into my friendly local pharmacist, Toby, to get antibiotics for my weekend on call. Perhaps foolishly, with legal guns being drawn, I asked what he thought of Goodman. We were alone, his staff had been leaving as I'd arrived. Trusting his discretion, I expressed my disappointment the police weren't taking Senga and Mrs

Mac's death further.

'Perhaps it's for the best. Mind you he *is* odd.'

'In what way?'

'He orders mountains of disposable gloves.'

'Disposable gloves?'

'We get his stock orders from time to time, but whatever else, they always request 6 dozen or more boxes of latex gloves, far more than anyone else. Does he have some rubber fetish maybe? I take it there's been no circulars instructing a new pair for every patient?'

'Ha, no! Curious. And we've swapped to PVC since that lass went into anaphylactic shock during a smear. Think Latex is on the way out. Hope you don't have rubber shares!'

'Well, I needn't worry if I had – Goodman orders enough for Britain!'

*

His first dawn in Switzerland is impressive. The view from their chalet, the highest on this slope, is superb. The peaks mute from sparkling, crystalline silver to flamingo pink as the sun rises. Everything below is blanketed white and pristine, apart from the black slash of the recently snowploughed track leading up. White is good. Clean. Pure. God-given. He breathes deeply. No pollution here: unlike in his fifties London youth. No murky fog. How he has risen above the chaotic existence that was his childhood. How he has seen the light, followed his destiny! He must dress before Lucinda arrives to make their breakfast. Pity she isn't living in as promised.

The chalet is spacious and spotless thanks to her. Such an upper-crust girl for menial work. Perhaps Daddy's allowance ran out? She is getting a cake for Christmas Day. Clara will like that. At home, they don't celebrate birthdays, he deeming them frivolous, expensive rituals. But yesterday, watching Clara and their son skiing on the nursery slopes, he had reflected on God's goodness in giving him such a beautiful, agile boy. And a stunning, virtuous wife, born on the Lord's birthday. With her slender figure, porcelain skin and refined features, she is his destined mate. Her chosen name is fitting, meaning bright and clear. And David is ideal for him - beloved, gift of God. This cake is not only a celebration, but a sacrifice of thanksgiving. It is exorbitant.

Retreating from his window, he hears only silence. No one has stirred. He dons his new ski-suit and goes out to sit on the veranda. Today he will board a train to Basle. It is a four-hour train journey, but he wishes to ensure the bulk of his accounts are satisfactorily transferred there. Gratifying that Oscar has supplied two new passports for the new accounts. They are also insurance against all eventualities, although he doubts anything will go awry. Nonetheless, he will keep more ready cash at home and ensure all visible practice records and accounts are immaculate. In the unlikely event that new pastures were merited, Basle is the destination of choice, not Geneva. His German is better than his French.

The recent irritations have not deterred him. Indeed, he feels more assured than ever in his calling, and ready to embrace new ideas. Like Plato says, only those of '*high marriage number*' should procreate, and with those of similar *worth*. He knows where he and Clara sit in that pecking order. In the past, Darwin's cousin Galton held flawed eugenic ideas, Hitler's were even cruder, but the weak and impure did need careful selecting out. His own solutions were nothing but admirable.

New candidates suggested themselves all the time. The old, of course, but recently younger, flawed individuals had attracted his attention, and those as yet unborn. He may alter his focus. He has acquired a stock of RU 486. The abortifacient drug sounded more like a Nazi U-boat than a medicine, but had worked well on Rana, his old partner

Jack's girlfriend. He'd spied them kissing in his car outside the station. Handy to keep a camera in the car. A hint at disclosure to his wife and Jack was off into retirement, leaving him in charge. Ignorant Indian student Rana had readily accepted the RU486 as a new two-dose antibiotic for urine infections. The tainted mixed-blood foetus was aborted in forty-eight hours.

These girls were sinful, these seducers of men who spawned hybrids of the pure races that God had formed. Like that Bishopbriggs receptionist, the malicious bitch whose allegation of harassment had lost him the Pearson partnership – she was co-habiting with a Kenyan! He pitied any child of that union.

But for now, he aims to enjoy a well-earned three-month respite from the Work, content in the knowledge that his elderly flock are devoted to him and that he has prevented many facing a senile, shrivelled old age past the Bible's three score and ten.

A voice from behind interrupts his thoughts. 'What are you doing out here, Dad? It's freezing!'

'Looking at the wonders of God, my son.'

'Oh. There's Lucinda!' Neil waves at the figure slowly climbing the hill then returns inside.

Goodman remains sitting, raises his eyes and prays. *Psalm 51:6-7.* 'Yet you desired faithfulness even in the womb; you taught me wisdom in that secret place. Cleanse me with hyssop, and I will be clean; wash me, and I will be whiter than snow.'

Turning to go in, he wonders if hyssop is a poison.

Twenty-Six

Closet Secrets

On Christmas Eve, I put a chicken in the oven, then turned to the day's post. On top lay an A4 cardboard-backed envelope, with 'Do Not Bend' printed in red. That music certificate of Katy's, I suspected. But slitting it open revealed a single photo. The kitchen chilled. My heart stopped.

In any other situation, the photo would have been an innocuous snap. It was a close-up, probably taken with a telephoto lens, and had a red felt-tip eye drawn on the back above the simple message: 'Pretty, aren't they?' The postmark showed Edinburgh. The date indicated it was posted yesterday, first class.

I tried to curb my panic as Mum appeared. Swiftly pushing the photo under the other mail, I asked, 'Did Ralph say anything about being late?' I thought my voice was calm, but Mum took one look at me, put on the kettle, and ushered me into the living room.

'Calm down. I'm sure he'll walk in that door any minute!'

'I think I should phone the police.'

'Ye Gods, Beth, it's only been a couple of hours!'

Her out-of-character swearing heightened my distress. I tried phoning the faculty a third time. No one answered. My imagination had Ralph in an accident or assaulted or in hospital or dead! In the current climate of suspicious deaths and harassment, no one around me was safe. I could no longer contain myself. As I lifted the lounge phone to ring the local police station, I heard a car in the drive. The front door opened. Slamming down the receiver, I ran into the hall, shrieking.

'Where the hell have you been?'

'Hi, pet!' Ralph, clutching a large blue bag, swerved round me to run up the stairs.

I yelled again. 'What are you doing?'

'Aha, that's a secret!' he shouted down. I burst into tears. The girls came down the stairs past Dan and regarded me as if I was a lunatic.

'Shall I get some Valium from your bag?' Katy might be harbouring ambitions of a medical career, but offering to medicate her mother at this juncture wasn't appreciated.

'Don't be ridiculous, Katy!' I sniffed into my hanky.

'You're like, freaking us out, Mum! What on earth is wrong with you?'

Ralph ran back down the stairs, took off his coat, flung it at the hallstand and nodded from the girls towards the lounge. 'Leave us a minute, girls, will you?'

Unusually, they complied. He grasped me by both arms and fiercely whispered, 'Beth, you'll have to get a grip. This is exactly what he wants to happen, whoever he is. And I think it's definitely a *he*. I was talking to Prof Sinclair today …'

'You were talking to the prof of psychiatry about me?' My voice reached a high C.

'No, silly, about the kind of folk who stalk, do poison pen stuff. I wanted to understand.'

I marched into the kitchen, Ralph following behind. Mum had diplomatically vanished. I handed him the photo. I saw fleeting alarm, but then he shrugged.

'Sinclair said it's likely an inadequate male with a grudge or a lonely, spiteful old biddy. What's reassuring though, is that he maintains poison pen threats aren't usually followed up. The previous letters haven't been overly threatening, but this photo is something else.'

I looked at the photo lying on the table, blew my nose and sniffed. 'This photo's not old biddy territory, is it?'

'No. Looks like it's from a good modern camera with telephoto lens.'

'That's what I thought. Oh Ralph, I'm sorry I lost the rag, but it's been a stressful week and I got no sleep last night on call. And then I get this – and you're late!' Ralph hugged me, which helped, slightly. 'I'm not sure what this photo means. It is recent, Ralph, that's Katy's new birthday coat. And it's at the school gates. Maybe we should speak to the Head?'

Ralph looked thoughtful. 'First, we need to speak to the girls. They think you've flipped.'

'OK, I agree.'

My mother reappeared. Ralph stooped to peck her on the cheek. 'So, what's for tea?'

'Beth has chicken in the oven. I've made roast potatoes and lentil soup. We could start.'

'Yum!' said Ralph, taking my arm and marching me to the table. He yelled through the door at the girls ensconced in front of the telly, 'Tea's up!'

During the meal, the girls recounted the week's classroom politics and social disasters. I took nothing in. When Mum went to wash up, Ralph announced, 'Family confab. Gather your ears, girls, we have something important to tell you.'

The girls sat back down.

'Now, today your mum got this photo.' He put it on the table. 'The chances are it means nothing, maybe some kind of sick joke, but we're phoning Susan's mum to start picking you up again.'

The girls looked at it, then at one another, then us. 'Why send a daft photo?' said Julia.

'Oh, it's to spook me. There've been anonymous calls and other letters, like one saying nasty stuff about Ellen, another telling the Health Board I was selling drugs.'

Katy shrieked with laughter. 'My mum's a drug runner? Cool!'

Ralph allowed himself to smile.

'It's sick,' said Julia.

'There haven't been any actual *death* threats, have there?' Katy wrinkled her brow.

Ralph patted her hand. 'No!'

'So, what have you done about it? I mean, can't the police find out who's responsible – like from fingerprints on the letters or tracing the calls?'

'They're looking into it all. As far as you two are concerned, just keep your eyes open and be careful. If you see anyone hanging about outside the school, especially with a camera, notify a teacher. We'll tell the headteacher about it, and the police tomorrow, but don't mention it to anyone else. Susan's mum will obviously know too. You should wait inside the playground till you see her, or us.'

'Och, Dad, we could just walk home together. Or with Neil. We're not babies, we know not to get into cars and all that.' Katy was cross. Julia didn't look happy either.

'Please just do this for us. After school, Gran'll be here every night till we're home.'

'I still say it's overkill.' Julia had her arms folded. I winced at her 'kill.'

'Listen,' I said, 'Ralph and I have made these decisions, so that's that! Loads of your classmates get picked up, no one will think anything of it. Come on, let's finish clearing up and watch Gran's video.'

By bedtime I was calmer, having managed, almost, to enjoy *The Hunt for Red October*. Even if, as usual, Sean Connery played Sean Connery, at least no one in the film was called David. Then, over hot chocolate, we discussed plans for the next week. We were all off, it being my turn to have the days between Christmas and New Year as leave. The girls had revision for post-holiday prelims, but some family time was essential. Ralph already had Boxing Day tickets for the Kings' panto, *Dick Whittington*. We settled on *Beethoven's 2nd* at the cinema for the 27th. Mum stayed over and was as tired as us, so we decided to miss the usual midnight watchnight service. The girls grumbled but we allowed them to stay up for the televised Royal Albert Hall thing, while Mum, Ralph and I went to bed.

Ralph climbed into bed and held me close. 'Stop worrying Beth, I'm sure Tim will sort Goodman. It's even possible this harassment thing isn't anything to do with him. Might be some lone crank.'

'But who knows my ex-directory number and address? OK, the notes to the surgery and Health Board might be from anyone, but that photo? I almost had a heart attack when I opened it! Drawing that evil eye under it too, that's like a voodoo curse – terrifying!'

'Well, it is designed for maximum scary effect. There are no such things as curses, but there are lots of nutters about. The only consolation is that the photo's not from Goodman. How could he post stuff from Edinburgh when he's in Switzerland? You sure there's no one else with a grudge? Some patient or relative or someone you've refused drugs to? Sergeant MacPherson phoned today ...'

'See, he's worried too, he's phoning.'

'He only wanted to check if we'd thought of anyone else with a beef against you.'

'Sorry, but I'm short on cranks, disturbed addicts or criminals. My list is mostly nice young families and retired folk.'

'Being retired doesn't stop people being cranks though, does it?

'Oh, let's go to sleep and make this taboo for the week! I've got to calm down.'

Ralph was now nuzzling my neck. I knew his plan. It was better than Valium any day.

*

Kilnglass Surgery

Early on Christmas Day morning, Brian turned the key in the lock and sped into Kilnglass to disarm the alarm. The last thing he needed was the police turning up. If he had his way, the alarm wouldn't go off in the police station at all, but Goodman was neurotic about burglars. Yet there was nothing of value left overnight and any drugs were well secured. It was some of those he needed. After giving old Bert Niven a shot of amoxicillin for his chest infection, Brian needed to give him a supply for over the weekend until the chemist opened. Stupidly, he hadn't checked his bag before going on-call and had none. Old boy Niven was an optimistic joke-cracking character, though at seventy-nine with Woodbine lungs he'd little to be amused about. Brian was quite fond of him. Lifting the master key from the cupboard at reception, Brian knew it was pointless looking in his own bare cupboards, or Kevin's, and headed for David's. He was bound to have some.

It was only when standing in David's room that he realised the flaw in his plan: the door master key didn't open the wall cupboards. He swore. The only alternative was to phone the hospital pharmacy and trail into town to collect them. Or risk Niven being admitted.

Half-heartedly, he tried his own drug cupboard key. With a jiggle and twist, eureka – it opened! Security-mad Goodman would crap himself. The three shelves of the wall cupboard were crammed: assorted brown bottles, tablet boxes and injection ampoules. Brian lifted out bottle after bottle with growing amazement. Pethidine, morphine, sedatives, anti-psychotics, codeine and di-hydrocodeine tablets, some for patients he recognised, many deceased, most being controlled drugs like opiates. Well, well, did Goodman have a secret habit, fed by drugs collected from dead patients? If so, how had he fucking dared to blackmail him about his addiction and get him to sign up into Kilnglass! Goodman's leverage wasn't going to last much longer though. Brian had managed to delete most of his incriminating fiddled opiate prescriptions from his old patient records as they transferred onto Kilnglass's system. Even better, he'd managed to snatch a look at David's accounts. There were two different sets of accounts with marked discrepancies between. Serious fundholding fraud. The Health Board and the taxman would be more than interested. Blackmail could go two ways! He felt a surge of resolve. Clean for weeks, back pain gone, and hell, he didn't feel tempted by Goodman's loot. Using it as ammunition was more important.

Now, what in buggery was his boss doing with this other stockpile? Insulin, adrenaline and atropine ampoules: all rarely used by GPs. He recalled using adrenaline only once in many years. And three boxes of potassium chloride ampoules? A hospital drug to put in drips for low blood potassium levels. GPs might occasionally prescribe potassium-rich, oral electrolyte sachets to the dehydrated, but never gave it intravenously. Patients needed hospitalisation if that ill. Dangerous stuff, potassium chloride. Could cause cardiac arrest. Brian froze as he caught sight of the label on one insulin pack: 'Mrs A. Chaudri.' The Spar woman who'd died. Why hadn't David returned it to the chemist? Beside it lay several packets of the abortion drug RU486. For what? As he shakily replaced the drugs as precisely as he could, he noticed a brown envelope tucked in at the side. On lifting it, photos spilled out. Photos of girls. He was sweating. What the fuck? Was David a secret voyeur? Or worse, a kiddie-fiddler? These girls looked mid-teens, pretty, well-developed, long-haired, long-limbed. The first photo had them playing netball in shorts, in a playground. Others showed them in blazers at school gates, possibly Balgrove? Fortunately, none showed them undressed. He peered. Was that Neil? Was David spying on his son? He shuddered. He was spying on David! Thank Christ, bold boy was away. Too much to hope he'd break his neck in the Alps.

Carefully, Brian replaced the photos in the envelope and returned it to its hiding place. Taking a card of amoxicillin from the top shelf, he saw a black linen roll. Reminiscent of his old uni dissecting kit, it was encircled by a woven ribbon tied in a bow. Unfurling it exposed three 2ml syringes with attached needles still in their original sheaths. Each syringe, held by an elasticated ring, contained a colourless liquid, and had a different coloured dot stuck on its plunger: one was red, one blue, one green. There was no explanatory code for the colours or clue to their contents. Refolding and re-tying the roll exactly, he replaced it.

He sat down, dizzy and panicking. What the fuck did all this mean? Any explanation he could think of for this odd assortment of stuff seemed highly unsavoury. He was sure the dangerous drugs wouldn't feature in David's DDA register and thus, were held illegally. The girls' photos showed them clothed, so not illegal, but definitely creepy. And the mysterious roll of pre-charged injections, what did they contain and for whom were they intended? The room was becoming very warm, though Brian knew the heating was off. This was too much to take in. He needed to consider carefully how this knowledge might best be used. Simply confronting David wasn't an option. He had to get out. Time was marching. He still had visits.

Driving away from the Kilnglass Surgery, Brian Nesbitt made two resolutions. One, he would no longer sign Part Two cremations but insist David asked a doctor from another practice. Difficult for David to argue with that, seeing as how it was the professional standard. Two, he'd watch for signs that David was 'using'. Christ! That should be easy enough for him. He congratulated himself for not taking any opiates and felt confident that elephant was heading to the horizon. But now there was a new beast to consider, what did Goodman need all that potassium chloride and insulin

265

for? Was he bumping patients off? Nausea gripped him. His old worries about Goodman shopping his drug habit to the GMC were small beer compared to the dangers of working with a killer.

Outside, snow was falling heavily. The roads were icy and un-gritted. Brian shivered and turned his car heating up to max. Thinking he was likely one of the few people dreading a 'deep and crisp and even' Boxing Day morning, he concentrated on the road.

*

We managed a 'David' taboo for six days. On the seventh, it dawned bright and sunny, though bitterly cold, as we set off from home to meet Rosie and James at Strathclyde Park, halfway between Edinburgh and Glasgow. Neither of us had time to travel through and spend an overnight, but Rosie was keen to exchange Christmas presents.

Strathclyde Park is flat, exposed, and windy, but with a big loch for walking round and some fairground attractions for kids. Nathan fed the ducks. Winston ran ragged trying to catch one. We had hot drinks and doughnuts from a van while Nathan honked madly in a toy police car ride. As Rosie stood supervising him, Ralph went to find a loo and James beckoned me to sit on a bench beside him. In the early days, I'd regarded James as a philanderer, but he'd morphed into a respectable devoted husband. We got on well now, though I was surprised when he put his arm round me and spoke intensely.

'Now, Beth. Ralph tells me you're worried about this chap with the two names.'

'James, if this is a pep talk Ralph's put you up to as a lawman, stop right there!'

'Lawman?' he laughed. 'Love it! Must've been great being a sheriff in the Wild West.'

'If you were a guy and didn't have to give birth in a draughty wagon, maybe.'

'Oh, sure, just joking. But Ralph told me all about your rascal. I thought Goodman and Truscott were unusual names and might be easy to find in court records. And when I searched, bingo!'

'Bingo?' I pulled away to look at him in interest.

'Found nothing on any Truscott, but there were several cases in England against a Stanley David Goodman way back in the early fifties which might be connected.'

'Well, Goodman has used all of those names in various combinations.'

'Precisely. This one resided in Kilburn, London and was done for attempted armed robbery – a botched bank job where a bank clerk died. The others got away.'

'Really?'

'Also found a newspaper piece saying he'd come over from Jamaica on the famous Windrush to Tilbury in 1948.'

'So, he was coloured?'

'Not sure that's relevant, but presumably. He was done for the robbery when a witness saw his face in the paper during his trial for attempted murder by strangulation of – wait for it – a Winifred Dorothy Truscott!'

James sat back triumphantly as if concluding a devastating argument for the prosecution.

'My God! That Stanley Goodman must be Goodman's father! Not sure it helps us, though. I mean, why change your name to that of an armed robber who tried to murder your mother?'

'I know. From what Ralph's told me, there's always more questions than answers wherever Goodman's concerned. What are the police saying?' James waved at Nathan.

'Nothing much, though they're looking into a creepy new photo of the girls I got sent.'

'Shocking. And the other letters?'

'No word. The phoning has stopped, but I'm very worried about the girls.'

'Sorry not to see them today. What are they up to?'

'Studying, supervised by Gran. They've done little since they broke up on Christmas Eve.'

A laughing, fresh-cheeked Nathan ran up to hurl himself at me, followed by Winston trying to leap up onto my knee at the same time, while licking the toddler. The dog was a big softy. No idea why Jean called him Winston: he's no bulldog. Perhaps it was ironic.

On the way home, I told Ralph about Goodman Senior.

'Ah, James said he'd something to tell you. But it doesn't really help our case against Goodman Junior, does it?'

'Suppose not, except maybe murder's in his genes. Is that a goer? Should have asked Rosie. She's met some in the psychiatric line of duty.'

'I'll let Tim know anyway. It's tough waiting about for police investigations.'

'Och, well, at least the girls are still off. No coming-home-from-school worries.'

'I've decided after the hols to collect them myself. January's quiet at the faculty. I'll work from home afternoons till we see what's happening. With prelims on, they aren't in every day anyway.'

'Haven't said anything to Dan about the photo. Should I?

'Let's tell him when he's up on Sunday. You know, if I catch the bastard doing this, I won't be responsible for my actions.' Ralph hit the steering wheel with venom. Unfortunately, he caught the horn. I jumped in fright. But at least that made us laugh. There wasn't much to laugh at.

When we got home, Katy shyly showed me a postcard from Neil saying, 'Having a lovely time, see you soon! Love, Neil.' Klosters looked gorgeous. How I wished with all my heart that his father would bloody well stay over there.

Twenty-Seven

Crime & Punishment

Kilnglass Surgery

He is pleased to see the garish, gaudy baubles have been removed from the tree. Abominations, Christmas trees, nothing to do with the Lord's birth. But one is expected to pander to patient expectations. Maureen is bending over some open cardboard boxes.

'Good morning, Maureen. You are in early. Decorations going? Excellent!'

Maureen turns, smiling warmly. The woman worships him.

'Hello, Doctor. Yes, it's Twelfth Night. How nice to have you back – and looking so well! Mind you, they say Switzerland is good for the health, don't they?'

'Not that I needed restoration, of course. As you know, for me, a healthy mind and a healthy body are a perennial goal.'

'Oh, of course! Everything will be away by lunchtime. The wreaths and tinsel are already packed, but I'm sorry to say the missing Baby Jesus has not been returned.' Maureen shakes her head. 'I think we will have to get a new nativity scene.'

'I will purchase one. And secure it! The world is becoming a sorry place, Maureen. The young have no moral compass. The theft of our Lord is sacrilege!'

Maureen shrinks down towards her boxes looking upset. Wondering if he'd raised his voice excessively, he cocks his head and smiles. 'A new hairdo, Maureen? Very becoming.'

She rises to pat her new bob. 'Thank you, Doctor. It's

easier in the morning.'

He divests himself of his coat and holds it out. She cradles it over her arm, always eager to please. Yet that 'Derek' had strung her along for fourteen years before marrying his secretary.

His room is unlocked. Frowning, he reassures himself everything is correctly in place: mail pile on the desk blotter, pens aligned as left, chair tucked completely at right angles under his modern pearwood desk. The cleaner knows the score. It is very cold with the premises having been closed for four days. He turns up the heater thermostat and consults his watch. Thirty minutes should suffice. At his touch, the computer whirs into action. Time to concentrate on clinical acumen, diagnoses, and treatment. The Lord's work is on hold. He buzzes to summon the first patient.

Dr Innes Cameron is an unfamiliar, tall, angular fellow who extends a hand across the desk, which David ignores. He nods towards the patient seat. For a doctor, Cameron is ridiculously casual in an open-necked shirt. His problem is a painful shoulder. When asked, he undresses swiftly for examination.

'You have a supraspinatus tendonitis.' Removing his gloves, David types out a prescription. 'Continue to use the joint or it will stiffen more. Take these anti-inflammatories after meals to help ease it. I trust you have no gastric problems?'

The man shakes his head.

'I shall make an appointment for physiotherapy. What kind of work do you do?'

'I'm a university academic, a forensic scientist.'

'How interesting. What is your interest?' Goodman removes the ibuprofen prescription from the printer.

'Fingerprint research. Currently we're looking at disposable gloves.'

'Gloves? Indeed. I've heard it is now possible to get

prints from paper, but gloves?'

'Forensics advances all the time. So far, we've found useable prints inside discarded PVC ones, though not latex. The criminal is going to have to work harder and harder to escape us!' Cameron smiles, accepts the prescription and stands.

Goodman stares. How portentous Cameron should arrive this very morning as he is considering switching to the new PVC gloves. A sign from the Lord. He will not.

'Goodbye, Doctor.'

As Cameron exits, Goodman types up his clinical findings and treatment. He writes 'Physio referral, Cameron' into his to-do list on the desk.

Next comes Matilda Jamieson, Tillie. A regular of no note. Or means. Tiny bungalow, no art. Nonetheless, balm for the ego.

'Oh, Doctor, I'm so pleased to see you! Did you have a lovely holiday? The other doctor gave me tablets, but they haven't helped my heartburn. I'm sure you'll have something better.'

Dependency shone from her eyes. 'Well, Mrs Jamieson, let's have a look at you. Pop up on the couch.' Donning his gloves, he watches her mount the couch coquettishly. Bloody woman, she's almost eighty! Even without potential pecuniary return, she might merit attention on age. But for the present he is restraining himself.

His third patient stirs him. A Miss Cara Nichol, of infinitesimal skirt and plunging v-neck sweater, visible nipples and lace dimples erupt through the flimsy garment. Matching lace knickers, perhaps? A whiff of scent proves heady as he bends to check her blood pressure. After cursory questions about periods and headaches, he renews her Ovranette. She may safely fornicate for the next six months. 'Thanks, ever, Doc!' Her thigh flashes black lace as she rises. Hussy. He will need Edinburgh next weekend. He has needs and has denied himself long enough. 'Each of you should learn to control his own body in a way that is holy and honourable.' *Thessalonians 4:3-4*. He has learned control. A recent visiting pastor from Illinois, one Harley McAdam, had agreed with his view that release in this way is not a sin. And that it is completely apt for delicate wives such as Clara to be set aside physically after childbirth. Interestingly, McAdam had read that Tibetan lamas believed sex re-charged and increased their spiritual energy: an interesting concept. In any case, next Saturday he must convey his gratitude to Zara for posting his letter. It had been a clever idea. And Zara is always obliging. And relieves him well. The story for Clara will be an Edinburgh meeting on heart disease.

He pauses to re-arrange his vitals. These Jockey shorts Clara bought are much too restrictive; thoughts of Zara have enlarged him. He recites *Corinthians*, 'No temptation has seized you except what is common to man.' He is but a frail human. Offering a swift prayer for strength, he assumes genial confessor mode and buzzes. A young mother enters. Her baby is wheezing. A reminder he must phone Con, perhaps meet him in Edinburgh for reassurance that the wheezy Lester woman's records were deleted. And the police satisfied.

*

Edinburgh

The following Saturday, Conor entered the Café Royale off Princes Street and scanned the bar area. It was quite dark as its mahogany furniture and stained-glass windows belonged to the Victorian era. He preferred the nearby, livelier Rose Street hostelries, but Goodman had suggested here. Spotting him, he moved over to sit at Goodman's small table. He knew he was late, but up until the last minute he'd still been debating whether to come at all.

Goodman smiled broadly. 'Conor!'

'Conrad, if you please. Or I'll call you Stanley.' Conor spoke quietly.

'Of course, sorry, old habits. May I get you a drink?'

'I'll have a pint of their beer of the week. Aren't you drinking?' Conor nodded towards Goodman's coffee.

Goodman waved for a waiter. He ordered the beer plus a Caol Isla for himself.

'I waited to have a drink with you. As my car is at Milngavie station, thought it best to keep to one.' He beamed. 'Isn't this pleasant? So, how have you been?' He sat back and folded his arms.

'I am fine, David, but I'm not sure I'm happy to see you!'

'Why ever not?'

'That business with the police about the woman who died freaked me out. And how many of those trial patients of yours were kosher? I mean, I'm not a stickler, but this thing's caused me no end of hassle.' Accepting his pint from the waiter, Conor took a long draught.

As he carefully wiped the rim of his whisky tumbler with an alcohol swab, Goodman asked, 'What did you say to the police?'

Conor shook his head. 'What you told me to say – so help me! Fucking fash it was, fudging number 266's paperwork, photocopying forms, forging your writing!'

'Come, come, it can't have been that bad? In any case, it was only to facilitate your study that I entered her as 'improved' in a month. I had no idea she might die prematurely. We couldn't risk someone checking. They'd blame the drug. Then me. Then implicate you ...'

Conor shook his head. 'We've had other adverse events, you know, but none fatal.'

'Indeed?'

'Anaphylaxis, arrhythmias, chest pains. But it doesn't matter. We're pulling it.'

'What?'

Conor knitted his brow. 'I've no choice. That H-H rep, Jane, got antsy. Said if I didn't record the other side effects, she'd go to the CSM. Any suggestion of fraud and I'd be scuppered. She's buggered off now, but I think she took proof. I don't trust her.'

'But I thought you and Jane were a couple?'

'We were. Then old enemies crept out of the woodpile, my ex-wife and her mate, Beth Semple. Think they collared Jane at our reunion. God knows what they told her.'

'I, too, have had occasion to cross swords with Dr Semple. She is a devious woman. A purveyor of spite. I feel it may be time she faces her Maker.'

Conor paused, glass in mid-air. 'I beg your pardon?' Had he misheard? Hairs on the back of his arms and neck prickled. Christ, he felt on edge. He needed more sleep, exhaustion always spaced him out. Goodman sat smiling at a stained-glass window opposite. Conor spoke abruptly. 'What did you say?'

'You know, Conrad, people standing in the way of the Lord's work may have to be removed.'

Conor stared across the table at this man, whom he realised that, despite having socialised with him for years, he didn't know at all. 'Removed? By whom?'

'Why, anyone who is a believer. Someone blessed by our Lord and chosen to act for him on this Earth.'

Conor wondered if whisky had been the only stimulant Goodman had had. His friend moved his gaze from the heavens back to face him and speak.

'But, Conrad, my purpose for coming here today is to voice my appreciation for your efforts and assure you that I'll be delighted to take part in any future trials and to be, henceforth, meticulous in my findings. And, I am indeed sorry about Jane.'

'Oh, no matter. Plenty more in the sea.' Conor downed

the last of his beer.

Goodman glanced at the wall clock. 'Is that the time? Excellent. Should manage the six o'clock train. Been nice catching up, hasn't it? Perhaps we can do it again? I'm through fairly often.' Standing up, he buttoned his coat and exited out into the rain.

Watching his departing back, Conor realised Goodman had never ever offered a handshake. Must be his germ phobia. The bold boy had always been a bit bonkers. But now, he sounded like he'd tipped over completely! That fat cop speering about the Lester woman had hinted at other cases under investigation. What had he meant?

Other past odd remarks Goodman had made swirled in his mind. Like those possible methods for murder he'd listed that drunken night in the study. And then there was the way he'd looked when talking of Kenneth Stewart's suicide, almost smiling? On that count, the more he considered it, the weirder that suicide seemed. Why top yourself just after winning a prestigious job, even if you were queer? Kenneth had trumped Goodman for that SR post. Did the bold boy have a hand in his death? In their old drinking days, when Goodman had been Stan, he'd always dissed queers. Maybe, he was actually a closet gay? God, what had that to do with anything? Conor was very tired, but his brain still reeled on. There had been a first wife who'd croaked it out at sea. Had that been an accident? Or had she, like Kenneth, been 'in the way of the Lord's work'? Jesus! Imagination in overdrive, he rubbed his face and strode to the bar. 'A double Islay malt.'

'Which brand, sir?' The barman was a fresh-faced, innocent youth, unscathed by life.

'Any bloody one. No, the one that's the highest proof!'

*

On the 5th of January I was due a half day for covering Hogmanay. Gerry was off all day, but our locum didn't turn up. Chaos ensued. My surgery ran for four hours without a break. Finally, I made it to the sitting room and brewed cuppas for Charles and myself.

'Thanks, Beth. How was the weekend?'

'Mr Banks finally died. Wife's coping and daughter's there. Three admissions. Haven't put them in the book yet. An appendix, a coronary and a DTs.'

'Oh? Who went bonkers?'

'That solicitor Bill McGuiness at Mugdock. Decided to go sober over Hogmanay, honestly! Found him pacing up and down thinking he was Napoleon, directing the battle of Marengo, his wife reckoned. He's a toy soldier buff with an attic full of battle re-enactments.'

'Really? I know Bill. Never knew he was into toy soldiers! Did he go in willingly?'

'No. Usual certifying palaver then police escort. Ambulance guys refused to coax him in after being on some human rights training day. Yet poor chap desperately needed admitted. Exhausted, a danger to himself and his family. I'll phone the unit to see how he's doing. Buckets of Parentrovite and sedation should sort him for now, but long term? Only he can kick the booze. Daughter was inconsolable. Ages with Katy.'

'And how goes your harassment problem?'

'Quiet, thank God. No more photos, calls, poisoned bones, or letters. Ralph's getting the girls from school for the next few weeks and Winston isn't allowed into the garden alone. All we can do. So, what's the score with these calls?'

Charles was scribbling on a pad while scanning the call book on his knee. 'Mostly coughs and temperatures. We can't possibly do only our own patients today, so I've divided them geographically.' He handed me a list of names and addresses.

'Right, I know most of these. I'm off.' I fetched my glorious coat, the cause of Ralph speeding past me with a carrier bag on Christmas Eve during my meltdown. It must have cost a fortune, but the navy wool and cashmere garment was the warmest thing I'd ever owned. Outside, I skidded across the icy car park to my Escort.

*

Elbowing in the door of Kilnglass, he doffs his hat, giving a departing patient a warm smile. 'Ah, Councillor Tweedale, how are you? I hope Catherine feels better soon.'

'I'm sure she will, Doctor. Thanks for leaving the prescription. I didn't want to risk waiting over the weekend. You know how she prefers to see you.' He tapped his watch. 'Must dash, catch the chemist.'

'No problem. Tell her I was asking for her.'

David is holding the door handle, obstructing the councillor's exit. 'Oh, one quick thing, when is the next council planning meeting? We have completed extension plans for the house, but the architect says the planners only meet monthly, is that correct? I'd like to get building started by the end of February.' When the money rolls in from that penultimate case. Slow buggers, executors. 'I'm adding a TV room, new gym and facilities to my basement.'

'It's next Wednesday. If your plans are ready, why not pop them through my letterbox?' Richard Tweedale pulls up his coat collar against the wind whistling through the door and hurries out as a smiling Goodman releases it.

Goodman is pleased. Another favour returned. It is induced obligation that breeds power, not fear and intimidation as others foolishly imagine. Today he feels recharged. He has resolved to take a rest from his plans until March 31st, ironically his mother's birthday. It will be something special, something new. A red, blue, or green method, already mixed and stored. No more utilitarian digoxin-heart-attacks or warfarin-strokes, albeit useful. Being so common in West of Scotland patients, they are rarely queried.

As he unlocks his room door, Brian passes wordlessly. Watching his hunched back head for the waiting room, David realises that they haven't spoken properly for some time. He hopes there has been no relapse in Brian's habit.

It is two days before he pins Brian down in the practice sitting room.

'How are you, Brian? Is your problem under control?'

'Mine is. How about yours?'

Goodman smiles coldly. 'What do you mean?'

'The hoarded opiates in your cupboard. And the fiddled accounts. I think it's time we discussed a partnership, David, don't you?'

Goodman stands erect. 'Why not, Brian? Let me think about it. In the new tax year, perhaps?' Snatching his bag and diary, he walks off.

A few weeks later, in the study, David enters another name into his book before retiring. In front of the bathroom mirror he notes his hairline is receding. An indicator of high testosterone, no bad thing. The resulting high forehead looks quite distinguished, and hopefully he may be able to spend less on frizz-reducing treatments in Edinburgh. He isn't bad for his age, indeed Zara complimented him last week on his physique. There will be years ahead for the Lord's work. A Bible quote from the *Book of Job* occurs to him: 'The Lord giveth and the Lord taketh away.' Loyal servants of the Lord are always blessed. They may have mocked Job, but after several trials he received reward several fold. Gratifying.

Twenty-Eight

Sins of the Fathers

Sometimes whole months disappear. Time is eaten up by living. The lonely tell me their days are tediously long. I find it hard to understand how people can become lonely. Though after listening to distressing stories all day, I sometimes need time on my own, mostly my life thrives on interaction with friends, colleagues, neighbours and the interesting characters I meet. Ralph considers me a people junkie, a collector of friends and contacts. He is amazed at my lengthy Christmas card list. But when you've had cancer, you appreciate that life is short and want to live it to the full. In my diary for February 1994, every weekend is busy: theatre nights, cinema, walking in the Campsies, meals with friends. I may have been trying to obliterate worries about potentially murderous colleagues, but nothing is listed in the Diary of Curious Incidents that February, it was a limbo. But the first Wednesday in March is asterisked.

In Scotland, Health Boards have Local Medical Committees, a forum for interchange of views between GP practices and Board officials. Every practice can send a representative. We normally sent young Gerry, but that Wednesday he was off skiing and with new financial initiatives rumoured, Charles wanted a heads-up for planning in order to claim promptly, so sent me. I sped into town and arrived early to find Gordon at the coffee machine. He handed me the cup he'd just made. This was the only coffee I ever drank. The tea, left stewing in flasks, resembled creosote.

'What are you doing here, Beth? Where's Gerry the Lad?'

'He's on the piste, not the piss for a change!'

Gordon screwed up his face. 'Ouch, bad joke.'

'Sorry. Charles wants info on the new health check programmes, to get a claim in early before the funding runs out!'

We sat down at the large shiny board table and Gordon offered me one of his cheese and pickle sandwiches. The room rapidly filled up. The primary care chairman and secretary took their seats. The agenda was long. As usual, I hadn't read it in advance. We were on item two: *Infection Control Measures*, which had bizarrely segued into the dangers of home water-birthing pools, when the door opened. Gordon clutched me, hissing, 'What the fuck ...'

Dr David Goodman strolled in and sat in an empty chair directly opposite me.

'Apologies for being late, gentlemen. And lady.' He gave me a head bow and a smile I didn't reciprocate. 'An emergency, you know how it is.'

Irrationally, I was angry that he'd appeared instead of Kevin Nixon, even though I was there as a substitute myself. We moved on to Child Assessment Clinic Protocols. Malcom Rae, lead clinician in the Directorate for Women and Children rose. I focussed on his presentation, studiously avoiding looking across the table, yet from the corner of my vision, I felt Goodman had his eyes fixed on me. His pen lay idle in front of him. He exuded boredom.

When Malcom left, there was a break. People headed for a coffee top-up or the loo. I remained seated. Goodman didn't move. Gordon pulled his chair closer, put his arm across the back of mine, sweetly protective. But it didn't deter the challenge from across the table.

'How is practice in Bearsden, Dr Semple? Must be difficult with such a reduced rota.'

'It's fine. We have a very professional team and Drumlea practice are congenial and reliable for out-of-hours help.'

His eyebrows raised. 'Indeed? I am so glad. And how is the family?'

'Fine.' I stood up. 'Please excuse me.' Pushing back my chair, I escaped to the ladies'.

When I returned (after counting to 999), discussions had started on a Suicide Reduction Initiative. Goodman sat taking copious notes but didn't contribute. The last agenda item concerned audits in practice and using Significant Event Analysis. The lady speaker from the Patients' Association advocated all adverse patient experiences should be logged with what happened, why it happened and what could be done to prevent it happening again. The emphasis was on complaint procedures for patients and sharing good practice in our annual Health Board reports. She was well-informed and forceful about transparency. And certainly forced Goodman out of his shell.

'Surely few of us receive complaints?' Goodman's clipped English voice rang out imperiously. 'And if we do, we deal with them appropriately in-house? Lodging findings publicly with Boards and other organisations leaves us open to misinterpretation of facts and vulnerable to litigation. Only *doctors* understand clinical practice. We have the power to treat as we see fit and cannot be pandering to all these patient organisations. It would not surprise me to discover that ambulance-chasing lawyers lie behind this initiative!' Throwing down his pen, he banged the table.

There was a telling silence while the committee digested this tirade. The GP Chairman, Denis Clark, was a grey-haired, gentle man, my epitome of a good GP: thoughtful, considerate, calm. But not today. He was flushed as he spoke.

'Dr Goodman, I may have picked you up wrongly, but I cannot agree that we are,' he swallowed, 'laws unto ourselves. We cannot be. We have to be transparent in our actions and our dealings with any adverse events which may affect patient care.'

Goodman shrugged. 'Of course, but I simply meant that we do this already. The solution must not become disproportionate to the problem. We are busy enough without filling out more forms for peccadillos to be picked over by vultures.'

'I beg to differ. However, I must insist you apologise to Mrs Sinclair who has kindly come through from Edinburgh today to speak to us. We cannot have her going away thinking our Board is too arrogant to address its shortcomings.'

Goodman's colour flushed minimally. I saw his fists and jaw tighten and eyes dart in all directions before eventually he unclenched his hands, smiled charmingly, and inclined his head. 'My dear Mrs Sinclair, no offence was intended, I can assure you. I do think, however, that perhaps you misunderstand our role.'

A pin dropping would have sounded deafening. Mrs Sinclair rose and left in stony silence. The date of the next meeting was announced. Members packed up papers and pens. Goodman lingered to speak to Denny Clark, God knows why. Gordon walked me to my car.

'You OK, Beth? What the hell was that all about? Do you think Goodman's paranoid?'

'Yes. And I doubt significant event analyses will ever bother someone like him, he'll only lie. His actions are beyond any audit and his significant events are calculated, not accidental. God, I'm frustrated at the lack of police progress. It's months now.'

'They not been in touch, then? What does Tim say?'

'Merely that investigations are underway. Think they're working their way through Dawson's list, speaking to relatives, and if they pick up anything they'll go in for the computers. Apparently, they don't want to spook him till they have evidence. "Softly, softly," Tim says.' I opened my car door and leaned on it. 'You know, the sight of Goodman makes me so depressed.'

Gordon gave me a hug. 'Buck up, girl. Leave it to the police. Now, you off at the weekend? Fancy a curry?'

'Sorry, I'm on this weekend. How about a week on Saturday at the Shish? Mum will be over, so bring the kids and leave them with her. She'll love it.'

'You're on.' I got a peck on the cheek: Gordon was worried. I drove away with my dad's voice in my ears, which often happens when I'm upset. *If there's nothing you can do, Beth, you have to be patient.* I harbour many such stock phrases that pop up in times of stress. Parents have an effect on you that lingers long after they've gone.

*

Neil was fed up studying and went down for a drink. His mother was in the lounge watching *Corrie*. The whoosh-clunk noise from the basement told him where his father was. That was one of his many faults: vanity. Neil suspected the keep-fit fanaticism on the bike and rowing machine was not, as his father maintained, about cardiovascular health at all, but about cultivating a muscular physique. He'd heard the girls at school giggling about 'abs' and 'pecs' like Brad Pitt's. Neil felt downright weedy. Goodness knows why Katy was keen on him. Feeling guilty, he took milk instead of Coke from the fridge and a banana instead of a packet of the crisps his mother hid in the pot cupboard beyond paternal disapproval. Dad would never look in a pot cupboard. He didn't cook. In fact, he didn't do a thing in the house. Except criticise. More and more, Neil increasingly resented the way he talked to his mother. 'Clara, get this!' 'Clara, why did you do that?' 'Don't be so stupid!' More like a servant than a wife. It made him mad. And some of those comments he made about patients, especially young girls, were really rude. Yet he was so holy on Sunday in church, where he used his old name. What was that about?

Climbing back up the stairs, he heard his father coming out of the basement and closing its heavy door. Then the study door clicked twice as it was unlocked and re-locked from inside. Why did locked doors hold such great attraction? What could he possibly not want his mother and he to see?

He needed a plan.

*

The Shish was mobbed. I was glad I'd booked a table. Dan was up with his new girlfriend, Madeleine, except Katy had sussed she wasn't *that* new. She'd been around for six months. Katy's seemingly artless inquisitions could be deadly, as 'Maddy' would learn if she became a fixture. Dan and she were staying at a hotel in town, though I'd said they could have the spare room anytime. I was pleased he'd found someone else. She was nice. He could do worse.

'So, what do you do, Madeleine?' Gordon was straight in.

'Oh, call me Maddy, please! I'm a psychiatrist.'

'Excellent! Dan needs one.'

'Old joke, Gordon.' Dan pretended to glare. The rest of us laughed.

'So, you were all at university together, I hear?' She had a wide smile, warm grey eyes.

'Graduated 1973 from Glasgow, except Heather, who was at Jordanhill Teaching College.'

'Secondary or primary?' Maddy stole Dan's poppadum. He didn't murmur. This relationship was serious.

Originally from Edinburgh, Maddie said she now specialised in prison mental health. Conversation drifted from Barlinnie Prison in Lanarkshire to Parkhurst in the Isle of Wight where she'd worked with armed robbers, rapists, and murderers. Not my favourite topics. The boys discussed death penalties and parole boards as she gave insights into the intricacies of the psychopathic and sociopathic mind. I became increasingly tense and began to feel sick. Gordon caught my eye to shake his head apologetically, trying several times to hijack the conversation off at a tangent, but a fascinated Heather kept plying Maddy with questions. Only one thing to do when you don't want to join in. I ordered another bottle of wine. Not sure I remember going home.

*

All week he'd been debating whether he had the guts, but by break on April 1st, Neil decided to sound out Katy. Tired of their classmates endless un-funny April Fool jokes, they'd moved out to sit in the cycle shed, sharing crisps.

'I'm thinking of breaking into Dad's study.'

Katy looked horrified. 'Whatever for?'

'Because it's always locked. It's intriguing. What does he hide in there?'

'Is it worth the risk? I mean, from what you say about him, he could go crazy.'

'I've been thinking about it for ages. Last Saturday, he even locked it while opening the door to the postman. Must be something funny in there.'

'OK, but how will you get in?'

'I have a plan. I'll do it when he's down in the gym and Mum's watching TV. The keys are in his jacket hanging in the hall. '

'What do you think you'll find?'

'I dunno, really. But like, once when the door was a wee bit ajar, I saw piles of jewellery on his desk. It looked like he was tying labels on it. I mean, why would he have that? Did he get it from patients? Or is he a cat burglar or something? He goes out late at night sometimes. Oh, he could be anything! I feel I don't know him at all!'

Katy reached for another crisp and leaned forward. 'I've

never said, but my mum thinks he's a bit dodgy. Thinks he might've let a patient die unnecessarily.' She looked round at Neil who regarded her openly, looking unfazed. 'Then someone poisoned Winston and we had some spooky letters and calls and stuff, which she thought might be from him. But the last one came while you were in Switzerland. '

At this, Neil looked horrified. 'Really? Why didn't you tell me this before? Remember he once asked me your surname?'

Katy felt a bit agitated. 'I hope he hasn't guessed she's my mum.'

'Don't think so. He seemed pleased it was Sheehan. I never twigged why.'

'Well, Mum thought we should keep it to ourselves, but the letters 'n' stuff seems to have stopped and Mum hasn't mentioned anything for ages. Now Ralph's stopped picking us up every day from school. Didn't you wonder about that?'

'Well, loads of folk get picked up for the dentist or shopping in town or whatever. And he collected you during the prelims, when we came out at funny times and lots of folk got picked up. Didn't think anything of it.'

'And then there was that time your dad's practice stopped helping Mum's at weekends. Still no idea why.'

Neil squeezed her hand. 'Heard him shouting at Mum about that. He's always shouting at her, and it's getting worse. Anyway, I've decided to look in the study tonight!'

'Be careful, Neil!'

*

Katy worried all evening. Her mum was rarely wrong, rarely distrusted anyone, but she plainly disliked and distrusted Neil's father. What if she was right about him being incompetent – or worse, evil? Neil said he'd a temper. Supposing he got really, really, angry at Neil? Kissing her mum goodnight, she almost said something, but decided it might be best to wait and see what Neil found.

*

It took Neil a few days in the end. Timing was all. Eventually, Mum was deep in soap city, the basement door closed, and at last he heard the whirr-clunk starting. Rower first. Bike second. Weights third. He had thirty minutes precisely. His father's right-hand jacket pocket, as expected, held four keys on a brass ring attached to a crucifix. The largest mortice key easily opened the study door. He closed it gently.

The room was a revelation. He'd been to art galleries with school, and could tell these were serious, expensive paintings and art objects. Yet his father was notoriously mean with money. The walls were silky. The furniture dark wood and heavy. But he'd no time to dally. Desk papers were boring accounts. A snow globe of Paris was funny. Not like his dad. A tacky souvenir?

One of the smaller keys opened the top left-hand drawer. He removed a red velvet jewellery roll similar to a black one on his mother's dressing table. Out tumbled sparkling bracelets, rings and necklaces. All looked expensive, some old-fashioned, some modern. Each had a little label attached by thin string. One necklace of jewelled elephants was labelled 'A.C.' and dated recently. One bracelet labelled 'D.T.' was dated last year. Carefully replacing the items, he spotted a padded envelope at the back of the drawer. It contained a driving licence for a Kenneth Stewart, a woman's wedding ring and six faded, circular, plastic hospital wrist-tags like the one he'd had for his appendix op. Putting it all back, he re-locked the drawer and opened the top right one which contained a smaller jewellery roll and a leather-bound notebook full of his father's old-fashioned, spidery script.

It took a minute to decipher the writing, but after five, he stopped and shut it abruptly. Who were these people listed? It was too shocking to contemplate, and he felt overwhelmed. There was also a woman's will and a bank book loose in the drawer. He didn't open them: he'd seen enough. Locking the drawer and then the door, he crept back out of the room as music signalled the end of *Coronation Street*. He dropped the keys back into his father's jacket and headed across the hall. Pausing at the basement door, he could still hear grunting, but taking no chances, he raced up the stairs. As he sat on his bed, his heart hammered against his ribcage. Bile hovered at the base of his throat. What should he do? He couldn't ask Katy. She went south on Saturday. He started to cry.

*

Goodman is not pleased, not pleased at all. This morning Brian had demanded a partnership. And a ridiculous profit share! Thinks he can get it in return for silence over the accounts. How dare he! Then this afternoon, the council had rejected his extension plans. Who were these 'objectors' whose views had been taken into consideration? He will appeal! The planning officer, some Derek Mason, is nothing but a jumped-up little jobsworth! Throwing his coat on the hall chair he marches into his study. He has not used it for a few days. Saturday had been relief in Edinburgh, while Church business had taken all day yesterday.

Pouring a Scotch, he sits admiring his art. Pictures never fail to soothe. His eyes rest on the desk. Curious, he could have sworn he'd left the Paris snow globe with the lettering facing the window. He walks round the room, but nothing looks out of place. With the new locks and only one set of keys always in his pocket, no one could have entered. He takes out his keys, unlocks the top right drawer and extricates his notebook. Downing his whisky, he pours another. Perhaps a few minutes thinking time before dinner.

He records the plan for Brian. Intended method? Good, old-fashioned dihydrocodeine. And the scenario? He'd call at his home to discuss the 'partnership'. His spontaneous response to his death? 'Such a shame, but not surprised the poor boy relapsed after Jackie rebuffed his proposal.' Maureen has already disseminated some gossip concerning the imminent proposal. And quite out of the blue, also furnished other interesting news: the names of Semple's daughters. And she has seen the younger one with Neil in the High Street. So, Katy is Semple's daughter? Useful.

But for the present, he must decide how best to deal with his planning rejection. A stiff appeal, of course, but it has made him extremely angry. Planner Derek Mason is not a patient, nor is Councillor Richard Tweedale. But wife Catherine Tweedale is. Indirect revenge on the wife means a satisfying lifetime of grief. There is only one other decision to be made. Red, blue, or green?

Twenty-Nine

Ghosts of the Past

The Easter holidays were spent again in Bristol seeing Ralph's father. The girls had Standard Grade and Higher exams immediately after the break, but we felt they might as well study at Wendy and Henry's house and benefit from a change of scene, plus light relief with Maia and Roland. Maia was three the week we stayed. The birthday party was wild. We flopped exhausted onto sofas when the guests had gone. The girls were bathing Maia and Roly before bed and the sound of laughter and splashing came down the stairs.

'So, plans for tomorrow?' Wendy liked organising.

'Long lie?' ventured Henry.

Wendy hooted with laughter. 'Like we've had many of them over the last three years?'

'There's rugby on. Might get Dad over if he's well enough and do a boys' afternoon in front of the telly. You up for that Henry?' Ralph stretched out his long frame.

'Sounds good to me!' Henry went to fetch another beer.

As for us girls, Wendy suggested we took her kids into Bath. I love the city. The Roman baths, the Georgian architecture of sweeping crescents, the Assembly Rooms, the Costume Museum. And the historic cafés and restaurants. It was a plan.

In one old café, we pigged out on Sally Lunn buns, a sort of cross between a brioche and a teacake, in the actual place where she lived in the 1480s.

'Must be great to be remembered for a bun! What kind of cake would you like named after you, Wendy?'

It was nice being daft for a change, far removed from

work and worries.

'A toffee meringue with hazelnut and chocolate filling!'

'Oooh, sickly. Roly might like it, though.' I grabbed a napkin to catch the regurgitated mess he was spitting out. But after I'd put it back on his plate, he swiftly picked it up again and successfully ate it the second time.

Maia wrinkled her nose. 'Roly's a pig!'

'If you wrinkle your nose like that you might end up looking like one yourself!'

Maia didn't appreciate my humour and started to cry. Wendy picked up Roly. 'Quick change my boy and we're off! Cool it, Maia, Aunty Beth's only joking.'

Going home, Wendy detoured via Alexandra Park. The kids snored in their double buggy as we sat admiring the spectacular view.

'So how are things, Beth?'

'What do you mean? With the practice or the kids or what?'

'You know what. Goodman.'

'Well, Charles and I were interviewed a few weeks ago by city CID about the original cases Charles reported, the one I refused to sign a Part Two for, and some others on the Dawson's list whom they thought we might know.'

'And? Action?'

I sighed. 'Nothing as far as I know. But Monty the undertaker tells me Kilnglass have been poor contributors lately. '

'Coincidence? Or has Goodman backed off?'

'No idea. He's not been back at the LMC either, according to Gerry. I do worry about his wife and son. If he is bumping folk off, what'll it do to them when it comes out?'

'She may be complicit.'

'Och, no way! She's more abused and cowed, poor thing.'

'Well, I know all about that, don't I?' Wendy sighed. 'On that topic, any word about Con?'

'Not a peep. Gone to ground. I wonder if that girl Jane did take her research fraud evidence to the Safety of Drugs lot? Though my bet is not. Con's always been slippery.'

'They're a pair, him and Goodman. I only hope they'll be caught out eventually.'

'If there is a God! Come on. It's cold up here. Sun's going down. Let's get back to the car.'

Next day we mooched about the house, discussing Henry's proposed holiday plans for hiring a summer villa in the Algarve. The girls were enthusiastic, and on prompting that we'd consider it seriously if the studying became more regular, they vanished to their room. Wendy was edgy, fussing over a dining table floral centrepiece, plumping up feather cushions.

'You OK?' I took a cushion from her and plumped it myself. 'Anything you want doing?'

'No thanks, Beth. Just tidying up for a guest we're having tonight.'

She didn't elaborate when I said, 'Oh, who?' but sped back to the kitchen where a smoked salmon, capers and salad platter were cling-filmed and put in the fridge, and a huge home-made pavlova was filled with cream, pineapple, and passion fruit. Half an Aberdeen Angus bull was roasting in the oven. And on a weekday night. My mum would've had a fit! I peeled spuds, chopped carrots and parsnips to roast, the least I could do.

Henry came and went from the TV room in search of nuts, beer and the TV guide. Ralph was snoozing on the sofa. The wee kids were in the sitting area of the kitchen with Duplo. The big kids were at their studies. I hoped.

'Who's the mystery guest, then?' I tried again.

Wendy was removing plates from the dishwasher and polishing them before stacking. 'Someone Henry's invited. I've never met her. She's due at seven. I'm off for a shower."

After this cryptic information, Wendy headed upstairs. I looked down at my faded jeans and splattered jumper and followed, detouring to warn the girls to brush their hair as there was a mystery guest.

'How intriguing! Is it some Royal relative of Wendy's?'

'No, some friend of Henry's.'

'How old is he?' Katy likes detail.

'No idea, just get ready and be down for seven.'

I changed into clean, smart trousers and a white angora top. Wendy met me on the landing in her dressing gown, a towel turbaned round her head. She had the small fry already bathed and clad in sleeping suits.

'Any chance you could give them their tea, Beth? It's in the microwave.' She put a fragrant Roly into my arms and urged Maia to follow me. Thinking of my new white jumper, I wondered if I'd got dressed too soon. Fortunately, I successfully remained stain-free despite Roly's spoon-flicking expertise. I'd just finished clearing up the kids' dishes and the worktops and was lifting Roly out of his highchair, when the doorbell rang.

'Hello, Wendy?' said a vision of loveliness: up-swept blonde hair, immaculate make-up, trim navy trouser suit and killer heels. Uncharitably, I predicted bunions from those shoes. Or potential retro-patellar arthritis of the knee.

'No, I'm Beth, visiting from Scotland. Wendy's upstairs.'

'Right. I'm Mel Jones, pleased to meet you.'

Ah! This was Henry's old flame! I now understood Wendy's flapping. Mel offered me flowers and wine.

'Sorry, I've no hands with Roly here. Come into the kitchen.'

Henry appeared and gave her an affectionate hug and a peck on the cheek. No old acrimonious break-up there, then. 'You two introduced yourselves?'

'Yep,' I said.

Maia was wrapping her arms round Mel's legs. 'Now

who is this sweetie?'

'That's Maia,' said Henry, rummaging in the fridge. 'Come on, let's have a drink. Are you driving, Mel?'

'No. I'm staying with my cousin, didn't I say? A ten-minute taxi ride away!'

'Excellent!' Henry opened a bottle of champagne with a bang as Wendy made an entrance in an aquamarine blouse matching her eyes, a pair of wide-legged silk trousers and patent Manolo's. I detected transient millivolts of tension sparking between her and Mel. It only lasted seconds. Then the girl held out her hand.

'Wendy? Hi, I'm Mel. Kind of you to invite me. Your kids are gorgeous!' She moved through to the lounge, impeded by Maia clutching her right leg.

'Come Maia, let Mel sit down.' Wendy took Maia's hand.

'Oh, I brought them something.' She produced two presents from her large handbag which Maia snatched, retreating to a corner, Roland in unsteady pursuit.

'Do you have kids, Mel?'

'Sadly not. I'm really Mrs Metcalfe, but it was simpler to stay Melanie Jones professionally, too much hassle changing all the certificates. Sadly, my husband died of cardiomyopathy the year after we married. But I have five nephews and nieces nearby I can invite over. Best of both worlds, you can always give them back!'

The evening was relaxed. Wendy's meal was delicious, as usual. We sat in the lounge after the girls returned upstairs and Maia and Roly settled down cuddling Melanie's new fluffy bunnies.

Henry sighed. I knew what was coming. 'Melanie, would you like to tell Beth about Truscott and the cases?'

'Sure. He was an odd bod, the Senior Registrar in the vascular surgical unit when I was a new sister. Said to be highly qualified, very bright. The boss wouldn't hear a word against him. Difficult to put your finger on what was wrong, but most nurses thought him creepy. Not sexually creepy, more skulking or staring creepy, like he was always guessing what you thought of him or something. Kind of smarmily charming mostly, but sometimes if you caught him off-guard, he had a … a look.'

'A look?' Wendy was intrigued. 'What, like evil? Or devious? Or supercilious?'

'All of those! And with some patients, he could be a bit sneering, haughty. Anyway, he often came in at night when he wasn't on call. No one else did that. Yet he had a wife and young kid! Currying favour with old Prof Armstrong was my guess. Truscott liked to hover, talk to patients, fiddle with drips and dressings and frankly, drive us nurses nuts!'

'But the cases?' I was impatient.

'OK. The first guy was Air Marshall Willard, ex-RAF, bit of a toff, but nice enough. Armstrong's patient. Elective op for repair of aortic aneurysm. Prognosis good. Found dead in his bed in the early hours. I had seen Truscott fiddle with his drip after midnight and disappear immediately afterwards. Because he was post-op, a post-mortem should have been done, but the family blocked it, said they were happy he'd had good care and the wife terrorised old Armstrong into letting it go. Said she couldn't bear the old boy being cut up.'

'But why should Truscott do him in?' Wendy shook her head.

'Personally, I wondered about an exchange between them I'd overheard the day before,' Melanie answered. 'Willard was slurred, full of morphine, and asked Truscott if he was a wop or a wog? He obviously thought it funny, but Truscott looked furious and stormed off.'

'Wop? What's a wop?' Wendy asked.

'It's from the war, I think. Derogatory term for Italians.'

'And where was Truscott from?'

'I'm not sure. Mixed race, I think, or even Eastern Mediterranean? He had dark looks and quite tight curly hair. But anyway, the second patient was Geoffrey Tilletts, who'd been in a while with a leg ulcer caused by peripheral vascular disease. Armstrong tried to improve the leg circulation with parasympathetic ganglia injections and so on, without success. Henry came to see him. Then Tilletts developed a body rash, diarrhoea and his hair fell out. He was a retired surgeon, a pretty demanding man, bit grumpy. I got the impression he knew Truscott from before. A nurse overheard Truscott baiting him about something but didn't hear exactly what was said.'

'What happened to Tilletts?'

'He, too, died unexpectedly overnight. Again, Truscott had been in the ward that night – though he wasn't on call.'

'Cause of death? And who certified him?' I could put a bet on the answer.

'Heart failure. Truscott certified him, like he did most of the ward deaths. I'm sure there were more than average while he was with us, often overnight. Several times, too, I suspected that he'd doctored records and drug Kardexes, though I never actually saw him replace any. The surgical nursing officer in charge called me a jealous bitch. She fancied him and thought I did too. He did suck up to her, was all over her, in fact. After the police came to investigate and no action was taken, things got uncomfortable for me, so I headed for Oxford.'

Mel had four people staring at her intently. No one said anything, but as I paused at the door heading to the kitchen, I had to ask, 'Was there a post-mortem on Tilletts?'

'No. His body was bequeathed for medical research and went that afternoon to St George's Medical School from where he'd not long retired as surgical professor. No relatives ever visited. Homosexual, I believe. Not sure if that's relevant.'

I wasn't sure either. 'Hands up for tea? OK, us girls. Coffee for the boys?' A show of hands confirmed orders. I went to sort out the kettle, the percolator and cheese and crackers. A few things fell into place: these were more possibly Goodman-attributable deaths, but the motives were obscure. Were old ladies for art or money, or just because he hated the elderly? But for these men, were perceived slights enough? And were Mel's two the only Bristol patients who'd died prematurely, or might Goodman have targeted more in other wards?

When I carried the tray in, the conversation had drifted to holidays. Mel recounted trips down the Nile and the Amazon. Ralph was captivated by her. She seemed honest, sincere, decent. Sad that she'd been maligned for whistleblowing. I liked her and hoped, like me, she'd meet someone for a second chance at happiness.

*

Conor was sorry he'd answered the phone. He must get one of the new ones that showed the number and identity of your caller so you could ignore people you didn't want to speak to.

'Good evening, Conrad.'

'What do you want, David?'

Goodman was annoyed. Conor sounded so unfriendly. 'I was just wondering if you were about next Saturday when I'll be through. Perhaps I might treat you to lunch?'

'Sorry, I'm busy.'

'That's a pity. How are things?

'Fine.'

'And your girlfriend, Jane, has she returned and seen the light?'

'No.'

'And has she reported the study irregularities?'

'Not to my knowledge. Anyway, I've pulled the drug, I told you.'

Goodman paused. 'And what is your next project to be?'

'Nothing of interest to you.'

'Well, I have something of interest for you. It is my intention to dispose of one of your long-standing problems.'

Con stiffened. This guy didn't get that he wanted nothing to do with him. But his curiosity was aroused. 'What do you mean?'

'Beth Semple.'

'Dispose? What do you mean?'

'You can choose the method if you like. Though, as she's not a patient, I might need to involve someone from London. I have a friend, Oscar, with connections.'

'Jesus Christ, are you mad? Oh, fuck off, Stan! And don't call again.'

Conor hung up so violently the receiver clattered onto the hall floor. After retrieving it, he felt so weak that he remained bent over for a few seconds. As he straightened, the mirror reflected his ashen face. Had Stan just offered to murder Beth Semple? Now, there'd been a time he'd thought about doing just that, but only 'thought'. Stan hadn't expanded on his quarrel with Beth, but Con was sure that if he did murder her, it'd be for his own gain, no one else's. Or might it be a bravado gambit to try and re-kindle their friendship? Surely, Goodman or Stan or David or whatever he called himself, couldn't imagine that? Stan had never been good at maintaining friends, and Conor himself had never been good at psychiatry, but he recognised insanity when he saw it. Tomorrow he'd change his phone number.

*

It is mid-April. Goodman is gazing at Christine Tweedale's records on the Kilnglass surgery computer. Date of birth: 1.5.43. Occupation: secretary. Past history: appendicitis. Pregnancies 1966, 1969. Sterilisation 1972. Recent endoscopy diagnosis: hiatus hernia. Not much of a life. His plan is now overdue. He had abandoned the April start for his new projects after Maureen had ingenuously informed him that week of police interest.

'Do the police regularly question relatives after a death, Doctor?'

'No. Why do you ask?'

'Well, my friend Stella has been questioned about the death of her mother two years ago. She was ours. Do you remember Betty Cockburn?'

'I don't recall her. Have the family made a complaint?'

'No, I don't think so, Doctor. Here's your tea. Two folk in.'

Uneasiness had wrapped around him. He had decided it was best to postpone his plan for Christine.

He walks out to greet her. Richard's wife is smiling, wearing a smart tweed coat which should be mothballed now, it's spring. He says little. With these older women you need say little. They talk. He prints a Losec prescription for her reflux, advises smaller frequent meals and suggest a return in a couple of weeks.

'Thank you, Doctor.' She puts the script in her handbag and removes her diary.

He brings up the surgery appointments for two weeks hence. 'Five o'clock on May 1st, Mrs Tweedale?'

'May Day? Fine.' She writes in her diary, gives a lash-fluttering smile and leaves.

She is still attractive, well-preserved. As so often. If times were different ... Returning to the screen he marks off as void the 'emergency' appointments following hers. She must be last. Already, he is trembling with anticipation. It never diminishes, the pleasure.

Thirty

Never in a Million Years

After a jolly week in Bristol it was back to porridge and old clothes and a strict self-imposed study schedule for Julia. Katy had a more lackadaisical approach. As there had been no further incidents, we'd relaxed the school pick-up, though still urged the girls to be cautious. Sergeant MacPherson reassured us that, in his opinion, our 'poison penner' had moved on. The Goodman Question languished on the back burner.

The week after Easter, Charles was away, Gerry was his usual semi-conscientious but not over-energetic self, and I was snowed under, rarely home before 7.30 p.m.. Mum moved in until Charles returned. On Friday evening, it's always a Friday, came disaster. I was about to switch off the computer when Ellen came running in.

'Sorry, there's one last emergency. Chest pain, temporary resident, a Mr Bradley Pitman. In his forties, quite dishy actually!'

'Ellen Dunn, listen to you! OK, send him in, but no more. Lock the front door now!'

I buzzed for the patient, feeling too tired to go out and greet him. The door opened to reveal the last person I'd have expected to see in a million years.

*

After band practice, Katy had marched Neil to the café, bought two vanilla ices and sat him down.

'Right, what's up? You've been weird since we're back.

300

I'm fed up with it!'

Neil was looking down, shoulders hunched. 'It's difficult to talk about.'

'What is it? You got some awful disease like syphilis?'

'No, don't be silly! Where'd I get a sexually transmitted disease?'

'So, you got a girl pregnant?'

'No! Don't make fun of me, you know I've never ... I wouldn't ...'

'Oh, for Christ's sake, cough it up. I'm losing patience!'

He picked up his spoon and put it down again, before biting his lower lip. 'I got into the study.'

'And?'

'You won't believe it.'

'Try me. If you don't tell me I'll strangle you, so help me God!

'Don't take the name of the Lord in vain!' Neil looked distressed.

Katy looked around then whispered. 'Does he have a dead body in there?'

'No! Of course not! You are making fun of me!' He was almost crying.

Katy sat with her arms folded, waiting.

'He's got jewellery, all labelled with initials and dates.

'Jewellery? Women's jewellery?'

Neil nodded. 'And there was a will.'

'Whose will?'

'A woman I've never heard of, her bank book too. But there's worse. He has a book ...'

'What kind of book?'

'A notebook with names, dates, lawyers, sons, daughters, paintings and drug dosages.'

Katy looked puzzled. 'Written by whom?'

'My father, of course. I know his writing. The book was locked in a drawer like the jewellery. I put them all back.'

'What do you think the book is?'

He took a deep breath. 'I think it's a murder book.'

*

I looked up in amazement. Conor stood in the doorway. He looked different. Still clean-shaven, fragrantly Armani-ed, in an expensive suit with silk tie, but, somehow, he was less assured, diminished? Or did I imagine it? Wordlessly, he moved across the room to sit, looking down, hands on thighs.

'What the fuck are you doing here?'

'Swearing, Beth? Not like you.' His slight smile looked rueful, not the usual self-satisfied smirk.

'And what's with "Bradley Pitman" – not very original!'

'Sorry, mind went blank. First name that popped up was Brad Pitt.'

'Anyway, you're obviously not ill, so what's this about?'

'I thought if I gave my real name you wouldn't see me.'

'Damn right, I wouldn't!' I felt myself flushing in anger.

'But I need to tell you something important.' His eyes were steady, open, anxious and looked straight at me. Disturbing. 'You know a Dr David Goodman, don't you?'

'Yes, of course, though I wish I didn't.'

'I have reason to believe he wants to kill you.'

I was stunned. 'Are you serious?'

'Perfectly, I'm afraid.'

'And why would you care?'

'Well, you've got kids. And murder? Well, it's big-league horrible. I think Goodman's mad. I know this sounds as if I'm nuts too, but from things he's said, I suspect he might've actually bumped off folk before. Like an old colleague who annoyed him. He's told me you made him angry and he knows we two have had issues as well.'

'Does he? Well, do you know Henry's had issues with

him, too? When he was called Truscott, Goodman was suspected of killing some patients in Bristol.'

'Well, his dead colleague I mentioned was in Bristol.' Con sighed heavily. 'Beth, I really think he means to do you harm. You'll have to watch out.'

'I'm touched you bothered to come.' I felt I had to admit it.

'Don't be like that. I'm not that bad. I couldn't have a murder on my conscience, I mean, you've got kids!' His distress was visible. I was dumbstruck. 'Mothers are so important.' He caught his breath. 'I woke up this morning thinking about something he said once about his mother. I thought he was joking, but now I'm not so sure.'

'What?'

'I think he killed her. Oh, and he has friends who are gangsters. One's called Oscar, down in London. Oh Beth, the guy's evil, trust me!'

My flesh was beginning to creep. If Conor thought Goodman evil, he must be spectacularly so. 'Have you been to the police?'

'No.' He put up his hands. 'I've been trying to keep a low profile. Bit of trouble at work.'

'Jane? I know. She came here. Has she reported you for research fraud?'

I watched him grimace before rubbing his face with the side of his hand.

'She made me pull an asthma drug. Probably right. It's all a mess.'

'Look, Con, it's late. I need to get home.' I stood up. 'But thanks for coming. I appreciate it.' I extended my hand, something I never thought I'd ever do. He clasped it. 'You know I've done a lot of things I'm not proud of. The drink. The cocaine. By the way, if you see Dan, say thanks. I never did thank him for saving my life. And I'm sorry, truly sorry, about Maia. I still have nightmares. I just didn't realise …

303

Anyway, take care.'

He looked so contrite I was moved. But not ready to forgive, I gave him a card from my bag. 'This is the DCI running an investigation into Goodman. Maitland's a good chap. If you do nothing else, please phone him, tell him what you know. You might save some lives.'

He pocketed it. 'Right. See you, Beth.' He left, quietly closing the door.

I sat back, overwhelmed. A repentant Conor, seemingly genuine in his desire to warn me to watch my back? Mind-blowing. Was there a contract on me with this Oscar? Christ, I had no idea what to do. I called Ralph, if only to speak to him without the girls overhearing. Exams loomed. Home was already intense. Katy had stormed out that morning vowing never to return.

Ralph was terse. 'Jesus! Get home!'

I flung my signed letters at a startled Alison in reception and ran, weeping, to the car. Someone wanted me dead.

After a numb weekend punctuated by police coming and going, DCI Maitland arrived at Monday lunchtime to notify me that this time, we could expect a home security visit.

'Could they come while the girls are at school, please? It's English exams tomorrow.'

'Sure, Dr Semple. We do think, by the way, that you shouldn't worry too much. It'll be more difficult for him to target you as you aren't a patient. We feel we almost have enough evidence now to apply for search warrants. The Fiscal's Office are clarifying some confidentiality issues.'

I grunted. 'Didn't take the Health Board long to access mine!'

'As we said, just be vigilant, take cognisance of your surroundings. Collect the girls from school again and maybe avoid going out at night presently.'

'But I do nights here.'

'I would strongly advise against it. Perhaps I could speak to your partners?'

I phoned through for Charles and Gerry, whom I'd called on Saturday morning about the threat. Gerry promptly offered to shoulder my out-of-hours slots.

'Happy to do them. Don't worry, Beth, it's going to be fine.'

But I was filling up. Maitland leaned over and patted my hand. 'We've nearly got him, I think, Dr Semple.' He leaned back. 'Oh, and by the way, he hasn't got a gun licence, we've checked.'

I started crying. 'But that doesn't mean he hasn't got a gun!' Gerry turned white and scuttled off, to return with a cup of tea and a whole plate of biscuits. The detective left. My tea was loaded with sugar and I couldn't drink it, but it was a kind thought.

Charles was standing with his arms folded, leaning against the sink. 'Think you should go home Beth, have a rest before evening surgery. Might be best, though, if you had company. I'll phone Gwen.'

'No need. Mum's there. She came on Saturday.'

*

Next day, Katy came out of the English exam pleased it hadn't been as bad as she'd expected.

'Sorry, can't do café today, Neil. Gotta go with Susan's mum.'

He looked glum. 'Nor me. Need to get home. Mum's not well.'

'Oh, sorry. What's wrong?'

'Don't know. She's sleepy and tired, taken to her bed.'

'Has she seen a doctor?'

Neil shook his head. 'I wanted to call someone, but Dad says he's given her stuff, she just needs a rest. He's sent in a sick line.'

'Is that allowed?'

'Well, she uses a different name for work, so they won't know Dr Goodman is her husband.'

'You done anything about that weird study stuff you found?'

'No. Thought best get the exams over first.' Slinging his backpack over his shoulder, he ambled off.

A troubled Katy waited for Julia at the gates and went home in Susan's mum's Rover. But once home, she was pleasantly distracted. Her mum was sitting eating freshly-baked cake. And Gran was making apple pie. Things were looking up.

'So, how were the papers, girls? I came home to see how you got on.'

Katy gave her a tight hug. Her home seemed so safe and secure, unlike Neil's. She swithered whether to say anything about Neil's mum, but decided not to spoil the mood. Besides, she might be fine by tomorrow. And Neil's book might not be what he imagined. It could be an outline for a novel.

*

I was relieved when the exams finished. All that could be done now was to wait for July and the results. But I was still wracked with anxiety about Goodman. The police had not been in touch apart from installing two CCTV cameras outside – one pointing down the drive, the other at the back garden – and the fitting of a burglar alarm, all accomplished during one school day. The girls didn't notice. We'd booked Center Parcs at Nottingham for the following weekend, the May holiday. Ralph brooked no excuses. We would go on Friday night, return on the Monday, May 2nd. I was persuaded going away was best. Ralph insisted it would divert the girls, if not me, from worrying. Hearing of the indoor swimming pools and bike hire, the girls were enthusiastic, especially since Winston and Mum could come too.

The day before we left, Neil came for tea. He was extremely quiet, and when asked about any holiday plans, he looked upset and shook his head. I changed the subject.

'How's your mum, Neil?'

'Not so good.'

'What's wrong?

'Dad says it's a bug. She's in bed.'

Though I now knew she was my patient, I couldn't offer to visit. I doubted Goodman knew she'd ever registered. And I still wondered why she did.

Katy saw him out. Returning, she stood twirling her hair. 'I know you don't like his dad, but I'm worried about Neil – and his mum.'

What could I say? 'Och, she'll probably be as right as rain in a few days.'

Katy went upstairs. Julia moved in to whisper confidentially, 'I'm worried about Katy.'

God, everyone was worrying about everyone else! I felt like screaming. 'Why?'

'She won't talk. Usually, as you know, she never shuts up. And she isn't playing her awful East 17 stuff.'

'I'm not sure that's a sign of any ailment, Jules. If anything, it might be a sign of growing up! It's probably the strain of the exams. We're all tired. Ralph's right, a weekend away will cheer us up.'

I couldn't help thinking, though, that I was running away from the problem, and I nursed a secret terror we might be followed. We let Maitland know our plans. He was the only one.

Thirty-One

Death & Drama

Center Parcs wasn't without incident. On the Friday night, as we took our window seats in the restaurant, I saw Goodman leaving.

Panicking, I was on the verge of phoning Maitland when Ralph sprinted after him. I was worried what he might do and just about to hit 'call' when, to my relief, Ralph returned, shaking his head. He was angry.

'You'll need to cool it, Beth. I followed your guy into the loo. Got funny looks for hanging about till he came out of a cubicle. But apart from his beard, that guy was nothing like Goodman!'

'But you followed him too!' I sniffed into my hanky.

The girls exchanged eye rolling glances. Ralph ordered fish and chips for everyone, then announced, 'Sun's shining. Bike ride in the morning, girls, with me. Mum and Gran are off to the spa.' He raised an eyebrow at me and patted Mum's hand. She tried to smile.

The girls took advantage of my distraction and hit the high-octane Coke. I sat feeling confused, foolish, scared, helpless and angry all at once.

Mum and I enjoyed our facials and massages next morning, then she opted to cook for the girls in the lodge on the Saturday night to allow Ralph and I to go for dinner by ourselves. A lot of wine was consumed. Ralph did his best to comfort me on our return. I slept a bit. Sunday was the pool, followed by a lovely long lunch and a walk. We got back to Rowanlea at 4 p.m. on the Monday.

I took Winston for a brief 'business' walk in the park

at five, emptied the suitcases into the washing machine and made the tea. After a laughing, lovely family evening of Monopoly, we flopped into bed by 10.30 p.m.. Life was going to go on whatever the Goodman outcome was. Ralph curled round me. I was physically and emotionally exhausted. Dreamless sleep for once.

*

Kilnglass Surgery

Monday May 2nd has arrived. The stage is set. Code Blue. The door opens. Maureen has his tea and Hobnobs.

'No mail?'

'It's May Day public holiday, Doctor, remember? Kilnglass is the only practice open.'

'Ridiculous! May Day is not a religious holiday. In fact, it is pagan, even Trotskyist! I see no reason to inconvenience patients by closing.'

'Yes, Doctor. Jocelyn and I are on for you. Dr Nixon has taken the few calls.'

'I hope Dr Nesbitt enjoys his weekend away.' In reality he doesn't care, but Maureen expects chat.

'Paris in the spring? So romantic!'

'I went once, on my first ...' he fakes a cough, 'when I was on honeymoon. A filthy place. No wash hand basins in the lavatories. And some water closets were only holes in the floor!'

'Oh, gracious!' Maureen's eyes widen. 'Mrs Goodman must have hated that! How is she, Doctor? I haven't crossed her path lately. I often used to bump into her at Asda.'

'She is unwell, Maureen. In fact, quite in confidence, Clara has a problem.' Maureen's face registers appropriate concern. 'I fear she is drinking to excess. Wine and vermouth. And recently, rum. I am concerned for the boy.'

'How awful, Doctor! If there's anything I can do. Perhaps

sit with her or take Neil?'

'You are so truly kind, Maureen, but it won't be necessary. I am dealing with it.' He dons his reading glasses and turns to the screen. 'Must get on.' He nods. She leaves.

The anticipation grows with each patient. He savours his plan. By 5 p.m., only he and Maureen will be here. This first time, it's difficult to predict timings, but otherwise, the plan is sound. He guesses it will be ten minutes before he should call Maureen, who will come running. As always, he is slightly giddy with anticipation. Doubtless explains his little lapses with Maureen. Mentioning his first honeymoon! And suggesting rum? No genteel woman like Clara would consider working-class rum! Unlike his own mother.

But Clara has been increasingly irritating too, of late. Questioning his movements, being disobedient, surly. Regrettably, the outcome is now inevitable. His plan is proceeding well. Disseminating rumours about her drinking has been easy and he's had her slurred at church, even one day hatless and flustered. He has altered the kitchen clock. Simple deceits. And easy to contradict her memory in post-service conversations, implying confusion. As belt and braces, he has placed wine receipts and empty bottles in the airing cupboard and made AA calls late at night. How simple to mimic a weepy, mumbling, drunk woman and give her name. He knows calls are recorded. She's weakening now. Soon he'll call someone in for 'advice.' Perhaps Beth Semple? The irony appeals!

He reflects on his life with Clara. Now she seems more like a plain Mary, the name she chose in rebellion against her parents' fervent Catholicism. She hated being called Marie-Claire. Though he had considered her a perfect wife, the virginal Clara has degenerated into a wilful shrew, transgressing Ephesians' exhortation that, '*wives should submit to their husbands as to the Lord.*' That truculence when he forbade membership of a Women's Guild group!

Gossiping with other women was unthinkable. He has sent weekly sick lines to her work. Fortunately, pharmacy access is no longer necessary for his future plans. By the time she's hospitalised, her liver failure will be untreatable, but from tonight he'd best start reducing the hepatotoxic phenobarbitone and phenytoin in case it is detected by drug screening. High-dose soluble paracetamol and vodka will suffice to keep her quiet.

He regards his couch patient. Syringe A, the blue mix, is working well. Christine Tweedale is lying silent and pale. He checks her fluttering, weakening pulse; life is ebbing. A little more time for safety. The triple appointment has been perfect, as has the choice of a quiet surgery on a public holiday. No attendant nurse to complicate things.

He sits back down to examine the latest registered-post package from Oscar. He now has medical papers to match his two fake passports, extra insurance to facilitate a new continental life should it be necessary. Though he's heard that police have visited a few more former patients' relatives, he's still confident they will get nothing. But the malicious rumour Maureen has reported as emanating from Dawson's is troublesome.

He places the medical degree paperwork into his bag and rises to check on his patient. It is time. Checking the time on his watch, he rises and opens the door.

'Maureen!' He shouts up the corridor. 'An ambulance, quickly! Mrs Tweedale has collapsed! She's had a heart attack!'

Turning back into his room, he hears her speaking to the emergency services. A few minutes later, as high-heeled shoes clatter on the corridor vinyl flooring, he moves back to the couch. Maureen appears in the threshold, looking upset, hand over her mouth as if to stifle a cry as she looks in the door which he has left ajar. He is going through the motions of CPR, but the minute she heads back to reception to await the ambulance, he stands back. The paramedics take almost fifteen minutes. Excellent. On hearing boots thumping along the vinyl corridor, he resumes rhythmic pressure on the chest of Mrs Christine Tweedale while breathing heavily as if he's been exerting himself for a while. The ambulance men rush in. Checking for a carotid pulse and finding none, they attach their defibrillator. No electrical activity shows.

'Stand back!' they cry. Electricity violently jolts her body. A feeble fibrillating line appears on the machine monitor.

From the side of the room, he watches them 'fry' her once more, attach a drip and administer adrenaline. But he knows, as they rush her out on their recumbent chair, that she is irretrievable.

He tidies the room, tearing off the torn paper couch cover, rolling out a fresh piece of the exact length and packing his stethoscope into his bag. Supposing Maureen is in the office preparing to go home, he is surprised when she reappears. With Richard. He had not considered that Maureen might phone him. How pointless.

'Oh, Doctor, was that her ambulance leaving? What are her chances?' Richard Tweedale is hysterical. Gratifying.

Goodman sniffs and wipes an imaginary tear. Hands clasped he speaks softly. 'I am so sorry, Richard, she collapsed during examination. I fear the chest pains she's been having have not been solely due to hiatus hernia.'

'Where have they taken her?'

'St Mungo's.'

'Come, let me drive you.' Ellen ushers out the sobbing Richard.

Goodman sits down to type in a computer entry for today and modify one from two weeks previously. He collects the scattered needles, syringes and ampoules from the trolley and drops them into his little yellow sharps bin, before utilising his master key and swapping his box with Brian's next door. Standing at the window he admires the surgery garden and savours a deep breath of satisfaction. Rubeniclast is untraceable, not even on the market. There are no standard tests for detecting it. A random selection of several sets of tablets he had kept, ground up finely, proved very soluble. At least some were not placebo. It had been a little gamble. But a small one.

Noting it is almost 6 p.m., he collects his bag and checks the office phone system. Irritated to discover Maureen has not diverted it to Kevin before leaving, he switches it over, sets the alarm and locks up. Tonight, he will decide on Dr Semple's fate. There are several possibilities.

*

Balgrove Academy

The day after the May Day holiday, Katy was grumpy at returning to school. Her fourth year Standard Grades had finished, so she had to return. The fifth years, including Julia, could stay off, as there were still Higher exams to come. Katy was even grumpier when she couldn't find Neil at morning break. But in the dinner queue, he had no escape.

'What's up? You avoiding me?'

'No, Katy. Nothing's up.'

'Really? Could've fooled me. We need to chat.'

'No, we don't. In fact, you're better off staying away from me.'

Katy folded her arms and looked fierce. 'Rubbish, I'm not having that! Bike shed, fifteen minutes or I'll never speak to you again, Neil Goodman!' Snatching juice and a packet of crisps, she hurriedly paid and sped outside.

She hadn't been there long when he arrived. 'So? What's wrong?'

'Oh, lots of things. Like I'm wondering if Dad's trying to poison Mum.'

'What?'

'He insists on making all her food and drink, wants her to stay in bed.'

'Why?'

'Dunno.'

'Does *she* think he's poisoning her?'

'She was cross when I suggested it, but I think she might. When she's not too sleepy, I think she puts stuff down the loo after he goes. I thought I saw some chicken and flushed it away.'

Katy couldn't think what to say, then asked, 'Why are you sure he wants to poison her?'

'It's just …' Neil fidgeted on the bench, looking anxious. 'The way he stands over her, urging her to finish what he's giving her.'

'Doesn't he just want her to get her strength back?'

'It's not that kind of *nice* coaxing. Hard to explain. Anyway, she isn't hungry. She's lost shedloads of weight.'

Katy sat up. 'I have an idea. Can you get some of her food or drink?'

'Probably. Why?'

'We've got some bottles like the ones John used to find out what poisoned Winston. I'll bring them tomorrow. But it sounds like your mum has to see a doctor.'

'Dad won't get one. She's too weak to walk now. And I can't drive!' His voice broke.

Katy thought he might cry and gave him a hug. 'I wonder if, maybe, you went back into the study, found something to prove he is up to no good, maybe really is a poisoner. I mean, I didn't believe it, but …' She paused. Neil's head was down in his hands. 'When he's out, couldn't we get that stuff you saw and then call an ambulance?'

'He'd kill me!

'I think I should tell Mum.'

'No!' Neil looked terrified.

'Does he hit you?'

Neil shook his head.

Katy fiercely crushed up her crisp packet. 'We have to do something for your poor mum. What time does he go into his gym?'

'Quarter past, half past seven.'

'Are there windows in this study of his?'

'Yes, big ones he keeps locked.'

'Right. Get in tonight, leave a window off the catch, and tomorrow after school we'll get in, suss the stuff he's got locked up and call 999 if your mum's still ill.'

Neil was shaking. 'She will be, but I don't know if I can do it.'

Katy gripped his hand. 'I *do* know! I'll bring the bottles tomorrow. There's no band practice after school and I'll tell Gran we're going to the café on the way home. We'll get the book and stuff, phone an ambulance, speak to the police, all before he's home and then you'll come home with me.'

The bell went. Katy gave him a hug and went to her class, resolving that whatever Neil did, she'd speak to her mother about this awful situation.

But that night, Winston had chewed the TV cables, and her mother was in a foul mood with stomach cramps. She shouted at Katy for the state of her bedroom and failure to put dirty clothes in the basket. 'I'm not your servant! I've had enough!' she yelled, before going to bed early. Katy didn't answer back. Her mum had been having a hard time. She'd tell her in the morning that Neil would be home with her tomorrow after school. And maybe why. With Ralph out and Julia buried in a book, Katy managed to fetch Ralph's camera from the hall cupboard and put it in her schoolbag. Seemed a good idea. Luckily, Ralph had shown her how to use it at Center Parcs. Then she collected four little plastic bottles with silver lids from the utility room stash. Though labelled 'Sputum', they said 'sterile' and were similar to the Winston sample ones. Briefly, she considered phoning to ask

Aunt Cressie what to get but concluded she'd likely phone Mum back and thwart the plan. She couldn't let Neil down. Perhaps Julia might know about forensic lab samples? But asking her was equally risky. She spoke to no one.

Next morning, with her mum up and out early for an emergency, Ralph took them to school. Katy said nothing. At lunchtime, she gave Neil the bottles. He buried them in his bag.

'Did you fix the window, Neil?'

'Yes. Wasn't easy. Don't think that window catch has been moved for years, needed olive oil to get it moving.'

'Smart thinking!'

'See you later.' He went off to PE, Katy to English. She sighed. It'd be a long day.

*

Oakfield Surgery

After Wednesday morning surgery, DCI Maitland phoned.

'Just updating you, Dr Semple. Not for broadcasting, but we are applying today for warrants to search the good doctor's surgery and home. The CID have reasonable doubts about eight deaths and have applied for one exhumation so far. I'll keep you posted. I'd advise you to continue to take care. We will be in touch.'

I felt elated. Then guilty, since people were dead. Then, almost immediately, afraid. What might Goodman do if questioned? My gut churned.

Around 2 p.m., Ellen and Charles came to my room and stood looking grim. They held up an *Evening Times* front page, emblazoned 'Suicide of Glasgow GP!' The photo was of Brian Nesbitt.

Charles was spluttering. 'This is poppycock! He's been clean for months, Beth. He wouldn't OD, nor leave a note saying he "couldn't go on" because his girlfriend rejected his proposal. Rubbish! He told me he'd bottled out of asking Jackie at the weekend – decided it wasn't the time.' Charles flipped a hand at the paper. 'Goodman's behind this, mark my words! I'm phoning Maitland.'

'He's just off the phone. They're getting warrants and exhuming and …'

Charles shot off. Ellen followed. Despite my terror, I managed to struggle through the baby clinic. As the last patient left, the phone rang and Ellen put through Julia.

'Hi, Mum. Was Katy doing something on the way home tonight?'

'What? Don't think so.' My heart somersaulted. 'Why? Isn't she home?'

'No. I phoned Susan's. She's not there. Shall I try Lisa and Nicole's house?'

'Please. It's probably fine. Gran there?'

'Yes, she's in the kitchen.'

'Fine, see you soon.' I was surprised how calm my voice sounded. With constricted chest and heart pounding my ears, I packed up and rushed out, blurting explanations at Ellen.

'Katy's not come home. Could you phone Ralph and the CID boys?' I thrust one of Maitland's cards at her.

With shaking hands, I fumbled the key into the car door and drove home well over the speed limit, breathing maybe only twice on the way and jumping at least one red light. Katy had still not arrived. It was 6 p.m.. Where the hell was she? Ralph's Triumph sped into the gravel drive. As I collapsed into his arms, the first police car drew up.

Thirty-Two

Lot's Wife

Rowanlea

A missing child numbs the brain and ossifies the spirit. The emptiness of your heart is unimaginable if you haven't been there.

My brain offered no plan of action, no solution. A sinking void had replaced my stomach. What if I never saw her again? I took a deep breath, chiding myself I was being ridiculous. I switched on the kettle. Before that moment I'd never understood the kettle-in-a-crisis ritual. Now I did. Pouring a glass of water might divert you for seconds, but fiddling with kettles and teabags and mugs and spoons and milk reaffirms you can move and act, and distances you from the enormity of your catastrophe for a longer period of time. Not long enough. I sat to sip but caught sight of Katy's saxophone case and my stomach void became a chasm. My brain detonated. She was dead. My happy, brilliant girl was dead. My fault. I became Lot's wife: petrified. What now?

The kitchen clock said 11 p.m., seven hours since she was last seen at school. Ralph was in the study with the CID. My further 999 call on getting home had raised a young buck who'd said, 'You're panicking unnecessarily, Madam. Most youngsters turn up within a few hours. They tend to party, forget the time.'

'Jesus, my daughter's never late! And our family have been threatened. Get Chief Inspector Maitland to 76 Cedar Drive – and move it! My brother's the Chief Constable!'

Well, in truth he was my brother-in-law, not brother, and

he wasn't Chief here, but in Lothian, but I had no time for petty details. He got it. I got Maitland within minutes. After that, the phone kept ringing. I couldn't answer it. Ralph did. Mum had tried to comfort Julia, who blamed herself that she hadn't waited for her sister at school. They were now upstairs in Katy's room.

Katy always called if she was going to be late. Though it was Wednesday, not Tuesday café day, Ralph had gone to Fanconi's. The handful of kids still there hadn't seen her, or Neil. I'd phoned all her friends, alarmed mothers, and interrogated daughters. The void was threatening to swallow me again, but I had to concentrate and not pass out. I breathed strength from my toes, trying to remember yoga relaxation techniques. Yoga brought back Jean. I started hyperventilating, my forearms tingling and my toes sprouting pins and needles. The door opened with its habitual creak, though tonight it sounded louder, menacing. But it was only Julia.

'Where's Dad?'

Julia looked so like my father tonight. I remembered his rage at me one night, twenty years ago, when I'd rolled in late from a dance, crashing doorstep milk bottles. How the world turns in ever-repeating circles of misunderstanding. I sent up a silent prayer for forgiveness.

'Still in the study with the police.'

'We had another look round her room. Nothing's missing.'

'Why would there be?'

'That's what they do on the telly for "missing persons," like, to see if they've packed stuff.'

'Oh, right. You sure she didn't mention plans for after school? Like with Neil?'

'Well she was very tête-à-tête with him at break. Now I think on it, she gave him a poly bag with wee silver-topped pots in it. Weird. Might it be important? I'm so confused.'

'Silver-topped pots?'

'Yes, like the one you got Katy to spit into when she had that chesty thing that didn't clear up. Oh, and you gave to the vet after Winston was sick.'

Sputum pots? I went into the utility room cupboard where I kept extra supplies for my bag. The shelf for specimen bottles looked barer than it should. 'So, what would Neil want them for?'

Julia shrugged. 'No idea.'

I stormed into the study. 'Any word?'

'We've gone through the list of friends Julia gave us and the numbers in the diary from Katy's room and phoned the hospitals. All patrols have her description and photo. You know, we'd normally wait longer than this.' Maitland was coolly professional, but his eyes were human.

'Never mind that, what about Goodman's house? Have they been there?'

'Officers called. Got no answer. All dark and the phone rang out.'

'She's with Neil. I'm sure of it. Get round there now and break down the door!'

'How can you be sure she's there?'

'I think she's collecting specimens from Neil's mum. She's sick.'

'What?' Maitland looked baffled.

My father's old grandfather clock in the hall chimed midnight. I explained about Julia's story of the specimen pots ...

'Why didn't she say this before?' Maitland was irritated and got on his radio. We piled into his car, though Ralph volunteered to stay in case Katy turned up. If Maitland was unhappy at having a teenager, a granny and a doctor mum with bag squashed into his back seat, he knew better than to say. The drive was short, but by the time we arrived, I was an atheist. What kind of God allowed a mother to go through this?

As we sat outside the silent, foreboding house, I realised that I hadn't known where Goodman lived. But reassuringly, Maitland and co did. He was on their radar. The uniforms banged on the door, then a constable walked to the rear. There was only one car in the drive: Mary's little Fiesta. No sign of Goodman's Jag. The garage lay open, empty, everything gone. Like him. And my girl. I allowed myself a sob. My hopes of finding her alive were evaporating. Where was Katy?

*

Westhaven, earlier

After school, Neil had led Katy to his house. They'd dumped their bags in the back porch and returned to the garden. After struggling to lift the window that Neil had left unlocked, they finally climbed into the study.

Neil used a tool he'd bought in the ironmongers to fiddle with the lock of the top right desk drawer. Katy was visibly impressed. He lifted out a notebook and opened it flat on the desk for her to take photographs. She took a dozen or so. The pages listed initials, cause of death, sometimes drug or relatives' names, a money sum, jewellery, or a painting by title, all in spidery, old-fashioned writing. Even without time to digest the entries, Katy knew this was no novel synopsis. Neil replaced the book, jiggling his tool again to re-lock the drawer. Katy high-fived him.

The left upper desk drawer was easier. From it, Neil removed a jewellery roll. All items were labelled. Katy took close-up photos of them before Neil replaced it and reset the second lock. She moved round the room, taking pictures of the paintings and sculptures.

'This stuff must be worth a mint, Neil!'

'I'm sure. Right, that's us all locked again. Let's get out of here!'

Neil closed the window. Katy was anxious it still looked slightly open. Neil wasn't. 'It's so high up he'll not notice. Anyway, he likes the curtains closed.'

'Right, now let's sort your mum. Which is her bedroom?'

Neil consulted his watch. 'Gosh, it's after five. Dad will be on his last patient. There isn't much time! He ran to the stairs.

In Clara's bedroom, Katy was shocked to see Neil's mum looking so yellow and thin, hardly like the woman she'd seen at school concerts. 'How are you, Mrs Goodman?'

'Not so good, my dear. I just need to get a bit stronger.' She tried to sit up but slipped back on the bed.

'I'll make you a hot drink and some toast!' Katy sped down the stairs before Neil could stop her. What was she playing at? Shouldn't they just phone for an ambulance? They'd have to leave soon. His mother gave a low moan. He must make her comfy, get to the phone. 'Oh, Mum.' He plumped up pillows. 'Have you eaten anything today?'

'Dad gave me soup at lunchtime. I've had a nap.'

'We have to leave, Mum. I think Dad's a murderer.'

Her eyes were sad. 'I don't want to think about it. Oh, darling! He alters my computer at work ...' Her lids were closing as she drifted off again. He wanted to pick her up and carry her out of the house, but knew he wasn't strong enough. Katy came back with hot milk and toast, but his mother was unable to take any. He slammed the side of his fist onto the wall. 'That's it! Ambulance, now! Hope they're quick. Go phone. I'll do a reccie to see if we can find what he's been giving her.' He careered round the bedroom and bathroom, throwing bottles and packets into a carrier he'd lifted from a chair. 'Come on, let's phone!'

As they ran downstairs, they heard a car pulling up on the gravel.

'*Shit*! In here!' He pulled Katy in through the basement door, closing it behind them. Down in the gym, Neil stared at a high horizontal window in horror. 'Where's the door gone? Buggery! He had men in a few weeks ago and I haven't been down here since. The bastard's bricked up the basement door!' He sobbed.

Katy was already pulling over the exercise bike. Standing on it precariously, she could reach the window catch but it was stiff, and she was at a bad angle. A door creaked. She froze.

'Neil? That you down there? What are you doing?'

Katy dived behind a large chest. Neil had no cover. He moved to the foot of the stairs.

'Coming, Dad! Just trying out your machines. The PE teacher says I need to bulk up.' He was at the top of the stairs before his father could descend.

'Weight training at your age can damage epiphyseal plates in your joints. Stay out of the gym. I'll get you proper instruction when the time is right.'

'Great, Dad.' He stepped into the hall and his father turned the basement door key and pocketed it. *Shit!* 'I've taken Mum up some milk and toast but she's not great. I think she should ...'

'I will go up. Put on some coffee.'

Neil sped into the kitchen. God, Katy's backpack lay in the porch, her camera on the table! Moving a shelf up, he stuffed the backpack into the oven. The camera fitted into a lidded soup pot in the Rayburn cupboard. Trembling, he spooned grounds into the percolator, mind racing. Should he run off out the back door to the police and take the camera? But he couldn't leave Katy. What if ... God! He took out coffee cups, started laying them out as his father appeared. He wordlessly poured a coffee and went to his study, locking the door.

Neil looked at the basement door. Could he pick it too? *Shit again*! His screwdriver was beside Katy!

In the basement, Katy looked at her watch: almost 7 p.m. now. Tea would be ready. Mum probably frantic. There was no phone in the basement. She couldn't budge the window catch. Pity she'd none of Neil's olive oil. But wait, Neil had left his little screwdriver! Could she shift the catch with it? Now, if she could only get above it ... The chest would be more stable than the bike. She started to drag it over.

*

The study is chilly. He turns up the radiator. Clara is very weak. Tomorrow he'll request a 'second opinion' from the Semple woman.

Neil will take it hard, no doubt. Plans need to be made for him. Of course, at sixteen the boy can be left. But not overnight when he has to be in Edinburgh. Boarding school again might be best. Perhaps the Northumberland college advertised in the church magazine? The expense is immaterial.

Taking out his leather journal, he records today's adventures but notes some page corners are curling. How so? He flattens them. Rising to pull the curtain cords to close them he catches a whiff of something. Oil? From what? Displaced lubricant in the sliding curtain track, perhaps? He returns to writing up his day. As he finishes, he hears a bang. A car backfiring? But this room is to the rear, away from the road. No, the noise was surely inside the house. Downstairs? Neil must have returned to the basement. Locking the drawers, he goes out to the hall to listen at the basement door before unlocking it and creeping down.

He senses her before he sees her. Fear, female fear. More subtle than the sweat of male fear, but discernible to the cognoscenti. Noting the chest containing his weights has been moved, he puts the light on and walks over. She is crouching behind. Ashen.

'My dear? What are you doing down here? How could Neil abandon you? You must come upstairs.'

He takes her by the arm, dusts her down and propels her up the bare wooden stairs. Neil is not in the kitchen. He must be with his mother. Goodman makes conversation and a cup of tea. 'We must phone your mother to tell her where you are. She'll be worried.'

He goes into the hall, leaving the door open. She hears him dialling.

'Yes, she's here, Doctor, safe and sound. I'll drop her back later.'

He returns and urges another cup of tea on her. 'A teacake perhaps?'

'No, thank you. Aren't you having some, Doctor?'

'Oh no, tea is for women! ' He laughs. 'So, what have you and Neil been up to?'

Katy's mouth is dry. She drinks the tea. 'I came to see how Neil's mother is. She's very ill. Needs hospital.'

As bold and interfering as her mother. 'Well, you know, Clara doesn't like doctors. But if she isn't better tomorrow, I'll insist. Now, I must go and ask her what she'd like for tea.'

*

After he left, Katy tried to rise but panicked as she found her legs didn't work. Falling on the floor, two realisations hit her. She should never have drunk that tea. And he had not asked for her phone number.

*

On his return he sweeps up the limp Katy and carries her

to the basement to deposit her back behind the chest. He strokes her auburn hair. This sleeping beauty's only fault was to be born to a devil. But he isn't merciless: his double-dose opiate cocktail means she will not suffer. Mounting the stairs, he locks the basement door.

His work here is done. Christine Tweedale is easily explained away, but not Katy in the basement. Today he'd overheard office whispers about a CID interview last week. Yet Maureen has not mentioned it. But he smiles. The authorities' growing interest added a certain frisson to today's pleasure.

Back in the study, he fills his large leather briefcase with cash, jewellery, and Oscar's passports, but on hearing Neil returning to the kitchen and opening the fridge, he goes through to meet him.

'Mum wants scrambled eggs.' Neil is whisking eggs in a Pyrex bowl. David never eats eggs. Infected with deadly salmonella! He observes this beautiful son who has brought joy to his life, though not as much as he'd hoped; too much of a mummy's boy. Taking Neil will slow him down, make him more easily identifiable. David silently returns to the study and waits with the door open. He sees Neil glance in, then hears the stairs creaking, one by one, as the boy takes the food up to his mother.

*

Neil was pleased to find Clara sitting up. She took a forkful of egg and smiled.

'I'll just go down and eat my eggs up before they get cold, Mum, then be right back up with a cup of tea!'

At the foot of the stairs, however, Neil found his father was waiting to usher him into the study. Even stranger, he then paid him a compliment.

'I am proud of the way you are looking after your mother,

Neil.'

Then, before Neil knew what was happening, his father was thrusting a glass of whisky towards his face.

'Dad, I don't want this. You know I don't like ...' Neil tried to push it back, but found he was no match for his strong father, who suddenly moved behind him to forcefully clamp his left hand over Neil's eyes and nose. Finding it impossible to breathe as the stinging liquid was poured into his mouth, Neil gurgled and choked in terror. But by the time his father loosened his grip, he was incapable of uttering a word, and, knees buckling, could do no more than sink to the floor.

*

Goodman watches his son give a last few weak sobs. It is a few minutes before the boy's eyes roll upwards and his mouth slackens into deep unconsciousness. Satisfied the dose has been enough, Goodman lifts his bag and leaves the study.

Clara never gets her tea.

Thirty-Three

Death's Door

I was consumed with frustration as the police stood outside Westhaven debating on the legality of breaking and entering Goodman's house. Leaving Julia and Mum whispering, I ran around to the back, where Constable Teviot was standing guard by the back door. It was half-glazed, part of a small conservatory. I lifted a rock and hurled it through the glass. Teviot watched open-mouthed as the glass tinkled into shards, then shouted loudly to his colleagues, 'Hey, there's a broken window. We're going in.'

Inside, the hall clock chimed one. The constable walked in front of me as I advanced, shouting, 'Katy!' Weak moans could be heard coming from upstairs. Saints be praised!

In a back bedroom, I found Neil's mother, Mary, though I almost didn't recognise her. Barely conscious, she was mumbling about 'Katy' and 'Neil' and 'tea.' After a brief examination of her frail frame, I rushed downstairs to telephone 999 for an ambulance. I thought it odd there was no phone in Mary's room, but I'd seen one in the hall on the way in. Obviously, Goodman didn't sleep with Clara. He'd need a phone when on call.

I saw more police had arrived and were clattering about. Nothing subtle about this house search, but they shook their heads when I asked if they'd found Katy. Back upstairs, I assessed Mary as jaundiced, cachexic, and dehydrated. She was tremulous and jittery, obviously in liver failure and looking ready to fit. But I couldn't risk giving an anti-convulsant without knowing what she's been given. Something must have poisoned her to have made her this ill in only weeks. I tried to rouse her to drink water.

The ambulance men soon arrived and were setting up a drip on Mary when I heard a door splintering and shouts from below. Running down, I saw Teviot and MacPherson standing over Neil in the study. On the thick carpet he lay pale, sweating and breathing shallowly. His pulse and blood pressure were low, his pupils tiny. Opiate poisoning? With nothing to lose, I snatched a shot of naloxone, an opium antidote, from my bag, shouting to Teviot to order another ambulance. But where the hell was Katy? Had Goodman taken her as hostage?

Within a few minutes of the injection, Neil started mumbling. Glory be! My diagnosis was correct.

'Katy! The basement ...' Lifting a limp hand he pointed through the study door to one on the other side of the hall.

Macpherson rattled the handle ineffectually then rammed his side into it. It gave, but not without him crying out. He clutched his shoulder and doubled up to appear several inches narrower, with, I suspected, a fractured collar bone. Teviot ran past him down the stairs calling 'Katy!' Before I could rise to my feet from tending Neil, my mother rushed from the hall down the stairs after the constable.

I heard Teviot shouting from the basement, as if he were trying to wake up a drunk. My mother appeared from the depths, breathless but smiling. 'Katy's there, on the floor. She's breathing. Looks just like Neil!' She then sat down heavily, back to the wall, and gasped. As she clutched her chest, I was torn between checking her and diving downstairs, but since my mother was conscious and waving me on, I shouted at Julia to leave Neil and sit with her gran, before I grabbed my bag with its last dose of naloxone and rushed downstairs.

Katy was worse than Neil. Completely comatose. Teviot was attempting CPR, but I pulled him back roughly. 'Stop that! She's breathing. She hasn't had a cardiac arrest!' Well,

I silently prayed, not yet. 'She's been drugged like the boy!' I jabbed in the naloxone, praying again. I only had the one dose. If it worked, then I would really believe there was a God.

The first ambulance took Neil and his mum, the second, Katy and mine. I wasn't sure whether or not Mum had had a coronary, but I wouldn't have been surprised. There was no room for heroic MacPherson with his broken clavicle, but one of the uniforms took him off to casualty. In the kitchen, the boys in blue were emptying cupboards. Teviot had amassed piles of packets and papers on the table and nodded at me.

'We're looking for a camera. Neil said Katy took photos of a murder book and jewellery they found in the study, though surprise, surprise, there's nothing left in there now. Neil said he put Katy's camera in a kitchen cupboard.'

'Katy doesn't have a camera!'

Teviot shrugged. 'Neil said she did. No sign, though. Maybe Goodman took it too?'

I sat down at the kitchen table beside an equally exhausted Julia. Suddenly, Teviot cried, 'Aha!' With a flourish, he pulled Katy's backpack from the oven. It didn't contain the missing camera, but did offer up empty silver-topped sputum pots and plastic specimen bags. They joined the heap of 'evidence' already on the table.

Chief Inspector Maitland came in. 'Thought you'd gone in the ambulance, Doc. Think they'll all be OK?"

'Well, Mrs Goodman is pretty ill. Neil's fully conscious, but obviously extremely distressed. Katy's still groggy but coming around. And Mum's paramedic cardiograph looked OK, so fingers crossed. And poor old heroic Sergeant MacPherson's gone in a car to casualty for an X-ray. Think he'll be off for a while.'

'Good show, Doc, thanks.' Maitland looked in the drawers under the cooking range and lifted several lids from several pots before triumphantly pulling a camera from the largest. 'Here we go!'

Ralph appeared, clasped me tightly and pointed at the pile on the table.

'Hey, how's my camera got there? Would know it anywhere from that tartan strap Katy gave me!'

'Neil says Katy took pictures of evidence with it, Professor. Brave girl.' Maitland shook his head. 'A near thing for those kids. Complete bastard! Fancy poisoning your own family?'

Ralph sighed. 'So, where is the bastard, Maitland?'

'We'll get him, Professor. Shouldn't get far. His passport was still in the study drawer.'

*

As he speeds down the M74, Goodman feels satisfied. Tweedale and Semple have been well punished. Only indirectly, granted, but perhaps more painfully than if they had simply been eliminated. Vengeance is his.

He feels satisfied his Scottish work is done. As *Philippians* says, 'He who began a good work in you will carry it on to completion until the day of Christ Jesus.' He will be delivered to new pastures, safe in the knowledge he's as rich as Jehoshaphat. If he gets bored, he can always practise again.

Basle is a good choice, with his fluent German and new passports conveying Swiss citizenship. He must think of an appropriate reward for Oscar. The matching fake medical qualifications must have been difficult.

He makes good time to Penrith where he discards the Jaguar at the station, and walks through town to take a room at a pub. He naps until 5 a.m., when he shaves his face and scalp before donning casual clothes and a baseball hat from his holdall. He feels an unexpected freedom from being smooth-skinned. Perhaps he will never re-grow his beard.

By 6 a.m. he is standing outside his chosen small rental company. Though seeing no security cameras, he retains his hat. But the mirror has told him he looks nothing like Dr David Goodman now. His new clean-shaven appearance matches his new identification. Clever Oscar.

He chooses an inconspicuous blue Escort. Though annoyed at the supplement demanded for taking it abroad for a week, he pays up. No point in attracting attention, becoming memorable by indulging in an argument.

At his second motorway service stop, he detects no cameras and dumps his holdall in a bin. Driving off, he glances in the mirror. 'Well, Dr Avis Freeman, let us listen to the radio!' He switches the tinny radio to full Wagnerian volume, and laughs. Oscar has always been a comedian. Avis means 'bird' in Latin. And he is, indeed, a free man flying! He pats the bulging case on the passenger seat. His first purchase in Basle will be a top-of-the-range BMW. With a decent radio.

Thirty-Four

Salvation & Retribution

5th November 1994, six months later

Replacing the receiver, my hand is shaking. I have to sit on the edge of the bed, eyes closed, to breathe slowly until my heart rate normalises. Could the whole sorry saga be nearly over? Tim seems confident. But he has not yet had official confirmation. The informant is surprising. Or maybe not. He'll have his own agenda.

Returning to the dressing table, I resume application of war paint. The foundation brush I can manage, but applying mascara is not easy with a trembling hand. Through the oriel window, brilliant starbursts light up the evening sky. Cascades of green, red, and silver are falling from the heavens. Guy Fawkes has always been a party night for us, but not this year. Katy has opted for a quiet family birthday dinner in Oktober, a nearby restaurant.

I cannot believe she is sixteen. As I quench the fluttering anxiety which often plagues me since we nearly lost her, a sudden shrieking rocket makes me jump and stab my eye. Katy comes into the room and laughs.

'Oh, Mum! What have you done?'

Through stinging mascara tears, I see she is clad in one of her recently acquired grunge outfits. The red mini-kilt is acceptable, but the Doc Martens wheedled out of my mother as a birthday present are hideous. So far, I have fended off the pleading for tongue-piercing, though it may be that now she can legally have one. And she could legally marry! But I thank God that she has no lasting physical effects from her terrible experience and the nightmares have abated.

Julia still insists on walking her home every day. Katy will certainly miss her next year when she goes to Dundee to study forensics.

Julia appears at the door to do a twirl before coming in.

'You look great in that dress, Jules!' I reserve judgement on the cantilevered Wonderbra and the Cleopatra eyes. And as for the neon-pink lipstick? Motherhood isn't easy.

'Thanks. Wow, look at that monster!' She points at a massive starburst filling the sky.

I nod while applying my subdued peach lipstick, deciding to keep Tim's news about our 'monster' to myself meantime. Best to be sure.

Large Catherine wheels start spinning in the park opposite. Poor St Catherine of the Wheel. How much cruelty has been wrought over religious belief? Guy Fawkes himself was a religious terrorist, surely? Why his Catholic restoration plot has been immortalised by annual gunpowder and burger extravaganzas beats me. It failed. He was betrayed. Now, it seems the dark plotter we uncovered has also been betrayed. Our villain's motives were obscure, but if it was infamy he sought, in the acres of press coverage he's had over the last six months, he's succeeded.

'Right, I'm ready, let's go!'

Taking her arm, I head downstairs to take my coat from Ralph.

The dinner is excellent, but I am distracted. When the waiter brings a cake adorned with a sparkler to our table, Dan reminds Katy of her fifth birthday party when she singed her mittens whirling round in circles with one. Mum is laughing at her cross face. I am so proud of Mum, taking her angina diagnosis with equanimity, glad, she says, that the Goodman debacle highlighted it at a treatable stage. Always one for silver linings, my mum.

Ralph remains my rock. He is blowing me a kiss across the table, silly boy! Dan looks well, though the girlfriend has not been evident lately. I don't ask.

Driving them home in our new Previa, I am surrounded by jokes and shrieks of silliness. Nice. But as I turn the key in the front door, the phone is ringing. Tim confirms Goodman is definitely in custody and that his wife and son have been informed. Katy has been upset that their new identity and address have been withheld from her, but perhaps it's for the best.

Calling my family into the lounge, I sit them down, just managing to say, 'Tim says they've definitely got him,' before escaping to bed. By the time I crawl under the duvet I am crying. Partly in relief that we can now sleep safely. But also for all the victims I could not save.

*

In an Edinburgh police cell, Goodman is laughing. He had judged it low risk to fly back as Dr Avis Freeman, and indeed, had passed easily through passport control at Basle and Edinburgh. His only error had been doubting that fleeting twinge of recognition he'd felt across Princes Street last night while alighting from his taxi at the Balmoral. He'd decided it was an illusion caused by tiredness and had swiftly checked in, confident of achieving his goals within twenty-four hours.

But at 4 a.m., as he was in cuffs and being led to a waiting police car, he had realised his observational powers had not failed him. He had indeed seen Conor Towmey, who now stood outside on the pavement, nodding at his captors.

He starts laughing. How he'd enjoyed spitting in Towmey's face, growling, 'Wanking bastard! You have no idea who you are dealing with!' None of them had, only the Lord knew.

And at the police station, how he'd laughed at their facile questioning and given them 'No comments.' He had also dismissed their offer of some two-bit lawyer.

Now alone in his cell, he decides he'll sing.

'*Oh worship the King, all glorious above.*' He has a great voice.

Next day, after he has declined to answer questions from the psychiatrist they've called, he is taken away in an ambulance.

He finds Carstairs State Hospital for the Criminally Insane is preferable to the cells, more testosterone-sweat and Dettol, less vomitus and urea. There is a good library. He will have plenty of time to catch up on his reading, much neglected recently, what with consolidating his wealth and looking for a Swiss mate. His new spacious Basle apartment requires housekeeping and he requires sex. A wife is the most economical way of providing both. On his return, he will choose one from the shortlist he has drawn up.

He knows his incarceration is temporary. Already, coded letters are on the way to his 'priest' in Kilburn. Oscar has the priest in his pocket and access to generous funds left with him for such an exceptional eventuality as this. Forward planning is all. Springing him from old, ramshackle Carstairs should be doable. Others have succeeded.

He harbours only two regrets. One, that last security box at the Royal Bank still contains substantial jewellery and bonds. Two, he has not seen Neil. There had been no opportunity to drive past his school at home time. New identities and locations hadn't fazed Oscar. He'll doubtless get him photos. On balance, he is pleased Neil survived. Not so, his mother.

A nurse appears with two small blue pills in a small plastic pot. He recognises them as the chemical straitjacket, haloperidol, and accepts them, smiling. He swills some water and tilts his head back. As she leaves, he removes the pills from inside his cheek and grinds them underfoot into the conveniently blue linoleum. He is not insane. He will not be subdued. They do not understand, nor will they ever know how many were chosen. How many were not the deaths they imagined. Smiling, he opens his Bible.

THE END

Acknowledgements

Writing a book is not a solitary task. Many people contribute to its gestation with support and encouragement, or by reading drafts and highlighting errors and plot turkeys! *Not the Deaths Imagined* is no exception.

Grateful thanks must go to my long-suffering husband for putting up with my long hours at the computer screen and for provision of food and drink sustenance. To my beta readers, especially Polly Beck and Grace McKelvie, for their enthusiasm and suggestions. To Garnethill Writers' Group, whose good humour and objective criticism during the book's development was invaluable. Particular thanks to its leader, Dr Catherine McSporran, always supportive and a great mentor and editor. And to the wonderful Greenock Writers Club, who are always inspiring. Special thanks must go to John Reid, my excellent Ringwood editor who has an exceptional eye for voice, pace and narrative. Also the other staff at Ringwood. And to the excellent John Harkins of Scottish Print, for his splendidly sinister cover.

Lastly, to Bloody Scotland 2019 for making me a Crime Spotlight-er, providing a terrific weekend and spurring me on into even more heinous crime writing. A shame about Covid cancelling Bloody Scotland 2020, but roll on '21!

About the Author

Glasgow-born Anne Pettigrew is a graduate of Glasgow (Medicine 1974) and Oxford (Medical Anthropology Master's 2004). A Greenock GP for 31 years, she is mother to two children: David, now a biotech MD and Susanna, in the diplomatic service. She also dabbled in complementary medicine, medical politics, book reviews and journalism in *The Herald* and medical press.

Always an avid reader, she wrote her first murder mystery at eight (medieval mayhem best forgotten) and in retirement took tuition at Glasgow University in order to write novels involving female doctors who weren't just pathologists, historic pioneers or Mills & Boon heroines. Runner-up in the Scottish Association of Writers Constable Award 2018, she was chosen as a 2019 Bloody Scotland Crime Spotlight Author - 'one to watch.' Member of several writers' groups and a short story competition winner, she lives in Ayrshire and enjoys good books, good wine, and good company.

Her debut novel, *Not The Life Imagined*, reviewed as 'well-written and lively', a rollercoaster tale of 60s medical students, discrimination and disappearing bodies, is available in paperback and ebook. She blogs regularly about writing topics on LiteraryGlobe.com and her own official website where you can sign up to receive a quarterly newsletter.

If you have enjoyed this book, why not leave a review on Amazon, Goodreads or at the bookstore of your choice, and help others discover the world of Beth Semple?

Find her at:

https://www.annepettigrew.co.uk

Facebook @annepettigrewauthor

Instagram anne.pettigrew.author

Twitter @pettigrew_anne

https://annepettigrew.literaryglobe.com/

Other Titles from Ringwood

All titles are available from the Ringwood website and from
usual outlets. Also available as ebooks on Amazon

RINGWOOD PUBLISHING
www.ringwoodpublishing.com
mail@ringwoodpublishing.com

Not the Life Imagined

Anne Pettigrew

A darkly humorous, thought-
provoking story of Scottish medical
students in the sixties, a time of
changing social and sexual mores.
None of the teenagers starting at
Glasgow University in 1967 live the
life they imagine.

In *Not the Life Imagined,* retired
medic Anne Pettigrew has written a
tale of ambition and prejudice laced
with sharp observations, irony and
powerful perceptions that provide
a humorous and compelling insight
into the complex dynamics of the
NHS fifty years ago.

ISBN: 978-1-901514-70-4
£9.99

Cuddies Strip

Rob McInroy

Cuddies Strip is based on a true crime and faithfully follows the investigation and subsequent trial but it also examines the mores of the times and the insensitive treatment of women in a male-dominated society. It is a novel about love and friendship and the need to break free from the ghosts of the past.

It is a highly absorbing period piece from 1930s Scotland, with strong contemporary resonances: both about the nature and responsiveness of police services and the ingrained misogyny of the whole criminal justice system.

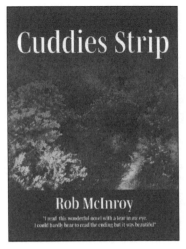

ISBN: 978-1-901514-88-9
£9.99

ISBN: 978-1-901514-68-1
£9.99

Inference

Stephanie McDonald

Natalie Byron had a happy life in Glasgow. She had a steady job, supportive friends and a loving family. Or at least, she thought she did. The morning after a date, Natalie wakes up inside a strange house, in a strange bed, sleeping next to a man named Jamie who claims he is her boyfriend. .

But this isn't her life and Jamie certainly isn't her boyfriend. Fearing she's been kidnapped, Natalie flees, but not one person on the island will help her. But there is one thing Natalie is sure of. She needs to get off this island.

ISBN: 978-1-901514-43-8
£9.99

The Ten Percent

Simon McLean

An often hilarious, sometimes scary, always fascinating journey through the ranks of the Scottish police from his spell as a rookie constable in the hills and lochs of Argyll, through his career in Rothesay and to his ultimate goal: The Serious Crime Squad in Glasgow.

We get a unique glimpse of the turmoil caused when the rules are stretched to the limit, when the gloves come off and fire fights fire and when some of their number decide that enough is enough. A very rare insight into the world of our plain clothes officers who infiltrate and suppress the very worst among us.

Ruxton: The First Modern Murder

Tom Wood

It is 1935 and the deaths of Isabella Ruxton and Mary Rogerson would result in one of the most complex investigations the world had ever seen. The gruesome murders captured worldwide attention with newspapers keeping the public enthralled with all the gory details.

But behind the headlines was a different, more important story: the groundbreaking work of Scottish forensic scientists who developed new techniques to solve the case and shape the future of scientific criminal investigation.

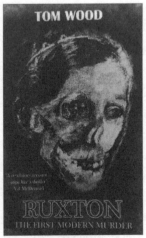

ISBN: 978-1-901514-84-1
£9.99

ISBN: 978-1-901514-71-1
£9.99

Who Shot Jesse James?

Alex Gordon

Jesse James – real name, Frank – shoots straight from the lip: the controversial gossip columnist makes a living sullying the reputations of the elite and, like his Wild West counterpart, is no stranger to infamy. He finds himself with no choice but to swallow his considerable ego and seek the help of his former colleague, freelance sports journalist and amateur sleuth, Charlie Brock. They soon becomes entangled in the mystery surrounding the identity of an enigmatic scribe - known locally as 'The Red Phantom'...

Murder at the Mela

Leela Soma

Newly appointed as Glasgow's first Asian DI, Alok Patel's first assignment is the investigation of the brutal murder of Nadia, an Asian woman. Her body was discovered in the aftermath of the Mela festival in Kelvingrove Park. During the Mela, a small fight erupted between a BNP group and an Asian gang, but was quickly quelled by police.

This novel peels away the layers of Glasgow's Asian communities, while exploring the complicated relationships between Asian people and the city.

ISBN: 978-1-901514-90-2
£9.99